CHILDREN OF THE DRYADS

Book One

Legend of the Singer

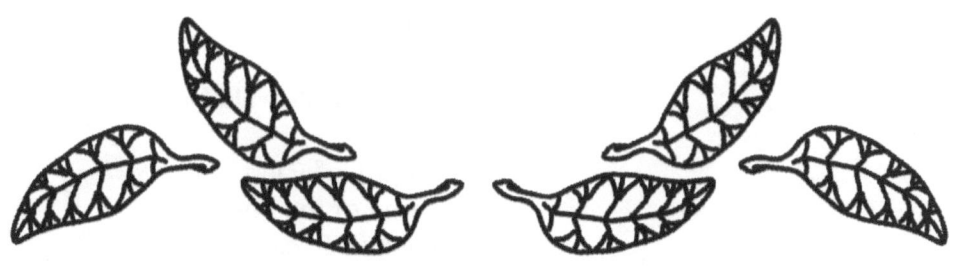

Kaarathlon

EPOCH OF THE PROMISE:
Dawn Unseen
EPOCH OF THE PROMISE:
Vision's Light
EPOCH OF THE PROMISE:
Wings of Healing
EPOCH OF THE PROMISE:
Darkness Bright*

Other

Kingdom of Light

Areaer Novels

Return of the Dragonriders

DragonBirth
DragonWing
DragonSword

Legend of the Singer

Children of the Dryads
Sorceress of the Dryads

Dragon-Mage
Heart of Fire
Scars of Fire
Healing of Fire*

Standalone Novels/Novellas

The Gifts of Faeri
Kindred of the Sea
Gryphon's Escape
Promise of Fire

* Not yet available

ISBN: 978-1-952176-12-8

[1] YOUNG ADULT FICTION / fantasy / epic
[2] YOUNG ADULT FICTION / social themes / friendship
[3] YOUNG ADULT FICTION / coming of age

Summary: When Tara-lin's father is called on a mission she doesn't think he can
survive, she secretly chases him and discovers that far more than just his life depends
on her magic.

Cover art and design by Raina Nightingale

www.enthralledbylove.com

Forward

Welcome back to Areaer! This time we will not be watching dragons so much, and our main protagonist will not be in shock from discovering all that she has believed and worshiped is wrong. Instead, we will see and learn about dryads and gryphons, with a main protagonist – the half-elven Tara-lin – who has no religion nor much interest therein. However, we still have the same enemy – the nightmare and its Dark Lord.

I look forward to your comments, and I hope you enjoy this journey of discovery with me!

Sincerely,

Raina Nightingale

PS. For those of you who love dragons, there will be more series about dragons in Areaer! In fact, look for Dragon-mage Book One, *Heart of Fire,* out April 16th, 2023.

Map of Ellenesia

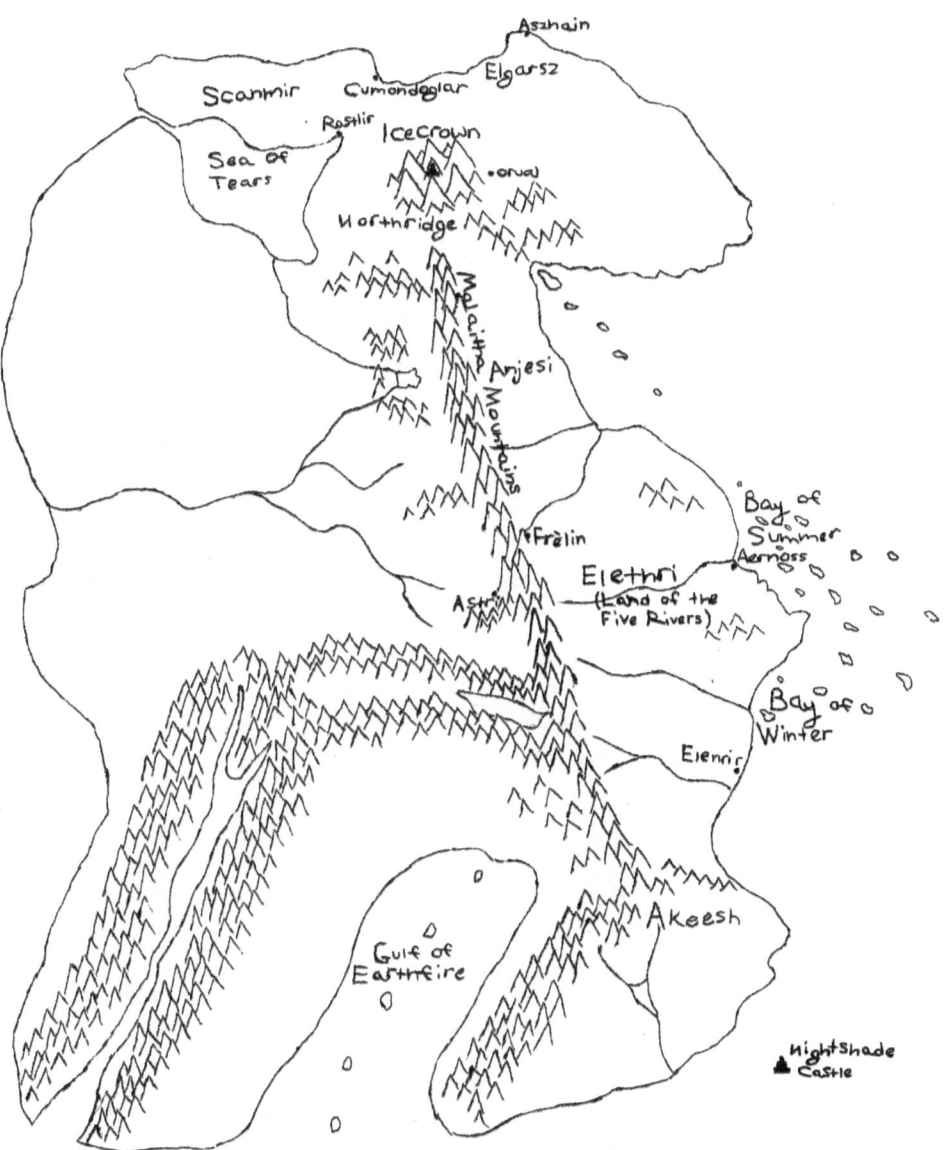

Aszhain

Scanmir   Cumondoglar   Elgarsz

Rostlir   Icecrown

Sea of
Tears   •oруа)

Worthridge

Malaitha Mountains

Anjesi

Bay of
Summer
Aernoss

•Frälin

Elethri
(Land of the
Five Rivers)

Ast—

Bay of
Winter

Elennir

Akeesh

Gulf of
Earthfire

Nightshade
Castle

Table of Contents

Chapter One – Elven Song

Tara-lin's hair, red like the newly-formed leaves of an apricot tree, thick and curly, blew about her face, raised by a rain wind. Beneath her eyebrows, each like a slanted red feather, shone eyes that were the green of cherry leaves in spring. Her ears tapered to points, difficult to fully cover with her hair. Her bone structure was fine but strong. Her small nose was rather pointed. Her skin was beige, her cheeks had a blush rose, and she had freckles. She was very thin, and only about five foot five, very short for an elf, but only barely tall for a human. Twenty-one years old, she had matured very quickly for an elf, but a little slow for a human. She was a half-elf.

She leapt onto a rock and, with the wind in her hair, began to sing. With the first words of her song the rain began to fall, and a shimmering rainbow soon appeared.

O sweet rain, falling softly
Come meet me here
Freshen the colors
Soften both light and shadow
Catch the sunlight
Reflect in brilliant hue
Through the mist shining bright
A rainbow shining through

From the sky o rain fall down
Soften the ground
All the little plants
Refresh with your gentle hand
So they can grow
Taller and lovely and green
So beautiful you know
And happily growing

Rain, rain, rain
Freshen the day
Beauty I couldn't say
Fresh and moist all the way

Shower down a rainbow
Sing in the leaves
Prepare the green to grow
Fall from sky to stream

Come and swell the little streams
Fall down so softly
Moisten now the earth
For young roots, and air refresh
From the skies fall
Refreshing silver curtains
On the earth, on us all
It's spring, time for freshness

Rain, rain, rain...

They were now wet, but only pleasantly so, for the rain was both warm and light. A beautiful double rainbow shimmered brightly. Amazement lit her parent's faces. Tara-lin wanted to yell, "What?!" at them.

Her mother exchanged a look with her father, and Eldor said, "I think you're a singer."

What?! thought Tara-lin. *How could I not be a singer, since I sing?* while her mother went on, "We've always known there was something special about your song, but a singer?"

Eldor met first his wife and then his daughter's eyes. "It's been fourteen centuries since the last singer."

Tara-lin nodded, confused. That was two elven lifetimes. "What are you two talking about?" she blurted out.

Her father spoke to her mother, "Lìrulin, it seems she is older than you thought at first. How shall we tell her?"

This was getting really exasperating. Tara-lin wanted to stomp her foot and yell, *"What is up with you two?"*

Lìrulin motioned for her daughter to come down. As Tara-lin leapt from the rock and sat in front of her parents, she began. "We didn't see until this morning, but your song can summon energy and, perhaps more importantly, direct it. In case you didn't notice, the rainbow first dimly shone when you sang 'catch the sunlight' and quickly brightened, as you sang of it. The wind varied in time to your song, as did the rain.

Tell me, when did you make up that song?"

Without thinking, Tara-lin answered, "This morning."

"Before or while you sang?"

"While. I have a question. Will my song call down rain anytime, or just this once?"

Eldor answered, "We don't know. It's been so long since the last singer, and besides, we have not studied the air. Probably, that is determined by many factors, not least the weather."

Tara-lin nodded. "How powerful is this talent?"

"We don't know, but *that* depends primarily on you," answered Lìrulin. Tara-lin's mother looked so beautiful. Her ruby hair fell about her shoulders and down her back. Her emerald eyes sparkled in her almost-white face.

Tara-lin rose, her silky green-tinged dress almost flowing as she rose. "So what happens next?"

"We don't know. You get to develop your ability."

"I don't know how. One question, is singing like wizardry?"

"Don't know. Probably in some ways and not others," replied her father. He rose to embrace his daughter. He was built much more thickly than either she or her mother, but was only a little taller than she was. His skin was a light shade of brown, his hair was dark brown, and his eyes were hazel.

"One more question," said Tara-lin. "Do all half-elven children have strange talents?"

"You should drop that 'one'. I bet you have a hundred, at least," said her mother with a hint of laughter.

"All children are unique," said Eldor. "And I'm pretty sure all children have talents."

"That wasn't an answer to my question, exactly," muttered Tara-lin. After another moment, she withdrew from her father's embrace.

She tried again. "Do other half-elf children have talents like singing or wizardry?"

"Persistent, are you?" said her father, with a glint in his eye. He looked like he still wanted to hug her. "That'll be great, as long as you're persistent about the right things. Or not so great if you're persistent about the wrong ones."

"Downright awful," added Lìrulin.

Tara-lin noticed her parents had once again not answered her question. She tried to approach it from a different angle. "Are humans or elves more likely to be singers?"

"Likely?" snorted Eldor. "No human or elf is *likely* to be a singer. Either he or she is, or he or she is not."

Tara-lin stomped her foot. Her parents were playing games with her. She hated these games. She liked answers!

Neither of her parents said anything about the stomped foot, but she knew they had noticed. She just knew.

"I'm hungry... I'm tired," she declared. "I shouldn't be tired. It's still hours before noon."

Lìrulin smiled a little. "You used your mind in a way you are not accustomed to. It's no wonder you're tired. C'mon. Let's have a meal."

"Yes, I believe that would be a good idea," commented Eldor.

Chapter Two – Missions

Tara-lin pulled her Elethrian cloak around her, and pulled the hood over her face, to keep out the rain, which was, by now, falling quite heavily. She sat on the foot of an old live oak, and tried to recall all that she could remember of how her parents met and married.

Her father, Sir Eldor, was a young knight then, no older than she was now, but nearly full-grown, for he was a fullblooded human. He had been called on a mission to discover and thwart the designs of the evil wizard, Falkur. With him was Lìrulin, her mother, who was incredibly gifted in the finding and use of herbs, as well as an accomplished archer. With them was Se'lorn and the drake-lizard, Tarunth. Drake-lizards were fire-breathing lizards, ranging in size from about that of a large kitten to that of a bobcat. Those who disbelieved in dragons thought that they might be the inspiration for the legend.

The trio set out from the Valor Hall in Astri, and journeyed along the Malaitha Mountains, through the Northridge Plain, to Orual. Along the way, they had some skirmishes with orcs and black drake-lizards. In Orual they uncovered little but rumors, giving evidence of a suspicious but unknown plot by Falkur.

The adventure led on into the Icecrown Mountains, and unendurable cold. At every step they encountered orcs and black drake-lizards. According to Eldor that was the worst part of the adventure.

Only by means of the Elethrian cloaks did they enter the wizard's Nightshade Castle. The most dangerous part of the quest followed. There Se'lorn was captured, and Tara-lin shuddered at what her parents knew befell him there, but he did not betray them. His drake-lizard Tarunth remained with Sir Eldor and Lìrulin as a message carrier, though he died within the week.

Several days later Lìrulin crept into the meeting of Falkur and his counsel, and listened long before she was discovered. There, at last, she understood Falkur's plot to forge an army of blackened dragons forced to bond with half-orcs. He wanted to force demons into the bodies of killed dragons and force the resulting monstrosity to bond to half-orcs under his control. Just as she turned to leave, she was discovered.

Tarunth told Eldor of her danger, and he came. Nothing withstood his sword, though he received serious wounds. At the last moment he thought of how to deal with the wizard. Quickly, he gathered some candles and lit the castle on fire – in so much as it was flammable material. He tore Lìrulin out of the grasp of the distracted wizard. Together they fought their way through the guard, and passed from the flames. They fled toward the sea, but within hours Eldor's strength deserted him, and he lay at death's door.

Lìrulin coaxed a fire from what wood she could get, and with melted snow bathed Eldor's wounds. Tara-lin knew her greatest anguish was her fear that Eldor would die – already they loved each other as more than comrades. Tarunth brought back what herbs he could, with his last few hours of life. As quickly as possible they made their way to the sea.

There they remained until Eldor regained his strength. Their mission was not yet completed. They still had to stop the evil wizard. But how?

At last Lìrulin persuaded Eldor to pass into the Nightshade Castle, again. In the middle of the night, when only the nightmare creatures roamed, and moving slowly to make full use of the camouflaging action of their Elethrian cloaks, they crept into the passages below the castle. Though they found not the dungeon, where, perhaps, Se'lorn was still held in torment, they found the hall where Wizard Falkur's 'precious' corrupted dragon eggs were held. (Tara-lin's parents thought they were not dragon eggs, but the eggs of an especially large variety of the drake-lizards, but they could not be certain. Maybe dragons did exist and these were some of their eggs.) But already daybreak must have been upon them. Quickly but cautiously they found the nearest torch, and set the hoard of blackened eggs on fire.

Unable to flee through the armies of evil again, the pair found a way into a crevice in the rock of the Icecrown Mountains. Knowing that there might be no way out, and that this could be their death, Tara-lin's mother and father wandered through the caves, hoping against all hope to see the light of day. They followed a trickle of water. At last, when both were near death, they emerged under the cold starlight, in a deep valley. There they slept.

Though weak and faint, Eldor had forced himself to arise and seek food. He had feared he would die before succeeding, but he returned with a cone of pine nuts, a rabbit, and two eggs. He managed to light a fire, and cooked the rabbit and eggs. When they were ready he had roused Lìrulin, and they had eaten together, and slept again.

When they had at last recovered, both were exhausted inside and out. Sir Eldor received leave, and went with his love to her woods. There they married, and there Tara-lin was born. There they still lived.

So, Tara-lin wondered, *why am I thinking about all this?... I've got it. I have unusual talents. Does this mean I will have to go on a mission? I don't think I like missions. In fact, I'm sure I hate them.*

She sat for a while contemplating missions, and knowing that, as a singer, *the* singer, sooner or later she would be called on a mission. At least, that was what all the stories she had learned, and even the history of her own parents, suggested would happen. Perhaps her parents might even ask her to go somewhere to train her abilities. Then again, maybe that would not happen, since there were no singers in the world and had not been any for a long time. But if she were sent somewhere, that would be horrible. She would not have any friends. It would not be home. She did not want to live anywhere other than where she did right now.

A man stood in the forest. He could be seen, or seen through, like a rainbow. He was robed in white, red, and gold light. His form and eyes radiated power. Tara-lin had no doubt that he was good, but in a way alien to her mode of being.

Tara-lin stood, instantly feeling like she recognized him, yet she knew she had never seen him before. She curtsied gracefully and asked, "What do you want, lord?"

"Be ready and do not hesitate, when you hear the call."

Before Tara-lin could speak, he passed out of the realm of her senses. What did *that* mean? Was she about to be called on a quest? She hoped not. Well, only time would show.

Tara-lin decided to get up and walk to the little house, without any haste. It was actually a tarp stretched between four pine trees and tied along the edges to four more, twenty feet above the ground. Nine feet above the first tarp was another, which served as a roof. Curtains fell from the roof-tarp to the floor-tarp, providing further shelter from the elements. The entire structure was made from the same material as her Elethrian cloak, and therefore nearly invisible. A rope ladder of the same material hung down, along the trunk of one of the trees, for her father to use. When she was in a hurry or extremely tired Tara-lin used it too, for she was not quite as adept at tree-climbing as her mother. However, right now she was neither tired nor in a hurry.

When she crawled into the house, Tara-lin saw three people. Sir Eldor, Lìrulin, and an elf she did not recognize.

Her mother greeted her quietly, hardly looking up. "Hello, Tara-lin."

"What's up?" asked Tara-lin, a little loudly.

"This is Fizzer, a messenger from the court," said Lìrulin. "He brings us news."

"What sort of news?" Tara-lin still spoke louder than necessary. "Good news or bad news?"

"Well," Fizzer looked sad, "Wizard Falkur is dead –" Tara-lin squealed happily, her mother sshhed, – "but his son – or one of his sons – is looking for a way to make himself a wizard by stealing the energies of various creatures."

"How do you know that?" Tara-lin blurted out.

"Princess Ithrìl has returned... and died."

"What?! Princess Ithrìl died exactly three hundred and twelve years before I was born."

"No," corrected Fizzer. "Falkur captured her. Instead of using her as a hostage, and maybe torturing her, he became enamored with her, and forced her to marry him. She had two sons a hundred years apart. Anakrim, Falkur's heir, and Keller, who wanted to fight his father's evil, and was killed. Anakrim was always his father's favorite, but both Princess Ithrìl and – Prince? – Keller were abused. When Falkur died, her living son let her go. However, worn beyond her years, she died hours after delivering her story."

"So," Tara-lin said, "an evil half-elf is the heir to the elven throne? And King Orenduil and Queen Alaria are not likely to live for another century."

"Yes," replied Fizzer. "An evil half-elf, who might be able to make himself a wizard. We are going to try to stop him from doing so. A company is currently being arranged for that purpose. Candidates will gather in the Valor Hall within the month. Sir Eldor, you are summoned, as a Valor Knight. Lady Lìrulin and Tara-lin, you are invited to visit the Valor Hall."

Sir Eldor nodded. "I'm actually surprised my leave was allowed to last for twenty-two years –"

Tara-lin interrupted. "How do you get these messages back and forth so fast?" she blurted out. "It's three and a half months to the Valor Hall on foot, and at least one on horseback. It's more than a month to Frèlin."

"They travel by means of a wizardry device," explained Lìrulin.

So that was what he meant. A quest. "I'll go," said Tara-lin. "But

I want to know why you're interested in me..."

"Lìrulin?" Sir Eldor locked eyes with his wife.

"I'll come. We'll see how I am in a month."

Tara-lin's eyebrows shot up. "What, Mom? Do you not feel well?"

"Not that sort of thing," said her father. He cocked an eyebrow at her.

"Your parents told me that you are a singer," said Fizzer, looking at Tara-lin. "I wonder how that will turn out for you, exploring and developing your talent with no one who really knows much about it, since the last singer died more than a thousand years ago."

Tara-lin nodded. Her mind was on something else at the moment, though. "So," she said as she stood, "When do we leave?"

"Tomorrow. It's pretty late already."

"How will we get there in time? You didn't bring an extra three horses, did you?" asked Tara-lin.

"No, I brought one." said Fizzer. "You and your mother are invited to visit; it's not Valor Hall business for you to come, and so you must provide your own mounts."

"We have one, and we might be able to borrow one from Earnrìl. If we can't, I'll stay," said Lìrulin.

Tara-lin wanted to say, "Me too." She had jumped to the conclusion she would have something to do with this quest, no matter whether she wanted it or not, and no matter whether anyone else wanted her. When one had unusual talents, one was always stuck with strange things happening around one!

Chapter Three – The Elven City

Tara-lin posted Neiler's trot with ease. Earnrìl, a friend of Tara-lin who was over twice her age in years, had ridden down to the sea, so Lìrulin stayed behind. Her father rode the horse Fizzer had brought, in a saddle. He could ride bareback rather well, but he did not like to do so all day.

"I don't like going on this mission," Tara-lin mumbled.

"What?" asked Sir Eldor.

"I do not care for going on the mission," Tara-lin repeated, slowly and loudly.

"What are you talking about? You're not going on this mission."

"But I am," said Tara-lin. "I'm a singer, and singer is an unusual ability. People with strange abilities always have to go on exciting, painful, and scary adventures. So I will, too."

"Not all are *that* painful. Besides, discomfort and exhaustion are not bad. Some of my moments of greatest awareness of inner peace have come while tired, or in pain, or both. Besides, I am not going to let my completely unprepared daughter who's still a child go with me into enemy territory, so that's that. You are *not* coming."

"But I am!" said Tara-lin, turning red all over. "You are an aging human, Dad! I am a half-elf and may live as much as a full seven hundred years! You aren't likely to live another *fifty* years, even if you don't get killed. And, if you do die on this thing, well, I am just too young to never see you again in a few months!"

"You are *not* coming," said Sir Eldor. "That is that. No one would even want you. You are too childish and would only make things harder. Besides, girl, I'm more likely to get killed with you around, trying to protect you, than if you aren't around. What if you get killed? Do you think I would want to see my daughter, who even if I had married a human should outlive me by at least twenty years, die before I'm fifty?"

Tara-lin shrugged. "You have no idea – and neither do I – what I might be able to do." Neither of them said anything for perhaps half an hour, except for a few comments Sir Eldor made on the trees they passed. Tara-lin was thinking about what he had said about pain and exhaustion. "How many missions, quests, whatever, *have* you actually been on?" she asked.

"Three, I think. There was the one I met your mom on. You know about that one. Before that, I had to help with the survival, restoration, and defense of a village burned by some of Falkur's minions. My first involved freeing the mayor of Hollen – I know it sounds like Hollin – from the influence – control – of one of Falkur's spy agents."

"This one sounds like the one you met Mom on. 'Go discover and thwart whatever that evil wizard is trying to do.' 'Go and stop that guy from stealing lives to make himself a wizard.' Hmm?"

"I already told you that you are not going on it, so you might as well stop worrying about what it will be like. Why do you even want to go?"

"Because I *will*, some way or another. I have an ability! Things always happen to people with abilities. If it's not this one, it will be another, and it won't be any better. Also, if this one is like the one you met Mom on, you will probably die and I will never see you again, since, even if it's impossible for me to accept or understand it, you are older and weaker than you were before I was born, and that one almost killed you and Mom then, when you were as young and strong as she still is! And it *did* kill that drake-keeper, Se'lorn. Why not you this time? I am coming! I will be with you as long as I can, since either way you will die while I am still young."

"Well, you're not coming," said Sir Eldor. "As I said, it will be harder on me and more likely to kill me if you are around."

For several more hours both were again silent, except for occasional comments about the flora or fauna. Then Tara-lin brought up again something her father had said that she couldn't understand.

"I don't understand what you mean about pain," said Tara-lin in a rather confrontational tone, "and, even if you don't want me to, I *will* end up involved in something like this sooner or later. It *always* happens to people like me. I'm *both* a singer *and* a half-elf."

Sir Eldor ignored her repeated comments about her talents and her supposed fate. "Don't fight *pain,* or try to avoid it or dull it with anger. You'll want to do so. Very much. It's such a relief when you learn not to. Even I haven't got that one down yet."

"Then how do you know it's a relief when you learn not to?"

"Because it's a relief when you *don't.*"

Tara-lin shook her head. She would never understand. She leaned forward and stroked Neiler's neck under her mane. "You don't understand either, do you?" she whispered. The animal turned her ears back to hear her voice.

Already Tara-lin missed her mother. But she knew what her

father would say if she told him. She could just turn around and ride back to her. While he would like to show her Frèlin and the Valor Hall, she did not have to come if she did not want to do so. The only problem was that she would miss him, too. She had never thought of this before, until she learned he was summoned back to duty, but he was a human. Her mother would live for decades and centuries assuming nothing killed her. Her father might live for three, maybe four, more decades. It was not that long. And, if he had to fight or go on a mission, he could so easily be killed! Then she would never seen him again. Neither, of course, would her mother. Thinking about it, she had realized he had aged. He was weaker than he had been. Struggle would weaken him more. Somehow, it all felt terribly distant, and yet terrifyingly close and real.

Besides, she *would* be involved in the problem, one way or another.

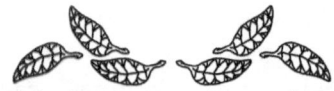

About two and a half weeks later, Tara-lin rode into Frèlin, the capitol of Elethri, forest-nation of the elves. Her father had told her that among men it was known as the Land of the Five Rivers. She had never been to a city before, and it both impressed her and made her feel uncomfortable. She leaned over, to whisper to her father.

He nodded. "Just wait till you see human cities. If you don't like this, you won't like them at all – even the best."

In the center of the many-tiered city, up against the mountain, was a tower of white stone, taller than the tallest of the trees of the forest. Above the point of the tower hung, as if floating, an orb of silver with veins of gold. Sir Eldor told her that it would glow at night, illuminating the city with a soft light. Tara-lin asked her father if all the elven cities were lit in the same way.

"Yes, child, but the elves are diminishing. It is not that their might in body or in mind is less, but they do not care to master or preserve the arts of old. Much has already been lost."

Tara-lin nodded. They had already passed through the wall of white stone, full of intricate carvings and decorated with silver. Here and there rose towers of white stone, imposing but small when compared to the central tower. Above each hung an orb like the one in the center, only smaller and often a different color. Her father told her that these also glowed. Scattered about were buildings of white stone, of various height and size, sometimes raised above the earth by pillars and reached by stairs. The roofs were usually silver, amethyst, ruby, azure, or cerulean. Everywhere pines, cedars, or firs grew clumped together, and Tara-lin saw the subtle signs of dwellings like their own. More obvious were the boards, often richly engraved and sometimes with gold or silver, nailed to one of the tree-posts and telling who lived there. Here and there an elf had made his or her dwelling in an oak or birch tree.

"Too many people too close together," murmured Tara-lin.

The paths were made with flat, shiny, almost-white gray stones. The city was laid out in a semi-circle around a prominent ridge of the mountain. At the back of each great terrace was a ring of water, not always the same width or depth, and sometimes with little isles, sometimes with fingers of water reaching far out into the terrace. At each crossing small wood boats, some decorated with gems, were moored. Long bridges of mossy white stone spanned the waters, and at the back of each terrace rose another, with a stairway that cut deep into it. Retaining walls of white stone held the earth up on either side. Much of the path from the gate to the central tower was these stairways.

At the entrance to the tower, which was even more amazing now that it was up close, they were admitted by the guard after brief, almost careless, courtesies. They entered the throne room, where courtesy demanded they visit the king and queen.

As she glanced at all the people all over the room, Tara-lin thought, Way *too many people in* way *too little space. I've never seen half this many people together!*

Tara-lin felt unbearably awkward and uncomfortable in the presence of the king and queen. She attempted an awkward curtsy, wishing she could vanish into thin air. Fizzer's announcement that she was a singer only made things worse. The king requested that she sing for them.

"You can do it," her father whispered in her ear.

Tara-lin nodded, but she was not so sure. Sing, of course. Sing with power? Not so sure. "I'm not sure I can sing like a *singer,*" she whispered back.

"Don't try to. I'll explain later," he whispered back to her hastily.

Tara-lin stepped back. She could not think of anything to sing about, except a clumsy warbler, who tried to sing but only produced grating combinations that rubbed everyone's ears raw. It was a children's song among the elves, but it was all she could think of. She felt the pressure around her mount. She raised her voice, which now quavered.

Little bird, little warbler
Tries to sing
But can only screech
Perfectly uncomfortable

Little bird embarrasses
Family
With song uncomely
No one can bear to listen

Tara-lin soon ran out of lyrics. She was sure there were more, but she could not remember them. She felt as embarrassed as the bird in her song. She just wanted to vanish.

Her father put his arm around her shoulders and whispered, "You did great, girl."

"I did?" she gasped. "I did *terrible!*"

"Not at all. You communicated. Everyone in this room can now identify with 'Little Bird.'"

After a few more courtesies, Sir Eldor and Tara-lin departed up the spiral stairway that curled up the inside of the tower. Sir Eldor whispered to her as they climbed, "Well, maybe not everyone can now identify with 'Little Bird.'"

"It was horrible," said Tara-lin.

"No, it wasn't. I'll explain later."

Chapter Four — Suspicions in the Valor Hall

At the top they found the magical device ready for them. A frame of treated oak wood with jewels of every color embedded in it stood against the far wall. The air between them was a black void, in which sparks of bright colors almost continuously appeared and reappeared.

"It's called a portal," said Sir Eldor to Tara-lin.

The portal was supposedly guarded — against intrusion from the other side — by dozing guards.

Tara-lin nodded. "Astri, right?"

"Yes, Astri is where the Valor Hall is located. Unless something has changed, this opens into the Valor Hall," said Sir Eldor.

"Okay," said Tara-lin. "So, what do you do now?"

"Well, only one person can go through the portal at a time." Sir Eldor turned to Fizzer. "Are you coming with us?"

"No," said Fizzer. He pulled a small scroll out of his clothing. "Take this to the Overseer of The Valor Hall, Sir Eldor."

"I will," said Sir Eldor. He turned back to his daughter. "I will go first. Wait a minute. Then go."

Tara-lin nodded.

"I will make sure the time works out fine," said Fizzer.

"Thank you," said Sir Eldor. He turned and walked into the blackness.

Tara-lin almost screeched as his body disappeared.

"It's okay, Tara-lin," said Fizzer. "You'll find him just fine on the other side."

"Yeah," said Tara-lin, but her body was shaking and her mind felt like it was melting. The time between when her father disappeared and when Fizzer told her it was now ready for her felt like it would never pass.

Tara-lin stepped forward. Her legs felt like they would melt. She stood before the portal and stopped. She felt a strange, thin vibration in the air that frightened her horribly.

"Go on, Tara-lin," said Fizzer.

Tara-lin turned and yelled at him. "You're not my father or my mother!" she said.

The guards looked at her. She risked no more time then. She darted into the portal and fell through.

Blackness swallowed her. There was no air. There was no

warmth. Her body was not even cold. Her heart did not beat. She could not breathe. She could not scream. There was only nothing.

Suddenly, as abruptly as the blackness had come on, it ended. Tara-lin was dizzy but she felt her body again. She stood on hard floor and could hear voices around her.

One of them was her father's.

It took Tara-lin a few moments to resolve her environment. She stood on a marble floor. The walls were built of blocks of white and blue stone. Her father stood several feet in front of her speaking to several men dressed in shining armor over which they wore white capes trimmed with violet. Sir Eldor had turned to her. Concern was clearly evident in his face. "Are you all right, Tara-lin?"

"Ah, yes. It was scary, though," she said.

Sir Eldor nodded. "I'd forgotten what it was like," he said. He turned to the others. "Sirs, this is my daughter, the Lady Tara-lin."

Tara-lin curtsied.

A tall man with silver-black hair nodded to her. "The Lord Vardan at your service, here. I am pleased to meet you, Lady Tara-lin."

"I'm pleased to meet you as well, Lord Vardan," said Tara-lin. She knew she sounded as awkward as she felt. She cast a pleading glance towards her father.

Sir Eldor nodded to her. "You're fine," he mouthed.

Tara-lin resisted an insane urge to stomp her foot. This was *not* funny!

The rest of the afternoon was spent in exchanging pleasantries. Sir Eldor learned that some whom he had once known and expected to be alive were dead, while others whom he would have expected to have died were still alive, notably Lord Sindragos, who had been Master of the Hall when Sir Eldor was last there.

Tara-lin was exasperated by all of it. In the exchanges of pleasantries, she soon forgot all about the mission and thought only about how vastly inferior this environment was to the woods of her home and the company of her elven friends and play-mates. It would have been so much more fun to go down to the sea with Earnrìl.

It was night. Tara-lin swung open the door to her father's room — hers was right across the hall — and stepped in, to hear him muttering, "That Fizzer! I should never have told him."

"You should never have told Fizzer what?" asked Tara-lin, closing the door.

"That you are a singer," said Sir Eldor.

"Why?"

"Because, though it's been almost fifteen hundred years, people remember singer as a powerful ability. Most will probably discard it as nothing like it's reported to be, especially after the way you sang there. Just well enough, they will think that to be a singer means nothing more than to be especially good at making people feel what you're singing about. It was so perfect, girl!"

Tara-lin smiled, pleased at his praise. She still did not quite understand what he was getting at, but she figured it out quickly. "Oh!" she said. "You don't want me to be in danger because anyone evil knows I might... be able to do... unpredictable... things."

"Something like that," said Sir Eldor. "But you are *not* going on this mission. Remember that."

Tara-lin shrugged. "You know it will be something sooner or later, and whether Fizzer had or had not announced it. People with strange and powerful abilities always have to do *something.*"

Sir Eldor fixed her with his gaze in a way that made her uncomfortable. "And how do you know your talent is powerful? Even among elves something could be greatly exaggerated in fourteen hundred years, and the talent was never uniform. Some were more powerful; some less."

Tara-lin smiled. Her father was not sure whether she was relieved, or did not believe him, or some of both.

After a moment, she changed the subject. "This place is stupid."

"It is, kind of. I never noticed it until living in the forest with Lìrulin and you. Even living in Frèlin wouldn't have done it. As you said, even Frèlin isn't quite right. There's so much pretense and fake courtesy and intrigue and so much that isn't natural. It's a wonder I didn't notice it before, and I don't know what I shall do with it now, for I am a Valor Knight and cannot just leave. There's so much going on that I didn't even notice as a young man, and I'm not, for the most part, sure who wants what and why." He shook his head. "At least, I suspect that the story about Princess Ithrìl is true, or mostly true, and there really is a Prince Anakrim who intends to steal the energy and magic from other beings to make himself a wizard."

"I can see why a man stealing other beings' whatever in order to make himself powerful so he can do evil things is a problem," said Tara-lin, "but I just never got around to asking this before: why does it matter that he is technically the heir to the throne in Frèlin? Can't the elves just decide they won't be ruled by a half-elf they don't like? Can't King Orenduil and Queen Alaria name someone else heir and denounce him? Can't the people just not accept him?"

Sir Eldor sat back and sighed. "All of those things *could* happen, if people would *do* them. They're *possible,* in that sense. Except that there is no provision in elven law for someone other than the blood heir to be named heir. In fact, it's explicitly illegal. The heir is always, if such a one is living, the eldest son of the eldest son. If there is no eldest son, it's the eldest daughter. It's a little more complicated, but Anakrim's claim is very clear. There are no disputations, and there is no one else close to the line of succession."

"Couldn't the elves say they don't believe he is Princess Ithrìl's son? That he just made that up?" asked Tara-lin. "And just pick a king from among their people?"

"If Anakrim is dead, then King Orenduil and Queen Alaria can name someone heir. Now, I don't like the idea of doing an assassination in order to circumvent an icky situation with the law, and I'm not sure what the politics between the elven throne in Frèlin and the Valor Hall in Astri is. I don't, however, mind trying to keep Anakrim from his scheme to gain power, which may be a scheme also to guarantee a long lifespan, because, as it is, it is highly unlikely for Anakrim to even know if he is likely to outlast the King and Queen, unless he knows that, naturally, he won't. Now, I don't know, and I don't know if anyone knows, if it is possible to prolong one's life with this nasty way of wizardry. Wizards do tend to live a little longer than other humans, though.

"But you asked, why can't the elves just throw out Anakrim's claim? Even make up, perhaps, that no half-human can hold the elven throne, so even if he is the son of the Princess he can't be King? I suppose that could be done, but it would have ramifications on the relationships between the elves and the humans. Some of the elves care only about the elven law and keeping the status quo; some of these would dearly like to rediscover their lost arts. Most of the elves don't, as far as we can tell, care one way or another about much except their comforts. The elves who care about elven law and magic would almost certainly accept Prince Anakrim as King, especially if he offered to help them rediscover and rebuild their magic with his own knowledge of magic arts. In fact, by such offer he would win a good portion of the elven youth to himself."

Sir Eldor sighed deeply, and then went on. Tara-lin held her tongue in check to keep from interrupting him with a thousand thoughts. She felt sad. He looked so tired and worn out, more tired than she had ever seen him before.

"The Princess' news is well-enough known, it would be hard to argue that Anakrim is not Crown Prince. And the elven law regarding the succession is carefully written, to make it very hard, if not impossible, to disregard someone's claim. I don't know why; it's probably buried in some bit of Elethrian history which I don't know, but it is that way. 'He wasn't raised by elves' is not an option; it's just *possible* that claiming no half-human can take the throne *might* work; also, it might have some leverage on those elves who really care about keeping and restoring their heritage, but the promise of helping them re-discover their magic would probably more than outweigh that in most of their minds; and he won't present himself as evil. He will present himself as unfortunate in his parentage and with a desire to be as elven as possible. And, most of the elves won't want to fight. If he claims the throne, and if he has powers to back him, they will just accept him. It would be too difficult and too bloody to resist him; then, when he starts to command evil things, they will obey him, once again, for the same reasons. Bloody civil war could result. There's so much here that I cannot forecast. But the situation is really bad, and there's something about the Valor Hall that I don't like. In fact, there's something I really don't like. Why hasn't your idea about how the ruler of Elethri must be a pure-blooded elf *not* been broadcast? But, perhaps that would not work; he might still claim to be their King when Orenduil dies, and then it's fight him or accept him, and a lot of people might accept him."

Sir Eldor lapsed into silence. Tara-lin watched his face with love. He looked so tired and overwhelmed. Defeated, almost. She wondered why. Suddenly, she said, "Dad, even if we don't succeed, it won't be your problem. You'll probably die before King Orenduil does, though I wish heartily that it won't be that way."

"So does your mother," said Sir Eldor, forcing a smile. "No, something else concerns me. If the Valor Hall is compromised, say, if Anakrim has his own people high in the structure of the Valor Hall, working for him, depending on how it is, those of us who use our minds and don't blindly do whatever is asked of us, trusting our superiors, but who think about what we're doing, will probably end up being assassinated or executed."

"Couldn't we run away?" asked Tara-lin. "We could fly back to Mom, and then disappear, couldn't we? Especially if I could learn how to shield our presence and confuse anyone who looks for us," she added, flashing a smile.

Her father smiled at that idea, too. "I don't know," he said. "Mom is pregnant, and they will look for us. Still, I suppose it could be tried. But I gave oath. I'd have to break my oath, and I won't." He dropped his voice. "Not while the Valor Hall might not be compromised. Not until I'm asked to do something wrong."

Tara-lin nodded. "But I don't want you to die!"

Her father was about to speak, but suddenly she jumped to her feet. "If they kill you, I'll, I'll, I'll k-kill them!"

"Let's hope it's not as bad as I fear," he said. "See what comes of sharing my thoughts with my daughter?"

"I *don't* think it's funny," said Tara-lin.

"It's not," said Sir Eldor. "But c'mon, relax, and I'll share about my interactions with people and point things out to you? I enjoy being with you. Having an elven wife and daughter makes me wish my own lifespan were longer, for you age so slowly, and I want to do and share things with you."

"I feel that way, too," said Tara-lin. "It's why I *am* coming with you on this mission, no matter what anyone, including you, say about it."

Sir Eldor chose not to push that issue at the moment, though he did not waver in his resolve that she should not accompany him. "Do you want to sleep in the same room as I?" he asked her.

"Of course," said Tara-lin. "We always slept in the same... tree-house, together, at home. It would be awkward otherwise."

"The humans around here would think differently, but come. I think we have sheets and bedding enough here."

Chapter Five – Escape from the Valor Hall

Over the weeks, more people arrived. Tara-lin was introduced to human ladies, and she found their company exasperating, for the most part.

It was not long before Lìrulin came to them. When Earnrìl had come back from the sea, she had borrowed her horse and ridden to them. It was now certain that she was pregnant. She stopped arguing with her parents about how she was going to go with her father.

One day, Tara-lin observed her mother and her father embracing. "I'd go with you, Eldor, no matter what, if I weren't pregnant again... You must not die! You must not leave me with our second child an infant who's never seen you."

Tara-lin stood still, feeling horrible.

"I don't intend to die," said Sir Eldor. "We don't know what this will be like, or what my role in it will be. But, if you don't want that, we *will* have to make sure you don't get pregnant again."

"I love you," said Lìrulin.

Tara-lin walked away. Just earlier that day, she had met a girl who did not irritate her as much as the other women – or men – around. Her name was Alis Luela, and though she spoke little she was definitely interested in what Tara-lin had to say about the animals and plants of the Elethrian forests. She was quieter than the other girls, and spoke little about herself and the other things interesting to them, and when she did ask Tara-lin a question it was about something in which Tara-lin herself had some interest.

It took Tara-lin about half an hour to find Alis. When she did she came up to the girl and, finding a pause in the conversation, said to her, "Would you like to come to my room and talk?"

Alis' face visibly brightened at Tara-lin's suggestion. "Yes!" she said. To the other young women she said, "We'll talk more later. It was nice enough."

Several minutes later, both were sitting on the furs that would have been Tara-lin's bed except that she slept in the same room as her parents. They were silent for a few moments, then Alis said, "How I would love your life, Tara-lin! I'd love to hear an owl hoot flying over my head as I sleep in a hammock high in the trees! I'd love to look over the edge and see a herd of deer go running by! I love to have hours to just sit still and let the rabbits get used enough to me to sniff my hands!"

"It's really nice," said Tara-lin. "Do you know how to ride a horse?"

"Alas, no," said Alis. "I groom them. I tack them up. I lead them. But learning how to ride? To really ride, so you can fly with the horse like the wind and soar over obstacles? No. After all, I can't be a knight, can I? It would just be a waste to teach me, I'm told, and distract me from my real life. It was hard enough for me to be allowed to learn how to care for them!"

"I'm so sorry," said Tara-lin. "Maybe, when this whole thing about Anakrim is over, I can take you back with me to Elethri, and you can get to do all those things. I'll teach you how to ride my very own horse by my very own self!"

"Oh, that would be so fun," said Alis wistfully, "but I can't."

"Why not?" asked Tara-lin.

"My parents wouldn't allow it."

"Are you that young?" asked Tara-lin.

"I don't know what that question means," said Alis. "I'm sixteen. Are you allowed to just run away and do whatever you want?"

"Well, there are some things I'm not allowed to do, but it's more that there are things I'm *not* allowed to do, and I'm going to do one of them anyways!" said Tara-lin. "I can go down to the sea with Earnrìl whenever I want to. I could do other things, too, and my parents wouldn't like it, but I might be able to get their permission to completely go off. Either way, I'm half-elf. But someday I'll be allowed to do as I like. I think I could, now. So that's why I asked if you were that young."

"Well," said Alis, "I'm old enough my parents want me to be married."

"What are you talking about?" asked Tara-lin.

"My parents want me to marry, and I don't want to," said Alis. "I *love* the idea of being able to, well, do as I like. Kind of like a man." At this point, she giggled nervously. "Not having someone I have to answer to, about everything."

"Well," said Tara-lin, "can you promise not to tell anyone something for me?"

"Umm, sure," said Alis.

"Okay. I'm going to run away and do something I'm not allowed to. My parents don't want me going with my father on his mission, but I'm half-elf and I'm going to live for centuries, and he's human, and may not live another forty years, if all goes well. So, I'm going to follow him. If you want, I'll take you with me," said Tara-lin.

"Sure," said Alis, then, "Can I ask you a question, Tara-lin?"

"Yes."

"How do elven women marry?"

"They marry whomever they want to marry, whenever they want to marry!" said Tara-lin. "That's how Dad and Mom got married."

"Tell me about it," said Alis.

So Tara-lin did so. Before long, she felt a lump in her throat.

Eventually, Alis said, "You don't have to tell me if you don't like."

"It's not that," said Tara-lin, and went on.

Finally, Alis said, "That is one terror of a story! Are you sure I want to come with you chasing your father on some mission to do something about a Prince Anakrim who wants to make himself a wizard? It sounds like it could get very nasty."

"Well, umm, do you have a better idea for how you want to run away?"

"How could I?" asked Alis. "I know precious little. I'll be looked for. I wouldn't know where to go. I wouldn't know who would take care of me and not turn me in. But, Tara-lin, will you also keep a secret for me?"

"Yes," said Tara-lin.

"I will *not* marry. I won't." Alis' voice grew low and her manner heated. "Right now, my family orders me around, but I never consented to it. I never made myself their child. I never promised to be their child. I will *not* make the marriage vows. I won't! I'll die first."

"Would it really come to that?" asked Tara-lin.

"I don't know," said Alis.

"Well, then, how much worse can it be to run away with me? After all, I can even do things. I don't know very much about them yet, but I'm not completely helpless," said Tara-lin.

"What kind of things?" asked Alis.

"It would be hard to describe them. You'll just have to see," answered Tara-lin.

Alis smiled. "That I would love to do," she said. After a long moment, she added, "Of course, though my father would hate it, he could not forbid it, so I could always take the service of one of the gods, and that way not have to marry, but it would be just as bad. I would be at least as bound."

"What's that like?" asked Tara-lin.

"I don't really know," said Alis. "The girls who do it don't get to interact much or play with the rest of us. Some who don't want to marry take that route, but I *won't*. I will not give control of myself and my life to someone else. They can take it; I won't give it. I want to see the sea. I want to ride a horse. I want to watch owls and deer. I won't voluntarily give that up."

"You shall have it," said Tara-lin. "You will come with me, and you shall have it. Even before the mission is over and we return home, you shall begin to have it. You will see all kinds of trees and bushes, you will see deer and foxes and owls and eagles and wolves!"

"That sounds so fun," said Alis. "If you figure out how, I really will run away with you."

Tara-lin laughed. "Thanks, Alis. But I think we should go to bed now."

"Probably," agreed Alis.

A week later, after Sir Eldor and his company had left Astri, using the power of her elven cloak, Tara-lin sneaked into the portion of the Valor Hall where the clothing and weapons of war were kept. After finding what she considered suitable camouflaging clothes for her friend, she walked across the room and stood before a table on which were arranged many swords. All had two edges and were of a metal which shone with a faint bluish tinge. Tara-lin tapped one of them upon the blade with her finger, and for a moment a wavering green flame sprang up from the blade around her finger.

She stepped back with a gasp. Ancient elven swords, the art of whose making was among the many things her people had lost. She knew, however, that of these swords some would flash a green fire, others a purple fire, or a blue one, or a yellow one, or yet a red one.

Tara-lin took one of the scabbards lying near, belted it around her waist, and sheathed in it a sword on the table which looked and felt to be the right weight for her. Then, trusting to her Elethrian cloak to conceal her theft, she left the room.

That evening, she invited Alis into her room after dinner, as they were wont to do. From under the furs, she pulled out a man's camouflage tunic, pants, and war cape which she had somehow filched.

"I'm sorry I can't get another Elethrian cloak for you," said Tara-lin to Alis, "but these will have to do."

"They're too big!" said Alis.

"Yes, I know, I've thought about that," said Tara-lin. "This tunic will hang over your shoulders. You can tie the cape as tight as you need it. The hood'll go over your head quite nicely. These pants will cinch tight enough they don't fall off. To keep from tripping in them, put the bottoms into your boots. It'll look funny, but it'll work. You're about the same size as I am."

"All right," said Alis. "I'll change."

When she had done so, she laughed. "This is so funny, and I'm sure I look as funny as I feel," she said.

Tara-lin shrugged. "I don't know. It's not important to me. You'll probably get to hear owls tonight."

Alis grinned, then said, "What about your mom? Won't she worry?"

"I hope not," said Tara-lin. "I quit arguing with Dad about how I'm going to go some days before she got here. I'm going to leave her a note that says that I'm going to go explore the area around here. Unless Dad told her, she'll have no reason to guess what kind of exploring I'm really doing."

"Uh-huh," said Alis. "So, umm, when do we go? Where? How?"

"I have, here," said Tara-lin, "two pouches which we can wear under our capes. The food in them should last us a couple of days. I have a little bit of Elethrian currency. But I should be able to find food for us. It'll be fine."

Alis nodded. "But when?"

"We wait a couple hours," said Tara-lin. "Then, when there's not too many people about, but it's not so late they'll wonder what we're doing, we go out... take a walk... and run!"

"Ah!" said Alis. "Sounds exciting. But what if we're caught?"

"If you have a better idea, share it. And, you don't *have* to come with me. Unless you have a better idea, I'm leaving tonight, whether you come with me or not," said Tara-lin.

"Yeah, I'll come," said Alis. "Of course, I'll come."

The two girls passed the time talking about various things. At one point, Alis said, "Is there a way we can get horses? I would love to get to ride one!"

"I doubt there's a way for us to get horses tonight," said Tara-lin, "but I might be able to figure it out sometime."

"So, something to do with your strange powers which you don't fully understand but which you've assured me you have?" asked Alis. "Can't you tell me something about them? What are they?"

"I'm half-elven," said Tara-lin. "Elves have... abilities that... well, it takes us centuries to really understand them, and it would be very hard to describe them to someone who has never experienced or seen them."

Alis rolled her eyes. "You sure you have them?" she asked.

"As certain as I am that I have an Elethrian cloak that will make me almost invisible in the wild, and it will hide me quite well even if I'm not in the wild," said Tara-lin.

"But I haven't seen that," said Alis.

"You will see it tonight," said Tara-lin.

The two were silent for a while, then Tara-lin said, "I think it's time."

Tara-lin pulled out her note and left it on her furs. Then, she and Alis went to the door and opened it. Tara-lin led the way, using her elven senses to lead them down passages where they would not encounter the few people still walking about. While a chance glance from the distance would not ruin their plan, she did not want them to be seen too closely. Alis, dressed in her camouflaging too-large men's clothes, would certainly wake suspicion.

Soon, they were in the Valor Hall gardens, completely abandoned at this time of day. With less caution – not only would no one be around, but Alis' garments would now camouflage her instead of making her look suspicious – they moved quickly through the gardens and to the garden wall.

"How will we get over that?" asked Alis in a hushed, scared tone of voice.

"This way," said Tara-lin. "You aren't as nimble as I am, but this should work. See that? I'm going to push you up, you will grab the top, and pull yourself up. Okay?"

"Okay," said Alis. She sounded uncertain.

Tara-lin grabbed her around the waist and began to push her up. "Help me," said Tara-lin. "Use your legs and hands to help me. Here! Now! Grab it!"

Alis scrambled to the top of the wall, then looked at Tara-lin. "I'm scratched. And how will you get up?"

"Your scratch will heal, Alis," said Tara-lin. "When you live in the wild, it happens. As for how I will get up, don't ask stupid questions so often."

Tara-lin turned, found a tree the branches of which grew near to the wall, and rapidly climbed it. She stood perilously on a branch that waved under her weight, gauged the distance between her and the wall, and leapt. She landed on the wall, several paces from Alis, who crouched in a fearful huddle.

"Now, how do we get down?" asked Alis.

"Easy," said Tara-lin, and swung herself over the wall, landing lightly on the cobblestone street below it.

"What about me? I'm not an elf!" said Alis in a hushed squeal.

"Come over here. I'll help you," said Tara-lin.

Alis scooted over.

"Now, sit with your legs dangling over the edge."

Alis did so.

"Now, slowly, start to slide down. I'll make sure you don't come down too quickly."

Alis did so, and Tara-lin helped her.

"Now, we're in the middle of the city," she said, beginning to sob. "My father says it's downright dangerous in the city at night for a girl like me. Maybe it isn't for a half-elf like you, but I'm human."

"Sshh," said Tara-lin. "We'll be fine, and we aren't in the middle of the city. I can feel which way the forest of the foothills of Malaitha are, and I climbed up the tower of the Valor Hall this morning to watch Dad and his company ride out. I know which way to take us."

"All right," said Alis, clinging to Tara-lin.

"If we had two Elethrian cloaks," said Tara-lin, as she began to lead Alis along, "there would be no concern or worry at all. My parents got into Nightshade Castle with Elethrian cloaks, and this isn't Nightshade Castle."

"So, you really think we'll be fine?" asked Alis.

"Yes, I really think we'll be fine," said Tara-lin.

Perhaps an hour later, Alis said to Tara-lin, "This city is big. And what about the gates? I remember hearing that the gates are always closed at night."

"That's no problem," said Tara-lin.

"It isn't?" asked Alis. "I wouldn't want to climb a wall like that again, and the city walls are a lot taller than the Valor Hall walls. They're more than three times as tall as I am, not just under twice as tall."

"It'll be no issue getting to the top, at least," said Tara-lin. "That part's easy."

"What about to the bottom?" asked Alis.

"Look, I really have an idea," said Tara-lin.

"All right," said Alis, but she sounded more skeptical than ever. About half an hour later, she pointed. "That's the wall!" she said.

"That's the wall," said Tara-lin. "Let's get closer."

"And what about those guard towers?" asked Alis.

"They won't be watching for two girls creeping over the walls," said Tara-lin.

Several minutes later, Tara-lin said, "Look at this house?"

"Yes," said Alis.

"We're going up on the roof. This time I'll get up first, then help you up."

Alis nodded. Tara-lin grabbed the overhang and jumped up. Leaning back down, she said, "All right. Give me your hands, and jump for it."

They walked along the roofs, climbing when necessary, until they stood on one next to the wall, which rose another seven feet above them. "This should be easy," said Tara-lin.

"None of this is easy," said Alis.

"Well, you're free," said Tara-lin. "No one will ever consider you property again. I'll go up first again."

Tara-lin sprang for the wall and pulled herself up. This time, she scratched some of the skin off of her hands. Then she scrambled back around to help Alis up.

Motioning to indicate the wall, she said to Alis, "This isn't so bad. It's pretty thick, so even you should feel pretty comfortable up here."

"I guess I do," said Alis, giving Tara-lin a smile in the moonlight. "But how do we get back down?"

Tara-lin smiled, then called, a low, whistling note that rose and fell gently and smoothly. Alis watched, entranced, wondering what was about to happen.

Before long, they saw a large shape coming towards them. Tara-lin continued to whistle. Alis sat down and drew herself together, shivering a little.

When the beast was near to them, Alis leapt up. "A gryphon!" she exclaimed. Turning to Tara-lin, she said, "I didn't know you were a gryphon rider."

Tara-lin was silent for a few moments, as the beast landed beside them. Then she turned to Alis. "I'm not. This is a wild gryphon. But I've called animals before, in the Elethrian forests, and I've seen enough gryphons, I thought I could call one, and here he is."

She turned back to the gryphon, and stroked his shoulders and mane. She thought he was a dark brown one, though she could not be sure in the lighting. After a few minutes, she said to Alis, "Normally, two don't ride a gryphon this size, but I'm only asking him to bring us down a short ways, so here. I will help you up."

The gryphon flinched a little as Tara-lin helped Alis seat herself on his shoulders. Then Tara-lin climbed up, behind Alis, and putting her arms around the human girl's waist, gripped the gryphon's body tightly between her legs.

Tara-lin whistled again, softly, and the gryphon turned and spread his wings. He glided down from the wall and landed, heavily Tara-lin thought. He shook himself, and both she and Alis fell off. A moment later he was in the sky again.

Standing up, Alis said, "I've reconsidered my request. You don't have to find me a horse. I will be more than happy if you can get me a gryphon."

"That's as hard a task," said Tara-lin. "That gryphon is wild. He will stay with his pack which lives in the Malaitha Mountains. Now, sometime, when I don't have my Dad to follow, and it's the right time of year, maybe I'll take you and we can try to see if we can find any young gryphons. You have to find them as hatchlings, or they won't bond to you, and gryphons are usually very protective of their eggs and young. It's hard for even an elf to get close to them."

"What about the tamed gryphons?" asked Alis.

"Their eggs won't be given to us," said Tara-lin. "Let's go, now."

Alis followed, much happier now. "I never thought I'd get to ride a gryphon!" she repeated over and over again. "I certainly never dreamed of riding a *wild gryphon!*"

As they climbed up towards the mountains, through wilder and wilder land every minute, Tara-lin said to Alis, "I've never ridden a gryphon myself, until today."

"You were right you could do things though," said Alis. "Did you know it would work?"

"I wasn't certain," said Tara-lin. "If it hadn't, I would have had to reconsider, maybe get down from the wall and find another way."

Alis shook her head. "The stakes are a lot higher for me," she said.

"I guess that's true," said Tara-lin. "And you have a lot less experience with stuff. I'll try to be more considerate."

Alis laughed. "More considerate? You're doing a lot for me."

"You've only made this barely harder, so far," said Tara-lin.

"Not for that gryphon!" said Alis.

"That gryphon isn't me," said Tara-lin. "Besides, he only did a little bit. It wasn't that hard for him anyways. You should see him hunt if you think that was hard!"

"I guess I don't know anything about anything," said Alis, "which reminds me: aren't the woods and mountains supposed to be dangerous at night?"

"Yes," said Tara-lin. "Even for me, this isn't exactly safe. But there's two of us. That counts for something. And, what *safe* way of running away from a life of subjugation to others' wishes can you think of, Alis? It's a lot safer than other things which might meet us following my Dad on his mission."

"Sometimes," said Alis, "I don't know why I let you talk me into running away with you. Then I remember seeing that gryphon fly in, and I know why. You told me I'd probably get to hear owls tonight. I rode a *wild gryphon*. How much better is that?" She laughed gaily. "I mean, how many people have gotten to ride wild gryphons?"

"I don't know," said Tara-lin.

Hours later, Alis said, "It's getting lighter."

"Yes," said Tara-lin. "If the Malaitha Mountains weren't between us and the dawn, we'd see the sun soon. As it is, how about we find a place to eat and nap a few hours before going on?"

"Are we going to go the whole way like this, sleeping several hours in the morning, and walking all night and most of the day?" asked Alis. "You might be able to, but I'm full human and I won't last that way."

"No," said Tara-lin, "just for now. We'll find a good place to sleep tomorrow night. Then –"

"What is that?" asked Alis.

"The morning cry of a hawk?" suggested Tara-lin.

Tired as she was, Alis jumped up and down. "So, in one night, I've ridden a wild gryphon, and heard both hawks and owls?"

"Yes!" said Tara-lin, smiling at her.

"Thank you so much, Tara-lin," said Alis. She embraced her

friend.

"Well," said Tara-lin, after she had let her go, "I am both hungry and tired and thirsty, and so are you, I'm sure. Let's find a place to rest, and then we'll drink from the water bottles we have, eat a little, and sleep a few hours. Then, we'll get up, and look for a better place to spend the next night."

"That sounds like a good idea," said Alis.

Chapter Six - Elven Kin

Several hours later, the sun almost at its zenith, Tara-lin shook Alis awake. "Time to wake up and go on!" she said.

Alis sat up and rubbed her eyes. Coming a little more awake, she said, "Can't you just call some gryphons, and ask them to carry us up to their caves, or whatever, and take care of us?"

"I'm not sure that will get us closer to Dad," said Tara-lin. "Also, I wouldn't trust my influence over a wild gryphon I'm not riding with you on his back. Besides, I don't think they would agree. They'll help us now and then, here or there, but their homes are their sanctuary. Remember when I told you they're very protective of their young?"

"Yes," said Alis.

"Well, that's where they keep their young," said Tara-lin.

"How do you know so much?" asked Alis.

"I don't," said Tara-lin. "I know nothing about court etiquette!"

"You know all the useful, interesting things. I know only boring things I never learned well enough for anyone around me... except for you."

"I don't care for you to know them at all," said Tara-lin. "Besides, there's lots more interesting things I don't know. But what I know, I'll teach you. That is, what I can. There are things I know – or, at least, can do – that I can't teach you. And I should let you know. Most elves are even more capable of those physical feats that astonish you than I am."

Alis rolled her eyes. "As much better than you as you are than me?"

"You could be better than you are, if you had practice, instead of being stuck taking lessons in court etiquette!" said Tara-lin. "Let's get going."

Alis got clumsily to her feet.

For the first few hours, Alis was constantly commenting on the things around her. She asked Tara-lin the names of flowers and trees, many of which Tara-lin did not recognize, being different from those in the Elethrian forests, but others of which Tara-lin did know quite well. They saw many different birds, and Alis asked about all of them.

Alis stopped and said to her friend, "Tara-lin, after you fell asleep, as tired as I was, I couldn't sleep for a while. All the singing little birds were just too beautiful.

"Then, I looked around, and for a moment I didn't see you. I know what you meant about the Elethrian cloaks, now."

Tara-lin laughed. "Well, let's keep on going. I want to cover as much ground as possible. Dad may stay longer in places we may pass through, investigating things or messing with politics, but they're riding horses at least some of the way, and I want to catch up with them."

"But I'm so tired, now," said Alis. "My legs feel so weak."

"That's what happens when you run away for freedom," said Tara-lin. "C'mon."

Another several hours later, Tara-lin stopped. "Hush!" she whispered, holding up a hand to Alis. She stood for a few moments. *It is just as I feared,* she thought, as she heard clearly, in the near-utter silence that followed her and Alis coming to a halt, the sound of a couple footfalls and a breath. *We are being followed, watched. If only we had two Elethrian cloaks!*

Tara-lin did not speak her fears to Alis, fearing that it would only freak the human out and make it even harder for her to do what had to be done. She did not even know herself what was following them. It could be the orcs who readily followed anyone, seeking to visit evil upon Areaer. It could be outlaws or bandits of some sort. She was not sure if it mattered which.

This glade is too open, thought Tara-lin, again leading Alis. *But if worst comes to worst, I might be able to hide both of us in my cloak. I also have the elven sword, but I won't trust to it, though I'll use it if I have to. I've never been taught how to use a sword. One place where my education is as deficient as Alis'!*

"What is wrong?" whispered Alis, as Tara-lin led her faster and faster up the hills.

"I don't know," answered Tara-lin. The next moment, the half-elven girl came to stop. Above her a tree spread out its arms. The boughs and leaves, something about the tree, made it look to her as if it were the limbs, or maybe even the facial expression, of some personal being. It was not the first time a tree had given her that look; in fact, it happened to her quite often, but in her current state of mind she could not help but be arrested by it.

Then she noticed that the sounds of their pursuers melted away.

She should have heard them in the silence as Alis stopped beside her, even over the human's panting, gasping breath. However, she heard only the usual sounds of the forest.

Then, something in the air wavered. Out of the shadow of the tree, or from behind the tree, or out of the tree itself, stepped a woman almost ten feet in height and very slender. Green leaves, intermingled with moss, covered her form, from her ankles to her throat to her wrists. Strings of moss fell from her head like hair and clung above her eyes like eyebrows. Her eyes were a green so dark Tara-lin thought at first they were black. Her skin was rough and a shade of brown, slightly darker than Tara-lin's own skin.

Beside her, Tara-lin felt Alis freeze, then whisper in a frightened tone, "What's that?"

"A dryad," answered Tara-lin, not frightened now, but awed. Dryads were a rare sighting even for elves.

The dryad paused, and as she did so she almost melted into the form and shadow of her tree again. Then she spoke. Her voice was resonant and musical. "Don't be afraid. I'm not going to hurt you. I don't hurt humans easily. I'm called Aumoura. What are your names?"

"My name is Tara-lin," answered Tara-lin, "and my friend is Alis Luela."

"Well, Tara-lin and Alis Luela," said Aumoura, "your pursuers shall not find you for the moment. I think it wise to give you something which will better hide you in the future. Alis Luela, come here."

Alis froze. "What's she going to do?" she asked Tara-lin.

"I don't know," answered the half-elf, "but I don't think it will hurt you."

"No, it will not hurt you," said Aumoura. "I am going to give you something like what your friend wears. It will not hurt. Now come."

Alis cast another glance at Tara-lin, then stepped forward, away from her half-elven friend. The dryad also moved forward, becoming more definite and distinguishable from her tree. She reached out and touched Alis, first upon the shoulders, and then again the air wavered. A nimbus of green light surrounded both dryad and human, and Tara-lin waited, watching. Though no such sound entered her ears, and she could not even quite imagine what it would sound like, she could not shake the sense of a song somehow related to the light and the dryad's work. It was not an audible hum or thrum, yet she was certain of such a thing. Something moved like a song.

Then Aumoura stepped away from Alis, and Tara-lin saw in a moment what the dryad had done. Alis' clothes were transformed; they still had the same shape, but like Tara-lin's cloak they would blend right into their environment.

"Your clothes will now mask your presence and can make you almost invisible in the woodland, even while you move, Alis Luela, though I do not think they will hide you as well in the structures built by men and others as the cloaks of Elethri," said the dryad.

Alis curtsied, a full, graceful, court curtsy. "Thank you, Aumoura," she said.

Tara-lin did not know what to say or how to respond to the dryad, but she said, "My people have not often seen your kind for a long time, Aumoura. Why do you grace us with your presence?"

The dryad laughed; it sounded like a low, soft wind. "You were in need of my help; else you might not have seen me. But, if I am not mistaken, you, too, are a singer. Your people have grown away from us dryads over the years, but you, I think, are closer to us. The ancient magic runs true in you. Unless I am mistaken and it was not you who called the gryphon?"

"It was I," said Tara-lin, "but I do not understand most of what you are talking about. Can you explain yourself?"

"I can explain myself," said Aumoura. "Perhaps, it will be best if I start right here. You are called a half-elf, unless I am mistaken?"

"Yes, I am called a half-elf," said Tara-lin. "My father is a human and my mother is an elf. That's part of why it surprises me that I should be closer to the dryad world than most elves – who are, I guess, only half my people, in so far as I am only half an elf."

"Exactly speaking," said Aumoura, "a half-elf is little more than a construct of the human and elven societies and speeches. Half-elves don't exactly exist. You see, elves are not really a separate race from humans. Elves are part-dryad and part-human. You, Tara-lin, are part-dryad and part-human. Singing is a talent you have from the dryad magic in your being. You, who have human blood in you, do not sing exactly as we dryads do, but your singing is very much like our magic. That, and the art of making the Elethrian cloaks, which it seems your people still have to judge from the fact that you are wearing one."

"Yes, my people still have that," said Tara-lin. "Every elf has one. But are our other magics, those we have mostly lost, also dryad magic?"

"Many of them are the combination of dryad magic with the human mind and position in the world, and thus far beyond our reach," said Aumoura. "I am glad you still have the magic of the cloaks, but most of your people's arts were never accessible to us dryads. Many and wonderful magics you made, but they were far too human for us, even if the humans could never have made them without blending their powers with those of the dryads."

Tara-lin caught Alis glancing back and forth rapidly between herself and the dryad. When a pause ensued, she said, "I never thought of *that* explanation. How very strange."

Aumoura looked momentarily confused to Tara-lin, but then she returned her attention to the girl. "If I am correct," she said, seemingly almost to herself, "you are a distant cousin of mine. This may make some things easier." In another tone, she said, "Tara-lin, there haven't been many singers in Elethri for a long time, have there?"

"Until myself," answered Tara-lin, "as far as I know, there haven't been any in fourteen hundred years."

"Well," said Aumoura, "you can rest here tonight. You will be safe under my tree, though I may often be invisible to you."

"Wait!" said Tara-lin.

Aumoura looked back at her.

"Does the fact I'm closer to you and your magic than most of the elves mean I'm likely to live at least a full elven lifespan?" asked Tara-lin.

Tara-lin could feel Aumoura inspecting her, thinking about her. "I don't... think so," said the dryad. "I can't tell for certain, but I think you'll live something in-between, very long for most humans but considered short by most elves. But I can't tell, and there've only been a few of what you call half-elves throughout history of which I know, that is, since those humans with dryad blood coalesced into a separate nation and a more or less uniform race. As far as I know, no one, not even a dryad, can tell how long what you call a half-elf is going to live. But when the dryads and humans first mixed there was a great deal of variety; it only gradually evened out into what is average among elves today. But I judge that you are nearly full-grown, but not quite."

The dryad partially faded into her tree, though Tara-lin remained keenly aware of her presence beside and through the tree. Then she noticed Alis' sleeping breath. The girl was already fast asleep. Tired herself, she took a sip from her water, and then laid down on the soft, leafy ground underneath the tree's branches and was asleep in a few minutes. As she drifted into sleep, Tara-lin was aware of the dryad's magic in the air and ground around her, something not fully audible but more like song than anything else she knew.

In Tara-lin's sleep, dream full of bright, colored shapes ran into dream full of bright, colored shapes, and in each of them a song replayed itself, over and over and over again, and every time it replayed itself it grew more solid and tangible and near to Tara-lin's awareness, but when she woke she could not remember it at all.

It was early dawn when Tara-lin woke. She felt at once the presence of the dryad, and, looking up, saw her standing in her tree, amazingly clear in the twilight of the dawn, surveying the forest. Taking her eyes from the dryad, Tara-lin looked on the sleeping face of her friend, Alis. After watching Alis' breathing for a few moments, she returned her gaze to the dryad.

A few minutes later, Aumoura leapt lightly down from her tree, to standing towering like a tree herself over the now-sitting Tara-lin. The dryad paused for a moment, then asked, "Why are you here? Elves don't often wander here, and I don't think you were raised here; I think I'd have known of you before the night you called the gryphon."

"My father is one of the Valor Knights," said Tara-lin. "He's on a mission to stop Anakrim, who is the only son of the only child of our King and Queen, from gaining unnatural powers for himself. I'm following him, since, well, he won't live that much longer by our standards, and I will. And I just have to." The look on the dryad's face made her lapse into silence.

"It is good that you follow him, singer," said Aumoura. "This Anakrim *must* be stopped." The dryad closed her eyes and seemed to battle some emotion or thing of that order. "He is stealing the life-energy of dryads; He *must* be stopped." Aumoura opened her eyes again and stared deep into Tara-lin's. "I just received news from a sister. You must follow your father and you must help him, with those magics that are yours because you are both dryad and human."

Tara-lin nodded. "I know. I'm going to try. But I still don't understand why or how I am a singer. I should be farther from you dryads, since I have less of your blood in me, than an ordinary elf, shouldn't I?"

"It isn't always like that," said Aumoura. "There is much that no one understands. At any rate, there *is* dryad blood in most of the humans here, just a great deal less of it than there is in the elves. When humans and dryads mated, most of their offspring mated with one another, and they formed the nation of Elethri, but a few vanished into the multitudes of other humans."

Tara-lin nodded. "But I still don't understand."

"Nothing is as simple as blood and descent, as we dryads well understand," said Aumoura. "You – your personality – your affections – your willingness – these things have a great part in who and what you are. I am not the dryad of this tree because it was *forced* upon me. The elves have grown away from what they should be; they have not grown away from their ancient magics because their ancestry failed them; rather, it is the other way around. They stopped caring, and, gradually, it changed them and caught up with them."

Tara-lin nodded. "I suppose that makes sense. It is something like some of the things Dad said, some of the conversations he and Mom used to have."

"Who is your mother, Tara-lin?" asked the dryad.

"She is called Lìrulin," answered Tara-lin. "She was involved in the mission to keep Falkur from unleashing a terrible evil on the world, along with the Valor Knight, Sir Eldor, who is my father."

"Why was she with that mission?"

"From what I've heard," said Tara-lin, "she knows more about herbs, their uses, how to find them, perhaps how to guess at their uses, than most elves. She's taught me some of it, and I know more than my friend Earnrìl, but that might not mean anything. Earnrìl might just not be interested. I think she was wandering around in this country, and she met Sir Eldor – that's my father – and they liked each other, or something, and he told her they would need the woodcraft of her people, and she agreed to go with him, and Se'lorn and Tarunth agreed to take her with them."

"Your mother was dryad-taught," said Aumoura. "She already knew more than most elves her age, and she spoke often to dryads. I am surprised she has not told you of this. I spoke to her once, and I suspect she spoke to more dryads as she journeyed north, and learned from them."

"Perhaps she thought it right to let me discover you on my own? To let you choose if you would speak to me?" asked Tara-lin.

"Perhaps, but there is another possibility. I now know your age within a year or two; you cannot be much younger than I think you are, which is about twenty, and you cannot be older than twenty-two. That means you have matured only a little slowly for a human. That is very fast indeed for an elf to teach all she knows and would like to pass to her daughter; fast even for an elf to understand and keep up with, I think," said Aumoura.

"Does she know that elves are part-human, part-dryad?" asked Tara-lin.

"I don't know," answered Aumoura. "I know now that I must help to ensure that you are able to reach your father and to track him, probably into the Nightshade Castle itself. When you leave me, I will send you north with many fruits and with herbs that even your mother might have difficulty finding. I will teach you all I can, and hopefully others will be able to teach you more, but you cannot stay long, for otherwise your father's company will get too far ahead of you. But I judge having them a little ahead of you will do no harm. Therefore, you will stay today, and tonight, and continue north tomorrow, if you agree."

"I do," said Tara-lin.

"Your friend stirs," said Aumoura.

Alis sat up. "Tara-lin," she said, "I had beautiful dreams."

"Cool," said Tara-lin. "I dreamt about something I can't quite remember but I almost do."

"You will remember when you need to," said Aumoura.

"Do you know what it is?" asked Tara-lin.

"Not really; remember, there is much about us that is incomprehensible to the other." The dryad stepped away, then paused. "Though I know now for certain that we are cousins of a sort; your mother was definitely kin of mine."

Chapter Seven – The Dream Song

"So," said Alis to Tara-lin, "what kinds of gods do the elves worship? How do they worship them?"

Tara-lin shrugged. "As far as I know, it is a common belief among elves that all things have some kind of a spirit or animating force or personality. Some elves worship dryads; they must have forgotten that they themselves are dryad-kin!"

"Not necessarily," said Alis, interrupting. "I know that many of my people think the gods have sometimes had offspring with men. But tell me more."

"Some elves worship the Sea Spirits or other things. Each elf does as he or she pleases in these matters, and I know little about them. Neither Mom nor Dad taught me much about whatever religion they might have known from their upbringing. Most of what I do know I know from listening to conversations between other young elves, or from Earnrìl," explained Tara-lin.

"Is there anything you worship?" asked Alis.

"No. Why should I?" Tara-lin shrugged. "Though, I did once meet someone who might be a god. He wore light of white and red and gold; perhaps he was made out of light, for I saw through him like a rainbow. He told me something I didn't understand about answering a call when I heard it. But I don't want to talk about it. Why the questions, Alis?"

"Because I want to know about you," said Alis. She looked down at her hands for a few moments, letting Tara-lin know this was not all of her answer. "Because... because, I'm a renegade. According to what I have been taught, what I am doing will bring shame on my family in the eyes of the gods and disgrace me for the afterlife." She sighed. "Women exist to belong to others... either to be married to men or to be the priestess-brides of gods. But I don't want that." She looked up into Tara-lin's eyes. "I want to do what *I* think is right."

"I understand," said Tara-lin, feeling uncomfortable. "That's what I'm trying to do right now: what I think is right."

"We've been taught that we're weak," continued Alis. "We're supposed to be weaker than men, both in mind and in body, so if we aren't guided – that is, told what to do and think," said Alis, bitterly, "then we'll fall prey to the deceptions and influences of demons. If we willfully go our own way, we're supposed to be exposing ourselves still more. 'It's for your good that you are to submit to us,' they all say. Even men can easily go astray and be deceived if they rebel against the authorities and teachers above them, to do whatever seems right in their own eyes." Alis shook her head, sadly. "That's my heritage, Tara-lin. One part of me tells me that can't be right; that can't be the truth; reality isn't like that; I've been lied to. The other part is afraid, afraid I'm walking right into hell."

"I'm so sorry," said Tara-lin, "but I'm not in the least bit concerned that what you've been taught is correct."

Alis smiled. "Thank you, friend."

Tara-lin thought that Alis still seemed unconvinced. "Alis," she said, softly, "how do *they* know they aren't the ones tricked by a demon? Any god like those gods *is* a demon!" Anger rose in Tara-lin's voice as she spoke.

"But what if – what if it is true? What if they'll strike you for such speech?"

"Let them!" said Tara-lin, rising to her feet. "Let them! Anything that controls by *fear* deserves to be defied. How are they better than Falkur – or Anakrim, then?"

Alis smiled weakly up at Tara-lin. "I'm glad you care for me, Tara-lin," she said, "but I'd rather not talk this way."

"If you like," said Tara-lin. "I don't care much."

"Thank you," said Alis.

Tara-lin shrugged.

A few moments later, Aumoura materialized above them. In her arms were bunches of berries and other fruit, which she quickly dropped in their laps. "Here, children."

"Thank you," said Tara-lin.

Apparently Alis was still thinking about gods. "Dryad, do you worship anything?" she asked.

The tall woman stood silent for a few moments, as if thinking. "There is a rumor," she said, "about someone named Shallim-Araldor, who, while not a dryad, is King of Dryads. I don't know what you humans call worship exactly; we need the rain, and thus the one who brings the rain, and the sun, and the earth."

"Are you allowed to think for yourselves? Do you have to obey male dryads and only do and think what they tell you to?" asked Alis.

"What?" said Aumoura, plainly not comprehending.

"Among my people," said Alis, "we are taught that for women to think for themselves and do as they think right is to fall into the snares of demons. Men can think for themselves and do what they think right a little more, but they, too, have to obey and only think what those in authority above them tell them to, for they too will fall into the snares. It's a little more complicated than that, but basically, is it like that among the dryads? Were you taught that?"

"No," said the dryad slowly, still plainly confused.

"Well," said Alis, "thanks for telling me. And thanks for the fruit."

"You're welcome," said Aumoura graciously. Then she turned to Tara-lin. "Am I right that you carry an elf-sword?"

"Yes," said Tara-lin.

"Good. The magic in it may help you, but I cannot tell you much about it, for though I sense it, and though much of it is based on dryad magic, it is too different from our magic. But it may help you."

Alis, her mouth full of berries, said to Tara-lin, "An elf-sword?"

"Thousands of years ago," said Tara-lin around the fruit in her own mouth, "my people forged magic swords. When the borders of Elethri were secured, and all the orcs driven out, the swords were kept as trophies and the art of their forging forgotten. Many of them were lost, but it seems the humans at the Valor Hall have a whole stash of them. I wonder if some of them use them, but without benefiting from the elven magic, for there is not enough dryad blood in them to make the magic work for them, or even, perhaps to sense it. I took one from that stash."

"Oh, I didn't know!" said Alis. "Can I see it?"

"Sure," said Tara-lin. She laid the fruit the dryad had cast in her lap on the carpet of leaves, threw back her cloak, and drew the sword. As it came out of the sheath, ephemeral and airy purple fire danced along its edges. She held the blade before her, long and straight and narrow, for the dryad and the human to look at.

"Wow!" breathed Alis.

"It will serve you," said Aumoura.

Tara-lin held it for a few moments longer for them to see, then sheathed it again, and grabbed another handful of fruit.

"Those swords are the heritage of my people," said Tara-lin. "Perhaps, sometime, I shall sneak into that room again, and carry all of them away."

"Do they all make that purple stuff?" asked Alis.

"They make it in every different color, and I doubt they make it in the hand of someone who doesn't have enough mastery or link with the magic of their forging," said Tara-lin. "The humans probably think they're well-made blades of a light, well-tempered metal, and don't know they're anything more. Goodness! They may not even know they're elven-forged, but I recognized them almost at once, and then I tapped one, and when the flame sprang up, I knew for sure."

The two girls looked around, and found that the dryad had vanished. But when she was done eating, Tara-lin had a feeling that the air was all a-thrum with some song-like magic. She rose and pressed herself against Aumoura's tree, closed her eyes, and felt.

Waking dreams, impossible to describe, passed through her mind.

A breath of cold wind on her face roused Tara-lin. She looked around her and saw that it was evening. "Hi!" said Alis. "So, you're awake now."

"I – I, uh," began Tara-lin.

"Never mind," said Alis. "*I* have been sleeping, and *I* only woke up probably about an hour ago. That's my best guess, thinking about how the shadows should move, but it could have been only fifteen minutes ago, or it could have been two hours ago. But it feels like it was all day."

Tara-lin gasped.

"What did I say wrong?" asked Alis.

"Oh, I'm just surprised that you don't know whether you woke up fifteen minutes ago or an hour ago, and you tried to track the time," said Tara-lin. "If you haven't noticed it getting a lot cooler, I'm sure it's been less than two or even one and a half hours."

"Well, thanks for explaining that to me," said Alis. "I have noticed it getting a little cooler. In fact, I'm a little cold."

Tara-lin sat down, rather ungracefully.

"Sore standing?" asked Alis. "I'm sore and stiff all over."

"Try to walk a bit," said Tara-lin. "It should ease your muscles some."

"I've done some of that. I was too bored waiting for you to... stir, so I walked around a little."

"I hope I've not been treating you too rudely, Alis," said Tara-lin.

"Not at all. Sometimes you get on my nerves a little, but I'm certain I get on your nerves a lot more than you get on mine. Besides, you're the one helping me run away, not me helping you. No, you've been a great friend, Tara-lin. Better than I... well, not than I ever dreamed, but than I ever really expected to have," said Alis.

"That's so sad," said Tara-lin.

"Not now, it isn't," said Alis. "I'm happy now."

"You don't miss your parents?" asked Tara-lin.

"I mean, I do... a little," said Alis slowly, when Tara-lin jumped in.

"I guess maybe you don't. After all, if they were going to force you to marry, or enter some kind of a monastery, and if you didn't take one of those two options, you didn't even know what might happen to you... they're not like my Mom and Dad at all. They don't deserve to be called Mom and Dad, anymore than those gods they worship aren't demons or non-existent," said Tara-lin.

Alis said, "You're still harsher, your judgments and speech are still harsher, than I'm comfortable with."

"Sorry, again," said Tara-lin.

Tara-lin felt the shadows and the air shift. Aumoura was coming to them. "Here, children," she said, "here is your meal for the night." She once again laid a bounty of fruits in the laps of the human and the half-elf.

"Do you ever eat yourself?" asked Tara-lin, then suddenly felt a sharp wave of embarrassment, as the dryad was sitting down and taking some berries for herself.

"It's okay," said Aumoura. "I'm not offended. But I think you learn very well. I have only a small idea what your capabilities are, but I think you will find them much more developed and much broader than they were last. I think you will *know* them, know how to use them, know what they are, much better."

"Thanks so much," said Tara-lin.

"It isn't much. I enjoy the company of elves; I wonder that many other dryads apparently do not, but I do. Besides, this Anakrim is threatening our existence at least as much as he is threaten-ing yours. So, I'm helping you to help us." Smiling brightly, the dryad said, "Don't be concerned. I'd do this for you even if that wasn't the case."

Soon after the meal, Tara-lin fell asleep. She was too exhausted, despite the similarity of her state for most of the day to sleep, to keep awake, even to hear the beautiful singing of some exotic species of nightingale, perched in an adjacent tree. Her dreams were still filled with strange and yet familiar, alien and yet deeply-resonating bright and colorful shapes and shadows, and a lilting something like a melody surrounded by several harmonies.

In the morning, Tara-lin was roused by Alis, who told her the dryad had already brought them their breakfast. Even after eating, Tara-lin felt, if anything, even more tired than she had the previous evening. However, she and Alis got up and continued their journey northward through the lower foothills of the Malaitha Mountain Range.

Over the next few days, Tara-lin grew increasingly frustrated. Not only was Alis sore and uncomfortable, but she was constantly tripping and getting caught. Even when she got along fairly, she was far slower than the elven-born and elven-taught Tara-lin. Tara-lin tried to be patient with Alis; in truth, it was not the younger girl's fault; she could hardly expect her to learn in a few days what she had had opportunity to learn in twenty-years. Even an elf, with Alis' experience, might not have gotten along a great deal better. Nonetheless, she was frustrated. Would her kindness to Alis mean that she would be too slow to find and catch up to her father, or to help him defeat Prince Anakrim, who, she now knew, threatened not only the stability of the elven kingdom of Elethri but the very lives of the dryads, her own kin?

Tara-lin knew that, despite her own fears, her friend sensed her frustration and unease and knew that it was, at least in part, occasioned by her own ineptitude at crossing forested and hilly terrain. Alis was grumpy, and would sometimes curtly remind Tara-lin, "You didn't have to decide to help me!"

"I'm glad I did," Tara-lin replied. "I just don't know how things are going to turn out."

Then, they were almost out of their food, taken by Tara-lin from the Valor Hall and supplied by the dryad. Tara-lin led again, as they descended the foothills and looked for a vale in which they would find a place to buy supplies with the money she had taken.

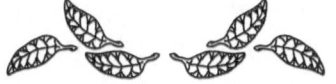

Tara-lin smelled the scent of smoke in the air. She stopped and waited for Alis to catch up to her.

"What?" asked Alis.

"Smell that?" asked Tara-lin.

"What?" asked Alis.

"Smoke," said Tara-lin.

"Umm, no. Should I? What does it mean? Is there a forest fire? Are we in danger?"

"No," said Tara-lin. "We're not in danger. I doubt it's a forest fire. And it's no surprise you don't smell it. I barely do. I suspect it of being the smell of cooking. Let's go."

A couple hours later, Alis said, "Are you sure we're going in the right direction? I still don't smell it."

"The wind changes," said Tara-lin. "We're going in the right direction all right."

"Okay," said Alis. "I can't wait. I hope I'll be able to spend *one* night in a real bed."

"The dryad's accommodations were pretty good," replied Tara-lin. "But c'mon."

"They were," agreed Alis, following Tara-lin. "But that was a while ago."

"Five days," said Tara-lin.

The night was settling in when Tara-lin and Alis made their way into the town. Tara-lin had instructed Alis to keep her hood over her hair and ears, far enough to obscure her face.

Tara-lin paused for a moment to recollect all that her father had told her of human towns and customs, then made her way to a large building from which many different voices could be heard. She passed through a large door-way into a lighted hall, very different from anything for which her experience among the elves could have prepared her. By this time, both she and Alis had already been assaulted by the smells of various and different foods, though more than a few of the smells were foreign to Tara-lin and some of them she had already decided she did not like.

With Alis, Tara-lin made her way over to a long table placed across the back of the room. She called, "We're hungry, and would like to buy food!"

A woman quickly came to her. "What do you want?"

"Whatever you have that's least expensive," said Tara-lin.

The woman named a price for loaves.

"That's exorbitant!" said Tara-lin. She had had some teaching from her father on how to handle these matters. "I'm not here to buy a hot meal, so don't charge me for the heat. I don't have enough coins to pay that much for every meal and live a week on it! What about," and Tara-lin named something a little under a quarter of that price.

"If I sold everything that cheap, I wouldn't be in business for a week," said the woman. "The loaf costs me more than that."

"Then give me one that isn't cooked for the wealthy," said Tara-lin. "No common man or woman can afford the price you name more than a couple times in a year. What do you charge the locals?"

The conversation went on for some time, until the woman said, "Fine. I'll sell it to you for," and she named a price twice what Tara-lin had demanded. "But where are you from and what are you doing?"

"From east of here. Going with a friend to visit south of here. I got a little lost on all these roads I'm not used to. We're cousins of sorts," said Tara-lin.

"Ah," said the woman with a delighted sigh. "By the way, customers get beds. I'll have someone show you your room. One for both of you, right?"

"Yes, thank you," said Tara-lin. When the woman turned away, Alis came forward, and they both leaned on the table while they waited. *I hope what I said works,* thought Tara-lin. *That woman is probably a gossip. Even if she isn't, half a dozen others heard what I said. Two young ladies traveling alone is bound to arouse interest, and though it's not likely anyone will guess I'm half-elf since I didn't show my ears and half-elves are very rare, I'll certainly arouse interest. Eyes a green rare indeed among humans and eyebrows a red just as rare. It'll get people talking for sure. Hopefully no one suspects who we are, since there's bound to be a search on for Alis.*

In a few minutes, a twelve-year old boy came to them with a tray on which were two loaves and a pitcher of water and two glasses. He showed them a room on the building's second level and laid the tray on a nightstand. Tara-lin and Alis thanked him, then went into the room and closed the door.

"At last! A bed!" said Alis.

"Only for one night," said Tara-lin. "I want it to be two more weeks and a lot farther north before we visit civilization again."

"Well, I'm hungry," said Alis. She cut a piece off the bread with a knife that had been provided and began to eat it.

Tara-lin stood for a moment in indecision, then decided to throw away all semblance of human court manners. She tore a piece off the bread and began to eat it, just like she would have in her elven home.

When the two girls had taken care of their needs, they quickly fell asleep. Though Alis was far more exhausted than Tara-lin, both were tired.

In the morning, while Alis was still asleep, Tara-lin went out and used some of her coins to buy as much bread and dried fruit as she could carry, as well as some milk and juice for her and Alis to drink that morning before leaving. She managed to preserve a few coins after getting what she wanted, and then returned to the room she and Alis shared.

Alis was still asleep, so Tara-lin woke her. After a little grumpiness, Alis thoroughly enjoyed the food, though she complained that it was poor compared to what she had eaten in her father's house. Tara-lin reminded her that she did not want to be in her father's house. After eating, they went down the stairs, intending to make their way out of the town and continue north along the Malaitha Mountains.

As Alis stepped down the stairs, a voice rang out. "Alis! My daughter!"

Everyone in the room froze. For a moment Tara-lin hoped that if they stood still enough they would simply vanish and they could slowly creep out. Then she knew it was a vain hope. Even if she could manage to move stealthily over those boards, she was certain that Alis could not do so, and she doubted even her ability to do so. Moreover, their clothes were designed to blend into foliage, not human buildings, and as such would not provide their best cover. Also, the room was very bright, which would not help.

Tara-lin turned to Alis. "If you want that superior food?" she asked.

"No!" shouted Alis. "I won't go back to being told who and what I am and what I must do with my life by others."

"Take her, and take that idiot who kidnapped her," commanded Alis' father.

Many of those in the tavern did not seem inclined to make way for him or to obey his commands. They stood gawking and doing nothing more.

"Do it!" the Valor Knight shouted, pushing his way forward himself. "As for you fool, Alis, you won't get that nice food. What did you think? That your pea-sized woman-brain wouldn't be led astray by demons and you'd end up in the infernal regions?"

He was drawing nearer. Tara-lin stepped in front of Alis, opened her mouth, and began to sing in a slow, haunting, creeping tune, barely audible.

> As ice grows on lonely banks
> As snow falls on fallow fields
> Dawn creeps lazy up the skies
> And stars slowly drift to sleep
>
> Don't watch as the sap grows slow
> Don't hear as sleep comes on fast
> Nightfall comes with stealthy dreams
> Your eyes close on outside light
>
> Your heart slows as silent snow
> A warmth as deep as winter
> Lulls you to a summer sleep
> Like winter's deepest silence

For almost ten minutes she sang. Almost at once the movements of the people in the inn became slower, drowsier, more clumsy. Some of those standing and gawking fell asleep almost at once and slumped down on chairs or laid themselves on the floor, further hindering the progress of those who would capture Alis. Her father stumbled, tripped, fell, struggled, cursed in a lazy, dreamy voice, and could not find the strength to get back up. Soon, he too was falling asleep. Still Tara-lin sang, wrapping her song around them in fold after fold.

She let the last note fade away, and turned behind her to where Alis had slumped down against the wall and sat on the stairs. In a rousing tone, she whispered, "Awake, arise, let us fly!" and shook Alis.

Alis looked at her dreamily. "Come!" she repeated, grabbed her friend by the hand, and made her way between and over bodies and chairs and tables, guiding Alis so that she would not trip over anyone. Once they were out in the open, they ran for the cover of the woods and hills.

Panting, Alis collapsed on the far side of a stream. Tara-lin stood, only breathing a little hard from the run. Her thoughts were a combination of elation, frustration, and fear.

Chapter Eight - Hospitality of a Young Tree

Tara-lin was elated because of the proving of the power of her song. She could imagine how proud of her, her Mom and Dad and Aumoura must all be. She was upset for related reasons. She had showed her power, and her enemies might learn of it! Even she had little knowledge of what it really was, how much and what she could do. It also upset her that the Valor Hall would learn where she and Alis were.

Alis looked up at her and asked, "What happened? When will they be after us?"

Tara-lin's eyes flashed and her face flushed as she spoke. "Even if they do come after us, they will not find us! They will be humans, bumbling around in a forest. We are protected by the dryad magic in our clothes. They will not find us! But, if things go as they may, they may not even try. The dreams of elves and dryads will fill their sleep, from which they should not rouse for an hour or two. Perhaps, they will realize the world is not what they thought it was and there is much they do not know and they will be ready to learn."

Alis shook her head as if she did not think that likely. "I'm so tired," she said.

"We can rest a few more minutes then. We should still be away as quickly as possible," answered Tara-lin. *The Valor Hall!* she thought. *What kind of a Valor Hall is that? My father was right. It is not what he thought it was, if it ever was!* So Tara-lin fumed.

Rising a little, Alis looked up at her. "What is it?" she asked in a worried tone.

"The Valor Hall!" said Tara-lin in an angry hiss. "My father's suspicions were not unfounded. But I don't think we want to talk about this right now."

Alis nodded. "You're probably right. We probably don't."

A few minutes later, Tara-lin said to Alis, "Let's go now."

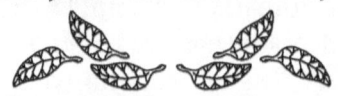

The tension, which both regretted, soon began again between the two girls. Alis was always hungry and she always ate more than Tara-lin, and she was always tired and, from Tara-lin's perspective, slow and clumsy despite the half-elf's constant attempts to gently teach her. They were not nearly so unsuccessful as Tara-lin felt them to be. Alis was soon traversing the wooded hills in the lower boundaries of the Malaitha Mountains with a skill and dexterity which would have amazed all of her previous acquaintances and which approached that possessed by humans who had lived their whole lives hunting and traveling such country. However, Tara-lin did not notice this. She noticed only that she wanted to find her father in time and to save the dryads from Prince Anakrim, and that Alis was far slower and clumsier than herself.

One night, Alis said to Tara-lin, "If you didn't want to deal with me, you shouldn't have taken me."

"It's not that, Alis. It really isn't," said Tara-lin. "I like you. I'd probably be lonelier than I am if you weren't with me. And when this is over, I intend to do something to give people like you options to... do what you choose!"

However, a few mornings later, Tara-lin looked at the remaining food, and said, "Alis, you eat twice as much as I do!"

"I don't like nothing but fruit," said Alis, "but why don't you look for a dryad and ask her to help you? From what I heard that other dryad say, they should all be eager to help you."

"That is an idea, Alis," said Tara-lin, grinning. "I wonder I didn't think of it before. Thank you. We'll do that today."

Several hours later, they were trudging up a particularly difficult ridge of the mountains, when Tara-lin thought she heard something. "Stop," she said to Alis, and stood silent for a moment, hardly breathing. *Yes. Men are coming after us,* she thought.

"Alis, into that brush over there," she said. "We're being pursued, but with these garments we should do well. Just beyond there is a flat, open place, in deep shadows. We will lay there. If they come there, just be still and try to relax. The dryad's gift will conceal you."

Alis nodded, clearly frightened, but she made no objections.

Tara-lin could hear their pursuers getting closer, but Alis did not notice the sounds of them until she and Tara-lin were both laying in drying, still green, grass and dirt.

With much noise, the men emerged from the thicket of brush. "They went through here, don't you think?" asked one.

"*Something* went through here, rather recently," answered another.

"How recently?"

"An hour? Two hours? Last night? But I think it was more recently than last night."

"There's no one in the bushes, right?"

Tara-lin thought the next speaker shrugged. "None but the very best of human hunters could lay hidden there from us. But who knows what that witch can do? She put a whole tavern to sleep."

There was fear in the next voice. "I don't really want to find her. They should have sent a bunch of priests with us. We should go back and say that the witch is hiding herself and the child she kidnapped from us, and demand that we need the priests to come with us."

"That's a good idea," said one who seemed to be the leader. "Do that, then. But make sure you really *can't* find them hiding in those bushes, and we search this whole area, first. Remember, they did give us some blessings of protection, so we should not fall into their snare."

They don't know I'm elven. Great! Tara-lin thought. *I bet Mom was wise enough not to suggest I might be involved or fit the description given. Instead, I probably grew weary of the Valor Hall and went to play with my elven friends. Goodness, am I even old enough to pull off such a thing?* As the conversation went on, she thought, *How I would love to sing out and show them their absurd gobbledy-gook doesn't protect them against the dryad song at all! But that would be unwise, so it will have to go for now.*

She and Alis lay still while the men continued to search around. When they were gone, Alis inched over to her and said in a soft voice, "What shall we do now?"

"Wait. I don't want there to be any more tracks, in case they should come back this way, and I don't know how to conceal or erase our tracks. So we wait," said Tara-lin.

"Aren't you in a hurry to find your father? Does this make that less urgent?"

"You're right, Alis. I will go and look for a dryad I can speak with. Come with me. Even if we run into them and are exposed, my song can protect us," said Tara-lin.

Thrice now have I truly used the song, thought Tara-lin, *and thrice it has achieved its meaning, each time more powerfully than the last. The first time, I brought the rain out of clouds almost ripe for it. The second, I called a gryphon. The third time I made men sleep and gave them dreams.*

Tara-lin led Alis, quietly and slowly, forward, always listening. Then she stood still, and sang softly:

Let my voice pass formless through the minds
Of those who know not union with the trees
But dryads fair and with your trees one
Hear my voice and answer if you will!

For as I seek to aid your freedom
Help from you to live and to survive
Nurture from you and your protection
From those who know not the peril near.

Tara-lin stood quietly, as the last note died into utter silence in the woods. "This way, Alis," she said. "Here is a dryad who speaks to me."

A few minutes later, Tara-lin passed ahead of Alis through a thicket and saw, standing under a thin, slender tree stretching to reach the sunlight, a dryad. This dryad was as tall as Aumoura and at least as slim, with skin a shade darker and just as rough, under which bunched hard, strong, straining muscles. A short kilt of peeled, aging bark girdled the dryad's hips, and thin strands of moss hung about and from head and chin and shoulders, down to the elbows. The knees also bore such dangling patches of moss, and lichen grew on knees and shins and on the arms and chin. Ears resembling those of elves but also resembling leaves, grew out from the sides of the head, and the eyes were a dark, sparkling red-brown.

"Welcome, child," said the dryad, in a voice reminiscent of a high, wailing wind, but much softer. "And who is this you bring with you?"

"This is Alis, a human who was seeking freedom from those who wanted to marry her against her will. She is my friend. I am Tara-lin, half-elf and singer." As she spoke, she saw a look she had never seen before, except that it bore a certain resemblance to a gaze she had seen somewhere – oh yes, the young men in the Valor Hall! Suddenly, she burst out in a different tone, "Oh! You are a male dryad. When Aumoura told me that elves are the off-spring of humans and dryads, I should have realized not all dryads are female."

The male dryad laughed. "No, but for some reason we *look* rather feminine to most humans and even, surprisingly, most elves. So it's not a surprise that you were confused for a few moments. But what do you need?"

"We need to be hidden from those who are looking for us, sent from the Valor Hall, and we need more food for our journey north," said Tara-lin.

"The Valor Hall?" asked the male dryad. "Why is the Valor Hall looking for you?"

"They say I'm a witch. As I said, I helped my friend here, Alis, run away. Then, they came after us, and I sang a bunch of people to sleep. So they think I'm a witch."

The dryad laughed again. "If they knew your power was the dryad song, I wonder, would they accept it, or would they think they have to kill the trees to keep us from having a dwelling place and life in Areaer among them?"

"I don't know," said Tara-lin. "They might even think the evil was dryads marrying men. After all, you dryads very rarely interfere in their affairs."

"And that more often in the past, though I think I understand now what I never did before: why a dryad might marry a human," said the dryad. "Though," he added, again laughing a little, "if they knew, they might think dryads are evil, and male dryads seduce vulnerable female humans! But what about when the woman is a dryad and the human is a man?"

Alis spoke up then. "The dryad might still be evil, a demon even. They have stories about women seducing men, witches taking advantage of men, maybe having sex with them in order to kill them, all kinds of nasty things. Either women are evil, or they're vulnerable to deceptions and corruption. According to them."

"How funny!" said the dryad. "So, they would think us demons who possess the trees, and in trying to drive us out of the world they think is theirs, they would kill both our friends, the trees, and bring death on themselves. Without us having to do a single vengeful action or even think such a thought. How very funny!"

"I don't see what's so very funny about it," said Alis.

Neither do I, thought Tara-lin.

"You don't?" asked the dryad. "Well, I don't know how I might explain it to you better."

Tara-lin broke in. "How do you know so much about what the humans think? Aumoura was completely confused by it when Alis tried to tell her."

"I heard that group that came looking for you talking amongst themselves," answered the dryad. "As I said, I am a young and wakeful dryad, inhabiting, as I do, a tree yearning for more sunlight."

"Does that have something to do with it, then?" asked Tara-lin.

"In a way," said the dryad. "But you have told me your names and I have not told you mine. My name is Manaear. But you said you were hungry?"

"Not right now. We had a good breakfast. Water we would like. We were going to look for a stream, when they came after us. We also need them not to find us."

"The last is no trouble to us," said Manaear. "Not I only but the other dryads here will not let them. I will bring you water. Rest in the meantime."

"Thank you," said Tara-lin. As the dryad left, she thought, *Does he like me? Does he want to renew the inter-course of dryads and men and marry a half-elf woman? Or is it Alis he is looking at? I do not think that is such a wonderful idea. There is pain and difficulty because my Mom is an elf and my Dad is a human. I think it could not be better, but only worse, if a dryad and a human, or even half-elf, married. And I understood from Aumoura that, when the elves were just beginning to be a race, their lives varied greatly in span, so that many unions were probably much as Mom and Dad's, except that no one really knew how long another would live. That could only make it harder.*

He is rather handsome, but he could not successfully woo me. I have no desire to lay with a dryad, as much as I love them, even if this issue of lifespans were not between us.

Alis' voice broke in on Tara-lin's thoughts. "What did he mean by saying he now understands why dryads and humans wedded?"

"He could imagine wanting to wed one of us. Either that, or he does," said Tara-lin.

"Well, I don't know about you," said Alis, "but I'm not marrying *any*one, not even a tree! I'm going to be a gryphon rider. The first female human gryphon rider in Areaer, probably."

"I'm not interesting in marrying a dryad either," said Tara-lin, "but a dryad is not a tree."

"Close enough for me," said Alis. She lay back on the most comfortable spot of leaves and ferns she could find and closed her eyes, while Tara-lin looked around, examining the trees of the thicket in which they lay, and discerning something of the nature and probable appearance of the dryads who lived in them. After about a minute, Alis said, "This dryad is not much like the other one we've met."

"There's no more reason for two dryads to be alike than for two humans or elves to be. I'm also pretty certain that Manaear is a lot younger than Aumoura, and he is definitely the other gender. Think how different the trees are. Why would you expect dryads to be more like to each other than humans are, or than trees are?" asked Tara-lin.

"He's just... not what I thought of," said Alis.

"Until I told you they did, did you even think dryads existed?"

"If orcs and bad magic exist, why not dryads and dragons?" said Alis.

"I've no idea that dragons *do* exist," said Tara-lin. "Falkur once said he had dragon eggs, but my parents think they were probably the eggs of an exotic and large species of drake-lizard."

"Is there a difference?" asked Alis.

Tara-lin shrugged. "Dragons are *supposed* to be creatures as huge as mountains who form such bonds with humans that for *either* to die is the death of the other."

"I know *that!*" said Alis. "Do you mean in elvish tales dragons bond to humans, not elves?"

"I wasn't thinking that," said Tara-lin, "but now that I think of it, we don't have as many stories about elf Dragonriders as about human ones. I'll ask Mom and Dad about it the next time I see them."

Alis laughed lightly. "They seem like nice people to me." Then she added, "But I can't imagine a dryad Dragonrider, though elves *do* seem to be, in a lot of ways, more like humans than like dryads."

"I'm only a half-elf," said Tara-lin, finding the subject amusing. "Though it is funny. Elvish legends suggest that elves are the elder race, elder than humans, but if elves are the children of dryads and men, then the human race must be older than the elvish one."

"That is funny," said Alis. "So, few of the elves know they are not a race separate from both humans and dryads, but the intermingling of the two races?"

Tara-lin was about to answer, but out of the shadows, ever suggestive of the magical life inhabiting the trees which cast them, came Manaear. "Here is our water," he said. "I hope you will like it. I have tried to make it such that humans will appreciate it." He held out a gourd filled with water and having a hole in the top.

Tara-lin let Alis take it, and as soon as she had done so, the dryad produced another, which he gave to the half-elf. Tara-lin put it to her lips and sipped. It was certainly a flavored water. The taste was mild, slightly sweet, and, Tara-lin thought, *brown*, an almost pastel medium brown. It was not really exciting, but it had a slight tang which, if it had been stronger, would have been harsh. Being rather thirsty, she took several long swallows and, glancing up, saw Manaear intently watching their appreciation of his gift.

"How do you like it?" he asked, and Tara-lin saw that Alis appeared to have finished hers.

"It's... it's interesting," she said. "I've never had anything like it be-fore, but I... I think I could get used to it, but I'll always enjoy our kind of water."

Tara-lin took another sip, thinking, *So is it she he's interested in, not me? Either way, he's a fool. He's handsome and beautiful in a very tree-ish way, but Alis has no more interest in, as she says, a tree for a husband than in many of the others offered to her, and neither do I. Of course, I'm not interested in anything of that sort at all. He could think I'm young, and the time it will take for me to mature is nothing to a dryad, I suppose, but* her? *He'll be sorely disappointed for sure, unless he's just making casual conversation with a guest. Which he might be. He cannot know well how humans interact, even if he listens and learns faster than the older dryads.*

Manaear turned to her now, and said, "And how do you, elven singer?"

"It has refreshed me quite nicely. Thank you, Manaear," said Tara-lin.

The dryad bowed the upper portion of his body in a way which struck Tara-lin as comic. The way his leaf-like mossy hair waved from his head and body and the whole way in which he moved looked rather like the boughs of a tree waving in a strong wind.

"Rest and sleep as you will. I will bring you more refreshments," said Manaear.

Before the dryad vanished, Alis said, "I think I will take him up on that offer. I'm always tired, and this feels almost as soft and comfortable as my old bed."

"I wouldn't mind sleeping some more, myself," said Tara-lin. So saying, both girls lay down. Once again, Alis, by far the more weary, slept before Tara-lin, whose eyes wandered over the trees and their shadows, but soon she too slept, and the dryads were clearer in her dreams and their song made itself more and more at home in her mind.

Chapter Nine – Council in the Thicket

Evening was falling when the human-kin woke to find that Manaear had laid a good meal on the ground next to them. Fruits and nuts laid there, as well as various different cloves, including garlic, and an onion. The gourds had been re-filled with water.

Alis was already awake when Tara-lin roused. She looked at Tara-lin almost guiltily, then said, "I tried not to eat too much, but every time I just *needed* to eat a little more. I'm so hungry. The onion is rather mild for a raw onion."

"It's all right," said Tara-lin. "This will be enough for me, and if we want more, I'm sure the dryads will oblige us. Remember: we go to fight for their lives." She reached out and gathered up a few cloves.

"That's it," said Alis. "I'm so scared. I'm not half-elf. I can't wield an elf-sword. I can't work magic, with song or otherwise. I'm helpless!"

"Well, we're still a fair ways from Nightshade Castle. We will worry about that when we get closer. Speaking of which, we need horses. Otherwise, we'll get there months after my father and those with him." Tara-lin did not share that she worried about Sir Eldor nightly.

Suddenly, she went still. Noticing, Alis asked, "What?"

"The trees. Dryads stir. They come," answered Tara-lin. She could feel the air shiver, see shadows melt and move. The air filled with living, vibrant song-like magic.

Manaear appeared then, and out of the deepening shadows of the evening – it was already quite dark in the thicket, other dryads appeared. *I do learn very quickly!* Tara-lin thought, as her mind effortlessly distinguished male and female dryads. There were far more female dryads. Perhaps that was why elves and humans both thought of dryads as female.

"We would like to see the elf-sword, child of dryads and men," said a voice both husky and sweet belonging to a female dryad with red berries in her hair. She was shorter than most of the dryads, with tendrils that looked very much like young branches covering her, and Tara-lin thought she was the dryad of a tree that was almost a bush.

Tara-lin stood and drew forth the sword. Once again it sang out an airy, purple fire. She could feel the intentness of the dryads' gazes upon the blade.

"It is indeed well," said the dryad again. "Its magic will aid your own and may offer you some protection. It will also help you to fight orcs and other nightmare creatures when you have to do so."

"Nightmare creatures?" asked Alis. "Does that have something to do with that wizard's castle? Nightmare or something?"

"Nightshade," corrected Tara-lin.

"Something?" mused the dryad. "Yes, something. Those who built and have dwelt in that castle serve with the nightmare. We think they are as much slaves of the nightmare as the orcs and other things they use are their servants."

"Why?" asked Tara-lin. "I mean, I've heard that most humans, and even elves, find the presence of nightmare creatures paralyzing and that it drives them mad. Why didn't my parents and Se'lorn suffer from this?"

Tara-lin felt the dryads glance around at each other, as if both puzzled and questioning the wisdom of sharing a secret. Then she added to her question. "Do dryads experience this effect to any degree?" Another thought flared up in her mind, and she gave voice to it. "Maybe that's what's wrong with Anakrim! Maybe being born and growing up around maddening nightmare creatures drove him insane."

"Maybe," one of the dryads agreed, in a soft voice which hinted of shyness.

"I hope, then, that there is something we can do for him," said Tara-lin. "If what I've heard of the nightmare creatures is true, then he is at least as much of a victim here as anyone else!"

A shiver went through the dryads. One of them said, "She won't fail us because of her pity for him?"

Another replied, "He must be stopped. That does not mean he must be killed or hurt. A cure is just as good."

A third, the voice of the female bush-dryad said, "Pity is the way of Shallim-Araldor. We are bound not to harm the humans, even though they kill our trees and ourselves. She proves the dryad blood in her is not corrupt. It would be ill if we placed our survival above compassion and worked death, for which our own magic is ill-suited, through another being!"

A fourth said, "Why do you mention Shallim-Araldor to her? We do not know enough to tell other races of him! And you share our secrets."

The second said, "Tara-lin is dryad-kin. She is not another race."

The fourth said, "She *is* another race. She is both dryad and human. And the other – Alis – is human alone. There is scarcely a drop of dryad blood in her veins."

"What I have done I have done," said the bush-dryad. "If they are to help us, they may as well know as much of what we know as we can tell them. What I have told them can do no harm. There may be things some of us know that we neither can nor ought to tell the human-kin, but it would be well if all knew that Shallim-Araldor is compassionate. There is too little pity or compassion among their kind."

"That may be exactly why we cannot yet tell them about Shallim-Araldor!" said the fourth.

"As I said, it is past. It is done. Arguing about it will not change it." There was a pregnant and uncomfortable pause, and the bush-dryad spoke again, as if responding to an unspoken objection. "For our sakes, she and her friend go to fight the nightmare. How can we not tell them this about Shallim-Araldor? Without him, they cannot resist the madness."

Tara-lin almost jumped in the air. "What?! My parents know about this Shallim-Araldor? And they did not tell me!"

"We know little about Shallim-Araldor. We have scarcely more than rumors. Lìrulin and Sir Eldor may not be *able* to tell you. They may have tried to tell you what they can. As you can see, there is opposition among us dryads as to whether others should even hear him mentioned."

Aumoura mentioned him to us, thought Tara-lin. *But she spoke of him as a rumor. These speak of him as someone known, but only barely. Which is it? Does she know less of him than they? Does she consider what they have said here to be rumors?*

She thought it probable that Lìrulin had *heard* the name Shallim-Araldor. After all, she had had a great many dealings with dryads, and *some* of them appeared to think their human-kin allies should know what they knew. Yet she might have shared the dryads' reticence to share their scanty knowledge with others, and she might have known nothing she thought worth passing on – or, as Aumoura had told her about other things, might simply not have gotten around to it yet, for, by elven standards, Tara-lin was very young indeed.

"Anyway," said Tara-lin, "why are you all here? What did you want to tell us?"

"Haste is needed," answered the bush-dryad, whom Tara-lin began to suspect of being ancient, "but we wanted to all watch over your sleep and dream with you, that you might learn as much as possible as quickly as possible. For the task set before you and your father is huge, and even we have no idea how to set about it. For you humans, killing Anakrim, while a major undertaking, is one which admits a great possibility of success. But you, Tara-lin, have other sentiments, ones more in line with our dryadic nature, which you share to some degree. We would also share with you knowledge: how to navigate the mountains, how to recognize when you are near the Nightshade Castle, perhaps even –"

A wail rose up from Alis. "How can I go with you? This is so dangerous! I will be killed or go mad!"

Tara-lin felt the dryads unite in a powerful and soothing song – except it was only so like a song Tara-lin could not help but think of it as a song, and there *was* an element of real song, but she sensed that much of the dryads' magic was not channeled through the song, though its heart was song. Manaear's voice moved through the song. "No one is forcing you to go into the Nightshade Castle. You may stay here, and we dryads will provide you with the best of our hospitality."

"If she's not too frightened," said Tara-lin, "I'd like to have her company for a little longer."

"Just as long as, once it gets really dangerous, I don't have to go on!" said Alis, only a little calmer.

"You won't," said another dryad. "Any dryad – or as near it as matters – will be willing to take care of you. Just don't take her up into the slopes of Icecrown. All the dryads there may be dead, or so near it they cannot be entrusted with the care of a human, by the time you get there."

"Yes," said Tara-lin, "but you must show me how to recognize the place. I'm sorry, too. I'll do all I can to keep you all from being killed by this Prince Anakrim."

"Thank you, Tara-lin, child of dryads and humans, elfling," said the dryads in chorus.

"One other thing, dryads, if I may," said Tara-lin, "how will *I* keep from being overwhelmed by the nightmare and going insane?"

"We have good confidence that you will, friend and cousin, for reasons which we cannot tell you, but which we assure you are there," answered the dryads.

"Well, thank you for that."

They moved then into a mode of conversation which was bewildering even for Tara-lin. At the end, she expressed her doubts about whether she had learned anything.

"You have indeed learned well," said the bush-dryad. "Aumoura has sent us tidings of you, and so we know you learned well from her. We cannot give you our knowledge in a way which is more suited to the human side of your nature. If we tried, you would learn less, for we would be able to teach less in that form. You will integrate the knowledge when needed, so that you may use it well. Not, perhaps, as perfectly as if you were pure dryad, but better than any other way and enough, we think."

"Very well then," said Tara-lin. "I will need a lot of sleep, I think, and I don't know how to make haste – unless I can get horses somehow."

"Try whatever you think will work. You will not be able to go mounted into the clefts of Icecrown."

"I understand. But it will get me *close* much faster, and that's *there* that much faster."

"We understand."

Tara-lin looked for Alis, and was then aware that it was so dark in this thicket that even she did not see very well. Nonetheless, her eyes faintly detected the form of the sleeping Alis. She lay down next to her friend and was, in a few moments, in a deep sleep which soon passed into one still deeper and walked by dreams.

In the early hours of the morning, Tara-lin found herself awakened. The voice of the bush-dryad sang over her, a whispering song. "Greetings, Tara-lin. I hope you feel well. I should give you my name. It is Beriririkirkirkitira."

"Oh my! What a name that is!" said Tara-lin. "Can you say it again?"

"Beriririkirkirkitira."

"I don't know how I'm ever going to learn how to say that."

"I will not be offended if you don't. We are asking so much of you already. And I thank you for being who you are. It would corrupt us further if our lives in this realm were to be saved by blood-shed on our behalf."

"Corrupt you further?" asked Tara-lin, not yet fully awake.

"Sometimes, here or there, a dryad is corrupted. Somehow, the nightmare gets into him or her, and she will respond to the harms humans have done to us and the trees by becoming vengeful. Our magic is such that our ability to harm is limited, but it is yet there. We can use the wind and the power we have over our trees to drop branches on people. Darker still, our song may be used to harm: to put darkness and misery in their minds and hearts, to lure them to their deaths and bring packs of wild animals against them to slay them. I do not need to tell you all the details."

Tara-lin nodded. "Do you think it is wrong – corrupting – when humans kill in self-defense or another similar cause – like this one?"

"I don't know," said Beriririkirkirkitira. "I know that humans in general have far less compassion and pity than they should, and find it far easier to kill than they should, and kill far more than they should. But I don't know if it's ever well for humans to kill. And I cannot tell you what you should do, either. But I thank you for being yourself."

Tara-lin nodded again. "What can I say to that? I *am* myself."

"True," said the dryad. She seemed to take a deep, slow breath, then said, "I want to know more about Shallim-Araldor. I have lived so long. My tree has been burned to its roots or fallen and then come up again many times. My desire for something or someone beyond, and to *know*, has grown with the years – years that seem not yet over. I do not know how many times my tree can fall and grow up again. Each time it happens, I learn something new. I love my tree so much."

"I told Alis once that a dryad is not a tree. Can you tell me more about the relationship between a dryad and his or her tree?" asked Tara-lin.

"I don't know if I can. Have you heard of the Dragonriders?"

"I think so," said Tara-lin, "but, to my people, the stories are all legend."

"There were Dragonriders on Ellenesia when I was young. It is hard to explain. Dragons are farther from us dryads than we are from humans. It was almost impossible for us to speak with any kind of clarity. I think they thought in a way unlike how either we or humans think. They bonded to humans – or an occasional elf, but such bondings almost always ended in great grief. They and their riders knew the other across any distance, felt what the other felt to a large degree, and when one died the other usually died, sometimes instantaneously, sometimes more slowly – most often instantaneously when they were old by the standards of their races. I would say that the relationship between a dryad and her tree is something like the relationship, as I understand it, between a dragon and rider, and something like the union of your mind and your body. But don't take it too exactly. I'm just trying to give you a vague notion, since that is the best I can do."

"I'll try not to take it wrong," said Tara-lin. "But how did the dragons disappear?"

"A terrible war was waged on them by the nightmare, and a curse was laid on them, recently to my thinking. They died in their eggs; they were born weak and frail and died young. Most of their females perished in their eggs, and quickly they died out. It seems to me not unlike the threat that now faces us, but I hope it does not succeed. If it does, almost all will die, for we dryads and trees sustain so much of the life on this world, and without dryads there will be fewer trees and sick ones. The nightmare and whatever is lord of the nightmare is so destructive and evil. It must hate Shallim-Araldor, who is Lord of Life!"

"About how many years ago were the dragons cursed? Are there no more dragons ever again?" asked Tara-lin.

"The dragons almost completely disappeared from this continent about eight hundred years ago. There may have been a few since then; I do not know, for we dryads were never close to the dragons."

"How did they all become legend then?" asked Tara-lin. "That's little more than an elven life-span."

"Perhaps, because the elves have mostly hidden in Elethri and interacted with no one but themselves for longer than that?" said Beriririkirkirkitira.

"It could be that," said Tara-lin. "But I'm only twenty. But, are there never again going to be dragons or Dragonriders?"

The female dryad was silent for a long time. Then she said, "I cannot be sure. I felt something – probably long ago by your standards – that makes me think the curse may have been removed. It was, say, nearly three, four hundred years ago. Such things are hard for me to estimate, I and my tree are so old. That is the other thing, the numbers I am giving you could be vastly off. And I think I feel a very faint sense of dragonlife in the energy of Areaer. We dryads are all inter-connected in a way, so if dragons again fly the skies above another continent, I might know through my brothers and sisters on that continent."

"Well, what did you wake me for? I should probably be sleeping, instead of talking about dragons," said Tara-lin.

"I told you at the beginning much of what I can say. I can only give you a little advice for what you might face: do not fear or hate. It is that which gives the nightmare hold over you. It will try to induce fear and hate in you. Resist it. *Be what you are.*"

"There's that," said Tara-lin. "Shortly before all this happened, or while it was beginning, someone came to me. It was weird – light, gold, white, and red. A man-like form. He appeared transparent, and I could tell he was powerful, and good, and alien. He said to be ready when I heard the call, and then disappeared. Do you have any idea what he was?"

Beriririkirkirkitira shook her head. "Not really. There are beings who call themselves the Ellenari. I don't know much about them. We almost never see them. By all accounts, they are strange indeed. They are messengers of Shallim-Araldor and, compared to them, even we dryads and the dragons have much in common. They can take on different forms. I don't know much more about them. I know of nothing else that what you saw might be, but there are many things of which I know nothing."

"Thanks," said Tara-lin. "I've wondered about that a lot. I thought it meant I needed to go on this quest or mission or adventure or whatever it is. Campaign."

"I can't tell you what it meant. But if it referred to a call of Shallim-Araldor: listen to that call!"

"Well, I should sleep as much as I can," said Tara-lin.

"A moment," said the dryad. She put her hands out and touched Tara-lin's shoulders. The half-elf felt a tingle begin at her shoulders and go all through her body. It felt like she was being infused with living energy. The air around her thrummed with an inaudible song of magic and life and vigor which she knew originated from the dryad. She was unable to measure the passage of time, and felt neither sleepy nor wakeful, but something which either was neither sleep nor waking, or encompassed both.

Then the dryad withdrew. "Sleep, Tara-lin. I feel about you as about a daughter. You will feel well tomorrow. Sleep."

Tara-lin lay down. The dryad's last word still sang in the air with soothing, refreshing magic.

That morning Tara-lin woke first. Birds were singing around her and the morning light filtered through the thicket. Something like ecstasy thrilled through her at the voices of the birds. Sitting up, she saw that a meal had again been brought to them by the dryads. She woke Alis, and both girls set about the meal.

Through a mouthful of nuts, Alis said, "I'm hungry for meat."

"Meat *would* be kind of nice, but I don't think dryads can provide it. We'll have to wait for a while before we can have anything of that sort."

"Yeah, I know," said Alis. "Maybe, we can visit an inn or something, run off with some meat, and, you know, if you have any coins left, we could leave some of them for whoever owns the place as payment?"

"Yes, I have some coins left. I'll think about it," said Tara-lin.

They finished their meal, and found that their bags had been re-filled by the dryads. Then, together, they continued on their way north.

"You said we were going to look for horses, Tara-lin?" asked Alis.

"We *are*. But you forget how recently we were chased. I want to get a little farther away first."

"Okay. Whatever makes sense to you. I think we would be less likely to be found riding away on horseback."

"Well, I don't want to go down and look for horses just yet. You forget there might be a description of me. And my coins are *Elethrian*. It will be a while before I'm willing to go down to get you meat, either," said Tara-lin, though another idea was forming in her mind.

"There ought to be a way for you to sneak away with horses without ever being seen," said Alis.

"Yes, and I may have to do something like that, since horses are not cheap, and I don't have a treasure in my money bag," said Tara-lin.

They walked in silence for a while. Squirrels and rabbits watched them from trees and grass, and sometimes raced across their way, and Alis often exclaimed with delight. Above them, they could usually see hawks soaring. Then Tara-lin said, "Alis, I thought of something you might want to know. What if the nightmare behind Wizard Falkur, now dead, and Prince Anakrim, a present threat, is the same thing behind all the religious stuff the Alliance uses to keep women in subjection to men and men in subjection to the temples and princes? It might be dangerous, but we're going to fight the same thing that's responsible for you having to run away from your family and for never having had any friends before me!"

"That's all fine and well, Tara-lin," said Alis, "but that doesn't mean I'm anymore suited to fighting it. How do you know I even have any protection against the nightmare – the madness, and all that?"

"All right," said Tara-lin.

"It disappoints you," said Alis.

"Not really. Yeah, I guess it does. I've not had a lot of friends. I don't know if I count Earnrìl my friend as I would like to count you my friend. Maybe. But I don't know. And she's the only other. I'd like your company. But I don't want to push you where you don't want to go. And maybe you're right. Maybe you're not ready for this conflict. Whereas I have been called to it, you were not. So it's different for you than for me. I'm not disappointed with you, Alis. Not at all. You've been great. I'm glad I met you, glad I ran away with you, glad to get to know you. That's all."

"Well, I too am glad to be your friend, Tara-lin!"

Evening was falling, and Alis turned to Tara-lin. "Aren't we going to start looking for a place to spend the night?"

"No," said Tara-lin. "Whatever dryad I ask will accommodate us."

"Oh!" said Alis. A few more minutes passed, then the human girl said, "This is great, Tara-lin! We sleep with dryads, we wear their woodland clothing, this is great! I'm so glad I ran away with you. Even though I'm hungry right now. And I'm still sore, though I feel much better than I expected!"

"I'm glad you came with me, too. It won't be too long before we stop for the night. As for you feeling well, I suspect one of the dryads worked on you some of her magic," said Tara-lin.

"Why didn't they do it earlier?" asked Alis.

"I see no reason to think all dryads have the same abilities, and one of the dryads we met last night – she told me her name and it's downright impossible, so I won't try to tell you it – has been around for a *very* long time. I don't know how long. I don't know if she knows how long either. But she was here when dragons flew these skies!"

"Oh!" said Alis. "So dragons are real? What are they like?"

"A lot like the dragons in the legends, and they *do* bond better to humans than to elves. Yes, they're real, or they were real. She thinks they live again, but their race was cursed and they at least *almost* all died," said Tara-lin.

"Oh, that's so sad," said Alis.

A few minutes passed, while the shadows deepened. "I wonder," began Tara-lin slowly, "whether dryads have longer names the older they get. Manaear is a shorter name than Aumoura, and he was a younger dryad. Aumoura is definitely a shorter name is Beriririkirkirkitira."

"What?!" asked Alis. "What's that name?"

"As I said," said Tara-lin, "it's impossible. And I don't know their names get longer as they get older. It's just a weird thought. Maybe she was always called that. But I wonder what Aumoura's name would sound like when she's older, if my thought is right? Aumourararoukoumumukou?"

Alis laughed freely at that. "Manaearaeraenraenmamara?"

"I thought you didn't like him!" said Tara-lin.

"I *don't*," said Alis. "You just didn't try out his name when he's five thousand years old, so I figured I'd give it a try."

"We really have no idea what the lifetimes of dryads are," said Tara-lin.

A few more minutes passed. Then Alis saw her step right to the side and touch a tree. In a soft voice, which bordered on song, she said, "Dryad of this tree, I request your aid on behalf of all your allies and friends."

A shuddering thrill went through Alis, for she felt the magic in Tara-lin's voice and words. Then a form materialized in the shadows, and the voice of a dryad, this time soft, whispering, and nearly inarticulate to Alis' ears, bade them welcome, rest, and be safe. Tara-lin, hearing the voice, felt a shudder herself, one that contained elements of ecstasy, discovery, and fear, all at once. The magic of this dryad was strange, wild, and strong.

It felt like dark boughs tossed around her, weaving an enchantment of confusing shadows. Something about it thrilled her, resonating with her, seeming beautiful and attractive, but it also frightened her. Nonetheless, she sat down and, with Alis, she began eating.

The conflict within her only grew. She longed, almost ached, to learn this dryad's magic, so familiar and yet alien, so enchanting, so gentle, it seemed, yet she was frightened also. Something in it seemed wrong, fierce, out of order and place. She could not quite put her finger on it.

Alis noticed Tara-lin's discomfort. "Is something wrong?" she asked, with real concern.

"I – I don't know," said Tara-lin.

Tired and torn within herself, she still fell rapidly asleep. Shadows, almost formless and yet definite, slipped through her dreams with a texture soft and fuzzy. Intermingling shades of gray, concealing here and there a color, danced and sparked on the field of her sleeping mind. They lulled and excited her, having always the sense of something that drew her, something enchantingly familiar and wholly alien, subtle, persistent, like a backdrop, like something she longed to learn, yet it felt wrong, as if a warning reached her through it, warning her away from it or from something in it. Always it repelled her.

Shadows fall and shadows grow.
Shadows creep and shadows war.
Some may be good, but some are evil.
Some are dreams, but some are nightmares.
Seek not the shadows, though they be destined
To find you and be your solace and joy
For if you seek the shadows, you will find the nightmares
And dwell within the labyrinth of madness
That is torment

Suddenly, abruptly, Tara-lin woke, as if a hand touched her – a hand of which the touch was perfect peace and vibrancy. A maze of hate surrounded her. Her mind was clear, crisp, with a perfect wakefulness that can be preceded only by some sort of sleep. She fought through the shadows, and knew at once where the hate was directed: Alis, and, in a very small measure, herself.

She sang then, though fear surged through her, for she knew that she, a young half-elf singer, battled a dryad.

Dance with the light, dance o shades
Fall where you belong and rest there!
Rise not from your graves

To cover the moon
And the light of the reborn sun
With hate and confusion that is not yours!

Desperately she sang, and her song passed out of language, even while she moved towards Alis. She drew Alis up by the arm, and the girl came awake. With strange presence of mind, Tara-lin stooped to pick up their satchels, and dragged Alis forward. Almost at once, the human fell into step beside the dryad-kin, and Tara-lin stopped singing.

In a minute, Alis stopped again. "What was that, Tara-lin? I feel so tired."

Tara-lin was almost spitting when she spoke. "That dryad – her name is Zànalin – *hates* humans. I don't know everything about why. I don't *think* she intended to do you harm, but be that as may, she was going to harm you. We must find another dryad who is not corrupted."

"Will you know how?" asked Alis.

"I know more than I did in the evening," said Tara-lin. "But are you all right?"

"I don't know. I'm too tired. I feel... weird, but maybe... I don't know. I'm tired."

"Let's go a few minutes further," said Tara-lin. "I, too, feel shaken."

She stood, then, and listening. "A-ah!" she said.

"What?!" asked Alis.

"Strange," said Tara-lin. "There is another here. One who hates me. It's horrible. How? But I know one who will shelter us. Come. It is only a little ways."

She led Alis down a short incline and stopped at a tree part-way down it. Touching the tree, and feeling a life sedate and comforting flow through her fingers, Tara-lin said again, her voice almost but not quite song, "Dryad of this tree, I request your aid for Alis and myself, on behalf of all your allies and friends."

"Welcome, elfling and human. Here you shall rest safe. May you rest well!" said a voice, much clearer than the last, strong and firm, like bark over an ancient branch, toughened by the passage of years and winds.

Tara-lin curtsied. Alis did as well, but she was already almost falling asleep again. She almost fell over as she straightened, and lay down at once. Tara-lin, however, could not sleep. She felt shaken, betrayed even. Alis was right. She felt strange. She sat down against the bark of the tree, but could not sleep.

At last, she asked, "Will Alis be all right?"

The dryad, whose form she had hardly glimpsed in the darkness, which was illuminated only by stars, though a moon would rise later that night, answered, "Yes, your human friend will recover."

"You are disturbed also?" Tara-lin asked the dryad, sensing something in her voice.

"Yes, elfling. I am Elkanakur, and this does not contribute to happiness. I have long known that Zànalin is unhappy and unwell, but even I did not think she would break the Pact. Perhaps, in a stray moment, she might harm a stranger she saw as an intruder, but not the allies of our people or a friend of those allies – not to one who came to her for protection and to whom she offered it! The Darkness grows. The nightmare infects more and more. It is not Zànalin only. Enkardur falls prey to it also."

It felt strange to Tara-lin, hearing the dryad's voice come from nowhere she could identify but, in some vague, indistinct way, from the tree at her back. But she said, "I think I felt Enkardur. If anything, I think he's more hateful than she is. But I didn't know to look for it until I met Zànalin. Though I felt uneasy about her – and powerfully attracted to her – from the beginning."

"We could speculate about why you found Zànalin so attractive, but even now I think Enkardur is less prone to duplicity than she is. His magic is less suited for it also. But I could be wrong, since I did not expect that of Zànalin. There are only a few who would break the Pact that... treacherously."

"Did she fully intend what she was doing?" asked Tara-lin. "If I am right, the existence of a dryad is almost a song of magic, and she might be unable to hate us as she does, and not do us harm when we sleep beneath her protection."

"You might be right," said Elkanakur, "but Enkardur would not do as much harm that way. We dryads differ greatly, and he is, in a way, my son, though that is to use a way of thinking about it which is not perfectly suited to the nature of dryadic life and formation. But if she could do that evil without intending it, it means the sway of the Nightmare grows and is more horrible and terrible and near than I thought. Though I wonder why you were so attracted to Zànalin. Your magic is not much like hers."

"I don't know," said Tara-lin. "Her magic felt both haunting, familiar, and alien. As I said, I was frightened by it, too. And I still feel shaken. I should ask, am I going to be all right? I feel so... weird... disconcerted. Betrayed, even. I don't know what I feel, but I definitely feel betrayed. I feel horrible."

"Yes," said Elkanakur, "I will do what I can to heal both you and your friend. You will be fine. If I miss anything, the other dryads from which you ask protection will do what they can. But I feel confident here. My nature, my magic, is perfectly suited to this. Can you hear it in my name?"

"I *think* so," said Tara-lin.

"You have a great name, yourself," said Elkanakur. "And you were betrayed. Though you took not insubstantial damage from the dryad, more because you were closer to her in the dream-sharing than because her hate towards you was particularly unbridled, you are dryad. Human as well, but dryad, and the dryad nature in you is very strong. She broke the Pact in so many ways, it's just horrible. I think you feel shaken more because that betrayal was so horrible, so unexpected, because the dryad in you recoils from an evil so alien to the dryad nature, because you know, on a primal level, the Pact, and the binding power it has on us. Yes, I think you are shaken and wounded more by Zànalin's betrayal of the nature you share with her and all of us, than by the direct effects upon you of her magic. But I will try to help you deal with that, also, in as much as is in my power."

"Thank you so much, Elkanakur. At least you have a name I can pronounce. I can hardly remember, even less say, the name of another I met. But, this isn't distracting you from taking care of Alis, is it?"

"No, not at all. And about the name, are you speaking of Beriririkirkirkitira?" asked Elkanakur, a laughter that sounded like leaves rustling gently in an unsteady breeze ruffling her voice.

"Yes," said Tara-lin.

"There are others with names as hard – to you – but only a few. I'm glad you like my name. I like you a lot. And you should go to sleep soon, so that I can impart to you as much knowledge of my magic as I can. It is so strange, teaching an elf singer! You are different... and not different. It is just really odd to us. But, as I said, you should sleep."

"Thank you again, Elkanakur," said Tara-lin. "I think I like your magic. A lot."

"You will. It is better for you than Zànalin's, though hers would be so wonderful if she were well. Now sleep."

"I'm just afraid. And, really, how could she do that? If she couldn't care for us, why not say no? This will slow us down, and it's for her life among others that I will be working!"

"Sleep, Tara-lin. I don't know what she thinks. Sleep."

Tara-lin curled up then. Quickly she fell asleep, but before sleep took her completely, she recognized the signature of Elkanakur, and knew she had been influenced by the dryad's magic.

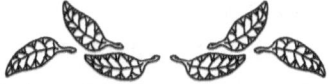

Strength flowed through her dreams, strong, slow, revitalizing. She felt as if she partook of the deepness of the tree's roots, sucking life and water from deep within the stabilizing soil. She felt as if she partook of the strength and sturdiness of both roots and mighty trunk and branches, made strong and fast by years of slow, patient growth, relying and focused on the water below, weathering the heat and winds and snows, rejoicing in the strong light of the sun.

In the morning, Elkanakur gently woke Tara-lin. "Don't be afraid, elfling. I judged it well for you to sleep in today. It will be good for you to wake in the warm and the light. And I have thought about your questions. But don't worry about Alis. She will be well. I think Zànalin harmed *you* on accident. She may have intended to do Alis no harm, but she did not like you for your humanity, but thought you would do better if Alis remained behind – with her no doubt – unable to distract you or hinder you in any way. I think she felt threatened by your humanity also, fearing that any attachment you have to humans damages your ability to help dryads and might be used to turn you against the dryads and the trees. After all, to her thinking, Prince Anakrim is elf, too – and even half-elf, as you elves and humans count it! She must forget, then, that you can help us only because you are elf, because you are both dryad and human, though it is likely that no one who is not both dryad and human could do – or even think of doing – what Anakrim is attempting.

"These, that fear death, are fools, too. It seems to me the fear of death is the greatest madness of the nightmare. It is the seed that allows this corruption. Death is no threat to me or to my brethren. I cannot explain it, but neither I nor my tree fears death. Nor can I think of it as death as humans call it. *Death* is the wrong concept for it, and one I understand only a little, mostly through my conversation with Zànalin last night. When we and our trees can no longer draw life from this world as we do now, we pass into another phase of life, one of which I cannot now tell you anything."

"It seems there's a lot you dryads know of which you cannot tell me anything."

"Someday, you will discover there is much you know of which you can tell others nothing. Perhaps, a day will come when much we could not tell others we can now tell them. Many of us dryads think that is so. I do not know."

"Does this thing you tell me about how you don't die have something to do with this Shallim-Araldor, of whom I hear a little, but also that you cannot tell me?" asked Tara-lin.

"Maybe," said Elkanakur. "Some of the dryads think so. I think neither so nor otherwise. New things have been revealed to me, for in Zànalin there rests a horror, or the fear of a horror, which is incomprehensible to me. I wonder, does *fear* create death? But I still do not know what death is or that it is. It may be no more than fear. I do not know. Nor do I wish to know. But I understand how she did you evil with that song of hers.

"Since last night, since speaking with you and with Zànalin, I wonder: is it wrong to ask you to go on this quest to stop Anakrim? I have had no part in it, but I wonder now if it is the beginning of an entrance into the fear of your race and, perhaps, thereby in your death, whether it is only a fear, or a reality created by your fear, or a thing you fear because it has come upon you – or whatever it is. I do not know nor wish to know. It seems to me that the nightmare is very devious indeed in its quest to destroy our presence here or corrupt our race. And it would be better for us all to leave willingly than to be corrupted in a flight from a passage which is no evil. For us, at least. I do not know what the passage is to human-kin. I do not find the horror even in what you call your own death, but how should I know? There is not a droplet of humanity in me. It may be a thing horrible in itself. I do not know. I keep saying that, don't I?"

"Yes, Elkanakur. But I don't mind," replied Tara-lin.

"Good," said the dryad.

As the dryad was preparing to speak again, Tara-lin interrupted, "Are you asking me *not* to go?"

"No, Tara-lin," said Elkanakur, softly, almost sadly she thought. "If you choose to go, it does not harm me. It does not harm any of us, I *think*. It is the participation in *fear* that would harm us. The attachment to remaining, as long as possible, in this phase of our life. That would harm us. I think it has already begun to do so. As far as I can tell, it is the beginning of the corruption of every dryad who has ever been corrupted. Apart from that *fear*, that attachment to this phase of our life, no dryad would ever be corrupted. As I said, I understand the corruption no more than I understand *death*. It is all unknown to me."

"It is not to me," said Tara-lin. "Not all, but much, of why I am here is because my father is human and will die soon compared to me, and I fear losing him while I am still young."

"That, too, is a fear dryads do not know. I mean, those of us who are well. I don't know what dryads like Zànalin and Enkardur fear or don't fear. But we find no horror or loneliness in it, though it may be horrible and lonely for humans and human-kin. Loneliness is hardly even a concept I know."

Tara-lin was silent for a few moments. Then she asked, "How did Beriri, uh, I don't want to try to pronounce her name right now, know about fear or hate?"

"I don't know," said Elkanakur. "Beriririkirkirkitira is a very ancient dryad. I don't know most of her history. She might have learned much simply from living that long and touching so many different beings through such a long life and thinking so long. I don't know if any dryad has ever been corrupted and then recovered in this phase. She's so much older than almost all of us; most do not live to half her age. Maybe she understands that you understand those concepts and that's all? Maybe she understands them from watching other dryads go corrupt. I don't know, though. These are just idle speculations."

"That's fine," said Tara-lin. "I was just wondering." She sat, curled up against Elkanakur's trunk, and said, "Do you never fear anything? Do you ever fear for Enkardur? You said he was something special to you – not a son, exactly, but like one."

"I do not wish the corruption for him. I wish him to be healed. But I do not know if I fear for even him."

"So then you don't fear more dryads being corrupted?" asked Tara-lin.

"Do I want it? No. Would I do anything it is right for me to do in order to stop it? Yes. I do not know what your question means. I do not feel *fear.* Perhaps some dryads do. Perhaps it is not even wrong. But I do not. I feel sadness," said Elkanakur.

At that, Tara-lin moved and looked above her. Standing in or through her tree, the form of the dryad appeared. She was tall, like other dryads, though not as tall as Aumoura. She radiated strength. She was clothed in green and white, and there was an aura of brightness around her, as if she welcomed the heat of the day. Her eyes were bright, a radiant blue with the light of noon in them. "You're a light dryad!" she said. "Would Zànalin be a shadow dryad even if she were good – well?"

"I do not know how to answer that question," said Elkanakur. "She would not be as I am. And, though seeing Enkardur might help you understand the question you just asked, I don't think it would be good for you to do so. For one thing, I think it would unsettle you too much to meet him."

Tara-lin nodded. Probably it would. In fact, part of how she felt last night could have been due to sensing his hatred towards her as much as to anything Zànalin did. She was quiet for a while, thinking over the events of the last night. "I think I've met this Shallim-Araldor you dryads speak of," she said.

"Really? Tell me what you can," asked Elkanakur.

"Last night," said Tara-lin. "It felt like everything I understand from the name and the various tid-bits I've heard from different dryads. I think he woke me so that I wouldn't fall under Zànalin's spell and would be able to take Alis and come to you."

"It could be," said Elkanakur.

"By the way, do you think it's wrong for humans to chop down trees for firewood and other useful purposes?" asked Tara-lin.

"I don't know. It is debated among dryads. Some say that we do not know, for we are not humans. Some say that we would know, and they would not, for they do not know what a dryad is or what a tree is, hardly even *that* such things as dryads and trees exist. A few of these say it is wrong, but not all. Certainly, it does not always even hasten our passage from this phase of existence; sometimes it returns to our trees, and thus to us, the vigor of youth. If it is done rightly, to the right trees, it is always thus. In some ways the discussion is, I think, a fruitless debate, for it changes nothing for us and does us no good."

"Doesn't it *hurt?*" asked Tara-lin.

"To be cut down?" asked Elkanakur, and again Tara-lin heard laughter in her voice. "I would suppose it does somewhat. It is not spoken of much among us. It seems a strange thing to discuss. Other things also *hurt,* if you would call it that. We – or at least I and some others – don't think about it much. I suppose it also *hurts*, as you say, when we cannot get enough water, or when it is too hot and dry for our leaves, or, I have heard for some, when it gets too cold, or a few other things. But why such a strange thought?"

"It is not a strange thought to me," said Tara-lin. "I think such things often. It seems important."

"Can you explain how?" asked Elkanakur.

"Can you explain how not?" replied Tara-lin.

Elkanakur laughed. "Not really," she said. "I can only say that I don't know what good it does, how it helps anyone to be what she should be or do what she should do or know what she should know."

"Well," said Tara-lin, "for us human-kin pain is very real. We feel it, and often we cannot ignore it. It drives us. We easily hate it and easily fear it. It – I don't know."

"Have you ever been in much of it?"

"Not much. But I fear it. I am concerned about it – what it will do to me, how I will respond. I'm sure there will be a lot more of it getting into those Icecrown Mountains and dealing with nightmares and getting close to Anakrim."

"Just a thought, but perhaps the fear is more of the problem," said Elkanakur.

"I think Dad said something like that to me once," said Tara-lin.

"I think, at this point, this conversation is becoming unfruitful. Come to me. Feel the light. Rest and wake at once. I want to show you something."

Chapter Eleven – The Starweave

Alis' voice interrupted Tara-lin's meditation. "Tara-lin! It's past noon already! I thought you wanted to move quicker."

It took a few moments for Alis' words to register. Tara-lin's mind was filled with indescribable, almost immemorable visions, of which the dominant impressions left later in her distinct and articulable memory were of strong clear light, of deep wells of strong water, of an almost flame-like motion or substance of life, frozen as it were in a single dynamic up-rushing movement, as if water and earth were to burn. Mixed with these were other impressions which she only later began to sort out and which, though she could pin in her memory to that time, were yet hardly remembered and certainly less describable.

Finally, Alis' words registered. "Elkanakur and I have been speaking. Traveling faster will do us no good if I do not learn or know what I must."

Alis nodded. "It's not I that am in a hurry. In fact, I like sleeping in a lot. I'm always so tired. I just thought you were in a hurry. To save the trees."

"Well," said Tara-lin, "I presume it is time for us to continue forward."

"I think it is," said Elkanakur, her voice a soft whisper in Tara-lin's ears, almost in her mind. "You have absorbed, I think, as much of what I have to share as we could hope. I will always call and remember you as *friend*, Tara-lin."

"Thank you, Elkanakur," said Tara-lin. "I, too, shall always remember you as a friend." She curtsied in the elven way.

"Now, eat a little. I asked a few other dryads to see about a meal for you, since I was occupied with other things," said Elkanakur. "May we meet again someday."

"Are you sure you never get lonely?" asked Tara-lin.

"I shall not be afflicted with sadness at your departure, however long it lasts, however I may enjoy your company or wish to see you again," answered Elkanakur.

"There are so many things I do not understand!" said Tara-lin. Alis was already wolfing down the food.

"I do not understand most things, either," said the dryad. "Now, eat, unless you are not hungry."

After eating and drinking, the girls walked for what was left of the day. As darkness fell, Alis grew nervous. "You won't make the same mistake you did last night, will you, Tara-lin?"

"No," said Tara-lin. "I know what I'm looking for – rather, to avoid – now, Alis."

"Good," said Alis, but Tara-lin could tell she was still worried.

That night, the dryad of a birch tree welcomed them. Her skin gleamed white even in the darkness, and Tara-lin knew her hair and accents would be a bright green, almost pale, in the light. Tara-lin and Alis ate and drank from their provisions, and the dryad told them she would see to it that they were fed in the morning.

In the cold hours of the morning, a voice woke Tara-lin. She recognized it at once as belonging to Beriririkirkirkitira. "I didn't know you were here!" she said.

"My tree is not here. She is where she always is. But I came to you."

"Why?" asked Tara-lin.

"I was given something for you by one whom I surmise to be one of the Ellenari. It is called the Starweave."

"What is a Starweave?" asked Tara-lin.

"Something I was told would help you. It comes from far away. Here. Let me show it to you."

The dryad's form moved, and something appeared in her hands that glinted and shone. It looked like lines of light that formed the pattern of a crystal's edges.

"It's... beautiful," said Tara-lin.

"Yes, it is. Have you noticed? It sings, but in a way very different from our song."

Tara-lin reached forward and touched it. A shock ran through her fingers, her mind, her whole body, when she discovered that it did not *feel* like anything after the manner of most things with which she came in contact. She could hardly say she *touched* it. It did not seem touchable in the normal sense. Instead she came into contact with an indefinable energy, but it was not even clear that this contact was through her fingers.

Beriririkirkirkitira noticed her bewilderment. "Yes," she said, "it seems like something from another plane of reality, another type of existence."

"Why do I need such a thing?" asked Tara-lin.

"I do not know if either one of us could comprehend the answer to that at this point in time," said the dryad, "but I came for more than to give this to you. I heard from Elkanakur that you have asked questions concerning me and about how I know some of what I do. I will not share my history with you. It would be too long and complicated to share now, though if both you and I live much longer in this phase I may sometime tell you more.

"Death holds no horror to most of my kin – that is, if you dis-count those who are also human-kin. I do not know how most elves feel. But death holds horror to most humans. I think all of them perceive it as something that is not what it should be, is somehow wrong. Over the years I have watched much; most dryads my age are reclusive and sleepy. I, however, am both young and old, probably because my tree has so often lost its top. Even those humans who accept death as the passage into another state of existence, one closer to the heart of Shallim-Araldor, the Ultimate Good, the Utter Life, feel about it in a measure incomprehensible to most dryads. It is hard for me to explain this, even to understand, Tara-lin. No dryad can die or give her life for another dryad. We see death as nothing so much as this: suppose you and a host of your friends are sitting on the banks of a river, enjoying a lovely meadow, abundant with sunshine and food. Downstream is another land, at least as lovely as the one you know, almost certainly even better. Every now and again a boat appears which is headed downstream, and one of your companions is called into the boat to go downstream. You know that sometime, sooner or later, you will all be called downstream. Going in the place of your companion would have no meaning for you, would it?"

"No, I don't think so. It certainly would not be thought of as we consider 'dying for another'," said Tara-lin, "but how do *you* know about human fear and horror?"

"In a way, because I have watched men and women who knew much of Shallim-Araldor, that I could vaguely sense was true yet could not comprehend myself, face death. There have been only a few of them over the ages, but whenever one has appeared of which I have known I have taken great interest and watched his or her life as closely as I could manage. I have arranged many things which it would be hard to explain quickly to you, but which have to do with the dryadic nature, to do so. I have watched other humans also, humans who, as far as they knew, knew nothing of Shallim-Araldor, humans who hated and feared and slaughtered. I have watched many humans. It seems to me... it seems to me... I don't know how to say this. I fear it is one of those things we cannot say because we know too little."

She paused for a long time, and Tara-lin almost thought she was done, but then she said, "Let me put it this way. The temptation to fear or hate is incomprehensible and impossible to most dryads. How can we fear or hate because of a passage from one phase of a good existence into the next? It is almost too simple to explain. But for humans, something has gone wrong. There are many speculations about it. Perhaps they were corrupted once, as individual dryads are corrupted, and so death changed for them. Arrgh! How little I know! Yes, I am saying this all wrong. I shall not try anymore, Tara-lin. I think the younger dryads were wise to warn me that I am too free in my speech, but since I went this far, I must try to correct my error. Yet, I cannot, for I do not know. I know – yet I do not know – that Shallim-Araldor offers only good. I have seen a love which we dryads do not know – not that we have not a love of our own – occasioned by human death. But something in my heart warns me. Many times I have seen humans, and sometimes dryads, compare what should never be compared. I do not know that the human love is better than the dryad love. I know only that the world would be incomplete, that there would be a good which did not exist, if either the human love or the dryad love did not exist. But, please, take no more from what I have said than I have said, and take even what you have heard me say very lightly. I do not want evil to come of my attempt to communicate with you. You are strange to us, for you are at once human, and almost a dryad. It is hard for some of us not to think of you as a child of our race, fit for instruction in those things we pass onto our children.

"No, my heart compels me to share. I will give you a parting thought. No, I cannot. How can I say it? Yes, I will try it this way. Even if harm is meant us – even if we feel that harm is meant – we feel no harm done to us. No, I have still said it wrongly. Let me say only that I think... that I think that the dryad perception of the world and the human perception of the world complete each other, help the other one to be what it is, that humans can learn what they are from dryads, and dryads from humans. Perhaps this is why humans and dryads were often drawn to each other and mated. The love of humans and the love of dryads are not as different as they at first appear, yet perhaps they are more different than they appear. Nothing can be said rightly. Perhaps the others are right, and nothing should be said at all."

Tara-lin nodded. "I hear you. But, how will I carry the Starweave?"

"You might not be able to touch the Starweave, but your touch can carry it as well as my touch can. Here. Take it."

Tara-lin again reached out her hands and grasped the Starweave. Again she was shocked, thrown off even, by its alien mode of presence.

"It hangs now in your hands," said Beriririkirkirkitira. "There are some of us who think it might come from distant stars."

Tara-lin nodded. Her mind was still spinning about the previous conversation. "Beriri, do you think we could meet again in the next phase, as you call it? That as humans and dryads inhabit the same world here, we will inhabit the same world after the passage?"

"Ask me no more questions, elfling," said the dryad. "I am not angry with you, but I have a difficulty here."

"I am sorry," said Tara-lin.

"It is well. I am not hurt, nor do I take offense."

"And thank you for coming, Beriririkirkirkitira."

"You are welcome, Tara-lin."

The half-elf was about to speak, when she felt suddenly something like a wind and knew that the dryad had departed and returned to her tree. She laid the mysterious Starweave in her bag, looked to make sure the bag held the magic item, and returned to sleep.

Upon waking, she checked again to make sure the Starweave was still there. Alis, who awakened when she stirred, looked from where she lay and asked, "What are you doing, Tara-lin? Is something wrong?"

"I'm just making sure it's still here."

"What is it?"

"The Starweave. A dryad brought it to me and said it had been given to her for me by a mysterious being. It's different."

Thoroughly curious, Alis sat up. "Show me it!"

Tara-lin opened the bag and held it out to Alis.

"I don't see it," said Alis.

"You don't? You don't see lights? Lines of light that kind of pulse and ripple, only those words make you think of water, and there's nothing watery about this light?"

"Oh," said Alis. "Yeah, I see some odd variations of light, just a suggestion. Weird. Can I touch it?"

"I don't know," said Tara-lin, but Alis had already put her hand in.

"Odd," she said. "It... it tingles. That's all. I don't like it, though."

Concern flooded through Tara-lin. Somehow, this artifact was extremely important, and she knew almost nothing at all about it! Would Alis' touch hurt it? She yanked back the bag from Alis and inspected it. It looked like it had in the night, except that the light was less pronounced. It was beautiful, though. She understood now why it was called the Starweave. A weave it certainly appeared, but the threads were not threads, nor was the weave one known to Tara-lin. Instead they were a form of light or energy that took on a structure reminiscent of the facets of a crystal. She reached in and touched the Starweave. It felt, as near as she could remember, just like it had the night before.

"Did I do something wrong, Tara-lin? WHAT'S GOING ON?!" squealed Alis.

Tara-lin put the bag down. "We're dealing with things neither of us understand well. Don't go touching and grabbing things that are *obviously* magical!"

"I'm sorry," said Alis. "Did I break it?"

"I don't know," said Tara-lin. "It doesn't seem any different to me than it did, but how would I know? I don't think even the dryad who gave it to me might know. I don't even know *what* it's supposed to do."

Alis nodded. "I'm sorry." She seemed to be near tears.

"It's all right," said Tara-lin. "I'm not angry at you. Just concerned. Probably it's not broken. And you couldn't have known. Just don't do it again."

"I promise I won't," said Alis.

"And I'm sorry I get upset at you so much, Alis," said Tara-lin.

The human girl nodded. "It would be really stupid of me to get mad at you. And I think I might have gotten upset my share of times. I don't remember right now."

Chapter Twelve – Song of Shadows

Alis and Tara-lin were trekking near the edge of the hills, trying to find level ground to travel. Suddenly, Tara-lin stopped, her elven senses picking up a subtle cue.

"What is it?" asked Alis.

"Men. Riders," said Tara-lin. "They come quickly. There are many of them."

"Are they looking for us?" asked Alis.

"I don't know. It would seem strange to put so much effort into finding us. And we are miles and miles from the last place they... know we were. In fact, from the last place we knew they were searching for us."

"Do we need to hide?" asked Alis. "Can you ask a dryad to hide us?"

"Not now. Not here. Not that fast. Yes, they're definitely coming this way. The dryads here will help us as much as they may, but they have not the skill or nature to hide us as quickly as we would need. The Elethrian cloaks will have to do. Alis, there." Tara-lin pointed.

"What?" asked Alis.

"Hide there." From then on Tara-lin quickly instructed Alis on where and how to hide. "Now, be still," she said, and turned back toward the nearest large tree.

She was somewhat uncomfortable. A troop of ten men, not more, was a different thing from a full cavalry unit, which this sounded like to her. Why they would send no less than twenty horses to look for her and Alis she did not know, but they were coming. There was no reason Tara-lin could think of for them to be riding in these hills other than to look for herself and Alis.

Tara-lin felt, rather than saw, the first rider crest the hill below her, and launched herself up at the branch above her. Another question flashed through her mind. Why were they riding so quickly? Horses couldn't sustain a continuous canter through these hills. Why were they running now? Why send horses at all?

Lying flat along the top of the branch, Tara-lin saw the horses coming closer in a wide-spread formation. The eyes of their riders looked everywhere, hither and thither, nervously observing as much as they could. They knew they were looking for something almost impossible to find. Some of them moved on. They spoke softly among themselves, so many different voices Tara-lin did not immediately understand all they said, but she knew she could understand what she put her mind to.

Another rider rode up. He spoke loudly and his voice cut through the muttering. "They should be somewhere around here. I saw the tracks not a half-mile back."

"I don't see any tracks around here," said another.

"This area doesn't hold them too well. You'd have to look very carefully, to follow it. Just fan out. They have to be somewhere around here. The trail they left was pretty consistent."

"How long were you following it, again?" asked one.

"I found it early this morning, after losing it yesterday afternoon. They're here. I just waited to ride to you until I understood the pattern of where they were traveling very well. As I said, it was a half-mile ago I left the tracks, and I ran to you, and we rode like the wind. Unless that witch sensed something and ran, she should be about here. She shouldn't have sensed anything until it was too late either, since she obviously didn't sense it when I was trailing her."

One of the men dismounted. He walked slowly, casting his eyes up and down. Tara-lin froze, pressing her face against the bark, tucking her hands under her cloak, as he walked under the branch on which she rested.

"That branch, there, there be something weird about it," said one rider.

"A bird's nest, maybe?" asked the man next to him.

"Maybe. It does look like a good branch for a nest," assented the first.

"This one?" asked the man passing under Tara-lin.

"Yes," said the second. "Not that it matters. It's gotta be a bird nest."

"Nah," said the tracker. "You probably found her. We know she hides *somehow*. She's been tracked and then completely disappeared just as she was about to be caught. She's got spells. She probably uses them to hide herself and Alis every night, but can't use them while moving. The only question is, is the bird nest her or the girl? It doesn't matter if we kill her, but we mustn't kill Alis."

"Who is she, anyway?"

"A witch. A servant of the demon lords."

No, thought Tara-lin. *I fight the demon lords. It is you who are deceived, who worship demons and not gods. It would be better if you worshiped Shallim-Araldor, the Lord of Trees, the King of Dryads. He, it seems, is worthy of worship.*

"Well, how can we get it down? A rope?" asked one.

Now that they're certain they found me, they'll never leave, thought Tara-lin.

"Someone could climb the tree. If that's Alis, she could get hurt, or even killed, if we forcibly dislodge her, especially if she's under a spell. That witch might, too, though her magic might help her, but we don't care about her."

Tara-lin's heart beat quickly. She was not sure if she was really afraid. They were certainly quite willing to kill her. If they could, they probably would, given how much they feared her. However, Tara-lin was not prone to panic. She remained still and thought quickly.

Then, softly, almost under her breath, she began a song.

> The haunting mist of dreams
> Another world overlapping this
> A haze that clouds the eyes
> And opens visions of ages far

A rope was pulled out of the bag, and thrown over the tree, and upon it a man began to climb. Tara-lin knew she could not let him reach her. Softly still, but almost frantically she continued her song.

> Weariness of thousand nights
> Opens eyes and ears to worlds unknown
> That float upon breakers
> From seas of light from forgotten times

The tone of the men's exchange began to shift. "This place is beautiful!" said one. "Don't let it distract you from what we're doing!" said another. From a different part of the hill, one said, "I feel so tired. It's been ages since I slept in a bed." "There is evil magic in the air," replied one close enough to him to hear what he muttered. A third, yet a little farther away, said, "It doesn't feel evil! It feels very nice here." Another said, "Evil always masks itself to seem good. Be ware! Don't fall for her magic. We know now she is here."

The man climbing the tree approached the branch, though he

muttered to himself, "I do not like this at all. I can hardly think about keeping my grip! I think I shall fall."

Without missing a beat in her song, Tara-lin reached under her cloak and drew the elven sword. As it exited the cloak, gasps of awe and fear went up, for ephemeral purple flames flared from the blade, almost hiding the hilt and the hand that held it!

A cry went up. "It is the witch! Kill her! Bowmen, shoot her! When she dies Alis will be released from her spells, and we will be able to find her!"

Still, Tara-lin felt no fear. She stood, swaying, upon the branch, the purple flame in her hand, the only part of her plainly visible, and continued singing.

> The world spins away from grasps
> Of hand and mind that sees it not, but
> Twists what little is seen
> Into parody of what is real
>
> Eyes, close on your delusions
> The real your mind renders invisible
> See, in dreams, a freshness
> Break through defenses, untwisted by clouded thought

Bows sang, and arrows sped through the air around Tara-lin, but the aim was off, as archers struggled to pay attention and could barely see their target – saw, indeed, only the sword she held.

The elfling crouched and, in a single bound, moved with speed none of them could believe of one upon a tree branch. She knocked the climbing man from the tree, bumping him hard with the hilt of her sword, and he fell. Still she sang.

> Fall the shadow, fall the shadow!
> Clouds as thick as shadow of the night
> Fall the shadow, fall the shadow!
> Hiding light that cannot be seen!
> Fall the shadow, fall the shadow!
> Blindness, terror, a formless stalking shade!
> Fall the shadow, fall the shadow!
> Fear in your heart, see fear that is not there!

Tara-lin's song rose to a haunting pitch. It became clearly, but indistinctly, audible to the men around her. "She snares us!" cried one, and several cried inarticulately. Those mounted fled on their mounts. Those on foot fled on foot. Tara-lin almost reveled in her success, and her song rose yet higher, sounding to those who fled like the keening wail of a terrible wind or a wraith. Long she held the last note, slowly letting it fade away.

Tara-lin sheathed her sword. Silently she observed that the horses who had no riders had not been frightened much, and were still in the vicinity. She would be able to catch them. She let herself down from the branch, and went to where she had left Alis.

She touched the girl. "Alis!"

Alis startled. She sat up straight, and, after a moment, said, "Are they gone?"

"Yes, Alis. You are safe now. And we will have horses. I only have to catch them now, and that is trivial for me."

"How can you do so many cool things and I can't do *anything?*" asked Alis.

"My parents told me all children are special and unique. I think they might have said all children have talents," said Tara-lin.

"That's not what I asked," said Alis. "Anyway, I want to see those horses."

"You will," said Tara-lin. "I bet you have talents none of us know about. And you've learned rather quickly given your exceptional lack of experience in the wild – from my point of view, that is, exceptional." She gave Alis her hand and helped the girl stand. Together, they walked towards where most of the horses had gone.

Alis wanted to help catch the horses, and Tara-lin soon discovered she had quite a knack for the creatures. The horses liked her and approached her readily, and she had a natural sense for when to push and when to back off. In all, six horses had been left behind.

Once the horses had all accepted them as friends, Tara-lin said to Alis, "Decide which one you like best. Then, we will untack the others and let them go."

It took Alis almost half an hour to decide. She went back and forth between several of the horses, letting them nuzzle her, blowing in their noses, and stroking them. It was obvious to Tara-lin that several of the horses were competing over Alis' attention. She also suspected that some of them had never known anyone who treated them as other than tools, important and expensive tools to be treated well, but tools nonetheless. Finally, Alis selected a large chestnut mare with an expansive and oddly-shaped white blaze across her face.

"She likes you," said Tara-lin, when Alis made her choice.

"They all do, don't they?" asked Alis.

"Yes," said Tara-lin. "You're good with horses. Quite good."

"As good as an elf?" asked Alis.

"Yes," said Tara-lin. "I doubt you have the experience of those elves who choose to gain it. You couldn't gain that much experience in your lifetime, since the lives of elves are nearly ten times the length of your own, but, yes, you are very good. As good as most elf children your age – I mean, the elven equivalent of your age."

"How old is that?" asked Alis.

"More than twice my own age," said Tara-lin, with a laugh.

"Oh. Wow," said Alis. "Anyway, which horse do you like best?"

Tara-lin stepped forward and grabbed the reins of a dark bay gelding with a narrow white strip down his face.

"That one's a beauty," said Alis.

"They will need names," said Tara-lin. "For now, let us untack these others."

"The name of mine is Makya," said Alis, walking along the side of the black whose reins Tara-lin now held. She expertly set about undoing the girth. It was clear to Tara-lin that she was more familiar with and better understood the tack these horses wore. As she crossed around the horse to the other side, while Tara-lin tried to keep the others from annoying the animal she held, Alis said, "What are we going to do with this stuff?"

"Drop it somewhere," said Tara-lin. "It can get ruined for all I care. We don't have any use for it and couldn't take it with us even if we might later."

"That I know," said Alis. "I'm just... not used to ruining things."

"I'm not, either," said Tara-lin, "though my people use much tack only rarely. But they don't need it. If they do, they can make more. But let's see if there's any meat in the saddlebags!"

"Good idea," said Alis, "though I bet they left all that stuff in their camp, wherever that was."

"Unless they were traveling to the next point at which they would make camp."

"There is that," said Alis. "But I think I have the saddle off now. Where should I put it?"

Tara-lin laughed. "Anywhere, Alis, anywhere! Just somewhere it's not right underfoot. Up against the tree? Just somewhere!"

"Sure!" said Alis. While she took the saddle away, Tara-lin quickly unbridled the horse and grabbed the next one.

Alis was unsaddling the last horse, when Tara-lin heard a call. "Can you finish this?" she asked the girl.

"Sure. Why?"

"A dryad wants to talk to me, I think," answered Tara-lin. With that, she turned and approached the tree, against which, her form distinguishing itself from and then fading back into her tree, stood the dryad, one who appeared to be, more or less, of Aumoura's kind. "What is it?" asked the half-elf.

"Be careful, singer. You are human, as well as dryad, so I do not know if it harms you as it would a dryad, but your song, just a few moments ago, was like the song of dryads who are beginning to corrupt."

"It was?" asked Tara-lin.

"Yes, it was. At least, it seemed so to me. It may not have been that to you. As I said, you are as much human as you are dryad, and even your song is as human as it is dryad – or, at least, so it appears to us dryads. It may not seem that way to humans. So I just want you to think about it. As I said, it might not be. Your mind is different from ours, and what I heard might not be what you did, or what those humans you sent away heard. I just want you to be careful that you not open yourself up to the Corruption, that you not indulge fear or hatred or blind rage and desire for the hurt of others, things I think are common among humans, though incomprehensible to most dryads."

"Thank you," said Tara-lin. "I'm not sure I understand, but I am becoming convinced of the existence of the being you call Shallim-Araldor. Mostly, I want the humans to realize what they think is truth is a lie and to actually open their eyes to reality."

"I know that," said the dryad, "and I sensed much of that in your song, but I also sensed something I did not like, unless I mis-sensed it: a desire to inflict pain. If it was so, I urge you to take care."

Tara-lin nodded. "So much is so confusing. But I will try. Shallim-Araldor is the Lord of Light." She turned and went to the horse she had chosen. She eyed the saddle and began trying to figure out how to take it off. Alis came around a tree with her chosen Makya, and said, "What are you doing, Tara-lin?"

"The obvious."

"Why? Aren't you keeping that one, whatever his name is?"

"Yes. I don't want to ride in this saddle. You might want to, but I am used to riding bareback, and this saddle looks uncomfortable to me, not to mention too big for me."

"All right," said Alis, "but I've never ridden before, and don't want to go bareback right away. I hear it's harder."

"I'm not asking you to do so. We'll keep Makya's saddle. Did you find anything nice in the saddlebags?"

"I was just looking," said Alis.

"Then go on looking. I think I can figure this out by myself."

A few minutes later, Tara-lin had succeeded in untacking the horse. Alis appeared again. She held up several chunks of meat. "Since I feel most need for meat, can I have more than my fair share of it?" she asked.

"Of course," said Tara-lin, "but I feel a hunger for it, too, so I'd like some. But let's just take the food, and split it tonight. I want to ride during the day."

"Okay," said Alis. She put the food back into a bag, and slung it behind Makya's saddle.

"Is there anything I should know about mounting a horse?" she asked, her hands on Makya's neck.

"How much have you watched people mount horses?"

"A lot. I've watched everything I could."

"Well, mounting is pretty easy, at least with stirrups. You'll do fine," replied Tara-lin. With that, she slung herself across the back of her steed and settled herself behind his withers. What should she name him? No name came at once to her mind. Oh well. He could do without a name for a day. She would think of one someday.

For now, she had to teach Alis to ride. They would not make much better speed if the horses only walked.

Chapter Thirteen - Ride to the Road

Tara-lin had spent a half-hour riding around Alis and instructing her, despite the fact the half-elf had only a vague idea herself of how one was supposed to sit the saddle Alis was using. Now, they were walking side by side, and Alis said, "Won't they find us again? Aren't horses easier to track than we are?"

"Yes," said Tara-lin, "but I have some ideas. If we ride right down a road with high traffic, no one will be able to tell *we're* there. Indeed, are you up to a long day today?"

"If we take a break to eat that meat, sure," said Alis. "I'd rather a long day than be caught, and I get the idea that last encounter was close."

"It was," said Tara-lin, "so, here is what we will do."

Alis watched her intently, with widening eyes, as Tara-lin continued. "We are going to go down onto the main roads. No one will suspect us of such a move. No one will be able to track the prints of our horses' hooves amidst all the other traffic on the road. You and I will keep our faces shadowed by our hoods, and so no one will recognize us, unless they both know us well and get close to us, and we won't let that happen. If anyone *does* try to stop us or talk to us, you will let me do the talking."

"Gladly," said Alis. "If we're gonna go, let's go!"

Tara-lin nodded and flashed a smile at Alis. "By the way," she said, "I've named my horse. Vonë."

"That's an elvish name?" asked Alis.

"Yes. Vonë is an Elethrian name. Let's go!" She put her heels to Vonë's side and brought him to a smooth jog.

Alis followed behind her, working to stay in a rhythm with her horse's gaits. On and on they went, and the shadows grew as the sun moved down the western sky. Alis grew incredibly sore, and struggled yet more to stay in rhythm with Makya's slow, gentle trot. The other horses had followed them for a while, but had now left them behind to fill their stomachs.

Alis rode up beside Tara-lin and said, "When do we stop? I'm hungry, and I'm sure the horses are, as well. At any rate, I have to work harder to make Makya keep up with – what's his name, Vonë?"

"Yes," said Tara-lin. "Vonë is his name. Soon. Another half hour. Then you can eat and sleep for a few hours, while the horses graze. But I want to be riding down a main road before morning."

"Aarghh!" said Alis.

"I know you're sore," said Tara-lin, "but this is my plan for how to not be chased anymore. At least, for how not to be found anymore. I don't know if they will ever give up chasing us."

Tara-lin's own thoughts were morose. Over and over again, she considered the dryad's warning. She did not think whatever she had felt or thought was exactly a desire to inflict pain, but she was not sure that all she had felt and sung was right. She *had* reveled in her success, in the fear she inflicted upon the would-be murderers. Perhaps, she amended her thought, they already *were* murderers. Just not murderers of herself or Alis.

Nonetheless, she felt confusion. What was she supposed to do? How was she to know what she was supposed to do? How was she to know if she had done wrong? A near certainty that she *had* done wrong settled upon her, but still no clear understanding of what she had done wrong or what she should have done instead. She wanted to cry. She wanted her mother to comfort her. She wanted her father to tell her what was right, or at least help her to figure it out. She wanted him beside her. Terror descended upon her, that she would be too late, or that something would happen, and that Sir Eldor would be dead, and she would never see him again! Then followed fear that the child Lìrulin bore would never know his or her father, that Lìrulin would be a widow and have to raise Tara-lin's brother or sister alone. Of course, Tara-lin would be there to help. If *she* survived. But what if Prince Anakrim succeeded? Then all would be horrible and Areaer itself would die!

She wanted to cry, but did not want to cry in front of Alis. The human girl was already emotionally over-wrought and, sometimes, hard for Tara-lin to get along with. Of course, Tara-lin knew some of it was her own fault. She often failed to take into account Alis' difficulties and hardships.

I should not be feeling like this, thought Tara-lin. *Normally, I don't feel like this. I've never felt like this before. Then again, I've never done this before, but, then again, I've been doing this for a while. I think it's been, well, about three weeks since I and Alis ran away from the Valor Hall. Oh goodness, that's three weeks behind! But, it hasn't been as close as it was earlier today before. But I didn't feel frightened or confused then. I just acted. But it seems I acted wrong, though in what way I can't find out. And, if I can't find out thinking about it* now, *how will I avoid it in the midst of the next battle? How will I avoid falling to the corruption and the nightmare?*

Yes, I had better not let Alis sense how I am feeling. It is too much like her own fears about what the gods will or won't do to her for running away from her menfolk. I don't want to stir that nest up again. But I really am scared. I guess I should ask Shallim-Araldor for help, but I don't really feel comfortable doing that. I guess, I don't think I can ask Shallim-Araldor. I know there is such a being, but I don't have any kind of relationship with him. I don't know if I can. It wouldn't feel real. I'd just be talking into the air if I asked Shallim-Araldor. If he wants a relationship with me, I think he'll know I'm willing, if he comes to me. I wouldn't know where to look for him. But I bet he knows where to look for me. But, I know if he's interested in that kind of thing with anyone. He's definitely not a normal *person. I don't even know what a relationship with him would be.*

She stroked Vonë's neck under his mane, and thought that none of these musings solved her problem. *Maybe,* she thought, *it comes of being both dryad and human, and there's nothing I can do that's right, no way not to do things that are wrong, since what's right and wrong is different for dryads and humans. But that can't be. Maybe it can, but if it is, I don't think it's all that's wrong. But I feel dirty. Sullied. Bad. What I did this morning leaves a sourness in my belly. Why? Is it wrong, or am I just being overly-sensitive for some reason? WHAT IS WRONG WITH ME?! I want to cry, but NOT IN FRONT OF ALIS.*

Dusk was falling. They were near the edge of the hill-country at the feet of the Malaitha Mountains. Not that the rest of the country in that region was not hilly, but the hills were more gentle and rolling a little further out. Tara-lin reined in Vonë. "Let's stop here for a moment," she said to Alis. "There's good grazing in this meadow for the horses, and they can drink from the brook. It's the first we've run across in hours, and they're probably thirstier than they are hungry."

Alis nodded, but she paused getting out of Makya's saddle. She was sore and stiff, but that was not all of it. Why did Tara-lin sound less perky all of a sudden? Her elf friend always sounded cheerful and positive. She slid heavily to the ground, and said, "Is something wrong, Tara-lin?"

Tara-lin took a moment to answer, while she undid Vonë's bridle. "No. I just have things I'm thinking about."

"Don't you usually have things you're thinking about?" asked

Alis. "Anyway, can you unsaddle and stuff Makya? I'm so stiff and I ache all over."

"Sure," said Tara-lin. "I can do that."

Stumbling across the grass to sit down in a place she thought looked comfortable, Alis said, "You really don't sound happy, Tara-lin."

"I'm not," said Tara-lin, turning to look directly at her friend. She decided to tell Alis something that did make her unhappy, but not the whole story. "I'm a half-elf. My father is a human. He's older than he was on the mission he met Mom on, and they almost died then. Even if he lives a full, even if he lives an extraordinarily long, human lifespan, he will die while I am still a very young woman. I don't know how it is Mom and Dad married each other, since I'm sure they both knew that my Mom would be a widow while still young, and possibly while their children were still babies. I guess they just fell in love, and that makes people do things that seem stupid to everyone else, but I don't know what that means. They *do* really love each other, though. They're so close and care so much for one another. And for me. But that didn't stop Sir Eldor from thinking an oath sworn decades ago, before he met Lìrulin, before he married her, before I was born, before Mom got pregnant a second time, means he needs to go off and risk his life on a mission he hardly understands because he swore a stupid oath to an organization that was probably corrupt when he swore the oath, but he didn't know it then, but he does know it now! – Anyway, I need to take care of your horse. Makya, not until I take your saddle off!" The horse was ambling off, and looked like she might be looking for a place to roll.

"I'm sorry," said Alis. "I shouldn't have –"

"You're right," said Tara-lin, snappily, chasing after the horse. "You shouldn't have. But it'll be all right."

"Yeah, I can see how that would make you upset. I miss my family a bit myself, and it seems your parents are so much better than mine. But I don't know what to think about oaths," said Alis. "When you get that saddlebag, give it to me so I can eat, please!"

Tara-lin had now caught Makya, and was working on untacking her. She did not respond immediately, but Alis spoke again. "How will we make sure the horses won't wander off and abandon us?"

"They won't," said Tara-lin. "I'll make sure of that, Alis."

"Yeah. You know quite a few things I don't," said Alis. "I'm just hungry, sore, and tired."

"In that order?" asked Tara-lin. She laid the saddle on the ground, wondering where she would leave it so it would not take too much damage, and took the bridle off.

"I don't know," said Alis. She paused and, while Tara-lin looked around for a place to rest the saddle, said, "I really don't relish the idea of riding all night."

"You relish the idea of being caught even less. And I don't know how much you liked having them hunting for us earlier this morning, but *I* did not like it at all. It was *far* too close."

"Yeah. It sucks you're a singer instead of a wizard. There're a few of them at the Valor Hall. They can *do* things. Not like you can. Different things."

Tara-lin was upset now. She turned to Alis and almost yelled, "You don't know what I'm talking about. You don't know the half of what I've done, or what I can learn, and I doubt you know what the real extent and limitations of wizard's abilities *really are!*"

"I didn't mean to make you mad," said Alis.

"I'm sorry," said Tara-lin. "Just let me find a place for your saddle, and then I'll get you your food. I think I'll eat some myself. By the way, Alis, the horses like us. Vonë likes me, and Makya likes you. And where is a better place than here? They will come when I call them as surely as the gryphon did."

"Sorry for questioning you," said Alis. "I guess we wouldn't have had the help of the dryads if you were a wizard instead of a singer, and I don't know what else. Sorry, Tara-lin."

The half-elf did not respond. Instead, she just brought the bag to Alis, opened it, pulled out some food for herself, and let Alis do what she wanted with the rest. She walked several paces away and sat down to eat.

"I'm sorry. I really didn't mean to offend you," Alis called after her.

"I just don't want to talk, Alis," said Tara-lin. "Leave it be."

She stood there for a few moments, munching on the meat, then continued towards the stream where the horses had gone. She wanted some privacy to cry. She hoped Alis would be asleep when she came back, and that she would be less upset in a few hours, since she did not want Alis to know more about her concerns and fears than what she had told her about her father. She was going to be very tired indeed by morning, but it could not be helped. She needed to cry. More than that, she needed her parents. She needed Sir Eldor not to die.

Without noticing it, Tara-lin drifted to sleep with the horses. She was wakened by Vonë pawing her gently.

Tara-lin started. "Hey, you stupid horse!" she exclaimed. He removed his foot and, after a moment, lowered his head to her. Gently, he brushed her hair and face with his nostrils. "Hey, I know you don't mean to be rude," she said, rising. Stroking his face as she came more fully awake, she thought, *Wow! I fell asleep.* "A good thing you woke me, Vonë," she said. "Else, who knows how long I would've slept. Let's see how long I *did* sleep."

Measuring the positions of the stars, Tara-lin came to the conclusion she had probably slept for about two hours, depending on when exactly she fell asleep. *Long enough,* she thought. Whistling, she called Makya, and then led the horses back towards where she had left Alis.

When Tara-lin shook Alis, the girl responded, grumpily and perhaps not even fully awake, "Do you *have* to wake me so soon?"

"Yes, Alis," said the elfling. "Otherwise, our plan won't work."

"To the netherworld with your plans!" said Alis, but Tara-lin shook her more vigorously and then dropped her down.

"Get up, Alis," she said. "I'll tack Makya up for you, but then you need to ride."

"Really? Will we trot the whole time? I'm still so sore! I don't want to trot ever again!"

"We'll trot until we find a largish north-south road. Then we can walk," said Tara-lin. "Now, wake yourself up."

She set about tacking up the horses, but discovered when she was done that Alis had gone right back to sleep. Alis was no less grumpy the second time she was awakened, but Tara-lin figured at least she would not fall asleep once she was on top of Makya's back. "You don't want to get dragged back to your family or put in a monastery," she reminded her curtly.

It was still several hours before they found the road Tara-lin was looking for, and Alis recurrently complained the entire way. Tara-lin tried not to be too harsh with her. After all, she was tired and somewhat sore herself, and until the previous day Alis had never even ridden a horse. Tara-lin wondered how sore Alis must be.

Finally, the two horses walked side by side. Alis said to Tara-lin, "How is this going to work? How are we going to stay safe during the day?"

"There are dryads even down here, and they will help us," said Tara-lin. "I'm hoping that our pursuers will not expect this move from us. Certainly, they will not be able to tell the traces we leave from those others leave, and so will no longer be able to follow us. That should help a lot. And I have other ideas for how to further confuse things."

"What?" asked Alis.

"They may try to follow us to the road and guess we continued north, since that was the direction we were traveling. Oh grief! Maybe they even think I'm trying to find refuge with all the evil things in the Icecrown Mountains. I hadn't thought of that. I wish I had. Still, when we find east-west roads, we will take one until we find another north-south road, then ride that one up. It will cost us some time, but less than we lose being caught, and less than we gain by being able to ride. That is, if you can acquire some stamina. Still, if we jog as much as we have since this morning every day, over flat roads instead of through mountainous terrain, we will make *much* better time."

"You seem in a better mood than you were in the evening," said Alis, yawning. "How is that?"

Tara-lin shrugged. "I'm still upset, Alis. I don't want to talk about it."

"All right."

Towards dawn, Tara-lin yielded to Alis' consistent requests to stop and sleep. To be honest, she was very tired herself, but she was also bothered enough she wondered if she could sleep. She suspected she could, given how unconsciously she had fallen asleep earlier that night. She found a dryad to offer them some protection, sang for a few minutes to the horses, impressing upon their minds to stay near and away from other people, but to eat well, and went to sleep. Alis was already fast asleep.

Chapter Fourteen – The Human–Friend Dryad

It was late in the evening when Tara-lin woke, her stomach rumbling. She sat up and looked around. Apparently, Alis still slept. She wondered if the human had gorged herself the previous evening. Opening the bag, she saw that was indeed the case. There was hardly anything left.

"Oh goodness," she sighed.

For whatever reason, she felt rather content and much less irritated than she would have expected. Perhaps it had to do with riding for a day and a night and then sleeping for a day. She sat there, considering what she should do. She was sure Alis would be almost as hungry as she was when she woke. The girl was ravenous.

"Tara-lin."

It was the voice of the dryad of one of the trees under which they rested.

"Yes?" said Tara-lin, looking up to see the dryad. She was a smallish-dryad, less than a foot taller than Tara-lin, with hair a shade of dark pinkish purple with highlights of green in it.

"I thought you would be hungry, so I have brought you food. It is not as good as that which my kin in wilder lands can procure, nor does it have as much variety, but I think it will please you well enough." Stooping down, she laid what looked to be a basket woven of grass in Tara-lin's lap. Inside the basket were thousands, maybe millions, of full, ripe, kernels of grain.

"No, Alai-ie-a," said Tara-lin. "This is wonderful. Alis will love it, too. Berries and roots and herbs are great, but we've had plenty of that for days. We will enjoy this a great deal."

"I flavored it with what herbs and spices I could find and procure," said Alai-ie-a. "I think you are right. I think you will like it a lot." Her voice was musical, with a high, quick beat, soft and floating.

Suddenly, a question formed in Tara-lin's mind, as she reached her hand into the basket and began eating. "Are you a very happy dryad, Alai-ie-a?" she asked.

"I am very happy," said Alai-ie-a. "I don't know if all the other dryads are as happy or not. I wouldn't know about that. I feel very young, though I don't think I really am all that young. But I feel it. The days and nights are always fresh. Everything whispers to me of new and bright goods always on their way to me, things of which I have hints but which I've never yet tasted, and always wondrous. I have a good life. I don't know that I have a better life than other dryads. But I'm happy. I usually feel like dancing and singing for joy. Why?"

"Because your voice – and the way you move – sound and look like that. Like you're always dancing or singing with joy. Like you're bubbling up with fresh happiness," said Tara-lin.

"I'm glad you hear it. I hope you feel it around me, too. I always want the humans, the farmers and their wives and their children, and the travelers, and the peddlers, and everyone who passes me, to feel what I feel, to be happy. I try to sing to them and dance for them, to show them, but I don't think they hear me very well. At least, very few of them ever stop to listen. You seem to me to be a lot like humans, even though you are dryad-kin, but you slept under my branches. Few do that."

"My kin do it a great deal. When I live in Elethri, our 'house', if you can call it that, is hung from the boughs and trunks of trees," said Tara-lin.

"Well," said Alai-ie-a, "I always wonder why humans have such a hard time being happy. Some of them seem very happy. I've known some very happy and playful children. I've met a few grown-up humans who tend to be happy, too. But, by and large, humans tend to be worried and enmeshed in the problems of their lives and tied down by I-don't-know-what! It's all very strange to me. I hope the Elethrians are the better for living amongst dryads. I think humans who live out here, not in their stupid cities where nothing grows, tend to be happier. I don't know if it has to do with being closer to us dryads. I wonder if we all, humans *and* dryads, would be happiest if we lived together in the right way."

"You're probably right, Alai-ie-a," said Tara-lin. "And I've met few dryads who seem as happy as you do, but maybe that's because I understand them less. Some of them are probably just happy in a different way. I think of Beriririkirkirkitira and Elkanakur, and perhaps a few others. As I said, I might not notice that some of them are happy because they're... *different.* I also met a very unhappy dryad named Zànalin."

"I think you're right in not trying to compare or measure who's happiest," said Alai-ie-a. "I'm just glad you could notice and receive my happiness. I suspect you're right that you have benefited as much, you just didn't know it, from some of these other dryads you have met. As for Beriririkirkirkitira, I've heard of her, though she lives far from me. She's something of a legend among dryads. None of us know how old she is, yet she is not reclusive like many of the aging dryads. Somehow, I don't think I shall grow reclusive either. I am, after all, less reclusive than many dryads younger than myself. I don't know if being less reclusive is a good thing or just a different thing."

"What do you know about Shallim-Araldor?" asked Tara-lin.

"I don't know that I know anything about Shallim-Araldor. We dryads tend to associate or tie that name to whatever we perceive as good, as happiness, as love or pity or mercy. I just know that I'm happy. The whole world *ought* to be happy, and I think a lot of it is kind of. It all feels like it is going to be happier, like something very happy is on its way, and every day it's nearer, and I get more of it. I'm not saying this right. But I told you already. There's a lot of evil, but, somehow, I just don't believe in it. I don't know if anything of this has anything to do with Shallim-Araldor. I don't know what, or who, or if Shallim-Araldor is. Just that... that I'm happy, and that I want everything else around me, and everything that's not around me, to be happy, and that everything *should* be happy. Maybe Shallim-Araldor is what will make all the happiness everywhere. Maybe Shallim-Araldor is the happiness. I just don't know that. But I do know what I know."

"Ah," said Tara-lin. "Thanks for telling me what you think. You are definitely a lot less reclusive than most dryads. Anyway, what do you think of this situation involving Prince Anakrim?"

"Prince Anakrim? Ah, I had forgotten that. I guess, by Elethrian law, he is a prince of your people. I had quite forgotten. Such things do not interest me and usually confuse me. But what do I think about the situation? What do I think about what?" Her voice, as usual, continued to be underscored by a hint of something that could turn into laughter – not the laughter of flippancy, but that of gladness – at any moment. "I don't really think about it. It's definitely a horrible idea. It has killed a few dryads, for sure. I don't really know why he has the idea. If the nightmare exists, maybe it's the nightmare's plan for separating humans and dryads, and all life, yet more, and spreading unhappiness." Alai-ie-a shrugged. "I intend to remain happy, though. If you're asking me what I think the right way to respond to it is, I don't know. I don't respond to it at all. I just live like I always live. I continue to enjoy life and be as I have always been."

"So, then, you're caring for me and Alis is... not a response to this?"

"Oh, not really," said Alai-ie-a. "I guess, maybe, I help you a little because you are counted dryad-friend, but, I mean, I'd speak to anyone who would or could listen. I *have* spoken to children sometimes. Usually their parents convince them that they just dreamed me up, but they usually come back to play in my branches. I don't think it ever occurs to most of their parents that I even *might* exist. I fed one little boy once. He's grown up now, and I think he either forgot me or thinks I was a dream. I see him now and then, but I cannot get his attention much. Once, I convinced him to have a nap and a picnic under my leaves, but even then I couldn't get him to acknowledge me. I don't know why humans tend to grow less perceptive as they grow up. It's not quite always this happens, though. There was an old lady I knew once – she died just this spring – who would come to me and speak with me in the afternoons. I liked her. But I think all the other humans she knew thought she was crazy, except for some little ones. That's what she told me. When she was dying, her family would take her outside and leave her under me since they knew she liked that, even though they thought she was crazy and had no reason for liking it so much. Then, I would sing to her.

"I think some children *almost* hear me. I've known them to play around me and to make up stories about me. It's kind of like they barely hear me and think it's their imagination. Often, a good deal of it *is* their imagination. I think these children – often somewhat older ones – don't hear enough to have much of an idea what they're getting unless their imagination gets involved. I just wish they found themselves hearing more and more as they grew, not less and less. Still, I think it's good for them and helps them to be happy to hear what they do. And I've known some adults who mostly lost the imaginative bent that allowed them to express what they sensed but did not, I think, completely lose their sense of me. Some of them might have sensed me a little better than they had when they were children, even if not well enough for us to really speak. And one continued to make up stories about me even after he had grown up. Sometimes, he would sit down and talk to me, even though I get the impression he did not think I could hear him and hardly even thought I existed. Certainly, he did not have much of a notion of me and missed a lot of what I tried to tell him. Mostly, though, I was just content to listen to him tell me about the things that interested him, that confused him, or that he thought. It was a most interesting and gratifying relationship and I think that, even though he did not understand it, it was as good for him as I found it to be for me."

Alis stretched and yawned. "Do I hear you two talking to each other? I'm hungry!"

"There's food," said Tara-lin. "I think you'll like it a lot. It's more like bread than anything we've had in a *long* time."

Alai-ie-a stooped down, picked the basket out of Tara-lin's lap, and placed it between the two of them. Alis immediately reached her hand into it to eat.

"If you're thirsty, I have water for you. I've already watered your horses," said the dryad.

"Yes, please," said Tara-lin. "I think we still have a little water in our water-skins, but we're definitely thirsty, and we wouldn't mind having them re-filled."

"Give it to me, and I will take care of it," said the dryad.

She returned with the water-skin full. "Tell me again, and I will re-fill it right before you leave tonight," she said, as she sat down next to them.

"You're different than any other dryads I've seen," said Alis. "And this food is delicious. Thank you so much for it. Why could you get this, but the other dryads couldn't?"

"Tara-lin told me I'm different, too," said Alai-ie-a with a smile. "As for the food, I am surrounded by fields of ripening grain. It's mostly still far from ripe, but with my arts ripening some and making it fit for your consumption is not a difficult task. My brothers and sisters you've met probably lived in the wild; thus, only those things which grow in the wild are available to them."

"Oh," said Alis.

The dryad looked around, seeing the shadows and the darkening sky. "We have little time, if you are to continue on your journey with the speed you desire. Let me sing to you now, while you finish your meal."

At first, Tara-lin hardly distinguished her voice from the sounds of the gentle breeze and the calls of night-insects and the occasional call of a bird. Then it distinguished itself, still soft, but higher, clearer, soon very clear indeed, and of a haunting beauty which was not quite ethereal. It rose and fell with a cadence that was sometimes quick, but never rapid. Tara-lin felt her body respond to the rhythm and melody. It was, she thought, the sweetest melody she had ever heard or imagined. She wanted to dive into it and rest in it forever. Happiness washed over her, sweet and fresh, and with a wholly contenting assurance of more happiness to come, always new and yet always a continuation and building upon of the happiness already given. She could not describe the feeling it awakened in her, as if everything in the whole world was, ultimately, in its heart and at its root, bursting with goodness. She thought she could lose herself in the song. It seemed to make the very air around her and the earth on which she sat more alive. It seemed to make *her* more alive. In many ways, the song was too primal to be captured or described. It was an utterly simple happiness, ready to embrace anything and everything in its mere goodness. No unbearable ecstasy accompanied it; only a sense of utter restfulness and contentment. It seemed to combine all the best of sleeping and of waking in itself.

As the night deepened, a pale blue light illuminated the shadows. In it, the dryad now stood, clothed in a bright, fresh, emerald green slip. The expression on her face was such that Tara-lin could find no name for it. It was like nothing she had ever seen before – except in glimpses on this dryad's face during their previous conversation. She finally decided to call it *Peace*. Certainly, the whole experience gave her a totally new, previously undreamed of, meaning for that word.

Then Alai-ie-a ceased singing. The song left something of an emptiness, a tinge of sadness, in Tara-lin, but nothing like the sadness that might be expected after the passage of such an experience by one who did not know the experience from the inside but had only heard of it. For something of the song remained in Tara-lin's heart, and at least the knowledge that such a wonder existed – except that, in the throes of it, she did not wonder. Once known, the peace, happiness, or hope could not easily be completely unknown and, if it were to be so unknown, would leave in its place a depth of horror and corruption almost too vast to comprehend, one to wither the mind and consume the soul.

"Let me fill your water again," said Alai-ie-a, and, now that Tara-lin's ears were open to it, she heard that the song was always present in the dryad's voice and was almost the whole beauty and enchantment of that voice.

Quickly, the dryad returned, from where neither Tara-lin nor Alis saw. Having had a moment to compose her thoughts, Tara-lin looked up at Alai-ie-a. "I think it would do wonders for Zànalin to hear you sing. Your song is almost the exact opposite of hers. Like it, I think, yet not like it. I don't know how to say this."

"Don't worry. Do we ever know how to say anything? But who is this Zànalin?"

"A dryad I met once. She is consumed by fear and hate, filled with a horrid darkness – but something in her song drew me, attracted me. Yet she cannot contain her bitterness. It lashes out at any human, or even human-kind, near her. She is...corrupting," answered Tara-lin, "but she is *such* a singer. Almost as if her whole being is a song. As I said, like you, but completely different."

"Call your horses, and you can get them ready while we speak," said Alai-ie-a. "As for this Zànalin. I don't know her, though I've heard of this Corruption. It has never caused me any concern or fear. But, if this Zànalin is as you say, I'm not sure she could understand my song. It might not... reach her. Oh, she would hear me *sing*, even though some humans do not, but that does not mean she would really *hear* any better than they do. I don't think you understand song, understand your own understanding, well enough to know what I'm saying. I'll try to give you an idea. She would know that I sang, but that does not mean she would hear my song, just as some humans don't know I sing, but hear my song at least a little. And I've met one or two who did not appear to know I sang at all but did seem to hear my song very well indeed."

"Speaking of singing," said Tara-lin, as she bridled Vonë, "do you know if my song –"

"I doubt it," said Alai-ie-a. "I... don't think that way at all. And I would never know how to judge whether or how or how much what you sang was right or wrong. It is impossible, even inconceivable, to me to sing anything other than pure goodness and happiness to anyone. I can only invite others into what I have and am. That is all I can say on the matter. I don't think much about right and wrong. Only about what you call happiness."

"How did you know what I was going to ask?" asked Tara-lin, slinging her share of their goods over her shoulder.

"Much what I was trying to tell you about song. It's not these words you hear, and I don't understand you primarily through the words you speak. It may not be a better form of communication than words – I do not know – but it is different. I would not be hindered at all in speaking to one whose language I had never heard before."

"Are you sure you never think about what's right or wrong?" asked Tara-lin. "Like, would you think murdering babies might be right or do you know it's wrong?"

"Whatever is motivated by the Corruption is, I suppose, wrong. I don't think of it that way or use that concept. As I said, I hardly even concern myself with thinking about the Corruption. I do not fear it. I simply be who and what I am – one who offers and sings goodness to the world and people around her. I often don't know whether what another does is in line with goodness or reeks of the Corruption. Sometimes, I suppose, I might. Perhaps, I even have. But I concern myself with it little. Ultimately, Tara-lin, even if someone tells you the answer to your question, I don't think it will help you, unless she tells you in a way that makes *you know*. Otherwise, you'll be no nearer to understanding what and who you are, and thus what your song should be, than you are now. I'm not sure you *could* understand the answer to your question and, perhaps, it is not all that important. What is important is only that the next time, the next moment, you know what you need to know about what you call goodness in order to do it fully with no admixture of wrongness – not whether you did so in the past or even how or in what you failed or did not fail in the past."

"Thank you for your wisdom," said Tara-lin as she leapt onto Vonë's back.

Alai-ie-a laughed. "I've never been called wise before. What even is wisdom?" she asked.

Tara-lin turned around and started. "What?! Do the other dryads think you're stupid then?"

"Is wise the only alternative of stupid?" asked Alai-ie-a.

"No. It's just hard for me to imagine anyone not calling that wise, unless he thought you were stupid and so couldn't see the wisdom."

"I think you are talking and thinking nonsense, Tara-lin. In fact, I think you will find you do not even mean the things you are saying." The dryad laughed again, and the elfling thought it was the most beautiful sound in the world. "Fare you well. May joy go with you. I wish you the best to the core of all that I am!"

As they rode away, Alis said to Tara-lin. "Her song was so beautiful. I'd like to settle down with her and stay with her forever. I'd like to listen to her song forever. But I don't relish riding at night under moon and stars."

"It will make people less likely to see us, and the story that we're traveling elves more believable if we travel at night. Also, neither we nor the horses will be hot, like we would be if we travel during the day."

Alis was not even listening to this last part. "Traveling *elves?*" she gasped. "I am not an elf!"

"No," said Tara-lin, "but if anyone stops us I'm going to tell them you are."

"Really? Won't that be suspicious?"

"We're young elves," said Tara-lin. "The people who want to catch us don't know I'm a half-elf. We're young elves exploring the world and, if someone asks, How come we never see elves out exploring the world, I can ask him how often he travels in the middle of the night! Besides, the world outside of Elethri is rather large. Why assume most of those young elves with most interest in adventure and travel and seeing the world would go north up the Malaitha Mountains? We chose to, but that doesn't mean most do."

"I'm not even remotely an elf," Alis groaned, "and I'm *not* interested in adventure or exploring the world."

"That's why you're to let me do all the talking. You will be my younger, shy sister I dragged out here with me. As for why two women are together, why, we're elves, and elves don't care so much about differences between men and women. As for not being interested in adventure, I thought you wanted a gryphon?"

"Yes, I want a gryphon," said Alis, "but I'm not sure I want to ride one. At the moment, I hate riding horses. I like Makya, but I *hate* riding. I'm so stiff I can hardly sleep."

Tara-lin laughed. "You slept very well today, and, while the dryad made us rather comfortable, the ground wasn't as comfortable as a downy bed!"

"I only slept because I was so utterly tired!" Alis retorted.

Chapter Fifteen – Still Pursued

Half an hour later, Tara-lin said, "I don't know how you could stay with Alai-ie-a. This area is too civilized, she has too many people around you. I see no way she could hide you for long."

"I know," said Alis with a huge sigh.

Tara-lin's mind was occupied with very different thoughts. In a fashion, Alai-ie-a's advice to her made sense and comforted her. It rang true, though she could not quite explain how. It seemed a solution, and the only possible solution. At the same time, she was just as confused and distressed as before, for it seemed no solution at all. How could she know what she needed to know? How could she know she was who and what she was supposed to be enough to know what was right? How could she know she was working towards, how could she even know how to work towards, knowing what she needed to know and being what and who she was? She growled.

"What's wrong?" asked Alis.

"Something that's my business," said Tara-lin.

"Was it whatever it was you asked the dryad at the end?" asked Alis.

"Something like that," said Tara-lin. A growl underscored her words.

A few minutes later, Alis said, "I really am so sore."

"You can get off and walk next to her when we're walking if you want," said Tara-lin.

"Why don't you?" asked Alis.

"Because I'm *not* sore, at least not very much. If you want me to, I might."

"I'm really sore of walking, too," said Alis. "At least, that's how I felt a couple days ago. And I always feel so sore and my legs are so shaky when I get off."

"Does it get better or worse the longer you're off?"

"Never tried for long enough to tell," said Alis.

"Well then, try, and whatever you like better, do," replied Tara-lin.

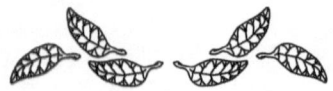

The dryads with whom they spent their nights provided them with food as well as water. Alis was pleased at the variety and types of food, ranging from grains to various fruits and vegetables, which the dryads living in civilized areas could provide. One day, Tara-lin explained to Alis that the elves often ate certain insects and bugs in place of meat, and then she asked the dryads if they could provide them with such insects – perhaps if there were any grasshoppers damaging the fields, they would love those, and ants would also do nicely. The dryads happily complied. They also provided the horses with supplemental grain.

Tara-lin spent some of the time actively instructing Alis on her riding. She insisted that Alis learn how to ride Makya at the canter, and on nights when a moon was out and more than just a sliver of a crescent, she had them canter stretches. Alis definitely took to dismounting Makya and walking stretches herself. One such night, she was walking alongside Tara-lin and Vonë, and said to her, "Tara-lin, it just struck me how unimaginable this is."

"What do you mean?" asked Tara-lin.

"Well," said Alis, "I just can't imagine what it must be like for you. You're doing all this in order to find your father – you're chasing him. I'm running away from mine. I can't imagine what it must be like for you. What it must be like to have a family you'd run after. And to think you encouraged me to run away from mine! I wouldn't have thought of it – let alone succeeded at it – if you hadn't helped me. And there's this other thing. Our fathers are both Knights of the Valor Hall. Right?"

"Yes," said Tara-lin.

"What will Sir Eldor do when he finds out you helped me escape... and that my father is another Knight such as himself?" asked Alis. Tara-lin's heart twanged at the concern in her voice.

"Nothing. I mean, nothing that will harm you," said Tara-lin. "I don't know if I told you, but he was developing suspicions about the Valor Hall and the intentions of the people who run it before he left. He'll just have his suspicions confirmed. No way will he give you back! Besides, you forget, he's not really a Knight such as your father. Remember, he married an elf and has been living in Elethri these past twenty-some years. He gave an oath, and thinks he needs to honor it by going on this crazy mission – and he doesn't even know what's really going on! But, as soon as he sees something that's definitely wrong, he'll have no part in it. Making you marry or join a temple would be definitely wrong."

"That's comforting to know," said Alis, but Tara-lin could tell she was not convinced. The half-elf decided to try again. "Remember how you told me you wouldn't have even thought of running away on your own?"

"Yes," said Alis, sounding confused. "What?"

"I haven't been raised like you have been, and my father is nothing like yours. I think it's almost an accident he ended up being a Valor Hall Knight."

"Look, Tara-lin, I just can't... imagine it," said Alis. "I hope what you're saying is true. I know you believe it. It's just unimaginable to me. And he *is* a Valor Hall Knight. You don't need to defend him to me. I'll find out that you're right soon enough."

"That you will!" said Tara-lin.

Another night, this time riding side by side with Tara-lin, Alis asked, "Do you ever notice it?"

"Notice what?" asked Tara-lin.

"That it messes you up to sleep during the day and be awake at night. You don't feel really awake most of the time, and you don't really sleep very well, either," said Alis.

"No, I don't notice that," said Tara-lin, an undertone of laughter in her voice. "I don't think that happens to me."

"Is that because you're part-dryad?" asked Alis.

"I don't know," said Tara-lin.

"You know," said Alis, after a pause of several minutes, "this is actually really nice. Etiquette and dresses and all the other stuff they thought girls needed to know in the Valor Hall wasn't really very interesting. I hated most of it. I'm sore most of the time, but when I'm not griping about how tired and sore I am, this is really nice. As you promised me, I've heard owls and hawks. I've seen foxes, wild rabbits, squirrels, and chipmunks. I've ridden a gryphon and spoken to dryads. I've seen herds of deer, I've learned about birds and different plants. And, I've actually got a horse and I'm actually learning how to ride!"

"You're learning very well, Alis," said Tara-lin. "You don't ride at all poorly."

"I don't?" asked Alis.

"No," said Tara-lin, "You don't. You've still got a lot to learn, but I'm thinking a lot of the difference between elvish aptitude and human aptitude is that elves live a lot longer. They might be children too small to learn things for longer, but they are children and young adults perfectly capable of learning for many times the span of a human life."

"I'd like to get to live that long," said Alis. "I want to be able to ride that well. I want to be able to climb trees and sneak through the woods that well."

"You'll ride as well as I do almost as soon as your muscles are all used to it, Alis! Isn't that good enough?" asked Tara-lin. "As for woodcraft, we've dryad blood in us. You might live twice as long as an elf, and still not match the skill we're almost born with."

"Ohh," said Alis, almost in a sigh.

"Still, I'd like to live that long and learn all those things and see them and stuff."

"If the dryads are right," said Tara-lin, "you will get to live that long. They seem to think that death is just a passage into another life where everything is more. So I think it'll be all right, Alis, and you'll get to learn and see and do everything you want to. Who knows, maybe you'll get to achieve even the wood lore of the elves!"

"Umph."

"You really tend to be cynical!" said Tara-lin.

"You don't really believe that, yourself," said Alis.

"I don't know what to believe," said Tara-lin, "or what I believe. Sometimes, I think it really sounds right, that it must be that way, that I believe that. Other times, I just... don't."

"Yeah," said Alis, "but, really, you shouldn't be thinking I'm cynical. The last time I worried about what I'm doing, running away with you, getting me in big everlasting trouble with the gods was... well, weeks ago, I think."

"You're still not absolutely convinced," said Tara-lin.

"When I think about it, I'm not. I just can't help it, for some reason. But mostly I don't think about it. I'm too occupied hiking and riding and being tired and sleeping."

Tara-lin laughed lightly, and Alis joined in.

One morning, Alis and Tara-lin sat on their horses and watched as the walls of city grew up before them in the light of the dawn. As they dismounted, seeking the hospitality of another dryad for the day, Alis said to Tara-lin, "Do you still have any of those coins of yours?"

"Yes," said Tara-lin. "Why?"

"This bugs we've been eating are good enough, though I *don't* like them, but I'm hungry for some real meat, and was wondering if you would be willing to go in there, or find a town, or whatever you think is best, and find some for me. The dryads feed us wonderfully, but they can't get meat!" said Alis.

"Yeah, I know that," said Tara-lin. She looked around, and her gaze settled on the Malaitha Mountains, outlined against the dawn. "Yes, I think we're far enough. Yes, I think I can do that, Alis." She turned and smiled at her friend.

"Thanks," said Alis.

"You're welcome."

"You're such a good friend, Tara-lin! I never imagined having such a good friend. And I'm not saying this only because you'll get me meat. Who else would've helped me run away or encouraged me that I even *could* live a life of my own?" said Alis.

"I like you, too, Alis," said Tara-lin. "I'm glad I met you and we get to be friends. None of the elves were really like me, either."

Alis nodded vigorously. Her tangled hair flew about her face. Tara-lin laughed.

"What's funny?" asked Alis.

"Your hair! I bet mine is almost as bad, but I can't imagine your hair looking like that in the Valor Hall! I can just imagine how your parents would react if they saw you now." She laughed harder so that she could hardly stand.

"Oh," said Alis, sputtering a little, but obviously far less amused.

Tara-lin leapt lightly down from Vonë's back. "Take care of my horse, Alis. I'll go right now. The dryad here will help you."

She took off, running in an easy, measured stride, towards the city. The dawn-breeze ruffled her hair and the feel of the early morning air rushing past her as her feet skimmed over the ground felt good.

When she got nearer to the city, Tara-lin slowed down and pulled the hood of her Elethrian cloak over her head. She would not want anyone to see her pointed, upswept elven ears before she chose. She moved into a press of farmers bringing their early-season goods to sell in the city, and made herself as obscure as she could. As she moved through the press, Tara-lin wondered if dryads sometimes mingled with men in just this fashion. Could any of them alter their appearance enough to not stand out too much? Somehow, she suspected such alterations were well within the province of certain dryads.

Sometime later, Tara-lin approached a merchant in the market. She looked at her bag and considered the fact that she would have to buy cooked meat. She could not buy freshed butchered raw meat, since she and Alis could not light a fire and cook it. When she got to the front of the line, she haggled with the merchant, hoping to get as much as she could for her coins.

When he saw her coins, he gasped. "These look... Elethrian. They must be counterfeit!"

"They're not counterfeit," said Tara-lin. "I'm an elf myself and I'm here exploring the flora and fauna of this region. I got hungry for some meat."

"I didn't know elves ate meat," said the merchant.

"We do, just not as much as some humans. Anyway, sell to me for a reasonable price, please. It would annoy me if I had to look for someone else to sell to me, and I know someone *will* sell to me for a reasonable price. Who wouldn't want to have some Elethrian coins to boast about to his neighbors? How many people in these parts ever see an elf, let alone speak to one?"

"You've got that right," said the man. "We're a little far north to be seeing your kind with any regularity. But aren't you a little short?"

Tara-lin pulled back her hood to expose her ears. "Elves vary in height much as humans do. I'm a little short for an elf, but then again I might still grow more, and I come of a short family. Anyway, will you sell to me?"

"Elethrian coins aren't worth any more than Alliance coins," insisted the merchant.

"Not *officially,*" said Tara-lin, "but you know it will be great value to prove you sold to an elf. It will increase your popularity."

When Tara-lin finally picked up the packages, an older woman standing in the line spoke to her. "Is that why you're not with your family? Because you're an elf?"

"Huh?" responded Tara-lin.

"You must be unfamiliar with our customs. How did you learn to speak our language so well?"

"Most elves learn languages readily. If we're at all interested, it's no trouble to learn your language," answered Tara-lin.

As she left the market, Tara-lin noticed she was being surreptitiously followed. She wondered why. It was very well-done, not the work of an amateur who wanted to follow an elf and find out what she did. This was a professional spy.

Tara-lin let him follow her for a while. She suspected he did not understand the natural awareness and subtlety of her race. It took some effort on her part, but she could keep track of him, when he disappeared and when he reappeared. Finally, she maneuvered into a crowd in such a way that there were several people between herself and him. She tossed the hood over her head and pulled it most of the way over her face, ducked quickly between two people, and threw herself down on the ground next to a house on the corner of an alley. A clothes-line swung over her, further disguising her form, as the Elethrian cloak camouflaged her into her environment. She understood more of the secret of the cloak now. It was more than simple camouflage. Song was woven into the threads, so that they naturally resisted the gaze of searchers.

She waited, picking out the spy's footsteps as he passed. She smiled to herself, picturing his expression on discovering she had lost him. She smiled again, when she thought of her own cunning. She had lost him here on purpose. On her way into the city, she had picked up on a short, somewhat convoluted, route, that opened up on a main street right before the gate. She was feet away from the route now... Tara-lin waited, until she could hear his footsteps disappearing in another direction, then got up and unobtrusively made her way into a dark side-street.

A lot of it was not so much cunning as luck. She had just happened to notice a curvy street exiting from the main road just after the gate. As she wandered on several of the main streets in the area, it became clear to her that it exited in another place, right around here. Actually, she was not quite sure this was the right one, but she was sure she could find her way from this street to the other if she was not right.

Tara-lin soon did discover she was not correct, and that the walls were higher than she thought she could climb in this lighting and at this time of day without being noticed. However, she did manage to find an exit that opened on another cross-roads from the one she had left. Her hood still over her face, she stepped boldly out into the road. Her bag was now hidden under her cloak, and the folds of its magical material concealed the fact there was a bulge against her hip. The cloak responded to her wishes and took on a slightly yellower and redder hue than it had earlier.

As Tara-lin passed the guards at the city gate, she saw a familiar form step out of the crowd. Without hesitation, she dropped down and rolled into the grass on the side of the road.

She almost laughed when the man stopped and looked around with obvious confusion on his face. She sang softly under her breath.

> The wind blows and shadows morph
> A movement seems a form that is not
> Return, return, the way you came
> I am a mound, a couple million blades of grass
> And the shadow of someone else's cloak
> I am a whisper of the wind, a breath of the breeze

It felt like minutes while he stood there. He even walked around and examined the side of the road. Once, his boot ended inches away from Tara-lin's knee. He walked up and down the road a couple of times and finally went back in. Tara-lin heard him muttering to himself, "If it's the half-elf witch, then she's used her magic to disappear again, and I won't find her. Darn it! How does she do it? But I could have been mistaken. Still, she contrived to give me the slip earlier. They ought to send a wizard after her!"

When he had gone, Tara-lin lay still for a few more minutes. Then she rose, her heart beating quickly now, with fear. She stole down the road towards Alis, considering this new development. Earlier, the common soldiers sent after her had not appeared to know she was elven-kind. Of course, she *had* used Elethrian coins in the village where Alis' father had turned up, but if they had discovered that and put two and two together, they should have known she was Tara-lin weeks ago. Moreover, it was probable that the lady she had given the coins had not told anyone, since it seemed the villagers mostly sided with her and Alis and against the Valor Hall Knights. Then again, someone would probably want to gossip about having found Elethrian coins, and a spy might have picked up that piece of information, so that could explain both the knowledge and the delay in the appearance of the knowledge...

However, it meant she had not completely lost their pursuers and that she could not go into a city again. Tara-lin hoped they would not be found. If they were, they would have to run for it. She hoped Alis could stay on.

When Tara-lin got to where she and Alis were staying that day, she found Alis awake, stroking and talking to the horses and waiting for her. She did not tell Alis anything about her pursuer. It was not like there was anything Alis could do. They ate and drank, and then went to sleep.

Chapter Sixteen – The Wind Song

When a week passed without any further signs of their pursuers, Tara-lin stopped worrying about them. It was not like they could be tracked by anyone except possibly a wizard. Tara-lin did not know what the particulars of wizardry were, so she did not know if a wizard might be able to find them. She also thought it possible a very good elf tracker *might* be able to follow them. She knew no human could, without the aid of magic or wizardry. The dryads covered their traces when they were gone so no one could tell where they had stopped, and dozens of horses and men and wagons drove over the roads they took each and every day.

Then, one morning, Tara-lin looked around them. To Alis she said, "We're rather far north now. I am still not certain how to find my father. I shall try to look for him shortly, but we leave the road now. Look!" She pointed.

Ahead, the Malaitha Mountain range ended rather abruptly in a region of rugged hills and cliffs. Across what looked like a huge rough gorge rose another mountain range, shaped like a crown, with peaks covered in snow and ice.

"The Icecrown Mountains!" gasped Alis. "I *thought* it was colder than it should be this time of year."

"That's because we're further north," said Tara-lin.

"Is it safe?" asked Alis.

"I will leave you in the care of the dryads in the woods at the foot of the Icecrown Mountains. Nyimia says it is still safe enough there. The dryads there are still strong. The dark magic has not yet sapped their vitality. If it becomes dangerous, they will lead you further south and into the places they remain strong, but, if Prince Anakrim succeeds in his foul plans, there may be no safe place left in Ellenesia."

Alis nodded. "And we're going towards *that?*"

"We discussed this already. It's not very dangerous until you go deep into Icecrown, where I must go. I will leave you where it is still safe. Let us go! A few more days now!"

"I'm going to miss you, Tara-lin," said Alis.

"I fully intend to come back alive," said Tara-lin.

"Yes, but it will be lonely, even for a few days, with only dryads for company, not that dryads make bad company – though some of them are much better company than others," said Alis.

"I'm glad you like me. I'll try to leave you with a dryad you can be friends with. Anyway, let's go!" She nudged Vonë with her heels, and the horse trotted. Alis followed behind. In a few minutes, they were cantering.

Excitement made Tara-lin's blood tingle. Fear might have mingled with the excitement, but mostly she felt intoxicated. She was so close now! It was time to begin looking for her father and his party. She was sure they had made good time during the last leg of their journey, and, though not much of a tracker by the standards of the elves, she was sure that, with the aid of her dryad magic, she could track her father's company into the Icecrown Fortress, Nightshade itself. If they had already got there. She did not really know what they planned, only that she must find them. She knew she was supposed to try to do something, too, but she did not know what it was. She was not too worried about that, though. Many times, the dryads had assured her that she would know what she needed to know when the time came. That was the way their magic worked. And she would find her father soon! She hummed as she rode, even after she slowed Vonë to a walk.

Alis looked at her. "Why are you so happy, Tara-lin?! Isn't it *dangerous?!*"

"I'm so close now. I'm about to be where I can begin looking for Dad. Even though I'm not a great tracker by elvish standards, I'm sure with the help of the dryads and my magic I can find a whole company of Valor Hall Knights. I miss both Dad and Mom, but I know I'll come back to find Lìrulin alive. She'll live for centuries more. Sir Eldor won't. It will be very nice to see him again!"

Alis smiled. "It must be so strange – and so nice – to have parents you'd *want* to see like this, that you'd be this excited to find. It makes me impatient to meet him."

"I thought you were worried he'll turn against you because of his oath to the Valor Hall," said Tara-lin.

"Oh, Tara-lin, you're no help at all! I am a little worried about that, I suppose, but why must you bring it up whenever I don't think it up? I'm impatient to meet him since I'd like to know what such a wonderful Dad must be like, and also because I want to know if he's what you make him out to be, since I've never seen that before – it's hard to believe. But why must you remind me of my doubts when I wasn't thinking them?" said Alis.

"Sorry," said Tara-lin. "I don't mean to... be a problem."

A scent blew past her on the wind. "Run!" she cried, kicking her horse into a gallop.

"What is it?" yelled Alis into the wind as Makya sprang forward, keeping pace with Vonë.

"Orcs, I think," said Tara-lin. "It's the tell-tale scent of them. But I suppose it could be another kind of Servant of Nightmare."

She cringed a little when she thought about Alis' fear. She did not want Alis to be afraid, to freak out. And they were not alone. The dryads would help them. If only they could make it into the woods...

Please, please, don't let myself or Alis be overwhelmed by the madness' stench. Please not Alis. She bent low over Vonë's neck and loosened her sword in its sheath.

The horses needed no urging. They sensed the horror almost as soon as the elfling had. *At least, I've never heard of a horse being paralyzed by the demons. They might have no strategy or tactics, but at least they'll run... they'll try to get themselves and their riders away, even if their riders are touched by the madness.*

Tara-lin saw the orcs falling out of the hills on either side of them. A whole band of them! *If you exist – I've never spoken to you before – I don't know if I am now – but I have to now. If you are, Shallim-Araldor, if you hear me, take care of us. We don't want to go mad. We don't want to succumb to the fever of hell. Protect us, if you can.*

What kind of song could I sing? Will it help if I draw this elf-sword? I will, if it becomes a close fight, but hopefully Vonë and Makya can carry us away from them.

At that moment, an arrow hissed through the air, then several more.

Oh no. They might be bad shots, but they could still hit us... or one of the horses, which is just as bad.

I'd rather be able to stand still to sing.

Tara-lin grasped the reins in one hand. She kept her seat over Vonë's back, and rested her other hand on the hilt of the elf-sword, which she drew several inches out of its sheath. She did not want to carry it naked, lest she accidentally drop it or cut Vonë with it. She had never trained to carry a sword while riding. She knew the rhythm of riding would interfere with her song, but tried to match herself to the rhythm well enough that it might work. Then, she began to sing.

Wind of the mountains

Wind of the hills
Come to my aid
Come to the aid of the trees

Wind of the mountains
Wind of the hills
Fly sudden swift
Turn the arrows' way from us

Wind of the mountains
Wind of the hills
Hear me now!
Gust and blow and swirl around!

Wind of the mountains
Wind of the hills
Come with wildness
Wild and fierce and changing oft!

Wind of the mountains
Wind of the hills
Come, wild and strong
Blow my way, gusts and torrents!

Wind of the mountains
Wind of the hills
Answer to my call
Answer the need of your dryads!

Wind of the mountains
Wind of the hills
Hear me now!
Gust and blow and swirl around!
Fly sudden swift!
Turn the arrows' way from us
Come, wild and strong
Wild and fierce and changing oft!
Come with wildness
Blow my way, gusts and torrents!

Blow sudden swift!
Turn the arrows' way from us.

So Tara-lin sang, and her song was rewarded rapidly. Perhaps, those trees which they passed joined her in it, but the wind answered, as if it had wings and a will of its own. Leaves blew around them. There was a musky scent of coming rain. There was noise in the tops of the trees, and it seemed as if the trees exulted in the wind rustling and rushing through their boughs and the sky above them. Dustdevils of dust and leaves rose from the ground. The horses, too, seemed energized, almost pleased, by the wind, which blew away from them the scent of the orcs.

This lasted for several minutes. Tara-lin was not sure how far ahead of the orcs the horses' gallop brought them. They were now climbing through more forested regions. Though the trees were still not thick, they swayed around them on every side. Now and then a whiff or the sound of an orc arrow reached Tara-lin's nose or ears, and she knew they had not left the orcs far behind. How many of them were there?

Then there was a creak and a crash. Twenty or so horselengths ahead of them a tall tree fell across their way. *That was close*, thought Tara-lin. Alis screamed.

"It's okay!" Tara-lin tried to call encouragement through the winds her song had helped to call. "You can jump it."

She thought she heard Alis scream, "My horse might be able to, but I can't!"

Tara-lin looked over her shoulder and met Alis' face. "Turn forward! You can! GRIP!" She herself had to face forward now. Vonë was only a stride away....

She had already driven the sword back into its sheath. Both hands were on the reins, and she went forward with the horse over the large trunk, gripping his shoulders hard between her knees.

A thump and a scream behind her told her Alis had fallen off. Makya raced past her.

"Makya! Makya!" called Tara-lin, trying to calm the horse with her voice. Alis continued screaming. "I'm going to be lost! The orcs are going to GET ME!"

"Get up," said Tara-lin, reining Vonë in. "Go and catch her, Alis. Do you see the orcs? No. Get up!" She turned and rode Vonë closer to Makya, who was slowing and circling around, crooning to the horse.

"Stop crying, and catch her," said Tara-lin to Alis again, this time more graciously. "You can do it. You can do it. See? She's even coming back to you."

In a few more moments, Alis was on Makya's back, and they continued their flight. *She's probably scared a tree will fall on her, too,* thought Tara-lin. *There's not much I can do, though. I only have so much influence. And I must not do anything that would cause the wind to slacken. We need the wind, all we can get. We need to* lose *these orcs. It would be nice if I could ask the wind to pick them up and throw them away, but I don't know if it can do that without hurting us.*

Tara-lin looked around her, and guided Vonë up a slope with few trees, most of which looked sturdy and relatively unlikely to drop limbs. This wind was wild, though, and she could hear more trees crashing. It made the horses somewhat wild, too. She wished she could reassure Alis. Horses tended to be rather smart in their own way, and if she did not try to fight with Vonë to make him go where he did not want to go, he was unlikely to lead them into the path of a falling tree right as it fell.

A thought came to Tara-lin then, and she smiled. The dryads and the wind were doubtless working on one team. The dryads probably intentionally dropped branches on the orcs. She did not think dryads were unwilling to fight the Nightmare Servants with violence, but only living beings, such as men, which, however corrupted they might be, had a life apart from the Corruption. That made it even less likely another tree would nearly fall on them or even across their path. Listening to the directions of the crashes, Tara-lin became nearly convinced of her theory. Yes. Her song and the dryads' worked together very well indeed...

This made her want to reassure Alis even more, but she doubted Alis could hear something so complicated over the wind, which was very loud. Then there was a strike of lightning behind them, and Tara-lin was certain it was serving them and the dryads against the orcs. She could *almost* hear the song of the dryads. For a moment she considered trying to help them, then she thought better of it. They were doing very well on their own, and she, part-human and inexperienced, might mess it up for them. Instead, she would try to listen and learn.

She only felt sorry that Alis would be terrified of the lightning, too, even though it was their friend if still a little dangerous to them. When the lightnings multiplied, some of them striking rocks above them, Tara-lin knew Alis would be frightened. She decided she would try to yell across the space between them and their horses. "Alis!" she called, looking over her shoulder.

She saw that Alis heard her.

"It's fine! They're fighting for us!" she called again.

This time she was not sure that Alis understood any of her words. She was sure Alis was afraid.

After a while, Tara-lin let Vonë slow down, as he was inclined to do. Soon, both horses were trotting. Alis rode up beside her, looking very frightened. "Is it safe now?" she asked, incredulous.

"It depends what you mean by safe," said Tara-lin. "I'm pretty sure the orcs are rather far behind, and cannot catch up to us. Most of the trees you heard falling was dryads fighting for us against the orcs. They can drop their limbs, and perhaps direct a few dryad-less trees to drop limbs or fall on the orcs. Some of them may even be able to fall on the orcs. For some, it may mean the end of this phase of their existence; for others, they may sprout up anew next year and live longer and grow to be stronger for it. The lightnings were somewhat less controllable, and therefore more dangerous, but they, too, were directed primarily at the orcs, and not at us. So, it wasn't as dangerous as you thought, but I couldn't figure out how to tell you, until the wind slackened a little, and we stopped running so fast."

"The wind doesn't seem slack to me," said Alis.

"It's not," said Tara-lin, "but it's not quite as wild as it was at first – or, rather, at its height. And, back there, it's still more wild than it is now. If it gets more wild here, we'll have to run again, since it will probably mean the orcs are getting closer to us, since it's them the wind is fighting," said Tara-lin. "The dryads sang, too."

"You will have to tell me if that happens, since I can't tell the wind is slacker," said Alis.

"Fine," said Tara-lin. "Let's keep trotting for a while, though. The horses might not care for it anymore, but it won't hurt them any."

"All right," said Alis. "You know better than me, I suppose."

Tara-lin flashed her a cheeky grin.

"About *some* things," said Alis. "I told you I was scared when you pointed out how close we are to the Icecrown Mountains."

"I really think you will be safe with some dryads," said Tara-lin. "I'll leave you here, at the edge of the Malaitha Mountains, if I can."

Chapter Seventeen – Betrayed

Tara-lin reined in Vonë. What was that? Had she heard something?

"What?" asked Alis. "I thought you –"

"Sshh!" hissed Tara-lin.

She sat there for a whole minute. There! She heard it again, even through the wind. Human voices. What were humans doing around here? It was a little wild to be a farmstead. Maybe it was a hunting party, but she had to go look. Maybe it was Sir Eldor's company!

An intuition, a whisper, reached her. She jumped from Vonë's back. "Stay here!" she said to Alis. "Watch the horses." Without waiting for her human friend to acknowledge her, she moved lightly in the direction from which she judged the sound to be coming, stopping every two dozen steps and listening for it. Something was making her very suspicious, but it was hard to tell what through the wind. Still, the orc company would make sense if her father's company was here, and Prince Anakrim, or whatever dark powers he served, had got wind of it.

She remembered things her father had said to her. *What if Anakrim has a spy in the Valor Hall?* With some alarm, she thought, *What if he knows about me?!*

She continued forward.

The voices became clearer, but still not distinct. She knew now there were three of them, and that none of them was her father's. Something about the tone made her think they were not from a hunting party caught in the storm she and her dryad kin had called, even though it was a not-unlikely size for such a party.

Tara-lin came to a crest, and dropped on her belly. She squirmed over it, and saw several men hiding in the shadow of a tree. *Now* she could hear what they said.

"This storm was unexpected. I guess we will have to wait it out," said one.

Another answered, "Unexpected storms happen in this region once or so this time of year, Talas."

"It will delay us, Gonar, though. We can't trek through it. Trees falling everywhere, lightning flashing. I hope it doesn't cause flash foods, because then we'll be swept away in this ravine where we're sheltering from the worst of it."

"I don't think flash floods are likely," said a third. "It will delay them, too."

"It will give them more time to notice we've vanished, and adapt," said Gonar.

Tara-lin almost cried out. They were wearing the crest of the Valor Hall under their cloaks. She'd seen it when Gonar motioned and his cloak flung wildly away from him in a gust.

What could she do? What were they doing? They must be traitors!

Tara-lin sat up and sang, hoping the wind would cover her voice.

> The sleep comes on you
> Like ice on a lake in Autumn
> Like the sun sets behind the North Pole
> The sleep comes on you
>
> The sleep embraces you
> Like snow blankets northern mountains
> Like snow muffles voices, and the bear's den
> The sleep embraces you

Tara-lin's song continued, at first slow and soft. The men below her said there was nothing else to do but sleep while they waited out the storm and slowly drifted asleep. Still, Tara-lin sang. Her throat grew dry and she became thirsty, but still she sang. She did not know what would happen if she stopped, if she would be able to pick up the enchantment where she left off. Slowly, she wove a spell of deep sleep, of dizziness and confusion, of suppressed thirst and hunger that they might sleep the longer, of many and confused dreams that might pass for reality in the fogginess which would haunt their minds for a while when they finally did awaken. As the sleep deepened, sometimes her song grew high and dizzying as she spun the various different parts of her enchantment. Around her the storm still raged and lightning flashed. Darkness began to fall. She was now very thirsty, but still she sang, deepening the enchantment, adding layer upon layer. Some concern for Alis niggled at the back of her mind, but she was almost certain the dryads would take care of her, and she pushed the concern aside. She had to focus on her song.

Finally, Tara-lin stopped singing. It was well past midnight. She was almost asleep herself. She felt like passing out as she stood. With some difficulty, she found her way to where she had left Alis. The girl lay asleep in a drier-than-usual spot at the foot of a nearby tree. She saw her plainly in the flashes of rapid lightning. The horses grazed in a clearing nearby.

Tara-lin approached Alis and the tree. She looked through the bags and found their water, which she drank greedily. She spoke to the dryad of this tree then. "Wake me when dawn draws near," she requested.

"Why?" asked the dryad, hardly materializing out of his tree.

"I must find my father, tell him what I have done, and warn him of the treason," Tara-lin answered. "Wake me when dawn draws near."

"I will," he answered. "Know that we know what you have done. Knowing the workings of human minds as we do not, there are spells you can weave, subtleties you can weave, that we cannot, though we have some understanding of what you do. Sleep, now. I will watch, and I will wake you."

As the dryad promised, so he did, wakening Tara-lin in the early hours of the morning, when the dawn was still mostly behind the mountains. She ate and drank quickly, then woke Alis. The girl sat up, rubbing her eyes.

"I leave you here," said Tara-lin. "If you and another dryad like each other better, you can stay by her tree, instead of by this tree. I'm sure the dryads will accommodate you gladly in facilitating you finding someone with whom you can be comfortable. They will also help you care for the horses. I know you feel unsafe here, after we had to run away from the orcs yesterday, but I think that will not happen again. I think they were wandering here for a reason. Either way, I am confident the dryads can protect you, and I *must* go and find my father. All right, Alis?"

Alis nodded, but Tara-lin was sure she was still sleepy. To be honest, she herself felt very tired. She wondered if she could wake up enough to find her father. She turned to the dryad again. "If she doesn't remember what I said, tell her."

"I will. We are all committed to helping you as much as is in our power and in accord with our nature," he said.

"Thank you," said Tara-lin.

"No. We thank you. It is our race which this Anakrim would enslave and destroy," he answered.

"And with your race, perhaps the life of this whole world," answered Tara-lin. "Still, I thank you. I must go now."

"I understand. Go now," he answered.

Tara-lin took the newly-stocked bag of provisions, hung it over her shoulder and under her Elethrian cloak, and ventured out of the shelter of the tree. The storm was still raging, but there were breaks in it. One showed a small patch of dawn behind the edge of the mountains.

This storm would make it harder to find her father. She stood silently for a moment, considering her options. She was sure the right dryads would know.

Tara-lin set off in the direction of the men she had enchanted with sleep. She found them again more quickly than she had the first time, and sat beside them for half an hour, adding another layer of her spells. Then she rose and addressed a nearby dryad. When the dryad responded to her greeting, she asked, "Can you tell me which way these came? – Unless you know where my father, Sir Eldor, is even now?"

"Yes, I can tell you which way these came. I do not know of Sir Eldor, however," answered the dryad. In a few moments, Tara-lin had learned the direction from which they came.

Tara-lin retraced it, speaking often to dryads along the way, to ask for the way when she passed the limits of the knowledge of the last dryad to whom she had spoken. Sometimes, a dryad she asked was older and sleepy, and did not know, and she had to ask around to find another. The sun had risen and the storm was continuing to abate by the time she reached a somewhat sheltered vale where it was obvious men had just made camp. She examined the tracks, and followed one pair of them.

The sun had risen yet higher when she overtook the man she was tracking. She heard him before she saw him. He was calling the names of his companions. "Hi!" she called.

He turned towards her voice.

Tara-lin stepped quickly nearer. "Who are you?" she asked.

"A Knight of the Valor Hall," he answered.

"The companions – Gonar, Talas, and another – for which you are looking have betrayed you. I am Tara-lin, daughter of Sir Eldor," she said.

"How am I to know that is true?" the man asked.

She flung her hood back and stepped towards him. "Come with me, and we will find Sir Eldor. He will know me," she said. "Has he ever told you about me? If he has, you will see that I at least look like his daughter."

The man stepped closer and inspected her. "You are certainly not an ordinary human. I will walk with you for the time being, but how do you know they betrayed us and were not lost in the storm?"

"I found them, and they were talking about how they were going to get to Anakrim to tell him you were here through the storm," said Tara-lin. "In what direction did Sir Eldor go to look for them? And what is your name?"

"I will tell you my name when I am certain you are who you say you are. You do indeed look like the daughter Sir Eldor described to me, but I do not know how you followed us or found us, and there are many evil magics and illusions in the Icecrown Mountains. Even though we are not yet there, it is best to be wary."

Tara-lin said nothing. She wondered to what odd superstition he might ascribe that he would think someone might gain power over him if he told them his name.

It was an hour more before Tara-lin found Sir Eldor. When he saw her, he cried out, "What have you done, coming here?!"

"Probably just saved your life," said Tara-lin. "And possibly this whole mission."

"At the risk of your own!" said Sir Eldor. "What have you done?"

"It is not a simple story. Put succinctly, you have been betrayed."

"By whom?"

"By those you think lost and are looking for," said Tara-lin. "Gonar, Talas, and another are traitors. They were going to tell Prince Anakrim you were coming."

The other Knight passed Tara-lin and stood next to his comrade. "This is your daughter?" he asked.

"Yes, Namdon, this is my daughter. She is a singer, and I don't know what she has done, and I wish she were not here, but she is no foe," said Sir Eldor.

"Well, then," said Namdon, turning and bowing to Tara-lin, "I mean you no discourtesy. I am Sir Namdon."

Tara-lin nodded. "I don't understand why..."

"It is a discussion for another day," said Sir Eldor. "Namdon is an old friend of mine. I know he can be trusted. There is also a sixth Knight with us. He was also searching for our lost companions, and we must find him. Then, I will ask you to leave and go back to Elethri!"

"I won't go," said Tara-lin. "You can't make me. But let us find your companion."

"I wish you would," said Sir Eldor.

"I cannot. You do not even know what this Anakrim is doing. He is trying to steal the lives of dryads to fuel his magic, and I have been charged by the dryads to do whatever I can to stop him, more or less," said Tara-lin.

Namdon turned around and gasped. "Dryads?" he asked.

"Yes," said Sir Eldor. "Dryads are real. My wife has spoken to dryads a couple times in the past, and it seems my daughter speaks to dryads also."

"You don't even know the half of it," said Tara-lin. "Elves aren't a separate race. We're part-dryad, part-human."

"What?!" asked both men.

"Yes," said Tara-lin. "It is *so* good to see you, Dad."

"It is not good to see you here, daughter," said Sir Eldor severely.

The rest of the walk back to the camp was made in silence.

When they reached the camp, the third Knight had returned. He rose and waved to his comrades. "Eldor! Namdon!" he called. "Did you find any of our comrades? Who *is* with you?"

"This is my daughter, Tara-lin, Cuthlin. I don't know how she found us. No, we did not find any of our comrades," answered Sir Eldor.

The men moved towards each other. Tara-lin walked beside her father. When they were close to one another, so that the four of them formed a tight circle, Sir Eldor said, "*She*, however, has reported to have found our comrades and, what is worse, to have found them betraying us."

They all looked at her. Tara-lin nodded. "Yes. Gonar, Talas, and a third, were having a conversation about how they could not travel to Anakrim's outpost in the storm, and that would give you more time to potentially discover what they were up to and adapt before you were overwhelmed by whatever force the Prince was planning to send against you."

"That would mean... the Valor Hall is compromised on a... *very* high level," said Sir Cuthlin.

"Yes," said Sir Eldor.

Tara-lin stood silent. She thought of Alis and Alis' father. No wonder an organization built with *that* was subject to infiltration, compromise, and take-over.

"How do we know any of us aren't spies?" stated Sir Cuthlin.

"I won't believe it of Sir Eldor," said Namdon. "We've known each other since we were young Knights, and he might have married an elf and lived in Elethri for the last twenty years, and he might have some very strange notions, but I can't believe him a traitor. He's absolutely true to his word and his oath."

"What about his daughter?" asked Sir Cuthlin. "No offense, but how do we know Tara-lin is not a witch, and that she captured our comrades? She is not even bound by the Valor Oath."

"Have you not seen *anything* in the way the Valor Hall is run that makes you suspicious?" asked Sir Eldor.

"Suspicious?" said Sir Namdon. "Sure. I'm not questioning your daughter, Eldor. I know you too well, even if it was twenty years ago. This is hard to believe, but I'm not certain it requires the level of compromise you're assuming, Cuthlin. These three might be plants, who've acted more or less consistently with their oath since they took it – at least, whenever they could be caught. Compromise? Sure. Lack of vigilance? Sure. But whole-scale treason throughout the entire Valor Hall? Not necessarily. Just a bribe here or there, a bit of laziness there in validating someone, and a couple dozen plants could be placed and rise quite highly if they're intelligent. Elves and singers and dryads is crazy, Cuthlin, but we knew we were dealing with wizards and crazy half-elves before we embarked on this mission. It's what the whole mission is about. The addition of a half-elf singer on the right side of things is... more crazy, but it's not wholly unbelievable. And she bears news from the dryads about what Prince Anakrim's methods may be..."

They all turned to look at Tara-lin again, and she felt uncomfortable. "I'm not sure about methods," she said. "I know nothing about the methods." She glanced at her father, and saw him nod to her. "The rumor I heard in Elethri was that Anakrim intended to steal the life and energy from other beings to make himself a wizard of sorts. It has become clear that the specific beings in question are the dryads."

"What are the potential ramifications of this?" asked Sir Namdon, stroking his lightly-bearded chin.

"We don't know for certain," said Tara-lin. "The deaths of many trees are likely. How far-spread the destruction will be is uncertain."

"All right," said Sir Cuthlin. "You've made your argument, Namdon. But I want to know something else. Tara-lin, what is the state of the traitors?"

"Asleep," answered the half-elven singer. "They will sleep for anywhere between two days and a week, and when they wake up they will be very confused. I don't know how confused. I'm hoping at least one or two of them will think they already went and told Prince Anakrim or whoever-it-is whatever it was they were supposed to, but I don't know."

"How is this possible?" asked Sir Cuthlin.

Eldor answered, "The ancient elven magic of the singers. They are nothing more than legend to us humans, but for the elves, whose lives are counted in centuries, not decades, they are somewhat distant history. The last singer, before my daughter, died fourteen hundred years ago, but I've seen her sing and have no doubt there is power in her song. But I have no conception of what powers she may have developed in the meantime..."

"Dryads taught me," said Tara-lin, taking her father's gaze.

"Dryads," said Sir Cuthlin, and let out a great sigh. "Can dryads be trusted?"

"We don't know anymore about dryads than about singers," Namdon reminded him.

"Some dryads can't be trusted," said Tara-lin. "But given that you don't typically find trees trying to kill you, I figure on the whole dryads are not untrustworthy, definitely not your enemies..."

Both Sir Namdon and Eldor threw back their heads and laughed. Cuthlin still seemed skeptical.

"This is a mess," he said. "If the Valor Hall is that compromised, why don't we turn around, quit, and go back and find some place to hide from all this madness?"

"Not me," said Sir Namdon. "It might be infiltrated, but I'm *not* convinced of its over-all compromise. I think there's still good people in it trying to do good things. And I think this Prince Anakrim is evil."

"But how will we do anything to stop him if we can't trust the Valor Hall not to set a death-trap for us?" asked Sir Cuthlin.

"Well, we have a half-elf dryad-taught singer with us, now. That's got to count for something," said Namdon.

Eldor turned to his daughter. "I expected you to be agreeing with Sir Cuthlin and thinking we should all go back," he said.

"I... I've promised the dryads to try to do *something*, I'm still not really sure what," said Tara-lin. She glanced around. "You were riding horses up till now, right?"

"Yes," said Sir Eldor, "but they bolted during the storm."

"They're probably too far away to answer my call at this point," she said, slowly.

"I don't know how far your power extends," said Sir Eldor. "I can only imagine they tried to go home. Weren't you riding, though?"

"Yes, and I could find my horse, and one other, but that's not enough to get us to Icecrown before Prince Anakrim knows something's wrong when his messenger doesn't show," said Tara-lin.

"One other?" asked Sir Eldor.

"A story for another time," said Tara-lin.

"There seem to be a lot of those with you now," said Sir Eldor, "and I still don't want you in Icecrown. You forget, I've been there."

"I do *not* forget!" said Tara-lin, stomping her foot.

"An old friend of mine, Sir Se'lorn, was tortured to death in there. I and your mother saw what goes on in there. I don't want my wife *or* my daughter anywhere near that mess again."

"*We* don't want you there anymore!" said Tara-lin, stomping again. "Besides, I am probably the least vulnerable of all of us! And I've got one of the ancient elf-swords."

"You do?" asked Sir Eldor and Cuthlin at once. "How'd you get it?" asked her father.

"That's a story for another time, too," said Tara-lin, "but, yes." She threw her Elethrian cloak aside and drew the elf-sword out in a fluid motion. Ephemeral purple flames sang along the length of the sword.

"So the elf-swords *aren't* mere legend!" said Sir Cuthlin. "What will happen if I hold it?"

"Just what the stories say," said Tara-lin. "Nothing. Try it." She handed him the blade. The purple flames vanished.

"You're right," said Cuthlin, handing it back to her. "I guess I believe in singers and dryads now."

Tara-lin turned to her father again. "I'm going. I promised the dryads. I'm a singer. I have to go."

"I do not like it," said Sir Eldor, "but I guess you *are* right. I couldn't stop you." He looked around. "It would be nice if we all had Elethrian cloaks."

"I can't arrange for that," said Tara-lin. "Elethrian cloaks mask our presence in artificial man-made structures somewhat better than what the dryads can provide, but I can arrange for us all to be clad better than we are now."

"But that still doesn't solve the issue of getting into Icecrown before Prince Anakrim becomes alerted to the fact his spies were incapacitated," said Sir Namdon, stroking his chin again.

"I guess I might be able to get gryphons to help us," said Tara-lin. "I don't know if they'd be willing to fly us that far..."

All three men gasped again. "Gryphons? You have a working relationship with *gryphons?*"

"I can call them with my song. One helped me get out of a city once," said Tara-lin. "It's a long story. I'll tell you all after we get out of Icecrown alive."

"*That* is what makes me suspicious," said Sir Cuthlin. "All these long stories she won't tell us."

"You wouldn't even know about these long stories if she was a spy," said Sir Namdon. "Besides, I really think the last person who might be working for Prince Anakrim is the half-elf daughter of Sir Eldor. There just wouldn't be anything in it. She'd also have to have been employed only very recently and... I don't see that happening. It's implausible."

"It's implausible that the whole Valor Hall is compromised, too," retorted Sir Cuthlin.

"As I said before," said Namdon, "the *whole Valor Hall* doesn't have to be compromised for what we're seeing. People just have to be lazy and greedy."

"Same thing," said Sir Cuthlin. "We took *oath*. And I don't believe that Anakrim would have had all three, or even three out of six or nine, of his spies on this one mission. If that was all he had, he would have arranged for only one to be used to sabotage this mission."

"There you're wrong," said Sir Namdon. "If he got wind of Sir Eldor being on this mission, he might have reason to fear. He might have committed all his spies to stopping it in one way or another. Two decades ago, when it was his father, the wizard, instead of himself, Sir Eldor and his lady Lìrulin got through his defenses and succeeded, along with the lizard-keeper Se'lorn Eldor mentioned just earlier. If Sir Eldor is coming, why shouldn't he expect interference from his wife or daughter as well – which is just what we have happening here? It seems elves and elf-friends are very good at these things."

Tara-lin glanced at her father, and saw Sir Eldor standing with such a forlorn expression on his face. She wanted to comfort him. He muttered under his breath, "We're going to have some *big* trouble," but she heard him.

He looked up at her, and said, "*Please.* I have no guarantee you won't be captured – you know what that means – or killed. I don't want you to die before me. *Please.*"

"I promised," said Tara-lin. "And I don't want you to be captured or killed either! And you're going to have *another* child. I don't have children. And I made a promise. I didn't give an oath to the Valor Hall. I made a promise to some dryads who will die if someone doesn't find a way. And... I just know I have to."

Something almost made her want to say she would return to her mother, just to make him feel better. But she could not say that. For one thing, she was almost certain he would die unless she went with him. Unless she could convince the gryphons to help them, they would not even get there before yet more defenses and traps were in place. Without her, they would be less able to detect traps. For another, she had to. She knew it. She did not know if maybe her father might understand how she knew it, but she doubted these other men could, especially Sir Cuthlin. How would *he* react to the knowledge that she had spirited Alis away from the Valor Hall?

"Really, Dad. I will be fine. I know I will," she said, smiling. "It's not even the same as it was last time. Anakrim is not a wizard, *yet,* and I *am* a singer. If I am with you, we have a fair chance of getting in and out alive, much better than you and Mom had before I was born."

"Nothing is ever certain in life," he said, embracing her. "I can't help but be concerned for you, Tara-lin." He looked away, then back into his daughter's eyes. "If you get captured by Anakrim, I'm going back in. He can torture me too, if he's inclined to do so."

"He won't torture me," said Tara-lin. "He *won't* capture me. If you lose track of me, know I just had to find a different way out. I *know* I can. I'm a singer, and I have abilities you don't understand. Even I don't understand or even know them all yet. But go back to Mom. She'll need you, and she'll have a child who needs you. *And I will be fine. I will find my own way out.*"

Chapter Eighteen – The Deathsong

"By the way," said Tara-lin to her companions as she led them in search of a dryad who would be able to transform their garments, "I'm thinking I'm beginning to understand the idea behind the Elethrian cloaks, but I'm not sure I can do it myself yet. It would definitely take me a long time, and I don't know if the result would be in any way superior to the dryads' work. I'm sure I could get good at it, but I haven't even tried it yet."

"It's all right, Tara-lin," said Sir Cuthlin. "Unless it turns out to be some bright color, it won't be any worse than the gray we're currently wearing."

"It *won't* be any worse than the gray you're currently wearing," said Tara-lin. "I've no doubt it will be vastly superior in all ways. It's just that, at this point, I can directly manipulate my cloak to some degree, but I've no idea what the result would be if I tried to imbue a completely new piece of material with the ability."

Tara-lin asked those with her to stay behind for a moment – except for her father – and approached a tree. She greeted the dryad, who greeted her in return, and then asked, "Why are you coming to me, with so many humans for company?"

"That is exactly why I'm coming to you, Gyenyah," said Tara-lin. "They are Eldor – that's my father, here's – companions, and I would appreciate it if you would do to their garments what Aumoura did to Alis' garments, in order to facilitate our ability to get into and out of Nightshade unmolested."

"I don't like revealing our arts to so many humans," said Gyenyah.

"They have all been betrayed by the Valor Hall, and this is necessary. They are my companions in the quest I have received from you – to stop Anakrim from killing you to increase his own power. Please, do not waste my time, but help me."

"Very well," said Gyenyah. "Bring their cloaks here to me. I do not want to be seen by anyone besides you and your companion."

Funny, thought Tara-lin. *Alis is okay, though, for some reason. Why? Now is not the time to ask.*

"So," asked Namdon, when that was done, "did I hear that we're going to ride gryphons?" He fingered his transformed cloak, wondering at the forest shades that rippled across it.

"If I can convince them to carry us far enough, yes," said Tara-lin. "I might have some work to do to convince them that it is in their own interests to help us." She turned to her father. "I think the dryad was right. Why am I even taking you with me? I can hide myself better, I am younger, I can find my way with my songs. I can do many things better than you can. You think I'm a liability. But I'm far less vulnerable than you are, Dad."

"I can't let you go into danger alone, Tara-lin. I didn't mean for you to be here at all. I'm still unhappy about it. My oath to the Valor Hall might be meaningless at this stage, if the Valor Hall is in the hands of Prince Anakrim or some other nefarious entity, but I won't leave you and I won't leave my companions. And, remember, I alone of us have been into and out of Nightshade before. I may be able to help us get in, and I may be able to help us get *out.*"

"But you are willing to leave Mom and your unborn child?" asked Tara-lin. "I'm sure he or she will want to know his or her Dad. You're old enough as it is. You'll live what, maybe thirty more years, if you don't get killed? That's so short! Depending on your child, he or she may be little more than a toddler when you die, Dad! I've grown up almost as if I was human. The next may grow up almost like an elf."

"I'm here now," said Sir Eldor. "I'm going with you, Tara-lin. At least Lìrulin and our child are safe for the time being. That may not be so, if Anakrim becomes King of Elethri."

"We'll flee if that happens, and I am here, with the aid of the dryads, to try to stop Anakrim," said Tara-lin, "but very well. I'm glad you love me. I'm not sure I'd even want you to go. It would be no fun trying to get into Nightshade and figure out what in the world I'm supposed to do on my own." She took a deep breath and swallowed, forcing back tears. Then she turned her face towards the peaks and sang a low, whistling call.

A flock of gryphons soon appeared in the sky. They came closer and then circled over the half-elf singer. There were nine of them, most of them black or dark brown with golden manes. For over half an hour they circled, sometimes squacking or making loud calls, and Tara-lin alternately waited silently and whistled her song.

Finally, four of them landed, and the others flew back the way they had come. Tara-lin motioned to her father. "Sir Eldor, this magnificent beast consents to carry you as far as he can fly and still return at sundown to his eyre," she said, and quickly introduced them. When Eldor had mounted, the gryphon took off. She did the same for the rest of her companions, and then got herself astride the shoulders of the smallest of the four gryphons. *Alis would love this*, she thought, *if only we were going the other direction.*

The gryphons were able to fly them over the Northridge Plain and land them in the foothills of the Icecrown Mountains. Tara-lin had had to coax them to go a little farther than they wanted, convincing them that most of their clan was still left to guard their home, but there came a point when they were absolutely unwilling to go any farther. They did not want to have to rest before they reached their mountain crags. Tara-lin sighed as they departed, and then turned to her father. "Do you know the best way up into these mountains?" she asked him.

"When I and Lìrulin first climbed up here, many ages ago, we came from the east, from Orual, not from the south. Later, we came from the sea, from the northwest. No, I don't know the best way in." He turned to look at her in the evening light. "You are really tired, Tara-lin."

"You know... I am," she said, and sat down heavily.

"When did you last sleep?"

"A few hours last night. But I hadn't slept the day or night before that. I'd slept the *day* before *that*," she said.

"And you've been working magic I don't understand," said Eldor. "We should sleep here. Thanks to you, we're not betrayed, even though I wish you weren't here, and we're days ahead of schedule and of our betrayers, even if they wake now. It won't stay that way – things always go wrong on missions like this – but it's a good start. And you need to sleep, Tara-lin."

She nodded. "I think you're right."

"Before we go any higher into Icecrown. It gets more dangerous the farther in you go."

"I think I'm thirsty, though."

"Then, drink from one of our water-bags," said Namdon. "Then sleep."

Tara-lin nodded. Her mind felt fuzzy, already. Her father gave her one of the water-skins and watched her drink, then took it from her. She lay down, pulled her cloak around her, and was fast asleep in a few minutes.

Sometime in the night, she drifted into half-wakefulness, and overheard her father and Sir Namdon speaking.

"You're right, Eldor. When we were young, we thought people were basically honest, and I think you've seen the full extent of what's rotten in the Valor Hall more quickly than I could, having been away from it for two decades. It's still hard for me to believe, but I was finding very suspicious things. I noticed that some of the Knights had gone up towards Icecrown in secret, and several suspicious-looking liaisons between principalities that I never got the chance to investigate. No, Eldor, I think this is worse than we were suspecting. I think they sent us up here *in order* to kill us, to get us out of their hair. Sir Cuthlin is young, and cannot believe the evil we know, but he will fight against it with all his might and with all the desperation of one utterly betrayed when he realizes it."

There was a pause, and Tara-lin's father said, "No, Namdon, old friend. That does not completely make sense. Why call me out of Elethri in order to kill me? Why not just leave me in Elethri where I know nothing and am not causing any trouble for them? How would they even know I was likely to be trouble, to be suspicious, if I were not involved?"

"They might not have," answered Sir Namdon. "Someone called all the Knights who weren't currently on mission, and recalled some who were, to the Valor Hall for this. Once you were *at* the Valor Hall, you were becoming a problem so, naturally, you were selected for this mission. It would have been hard to explain not selecting you, since you've been in Nightshade before."

"I've been in Nightshade before, but I'm older now, as my daughter delights to point out. And I would think I would not be highly trusted after hiding in Elethri for two decades," replied Sir Eldor.

Namdon's voice was slow now. "At least, there was a very easy and natural excuse for sending you on this mission. But I don't think we're the first to be sent, not to succeed, but to be slaughtered. I've noticed some strange disappearances of Knights over the last couple years, and while some of them might have been spies moving around, I'm almost certain some of the disappearances have been the slaughter of more-or-less honest men. The situation is more complicated than I care to fathom, and after what you've talked through with me, I'm coming around to your understanding."

"More than coming around to my understanding," said Sir Eldor.

"You're the one who theorizes this was nothing more than an elaborate plot to kill the three of us."

"If I know you at all, you were thinking it. You just didn't say it," replied Namdon. There was silence for a few minutes, then Namdon's voice resumed. "No. What bothers me is that Anakrim must have multiple traps in place to kill us. I can't imagine he isn't actually concerned about you and your family's potential ability to thwart his plans, given the success you've had in the past. I'm sure those three spies were not the only trap laid for us."

Tara-lin wanted to rouse, to explain the band of orcs she and Alis had almost been caught by, but she couldn't seem to make herself speak. She only grunted and turned over.

Later, her dreams were filled with the songs of weakening and dying dryads – low, soft, inexpressible, reaching deep into the earth and far into the winds and the air, as if looking for something to hold on to or something into which to give its last remaining energy and life, to renew the world rather than be taken from it. Here and there threads of fear, dread, and desperation tinged the song, sometimes achieving dominance for a moment, but mostly the song was a reach, either for something to cling to or for some way to return into the earth as renewing life, to give birth to more dryads, instead of being drawn into the web of Anakrim's magic.

I'm coming, she thought, and recognized another piece of the song: clear, if weak, it rose above the rest. It was scarcely tinged with human defiance, though for a moment Tara-lin's sleeping mind took it for such. It scorned the evil net set for it, and reached for the skies above, rejoicing to transplant its life in a higher sphere. It knew it could not be corrupted by the fear and evil of the nightmare to which the elven Prince was himself enslaved. It knew that it would outlast that nightmare and finally triumph. It knew the nightmare was nothing. It knew no concern, no fear, and no worry. It knew only life, finally and ultimately, inherently, triumphant – life that triumphed without effort or strife, that simply endured by being life, out-living death. It was not fatalistic. If it could endure in this sphere, it would do so. If it could outlast the magic of Anakrim, it would do so. If it could not, it would find itself growing again in a wider world, and from that world life would spread to all worlds.

Light filtered through the trees. Tara-lin woke to the smell of something cooking. It was mid-morning. She jumped to her feet.

The three men stood around a small fire by which they were cooking a rabbit. Her father turned to her and smiled, "Hi, Tara-lin." There was sadness behind his smile.

"Why are you cooking?" she asked. "Won't it draw attention?"

"Hopefully not here. We're not really in Icecrown proper, yet. We'll all enjoy some good food, and we don't want to run out," answered Namdon.

"All right," said Tara-lin. "I hope you're done soon, so we can keep on going."

"Is something new wrong?" asked Sir Cuthlin.

"I hear the dryads' deathsong in my dreams. They are failing in this region. Every day we tarry, they have less strength with which to help us," said Tara-lin.

"Would there be any gryphons in the peaks above us who would be willing to help you? If what they don't like is being far from their homes, just a few hours flight farther in – closer to their nests, actually – would be nice," said Cuthlin.

"I didn't want to ask the gryphons for help once we got into Icecrown. I wouldn't want to expose them to the wrath of Anakrim, and I'm pretty sure he'll have them hunted and killed if he finds out they're helping us," said Tara-lin.

"It might *not* be easy for him to do so," said Sir Eldor. "He's not a true wizard. From what we know, he's trying to build power. He probably does not have that much. I don't think orc armies are terribly effective against gryphons. The other thing is, would he be looking for us to arrive on gryphons? How carefully is he watching this area of Icecrown? A few hours' flight would bring us much higher and save *us* a whole day, but would leave us still days away from Icecrown. We do potentially expose the gryphons to his wrath, but I think he will not find the resources to destroy the gryphons in a few days at the same time as trying to keep us out of nightshade. I would think it would be better to speed this process up yet more, to be in nightshade before he's looking for us in Icecrown."

"Very well," said Tara-lin. "Are you willing to trust yourself to a gryphon far away from me? I think it's better if we don't fly as a group. We're less likely to draw attention to ourselves – the gryphons are less likely to draw attention to themselves. I'll ask them to fly high and rather far apart, but to land us all close to each other."

"If you can, that's great," said Sir Namdon. "I don't exactly feel safe with a wild gryphon, but on missions like these there is no safety. I agree with your father. For now, speed is our stealth. But I find it odd working with an elf – or half-elf – singer. It's stranger than working with a wizard."

"I don't know," said Tara-lin. "I don't know anything about wizardry. Have you worked with wizards before? Anyway, let's eat."

"I've not worked with wizards a lot, but there are some wizards associated with the Valor Hall," said Namdon. "Singers are hardly even legend among humans. They're myths of the distant past. You might not be acquainted with wizardry. I don't know if elves are ever wizards, and you *are* a singer, so it's not strange that you would find wizardry stranger. Cuthlin, check if the rabbit is done yet."

"I think it is," said the youngest of the three Knights. "But, if Tara-lin is concerned about stealth, would it be better to ride the gryphons in at night? Would they be willing to fly us at night?"

"I've ridden a gryphon at night," said Tara-lin. "I think they might. I don't know how it would affect how long or far they'd be willing to carry us. They might not want to go far from their territory at night."

"Would it be helpful, though?" asked Eldor. "The nightshade creatures tend to be more active at night – to them, night is as day is to us, and day to them is more like night to us. He does have human minions or allies or whatever, but I think day might be best."

When they were done eating, Tara-lin said, "I really don't want to call the gryphons this soon again. I just don't want to."

"It's your choice to make," said Sir Eldor. "I don't know what you know or don't know, but only you *can* call them, so you get to choose."

"I won't. Not just yet," said Tara-lin. "Let's go."

She picked up her bag, pulled her cloak over her head and about her shoulders, and took a step forward. Behind her, Sir Namdon fell into step beside Sir Eldor. They let themselves fall behind the singer, and spoke quietly.

"Is she concerned about the gryphons, or is it something else?" asked Namdon.

Her father shrugged. "She is tender-hearted. I'm sure she is concerned about the gryphons, but I don't know what skills she might have developed or what she knows. I wish she weren't here, but it's no good trying to stop her. She'd follow us anyways."

"I can see that," said Sir Namdon. "She certainly is determined. But is her determination, her apparent fearlessness and confidence the result of complete ignorance and childish naivety or is it true confidence? I wouldn't want her to turn into a bundle of nerves at the first real peril."

"I don't think she will turn into a bundle of nerves at the first peril," said Eldor, "but I don't know how accurate her comprehension is. Several months ago, when we were riding to Frèlin together, she talked on and on to me about how she was going to have to go on a mission sometime because she was a singer, and these things always happened to people with extraordinary talents, and her feelings about pain. I've no idea what the journey from the Valor Hall to this point may have been for her. I'm certain some interesting things happened that I don't know about yet."

"Whatever she might have encountered on her journey, it can hardly compare to what's inside nightshade," said Namdon. "Valiant Knights are sometimes turned into useless cowards and madmen there."

"In that sense," said Eldor, "there's no guarantee. I, myself, am not happy about going into nightshade again. Given that the Valor Hall is trying to kill us, I probably wouldn't, except that she is going. I wouldn't even believe what I'd heard about Anakrim and how evil he is, unless she had her sources from the dryads. I and my wife have always found dryads to be reliable, and I don't think they *can* be compromised the way human organizations can be. I suppose I could be wrong. After all, I didn't think the Valor Hall could be substantively compromised when I was Cuthlin's age, but... whatever might go wrong with dryads, I don't think *that* can go wrong with them. They have no society to speak of in any usual meaning of the word."

"I get you," said Namdon. "I've never been to Nightshade before and, given what I've heard, I suspect my trepidation is nothing to yours. I wouldn't go, either, given what we know after putting both our heads together, except that I won't abandon you. I consider my oath to the Valor Hall useless, but I'd be forsworn if I abandoned a friend and brother. But she's heard your and Lìrulin's story a dozen times before. Why does she display no fear? We, Valor Knights, have been trained not to show it, yet here we are talking about it. She seems... singularly unaffected, except for one comment to you about it being no fun to sneak into Nightshade by herself."

"She's changed a lot since I last saw her," said Eldor. "She's definitely growing. I told you, she was deathly afraid of Nightshade, or at least imagined herself deathly afraid, a few months ago."

"She looks lonely to me," said Namdon.

"I think she is," said Eldor. "She's very alone in this world, and I don't know what she's done in the last few months. I think she'll tell me a lot of it when we have some privacy."

They were climbing up a rather steep ridge at this point, and Tara-lin, who was several paces ahead of Cuthlin, who was somewhat ahead of them, turned and look straight at both men in turn, then turned and continued leading them up the incline.

After she turned, the old friends glanced at each other, then followed. A few minutes later, Cuthlin called back to Namdon. "Her woodcraft is good."

"It really is quite impressive, isn't it?" responded Eldor. "I guess I don't notice it as much, since it's no better than my wife's, and I've been living in Elethri for a while. I couldn't match her woodcraft, but I've picked up a lot of the art myself."

"That's gotta have been fun," said Namdon, with a sigh.

Ahead of them, Tara-lin's tinkling laugh could be heard.

She was glad that they were well aware that she did have *some* abilities. She was displeased with the situation regarding her father. She had first set out to find him, to go with him, but she was concerned for him. She wanted to live a long life with him. She did not want him to be worn out and die sooner than necessary. In other regards, her state of mind was hard for even her to analyze. Her communication with the dryads had rubbed off on her. Dread of the certain but unknown horror she would find deep within Icecrown was offset by something else for which she had no word, but which she thought was very like indeed the typical dryad attitude towards death and pain – not that dryads really experienced death and pain as many men seemed to do. She could not put a word to this attitude. It had something to do with Alai-ie-a's song. It had something to do with what Elkanakur had shown her. It had something to do with Shallim-Araldor. It had something to do with what Beriririkirkirkitira had told her. It had something to do with the deathsong she could still feel in the air around her, floating down from higher up and deeper within Icecrown, but touching even the woods around her with its indefinable touch. Elkanakur was right. Death? No, that was the wrong idea. Perhaps, Elkanakur *was* right, and it was fear that made death. Passage from this world to another there would always be, perhaps, and it might be attended with more or less pain, but perhaps fear created its own horror.

Thus, Tara-lin's state of mind was somewhere between horror and dread and something else to which horror, fear, and dread were completely alien. She wondered if this was related to what Eldor had told her about not fearing and fighting against pain. Sometime, she *would* have to ask him if and what he knew about Shallim-Araldor. But maybe he knew nothing about Shallim-Araldor, or at least not directly and not by that name. For who, even among dryads, had ever been farther from fear or hate or death than Alai-ie-a?

Tara-lin stopped, and when they had caught up with her, she grabbed Sir Eldor's hand. "Come with me, Dad," she said and, after leaning against him for a moment, again led the way. He followed close behind her, while Namdon and Cuthlin trailed a short ways behind them.

After several minutes, panting slightly from the climb, Eldor said, "You heard what we were talking about back there."

"Some of it," said Tara-lin. "Not all of it. I was too busy trying to forecast the best way forward to be paying attention to what you were saying for the most part."

"But you did hear," said Eldor.

"As I said, only some of it. My senses are more elven than human. You know that. If you really wanted me not to hear, you know you have to do better than that. Sometimes, I really can't help hearing. I *do* have to pay attention."

"I'm not mad at you, Tara-lin. I'm not even upset if you overheard. You know I'm upset you're here at all."

"You *ought* to be upset *any* of us are here at all," said Tara-lin.

"That's true enough," said Eldor, his speech broken by his breathing. "But after you caught up with us, and I and Namdon had a good long chat together last night, I'm done with the Valor Hall, and I'd be done with this mission altogether, if you weren't determined to go because of the dryads."

"Speaking of that talk you had last night – I hope you aren't upset I overheard you in my sleep – there already have been multiple traps set for you. Shortly before I found you, I ran into a company of orcs. They chased me, and that's how the storm happened. I sang it into being – of course, the dryads helped me with it. I can only guess they were supposed to take you out after the traitors left you, probably just that morning, about the time I met them."

"That's... interesting. I guess you've saved our lives at least twice now. Look, Tara-lin, I acknowledge that it's been very helpful that you followed me against my own wishes... but it wouldn't have been so helpful, I think, if you had somehow been allowed to come *with* me. Nonetheless, I'm not happy about the situation. I'm not happy you're here. I'm not happy any of us are going into Icecrown. I never was happy about that, but I really didn't want you coming. I'm not happy about the treason in the Valor Hall. I just hope your mom is safe."

"She probably is," said Tara-lin. "She probably returned to Elethri. I doubt anyone in Elethri is much interested in her."

"It depends on how deeply Anakrim has infiltrated Elethri, and I can easily believe that he has his spies placed very highly and broadly throughout Elethri," said Eldor.

"Not likely. The elves might be lazy and complacent, but they are elves. You can infiltrate the Valor Hall with any human. You have to turn elves before you can infiltrate Elethri, and as complacent as the elves might be, I don't think very many of them would do that," said Tara-lin.

For a few minutes, her father concentrated on catching his breath while he climbed. Then he said, "It's pretty amazing if you sang up that storm. You must have really developed your song."

"I have," said Tara-lin proudly. "Dryads taught me. But, as I said, the dryads *did* help me with that. And you knew already I'd developed a lot. How else could I have sung the enchantment on those spies?"

"I guess I really don't know," said Eldor. "I don't understand your talent. I couldn't inference that the sleep enchantment you sung on the spies was so much more difficult than the storm."

Tara-lin laughed lightly. "Oh, I sung the enchantment on the spies for, what, eight hours straight? I don't know. At least that long."

"No wonder you were exhausted."

"I still am, and I am getting cold," replied Tara-lin.

They scrambled up a particularly steep patch of the incline, and stood to watch the other members of their party follow. "It is colder up here," said Eldor.

"It's a good thing it's not any later in the year," said Tara-lin.

"Yes," her father responded. "The snow levels are probably the lowest they're going to get. Another couple weeks, and it will start snowing."

Tara-lin lead them for several more hours. Even when darkness fell, she led them for another hour. Behind her, she occasionally heard Namdon and Cuthlin discussing the oddity of being led by an elf through wood and mountain. "We're traveling reasonably quickly," said Cuthlin to Namdon. "She's doing a good job of navigating in the dark."

"From what I've heard, elves have much better night-vision that humans do," returned Namdon. "Creatures who have vastly better abilities tend to do poorly at accommodating those with lesser abilities, though, so I'm surprised that she's leading us a way which is not too difficult for us."

"She's half-elf, and Eldor is her father. She might be used to our needs," said Cuthlin. "But I'm uncomfortable traveling in the dark."

Tara-lin lead them for another ten minutes, then stood. "I think this is a good place," she said. "There's a rock which has been facing the sun all afternoon over there, against which we can find shelter. We'll be as warm as can be expected at this altitude and at this time of year."

"Did you know this was here?" asked her father, surveying the place she had chosen by the faint light. "How?"

"I don't know. I listen to the dryads, and I've already developed a feel for the general patterns in these mountains," she said. "But you're right. I am tired." Sitting down next to the rock, she said, "That's part of why I'm in such a hurry. Much of what I know – much of what you would see as 'my power' – is tied to the dryads. When their life fails, when their energy fails, they can't help me, and I can't follow their lead – their song, their knowledge. Anyway, I'm hungry as well as tired."

"And you are definitely *not* a Valor Knight," said Sir Namdon.

Tara-lin glanced at his face. "Is that supposed to be a joke?"

The Knight shrugged. "I guess. Everything about the way you talk and move shouts that you're not from the Valor Hall. But then, no woman ever has been a Valor Knight, though I think there have been a few elven knights throughout the years."

"There have," said Sir Eldor. "I wonder why none of *them* were chosen for the mission we have recently aborted."

"Aborted?" asked Cuthlin.

"We're not going to report back to the Valor Hall," said Namdon.

"Oh, that," said Cuthlin. "Give me some time to digest what you've shared with me, Namdon."

Tara-lin wanted to ask her father when they could have some privacy to talk, but she did not know if it would be safe to move far enough away from their companions this far into Icecrown. However, by the time she was done eating and drinking she was almost asleep.

Tara-lin woke early in the morning and found Sir Cuthlin standing watch. She sat up. He glanced behind him for a moment, then turned his gaze outward again. "You're already awake, Tara-lin?" he asked.

"Yes. Why wasn't I given a watch?"

"We discussed this last night after you had fallen asleep. We have been trained to stand watch; you have not. We don't know how disrupting your sleep or depriving you of sleep will affect your talents, either. What we can do is watch. What you can do is lead us down the best trails. The time and energy you save with your woodcraft makes up for not standing watch."

"Oh," said Tara-lin. "I want to get moving as quickly as possible."

"I was just going to wake everyone up."

Tara-lin stood. "And I think I could stand watch as well as you, too. Or close enough. Everyone would be sharper if we split it up more, wouldn't they? Even if I haven't the discipline, my eyesight and hearing are very good."

"No doubt," said Sir Cuthlin. "Maybe you can watch tomorrow night. But I don't know how little sleep you've been getting catching up with us. You'd hardly slept for days before finding us, if I recall what was said correctly. Anyway, let's wake up the others."

When everyone was awake, they took out some food and water, and decided to eat while walking. Once again, Tara-lin walked with Eldor. "Did you tell them they could watch better than I could?" she asked.

"Tara-lin, you're not supposed to be here at all! I want you to sleep, girl. You're driving yourself silly with your need to help the dryads. You're my daughter, silly-heart. And your idiocy might think your elven senses make you a definitely superior watcher, but a lot of discipline is necessary, and you might excel in that in some areas, but you've never practiced."

"It's not just my senses!" said Tara-lin. "The dryads would know, and the dryads can tell me. They might not be able to tell the others."

"Well, hopefully the dryads can tell you in your sleep, then," said her father.

"You don't understand!" said Tara-lin. She stomped, then continued. "When I was flying up here, I stayed with dryads every night. They... protected me, covered my traces. These dryads are weaker, and there are more of us. They might be able to shield us a little, but not as much. And I don't know if I could hear that sort of thing from them in my dreams. It's hard for most of them to think, to communicate, that sort of thing anyway."

Eldor was quiet for a moment, and Tara-lin wondered if she had offended him. The going was pretty level at the moment. "You... needed... protection?" he asked.

Tara-lin still didn't know how Sir Cuthlin would respond to the news that she had helped a Valor Knight's daughter run away. Speaking of that, she wondered how Alis Luela was doing with just dryads and two horses for company. "I was pursued. In the last city I visited, someone was waiting for me, who seemed to know about me, and wanted to capture me. I think it might have something to do with the Valor Hall being compromised, though how they would know I'd gone after you I don't know. I managed to lose him."

"You were pretty vocal about wanting to come with me, at first," said Eldor. "When you disappeared, they might have guessed where you'd gone."

Tara-lin shrugged, then said, "It seems I am very good at messing things up horribly. It could be a big problem if Prince Anakrim knows I'm coming."

"I agree that it's very unfortunate," said Eldor, "but there's a high probability he does not guess that you are a singer, or what power your talent can be. That stunt in King Orenduil's court was not very impressive, when it comes to magic."

There was silence between them for about half an hour, and Namdon and Cuthlin were not talking. They did not talk most of the time. Threading her way up a ridge, Tara-lin said to Eldor, "Can you wake me up tonight? At the end of your watch, perhaps?"

"You want to watch? Still?" asked Eldor.

"I think I am recovering from singing and not sleeping for a couple of days," said Tara-lin, "but it's more than that. I want to ask you a few questions."

She waited while he came up to where she stood. "Sure," he said. "I can do that."

She smiled and grabbed his arm for a moment, before continuing.

Namdon said, "Is there an easier way? This is pretty rough."

"I agree," said Tara-lin, hardly looking back. "I'm pretty sure we could go a long looping way around, and still have to climb pretty steeply at one point, or we can cut up this way, and be up there" – she pointed through the trees to a gap between two mountains – "in a few hours of very steep going. We should get to the top by evening, as long as we don't run into something nasty first."

"Do you expect something nasty?" asked her father.

"I don't know," said Tara-lin. "I can feel that something is not right, and it's definitely not the deathsong of the dryads, which I find at once deeply disconcerting and strangely comforting. Some of the dryads are evil, though. I'm trying to avoid those – to stay away from them."

The air grew colder as they climbed. A chill wind blew in their faces. Even Tara-lin's legs grew sore and heavy with the exertion of climbing the mountain in higher airs. Her lungs burned. No one was talking anymore. She stopped often and waited for the humans to catch up. Watching her father struggle, a lump formed in Tara-lin's throat, even though Sir Namdon had just as hard a time. She wondered how hard it must be for them, for her lungs felt the rarer air and her legs were shaky, and she got to stop for a few moments while they caught up. Maybe she should have taken them the easier way around, even though it would add an extra day... How could she have forgotten the age and limitations of her human father?

Tara-lin could not stop thinking about the question she wanted to ask him. How had he resisted the nightmare madness? She wanted to know. Did it have something to do with Shallim-Araldor? He had never really explained how he had endured Nightshade any of the times he and her mother told the story. Lìrulin had never shared it either. Had they thought her too young for it? At any rate, she needed to know now. She figured what he had said about accepting pain was part of it, but she knew it was not all of it. She felt a strange urgency, and also a terror that disaster would come upon them because she had voiced her desire to come with her father on this mission. *I am so useless and horrible,* she thought to herself. *I make the stupidest mistakes.* And she really *ought* to have known better. Her father had explained to her after Fizzer had told the court that she was a singer that it was really better not to give things away. Unless... unless she was wrong about elves being hard to turn, and Fizzer was a spy, an agent of this Anakrim... Even so, she should have known better than to talk about her desire to follow her father in places or times where she might be overheard, even at the Valor Hall. After all, Eldor had even confided to her his concern that the Valor Hall might be somewhat compromised.

Tara-lin shook her head. She could not get out of it the idea that Fizzer was some sort agent for Prince Anakrim. But, how? It seemed to fit in, somehow, but she was not quite sure how it fit in. Neither did she understand why an elf might be working for Anakrim. But, then again, how did Valor Knights turn out to be traitors?

What a fool I am, she thought. *Maybe Lìrulin is in danger. Oh well. There's nothing I can do about it now. And I'm pretty sure the dryads will help her, too, so the danger shouldn't be too great.*

Soon, they were trudging through snow. That made the going yet more difficult. Tara-lin tried to use her feet to clear the snow for those coming after her, even though it made her feet cruelly cold. She was pretty sure she could use her song to do something, but she had two reasons for not wanting to do this. One was that she did not know what the ramifications of such magic would be. The other was that she was now very near indeed to Nightshade and did not want to reveal her power before it was necessary.

I am a fool, she thought. *I should have taken their advice and asked the gryphons. As Dad pointed out, it would have gotten us here faster, and it wouldn't be wearing him and the other two out, like this is doing.* She fought back an impulse to cry.

After trying to compose herself, so her voice would not give her emotions away, Tara-lin asked, "Should we stop as soon as there is an appropriate place?" She feared her voice had given her away.

"If the next appropriate place is too far away to reach by nightfall, I would say yes," said Eldor. "Typically, I would say traveling at night in these mountains is not a good idea, even if you are what you are."

"And none of you are," said Tara-lin. She paused for a moment, trying to collect herself again. She was on the verge of tears.

"Is something wrong?" asked Eldor.

"I don't know, yes," said Tara-lin. "I was really asking, Do you need to stop as soon as possible?"

"No," said Eldor. "I can easily manage another two hours."

Easily. Yeah right! thought Tara-lin. The other two expressed their ability to continue.

"Seriously," said her father. "Is something wrong? Do you sense something I don't?"

"I'm just afraid," said Tara-lin. "I feel horrible. I am so stupid. I shouldn't have let anyone at the Valor Hall hear I wanted to come, or guess it. I should have acted all... I don't know. And I should have just called the gryphons like you all were suggesting." She decided to keep her fear about Fizzer to herself. How would it help them do anything they were trying to do? If they got out of Nightshade alive, she would tell, but for now, she did not think it was pertinent knowledge, but only a distracting problem – one more thing to worry about but about which they could not do anything.

"I don't know if you should have called the gryphons," said

Eldor. "And you're not stupid. You can do some things, and you don't know about others, and you are *very* young. You might not mature in a consistent way either, being half-elven. You've done great, Tara-lin, and you have your own unique strengths and weaknesses, strengths we wouldn't be alive without, and we don't even know if calling the gryphons wouldn't have precipitated its own disaster. But let's keep going."

Tara-lin nodded. "Thanks," she said. She held out her arms, and Eldor hugged her. When they stepped apart, she was struggling to keep from sobbing. *Do not die, do not die, do not die!* she begged in her mind. *Please, don't die because I messed something up!*

Tara-lin hoped that the shaking of her shoulders was not great enough to betray her sobbing, as she continued to lead them.

"Tara-lin," said Eldor, directly behind her, "we're getting closer to Nightshade. You've never been here before and don't know what to expect. Some of the things you are feeling might have something to do with the proximity of Nightshade."

Somehow, that did not comfort her at all. It *did* convince her that she needed to ask him her questions. As soon as possible. But she did not know if he would be comfortable being asked in front of Namdon and Cuthlin. She kept remembering the dryads' reluctance to talk about Shallim-Araldor.

The snow grew deeper, and it was no longer feasible for Tara-lin to try to push patches of it out of the way. She looked around her, constantly trying to plot the easiest course to the top for her human companions. She shivered a little under her cloak, and hoped she would be able to find a good place for them to stay – hopefully, one sheltered enough for them to build a small fire, but she did not know if that was a good idea inside Icecrown. It would be nice if she could find a cave...

She was almost surprised when she found herself at the top of the ridge. Looking around her, Tara-lin saw the snow reflecting the light of the sun, which was kissing the western peaks, purple and red and blue. The colors shimmered on the white icicles. It was enchantingly beautiful! In a flash, Tara-lin knew that these Icecrown Mountains ought to be a place of loveliness and beauty, of goodness, not a haunt of evil – that somewhere within them ought to rise a white castle of icy and snow-flecked loveliness to reflect the sun and the stars, not the horrible Nightshade, which even now her eyes descried, rising black and ugly out of the sides of one of the opposing mountains, across a wide vale.

Chapter Twenty – Shade of Night

Tara-lin stood, observing the ice-crowned mountains, the vale, with its wood and meadows and ridges and streams and lakes, below them, and across from them the horrid black Nightshade Castle. It rose against the mountain, sprawling formations of black rock at its foot, out of which it rose in a labyrinthine nightmarish shape, bulbous and strange and horrible. The very sight of it struck fear into Tara-lin's heart and, after a moment, she remembered her pity for Prince Anakrim. What kind of dwelling for a man or an elf was *that?* It looked like a haunt of evil spirits, a place for horrible, misshapen monstrosities, not a place any man would choose for his dwelling or build to be his castle – no matter how much his natural affections for friends and family and other creatures had been marred into lust after power and dominion. She remembered that the elven history told that Nightshade had existed long before Wizard Falkur was ever born, let alone found it. She knew it had been built by no man or elf, but by the Lord of the Nightmare in order to capture and enslave men and elves.

She desperately hoped she would not fall under its spell.

While Tara-lin thought these things, the others walked up and stood beside her. She almost felt her father's trepidation as he stood next to her and took in a deep breath. "Nightshade," he said, softly, almost under his breath, with horror in his voice.

"Yes, Nightshade," said Tara-lin. "How will we resist its influence?"

He turned to her with terrible concern written on his face. "You feel its influence?"

"I am horrified by it. It is the work of no man or elf; it is horrible and ugly. It repulses me. But how did it ever attract any man or elf? It is not the kind of thing anyone would choose for his dwelling!"

"Good," he said. "I am glad you see that. I had not thought it quite so clearly myself, but it is repulsive. I, myself, have never been attracted to it, though I have felt strange things. When I thought I was lost, I found something to which I could hold and, more, which held onto me. I cannot describe it, but it is the one thing in which I believe. I do not know how to, or even if I can, lead anyone else to that thing. I can only hope that you all find it. I would never suggest coming to Nightshade in order to find it, but I don't know how else I would have encountered it, and it has changed me and my life though I cannot name or describe it."

Tara-lin nodded. "I wonder if it is the song of Alai-ie-a," she said.

"Perhaps. I have never heard the song of Alai-ie-a. Let us find a place to spend the night, sooner rather than later. I do not like this view," said Eldor.

"It ought to be beautiful," said Tara-lin, stepping down, but towards one of the mountain walls. She glanced around her again, moving her eyes quickly over the horrible bulbous castle. "I think it once was beautiful. I hope it will be beautiful again."

"Yes," said her father. "I had that thought once before, when I was in Icecrown before you were born. It ought to be a place of wonder and awe. It's a strange feeling – to see something of such indescribable beauty and such haunting goodness which ought to be in a place dominated by such evil."

As the sun went down behind the mountains and the cold began to rapidly increase, Tara-lin thought it would be so cold they would not be able to sleep. She looked constantly over her shoulder, and the Valor Knights noticed. "Do you sense something?" asked Sir Eldor. "This is a horrible place," said Sir Cuthlin.

"I don't know," said Tara-lin. "I think we might be sensed... followed, but not too closely. The dryads here are sickly. I can still hear their deathsong, but it is faint. The impressions I get from them are vague. Look around – do you see? Even the few trees here are not happy."

"No, they are not," said Cuthlin. "Will they die when the dryads do?"

"Some of them will," said Tara-lin, "but not all trees have dryads. I do not know if dryadless trees need the dryads of those around them, or if some trees which have once had dryads can live without them."

"I agree with Tara-lin. Something is wrong. When I and Lìrulin sneaked into Nightshade with Se'lorn and Tarunth, we encountered resistance and foul creatures every step of the way. So far, we have not met anything. I cannot attribute it to us having been betrayed by the Valor Hall also, last time, and Tara-lin is no better a woods-woman than my wife. We should have encountered something by now. There is a reason..."

His voice trailed away into silence. Tara-lin continued to lead them onward, glancing around constantly. Several ideas came to her mind, but she still did not want to use her song yet. She did not know if the ideas would work.

Soon, they were walking along the side of a mountain, with a few trees next to them. The rock was warm to the touch, the light of the setting sun having only just left it. Nonetheless, a cold, chilling wind blew past them. Tara-lin was looking for something cave-like, or even some protrusion that would offer some more shelter and lasting warmth.

A tree, narrow and straight, growing out of the side of the cliff captured her attention. Tara-lin stopped for a moment, bending her head back to look at it. It had obviously suffered, but was in better condition than most of the trees. She felt as if it called to her urgently.

Silently, she beckoned her companions to follow her, and briskly moved towards the tree. A movement in the mountains above and an answering movement in the brush and rocks below caught her attention. She broke into a run, and slammed hard against the tree. She tried to turn, but could not move...

Desperation came over her, and then she heard the voice of the dryad, very quietly. "I am not strong enough. Stay here with me, Tara-lin. I am not strong enough to shield or protect them, and without our strength even your song will avail little in this circumstance. Wait. I will shield you from the nightmare, and then you must go after them."

But my father will die! she thought. She could not speak. Held in the dryad's magic, her heart hardly beat, she hardly breathed. She knew her consciousness and life had been temporarily adjusted and moved more slowly, as dryads were wont to be. She understood now, fully understood, their sleepiness, their lack of accustomization to the ways of human society, their different mode of perception, their difficulty with swift and isolated events. She did not even know how much time passed while she thought this.

"Even if the others had reached me, I do not even know if I could have shielded anyone but you," the dryad continued. "They are too unlike me, there is too little, if any, dryad blood in their veins. But do not fear. I understand not the fear of men. Worlds within worlds lie before us. If you could only see it, this Icecrown Vale is a place of such wonder and awe, such beauty. But you will go after them, and you will rescue them, and you will help this world be what it should be, you will help us dryads remain, you will help Icecrown be Icecrown."

Tara-lin wondered if the dryad was aware of her acknowledgement.

Suddenly, Tara-lin sensed that the magic had released her. She looked around. It was dark now, but her eyes quickly adjusted, and it was not hard for her to find the way which their captors had carried off her father and his friends.

Something within her made her want to run after them and attack the company of orcs as quickly as she could, but she knew she could never fight such a large company. She also knew she would need to eat and drink sometime. She undid the pack she carried and found both water and food in it. She drank and tried to eat, but discovered that she could not stomach more than a few bites. Putting the bag over her shoulder and under her Elethrian cloak again, she set off down the trail.

How will I avoid being ambushed myself, this time? she wondered.

Tara-lin wondered if, with all the things she knew now, if an orc company came upon her, she couldn't simply drop down, or against a tree, and *will* her Elethrian cloak to completely camouflage her presence. She might even be able to partially shift herself into that more dryadic way of living...

Even in the night, the tracks of the orcs were easy to follow. Tara-lin wondered how she could catch up and rescue them. Even if she could catch up, how could she take on such a large band of orcs? She was not even an archer like her mother. She was almost certain that, after the trouble her parents had caused his father, Prince Anakrim would order them killed right away. She wondered why he had ordered them captured instead of killed in the first place. What could he possibly want with them?

Several times, Tara-lin pressed herself against a tree and waited, hardly breathing, while creatures passed her. She took refuge in the song of the dying dryads from the cruel touch of fear and hate that crept into her bones as the nightmare creatures passed her. She wondered how she would survive it in Nightshade at all. Hopefully, she would find that thing of which Eldor had spoken. Was it the same as Shallim-Araldor?

When they passed, she continued following the tracks of her comrades' captors. She had almost no hope. She wondered how she had thought it was even remotely possible that she might be able to stop Anakrim from whatever it was he was doing. She realized she never had thought it was possible. The dryads had simply asked her to do so and told her that, when the time came, she would know what to do. Well, a time had now come, when *something* was necessary, and she did not know what to do. She supposed it was not *that* time, but still, she did not know what to do.

Sometime towards the morning, exhaustion overcame Tara-lin. She pressed herself against the ground and waited for some dark, terrifying creatures which struck horror and despair and self-hatred into her heart even though she did not see them, to pass. Many of the trees around her were definitely dying, and the deathsong of the dryads was weak indeed. The despair passed, as the dark creatures moved past her – their stomping feet passed within inches of her fingers – and she passed from it into a sleep. The slower form of consciousness into which she delved to further conceal herself passed readily into sleep, at least for one with as much human blood in her as Tara-lin had.

It was, however, a light sleep, and Tara-lin woke as soon as the beams of the sun filtered through the wood in which she lay. She heard the sound of a stream nearby and wondered if its water was suitable for re-filling her skin. She went down to the stream, and decided to try. She had not heard anything from her parents about avoiding the streams in Icecrown Vale. She drank and ate a very small amount, then found the trail of the orc company and continued to follow it.

The sun was well into the sky when Tara-lin realized how close she was to Nightshade. There was an imperceptible darkness about the air and when she looked up she could see the horrible bulbous labyrinthine towers above the tree-tops. It looked like some horrible monstrosity, something part spider and part snake, and perhaps part some obscure insect or octopus too. *How can anything live in there?* she thought.

Tara-lin forced down the fear and desperation she felt, and tried to absorb into her heart the final hope in the deathsong of the dryads. Hearing their song, she knew that even if they misunderstood her, if they told her falsely that she would know what to do when the time to do it came, yet they meant her and all things no harm but infinite good.

It was a little past noon when Tara-lin stood at the edge of the wood. A large treeless plain stretched out before her. Leaning against the mountain, was the bulbous horrible castle. It sprawled along the ground in a twisted mounded shape and even when the main body of the castle disappeared under the earth, she could see small little bulbous towers and twisted mounds rising out of the ground and disappearing again, some of them larger than others, some of them connected to each other by odd passage-ways, some of these passages towering above Tara-lin, some of them so small she would have to stoop, or even crawl, to get through them – if she could get through them at all.

Despair washed over Tara-lin afresh. She saw no entrance but, even if she had seen an entrance, she would have felt this wash of despair that threatened to submerge her. It was almost as if the Nightshade Castle were a horrible thing, alive except that it was too horrible to be alive, and that it was aware of her and watched her. She could not fight it! Would it not claim her soul, too? But, no! It had not claimed the soul of the Princess, Ithrìl, even though she had been imprisoned here for centuries. It need not claim her own soul, Tara-lin thought, trying to believe it, trying to gain confidence. Even when she listened for it, she could barely hear the dryads' deathsong.

No, she said to herself again, trying to believe. That *thing* was not all there was. It was not the ultimate power. Greater than it, and more real, was that of which Alai-ie-a sang.

Tara-lin could not drive out the cold emptiness from her heart. She could not tell herself why, but the Nightshade Castle struck utter despair into her soul. *Shallim-Araldor,* she thought, hoping she would be heard. Should she turn back and abandon the world to whatever evil was being brewed deep within that thing's utterly corrupted and corrupting heart?

No! She could not abandon her father. At the last, he had come to this for love of her, not because he abandoned her. And even when he had left her and her mother, it had not been to abandon them, but because he was trying to be honest and true. Again, at the last, he had come to this place of torment which he feared for love of her. She could not abandon the dryads, either. She had promised them. And she did not yet know that their word would prove false. She did not yet *know* that she would not know and be capable of the thing necessary when it came time, even if she could not believe or see how she could know and be able.

There was nothing for it, except to go forward, no matter what fear or despair chilled her heart and tormented her mind.

Feeling as if at least one eye of some horrible and thousand-eyed monster watched her, Tara-lin stepped out from the scant trees, moving slowly, willing her Elethrian cloak to camouflage her at every step she took. It took her hours to cover the distance between the woods and the massive bulk of Nightshade Castle. When she did so, she barely perceived the lines that marked the massive doors of the castle, doors through which doubtless her father and his friends had been taken, doors which she could not open. She doubted the gates of such evil would open to her song.

Tara-lin stood there and stretched out her hand, her finger-tips inches away from the doors. Even so, she would not want to yet reveal herself and her song. If she could find no other way in, then she would try to sing to these doors and command them to open, but only as a last resort.

She turned away to look for any entrance, anywhere. She spent hours slowly searching, but finding no doors on any of the odd protrusions. The more she snooped around, the more it seemed to Tara-lin that the Nightshade Castle was not an inert chunk of stone but some corrupted and monstrous thing – maybe the heart of the Corruption itself. At last, she decided to sing something that she hoped might help her find a way but which she also hoped would not reveal herself, not being a direct action upon the Castle. Just as she resolved to sing this, her eyes glanced upon the rock of the mountain itself. Perhaps there was a hidden entrance there. It was not likely. Probably every entrance was sealed and shut, but perhaps...

She did, indeed, find a hole in the rock which went in. Tara-lin was not hopeful that it connected to Nightshade Castle, but she thought she would give it a try. Terror raced through her mind, as she considered all the time she had lost, first a few hours sleeping, now hours searching for a way in. She absolutely dreaded the thought of finding her father dead or tortured by Anakrim... and why would the Prince want him alive anyway?

Sometimes Tara-lin had to crawl, but other times she could walk upright. It was altogether unpleasant, for she had no light, but since she did not encounter any junctions, she was not concerned. She could always turn around, and there was no place for her to go wrong.

Suddenly, a mighty chill swept over her. She recognized the presence of some creature of the Nightmare. Where could she hide? Where could she go? Nowhere. The passage was not wide enough for her to get out of the way. She drew forth the elf-sword, and its ephemeral purple flames lighted the dark passage. For a moment she felt comforted, then she sensed a deeper shade coming down the passage.

The chill deepened. Cold raced up her arms and legs. Her blood seemed turned to ice. Her mind was altered, too. For a moment, she was naturally afraid. Never before had the proximity of these evil creatures affected her so strongly. She had been, many times, within feet, even inches, of orcs, and it had not been like this. But this... this was still yards away.

Maybe it was because she was now *inside* Nightshade Castle... no, she was not inside Nightshade Castle. The rock was still the rock of the Icecrown Mountains, not the rock of that horrid monstrosity of corruption.

Tara-lin opened her mouth and sang, desperately fighting for her sanity, for her life, for her very soul. She sang of life, of love, of light, of heat. She sang of her memory of hearing Alai-ie-a sing. She sang of Elkanakur and what Elkanakur had told her. She tried to pour her whole being into a desperate song of goodness, to cling to goodness and life, to reality, to the dreams that were real. She tried to throw herself into the song and away from the nightmare. She felt herself failing. The wraith seemed to be a song itself, a song of horror, a song of death, a song of despair, a magic of evil, of an existence in which there was not even a memory or thought of good to desire or to despair of gaining. It crushed her and her song, stealing the life out of the song, silencing even her thoughts.

Tara-lin felt as if her body was turned to ice, but there was almost no pain in the cold, though the cold was all torture. For a moment, her mind resisted the thing once more, but it drew near. It stumbled over her burning elf-sword, then passed on... Coldness. Hate. Rage. Fear. Terror. Despair. All these passed through Tara-lin's mind and soul in progressive waves of numbing evil. She felt herself – no, she felt not at all – but she slipped into the formless evil wraith. Only for a moment was she capable of resistance, then it was as if she melted into the shade, into the coldness beyond all cold. It was not hate. It was not rage. It was not fear. It was not even despair. It was to all these as Alai-ie-a's song was to love, to life, to joy, to happiness. It was beyond misery. It was all misery. It was misery too great to be felt. It swallowed her up into itself. It knew no light against or without which it was dark. It knew nothing for which to hope which allowed the possibility of despair. It knew nothing opposed to itself which it might hate. It knew no end which might be feared.

For another moment, Tara-lin weakly resisted the wraith, but that passed almost without existing. Her body responded to the presence of the wraith, as it passed through her, enveloping her, and there was a moment of pure torture, flaming, burning, horrible cold, and worse than cold, that wracked her whole body in one wave of stabbing, terrible pain, pain that would kill her if it lasted for a moment longer... Her whole body rebelled against the presence of the possessing wraith, and for a moment she was consumed in the torture of the contact, pain beyond all thought, obliterating pain, and yet that torture was the last cry or existence of her soul against the wraith, the cold, the thing so evil it could not know evil.

Then the wraith drew back, itself knowing what little pain such a wretched existence could perceive – for it was all pain, and, in being all torture, could no longer recognize torture.

Tara-lin's hand fumbled in the bag she wore over her shoulder, and a tingling warmth, a breath of life, returned to her fingers. It was pain, but it was also pleasure. She touched the untouchable Starweave.

Slowly, Tara-lin grasped the Starweave, hardly yet aware of what she was doing, but knowing only the tingling sensation of life in her fingertips. The wraith still clung to her, death and coldness and torture and the despair behind all despair still gripping her, flowing like ice in her blood and bones, but her soul and the Starweave touched, and she was not lost, though she did not yet know it. Her hand brought the Starweave up to her head and, dropping for a moment the elf-sword, she bound it around her head with both hands. Some of it fluttered past her eyes.

In that moment, the wraith completely released her. She found that, even without the light of the elf-sword, she could perceive the passage in which she walked, though it was not sight as she had hitherto known sight. Her whole being tingled with life, as if she had been brought back from death or even hell. Most of all, her mind and heart tingled with an inexpressible life. It was as if she had passed into a new mode of existence, into the life of another world. It was not unlike her experience when the dryad's magic called her into a more dryadic existence, but that, she had known, even then, was only for a moment. This was more, so much more, more all-encompassing, reaching far deeper, even into her soul, transforming not only her outward perception of the world but her inward powers and senses, irrevocable – as hearing the song of Alai-ie-a was irrevocable.

Tara-lin looked, and saw the wraith almost cowering before her. She stooped and picked up again the elf-sword and advanced towards it.

The wraith cowered, shrinking, as if it could pass through the stone. Then it lashed out. For a moment Tara-lin felt the touch of coldness, of incomprehensible despair, but then the thing recoiled, as if burned in its contact with her. It seemed to writhe in unimaginable torture. A strange emotion coursed through Tara-lin. Something like hatred and something greater than pity mingled in one. It felt at once an act of destruction and an act of mercy as she stepped forward, her sword preceding her, and pierced the wraith.

There was one piercing immaterial wail which was not truly a sound. Unthinkable and pure torture realized itself in the wail, yet Tara-lin did not cringe or even flinch, though the sound – if sound it was – hurt a little.

Where the wraith had been, for a moment the Starweave hung across the cavern.

It was at that moment that Tara-lin realized she was seeing through the Starweave. It was around her and through it she perceived everything.

Chapter Twenty-One - Surprises in Nightshade

Tara-lin felt hope now. She could not explain it, but her spirits were buoyed. Still finding the passage uncomfortably cramped, but greatly comforted by the light that was not light, she continued down the passage. She could not explain why, except, what else was there to do? She thought that now, even if she stood before the gates of Nightshade again, she would not feel despairing.

It was not long before she perceived a gap in the side of the rock. Peering through it, she saw that it opened on the horrible substance of the Nightshade. She wriggled through it, feeling very vulnerable and experiencing some measure of fear, since she was absolutely defenseless in this position. Her body hardly fit through the crevice, and it was all she could do to wiggle through. It was an uncomfortable process.

Finally, Tara-lin was through the hole. She got to her feet just as a pair of orcish guards came around the corner. In a moment, the elf-sword was in her hand, flashing its purple flame, and she saw the orcs draw back. The legendary works of old times, the elf-swords had been forged for combat with the nightmare creatures. On some of the nightmare creatures they were almost completely ineffective, but orcs were one of those types on which they had most effect. This had not wholly pleased their makers, for while it was convenient to be able to fight orcs better, orcs were readily slain with normal weapons.

Tara-lin herself was uncomfortable. She had never been trained to fight with a sword, knew nothing of what she was doing, and there were two of them! She stepped forward, since she could not think of a better thing to do, rolling on the balls of her feet, ready to spring in any direction. One of the orcs stepped ahead of the other, his shield and sword held before him, and Tara-lin parried his thrust, throwing his blade far off to the side. She stepped back at once, and realized her mistake almost as quickly. That had been a perfect opening! Now she would have to fight them two at a time.

Amazingly, she felt only a moment of despairing fear. She moved towards the wall of the wide passage, not wanting to allow her opponents to position themselves on opposite sides of her, and thrust aside their blows. They were amazingly cautious, and she knew that if she knew anything about swordplay she would have been the victor by now, but she simply did not know what she was looking for, or how to move, and usually only saw opportunities after they had passed. She suspected many of the opportunities completely escaped her notice.

Finally, the orc on the right struck at her. Tara-lin parried and, this time, she was ready. She moved to her right, his left, and was past the striking range of his sword before he could strike. Dread ran through her as she wheeled around and tried to drive the elf-sword into his side, underneath his shield. Slow and clumsy as he was, he had already moved, and she swiped him across the lower back, her sword mostly glancing off his mail.

Tara-lin cursed under her breath. She was terribly inept, but there had not been time to learn swordplay from her father even if she had asked. She jumped back, away from his blade, and frantically tried to locate the other orc. It was taxing to have to pay attention to two blades... and, to make matters worse, both her opponents were armored, and she was not!

The orcs came at her as one, as if by chance – as often as not, they got in each other's way, but Tara-lin could never predict the course of their actions or blades. Both swords swung at her, from different sides and at different angles. Her mind froze the image desperately.

On an unthought and instantaneous impulse, Tara-lin moved to her left, the right of whichever orc was now positioned on the right (she saw no difference between them) and drove the elf-sword into his arm-pit. The moment of hesitation in her hand was overcome by the eagerness of the sword to penetrate orc-flesh. He cried out and fell forward, unable to move sword or shield or redirect the motion of his body in time to guard against her sword. The weight of his body on her sword almost yanked the weapon out of her hand. Tara-lin grasped the hilt tightly, unable to wait for his body to slip off the smooth, narrow blade so she could face the next orc...

The other orc was coming at her from the side. Tara-lin barely got her sword up in time to parry his blow. She felt the shock of it run up the blade and into her wrist. She drew back. Now she did not have to worry about enemies on either side of her. She just had to wait until... there! He swiped with his sword and his whole body was exposed. Tara-lin thrust.

Somehow, she missed. Her aim was wrong, and she struck his armored breastplate, instead of that gap in his armor on his side and above his belt! Her sword rang on the chain-mail and, while she knew he felt the impact, she also felt it and was out of position. She also, for a moment, did not see his sword. She staggered and fell, her body falling hard against his legs. She concentrated on keeping her grip on her sword, then rolled away from him.

It was a good thing these orcs were stupid! He looked confused for the barest moment, while she got to her knees. Then he came at her. Cursed position! She was far less mobile on one knee than standing. She lashed out and met his sword and, once again, the shock traveled up her blade and into her arm. She was beginning to be afraid and a little desperate. If any more came through right now, she would die before she could do anything!

The next time he attacked with an over-handed blow, she struck at the sword, trying to deflect it up and away, and went for his throat. If she failed, she died, but she had to end this sometime, or she would make a mistake, or more would come, and she would die just the same.

Tara-lin's sword pierced his throat, and she flung herself to her right, his left, out of the way of his body and sword. Quickly, she came to her feet, panting hard.

She did not think she would survive another encounter with orcs unless she learned more about using this sword first, and she did not think she could survive another encounter with orcs if the orcs had bows.

Tara-lin stood against the wall for a moment, trying to catch her breath, and then continued down the passage. One way was as good as another, so she had to guess, and her body ached to be moving. Her heart raced in her chest. She almost couldn't believe it. She had fought two orcs in hand-to-hand combat and won! It felt... strange. She was still a little frightened, but not much, anymore. She would just hope she did not have to crawl through any crevices and, if she did, no orcs came around the corner, and that her Elethrian cloak would conceal her when she met whatever guards wandered these halls. Besides, even if she did have to fight orcs again, she *might* live through it. After all, she doubted she was a worse hand with the sword now than at the beginning of the fight – she felt that she had learned *something* – and there was always the chance the next orcs would make as many mistakes as these orcs had. Still, she did not want to trust her life to that.

How am I supposed to thank you for the Starweave, Shallim-Araldor? Tara-lin wondered. The dryads had said the Ellenari served Shallim-Araldor, and Beriririkirkirkitira had said the Ellenari had brought the Starweave for her. She was sure that Shallim-Araldor cared about her and that the Starweave had been a gift from him through his servants, the Ellenari. She still wondered if it had been one of the Ellenari she had seen at the beginning of all this, who had said something about being ready to answer the call. Weren't the Ellenari specifically supposed to be his messengers, or did she remember that incorrectly? She was very glad for the Starweave, though. She wondered if there was a way to thank the Ellenari, too, preferably whichever one had gotten or brought the Starweave. She thought she had already thanked the dryad with that impossible name.

She hoped she found her father in time, but she had no idea where she was looking. For all she knew he was already dead, or being tortured. Her heart quailed at the thought. *Please, no! If you hear me, Shallim-Araldor, please, no!*

Tara-lin recalled the encounter with the wraith. Her father had been into and out of Nightshade before. She did not think he would be infected by the horror of the nightmares, but she hoped Namdon and Cuthlin were all right. *We walk amongst fates worse than death and torture,* she thought. *I never realized that, listening to Mom and Dad tell about their adventure inside Nightshade and Icecrown... that perils worse than death by torture are all around us. Did they think I was too young for them to share it with me? Was I just too young to hear it – too stupid? This is so horrible! I could prefer my friends to be tortured to death over some of the fates that threaten us! Oh, this is so horrible! Alai-ie-a, what would you say to this? What would your song sound like here? What is the truth? Oh, Shallim-Araldor, are you here? Are you real at all? What are you? What is your power?*

Twice more, Tara-lin heard orcs coming down the passage. When she did so, she pressed herself against the wall, and willed her breathing and heartbeat to slow and her Elethrian cloak to blend her into her background. She noticed once that the orcs probably needed to have *some* light, and that there were torches set here and there against the walls – enough that some areas were brighter, but these were few enough that, in general, the lighting was such that even an elf would find it hard to see, unless, of course, that elf wore the Starweave about her brow.

The passage split several times, sometimes coming to an end where there were two ways to choose from but the passage did not continue on straight, not that it was usually straight. Turns and curves were not uncommon. Once again, Tara-lin simply chose a passage, unable to think how to determine which way was best. For some reason, she was no longer concerned about being able to retrace her steps and find her way out. Perhaps, she was confident that she could use her song to find her way out if there *was* a way out or in.

Tara-lin was walking along a passage, keeping close to the wall, when she noticed that there were now doors cut into the wall. She wondered at first if it might be in a room like these that her father and his friends were held, but something made her unwilling to try to open the doors. She ran her hand along the wall, walking close to it in case she quickly had to hide herself, and continued on. A thought came to her. *I bet it's close to evening now, if it isn't night already.* She was hungry, tired, and thirsty. Well, there was nothing to be done about the tired part. Tara-lin simply was not going to sleep in the Nightshade Castle until she absolutely had to. She did however sit down and try to eat and drink. She found she could eat better than she had been able to eat that morning, though she still could not eat very well, but she did drink. She decided not to drink too much, since she would not trust any water she found within Nightshade Castle itself, she did not even know if there was water to be found inside Nightshade Castle, and she did not want to run out of water if she could help it.

Then Tara-lin rose and continued on. *I really want to find my father, but I have no idea how I would do that. What a stupid I am! I ought to sing a song.* She shook her head in bewilderment. *How did I not think of that before? Oh yes, I'm supposed to be doing two things. Finding my father and stopping Prince Anakrim from stealing the lifeblood of the dryads. Well, I have no idea how to do the latter, so I'll start with the former...* While she thought this, Tara-lin had been continuing to move along the wall, and a ripple caught her attention. No, it wasn't a ripple in the unliving stone under her hand.

What was it then?

Tara-lin stopped, standing still, listening with all her senses. There it was again! No, it wasn't a song. Yes, it was like... no, it wasn't like the dryad song... yes, there was that feel in it again! Magic, certainly... Where was it coming from?

Tara-lin continued to run her hand along the wall. She came in a moment to another door. Yes, it was stronger here. The door almost vibrated with it. Yes, it was like the dryad song, like her own song, but wrong, very wrong. She opened the door, surprised when it was not locked.

Tara-lin had only a moment for her surprise about the door. At once, an orc and a wraith were in her face. The elf-sword was in her hand almost as quick as lightning, and next moment the wrath cried out its long, piercing wail and was gone. She dispatched the orc almost as quickly, thrusting his sword aside and swiping off his head with her own blade.

Tara-lin surveyed the room. On a table, in the middle of it, lay a... man? elf? half-elf? Tara-lin had seen many elves, and the features of this being reminded her more of many men than of most elves. Nonetheless, the ears were upswept and pointed, and some of the facial features were distinctly elven. His hair was pale yellow, almost silver, and his skin was only a little less pale. Around him on the table lay various strange instruments, which Tara-lin recognized almost at once as magical.

Next to the table stood another who could only be Prince Anakrim. His hair was purpler and darker than Tara-lin's, and his eyes were a deep amber brown. His skin was as light as that of the man on the table. When Tara-lin's eyes met his, she saw first shock, and then a strange, twisted pleasure, in his face.

Tara-lin was surprised at the words that came out of her mouth. She instantly saw that what she said must be right, but she had not realized it. "You're torturing your brother." *Brother? It must be the Princess' other son, presumed dead!*

"Torturing?" asked Anakrim. "Do you see instruments of torture here?! But how very pleased, if a little surprised, I am to see you. I had wanted to meet such a personage as yourself!"

Tara-lin stepped forward, completely ignoring Anakrim, though she kept an eye on him. The Prince Keller was bound to the table, and Tara-lin wondered if even her elf-sword could sever those bonds. She stopped, a foot away from the table, and sang.

Slowly her song rose in power. The vibrations filled the room. The bonds snapped, and the half-elf's eyes fluttered open. For a moment Tara-lin saw their color: a pure blue, like a bright sky with a slight haze of clouds over it. Then they closed again.

She sensed Anakrim move almost before she saw it. He, too, began to sing, and she changed the tone of her song to combat his own. In her hand still blazed the elf-sword, and its flames flickered in time to the rhythm of their combat.

Towards her Anakrim moved, the fear in his expression growing all the time, and Tara-lin did not bother to ascertain the shape of the object he held in his hand. Vaguely she ascertained its purpose, and knew it was a weapon of torment and of stealing power. More than that, she knew simply that she must not let it touch her. She was too consumed with her song to think of much else. She moved quickly, and knocked the object out of his hand with a swipe of her sword. It shattered against the wall.

Fear grew and transformed into anger, and the rage blazed in Anakrim's eyes. He changed his song, moving to another chant, and Tara-lin knew now that she faced magic beyond her ability to sense or counteract. "Wake! Live!" she said, moving to the table. With the hand in which she held the sword, she knocked yet more of Anakrim's instruments to the floor, and they shattered. With her other hand, she grasped the hand of the still-faint Prince Keller. He rose in response to her touch, and she fled from the room, half-dragging him. He wept, as he followed her, and only as she exited the room did she hear what he was saying, "Mom! Please! Don't leave me! I love you! Don't leave me, please!"

Mom? thought Tara-lin. *What does he think? Who does he think I am?* His grip on her hand was painful. She was sure her hand must be bruised. She hoped he would not hurt himself on her sword. He certainly seemed crazy, but what did she know about what effects living in this horrible castle might have on people, or what effects Anakrim's dark magic might have on people – not to mention Falkur's magic? And hadn't Fizzer mentioned that Ithrìl had reported that both she and Keller had been abused? Apparently, though, she had been mistaken about Keller being dead, or had had another son she didn't tell them about – or that Fizzer didn't tell them about – for this was definitely a half-elf, and, Tara-lin thought, Anakrim's brother.

Several steps later, Tara-lin realized that Anakrim was not following them. She could still dimly sense his magic, but it seemed to have changed. What was he doing? She wished she knew! She wished she knew what she could do to stop him – to stop him from killing the dryads – but she could not do that right now. Right now she had to get herself and Prince Keller away from him, and she had to find Eldor and the others.

Just then she realized that she had known more than she had any right to, battling with songs in that room as she stood at the foot of the magic table on which he had bound his brother. She had heard a little about combat songs in the old legends, but she had not known she knew anything of the art. Doubtless, it had something to do with the way the dryads had taught her.

Tara-lin's song failed. She tried to convince Keller to rise and follow her.

"No!" he screamed. "Don't drag me away! Don't hurt me! Take me back to Mom!"

He is *crazy*, thought Tara-lin. *What am I going to do?*

"I won't hurt you, Keller," she said gently. "I'm trying to take you away from those who hurt you. I'd take you back to your mom, but I can't. I don't know where to find her." Tara-lin figured that was as much of the truth as Keller could understand, or needed to hear, in his demented state.

"They hurt me all the time!" he wailed.

"I know they hurt you, Keller," said Tara-lin. "Come with me. I'll take care of you." She held out her hand to him, which he had thrown away.

Tara-lin winced as Keller took her hand again. "Thank you, Mommy!"

She figured she could not explain to him that she was both a friend and not his mom. "You can walk now," she said. "Get up."

Keller rose, still gripping her hand tightly. Tara-lin felt uncomfortable. How could this large half-elf, significantly larger and older than herself, be calling her 'Mom'? Something about all this felt very wrong!

She thought about turning back and trying to take him out the way she had come in, but she thought almost at once that he would not fit that way, being much larger than herself. Also, she still needed to find her father and Namdon and Cuthlin.

Tara-lin did not sheath her sword. She hoped Keller would not hurt himself on it, but she felt much safer with it in her hand, especially since now that she had Keller with her she could not hide. She still marveled at the speed, ease almost, with which she had slain Anakrim's orc guard. She wondered if he had any human slaves and, if so, where they lived. She did not think she could kill them as easily as she killed an orc or a wraith – it was almost pleasurable to kill wraiths! In fact, she did not know if she could kill humans at all.

Another pair of orc guards came around a curve in the wall, and a screech of "No! Not the dungeons again! *NO!*" sounded from right behind Tara-lin. She was shocked for a moment, even though she should have been expecting all kinds of strange and violent reactions from Keller by now.

Tara-lin felt power behind her, then a blast took her off her feet and sent her sailing across the hall to land on the floor. *What was that?!* she thought, as she got to her feet, instantly knowing she was going to be very stiff and sore. *I didn't know orcs could cast magic!* she thought, then, as she came to her feet and recovered her senses, she saw that the orcs had been almost as affected as herself. She hoped she could get to them and destroy them before they regained their composure. She sprinted.

From behind Tara-lin, the screams continued. "NO! Not the dungeons! Don't hurt me! MOM! Where are you?! YOU PROMISED! Mommy, save me!"

Tara-lin tried to ignore the screams. Right now she had to kill two orcs. After that she had to figure out what was the cause of that blast and deal with Keller, but first she had to kill orcs!

Tara-lin charged towards one of the orcs. He staggered to his feet, but then saw the flaming elf-sword, and the moment of shock and fear at the sight of the elf-sword gave Tara-lin her chance. She quickly dispatched him, but she still had to deal with the other. She wheeled and saw him coming towards her, already recovering from the shock and terror of the elf-sword.

She heard footsteps coming around the corner. *No! No! Not more orcs!* Tara-lin thought in near panic. She could not fight two... no, three... more orcs at a time. That would be four at once!

At least she was close to the wall. Maybe she could manage if she could keep them all in front of her. She decided to get closer to the wall so the newcomers could not get between her and the wall.

A shout – a very human shout – startled her. "It's Tara-lin! Eldor!"

Tara-lin almost dropped her sword she was so surprised. She barely parried the blow coming at her.

Several strikes and parries later, someone else's sword pierced the orc from behind.

"I see you need someone to teach you how to use the sword," said Eldor, looking incredibly beat, and staring at her. Then, he shook his head, as if to clear it. "But what is that screaming?"

"Come. Let me show you," said Tara-lin. "It's Keller – the other son of Ithrìl, the one presumed dead. He's crazy. Oh, and I don't know why this happened, but I was fighting those orcs all the way back here because this *blast* hit us. Would it be possible for Anakrim to be able to hit us while we're far away and out of line of sight with a blast?" She was leading them back towards the still-wailing Keller.

"I've never heard of any wizard being able to do it," said Namdon. "Blasts, wizards can manage. I've never heard of wizards throwing blasts at far away people they can't see, but that doesn't necessarily mean... by the way, what is he yelling about?"

Keller was thrashing on the floor. "No! Don't hurt me! Mom, where are you? I need you to save me! Protect me! *Him* and Brother are going to hurt me again! Please, *MO–OM!*"

"It's all right, Keller," said Tara-lin. "These are men who will help me take you away from the men who hurt you. They're my friends and they're nice men. They don't hurt children. We just killed and got rid of the bad things that scare and hurt you, Keller. They helped me do it."

"Oh, Mommy!" cried Keller. He got up and took the hand Tara-lin once again extended. Once again, she winced as he gripped it.

Eldor and Namdon exchanged glances. Then they looked at Tara-lin. "What are we going to do now?"

"Do you know the way out?" asked Tara-lin.

"I think we might be able to find the big doors they brought us in through," said Namdon.

"Yeah, I think between all of us we can do it," said Cuthlin. "Especially if Tara-lin's excellent navigating skills are any good when one is on the inside of a mountain instead of the outside."

Tara-lin shook her head. "I don't know," she said. "I'll try. And I think I might use a song to help."

"We're going out?" asked her father. "Did you figure out a way to stop Prince Anakrim?"

Tara-lin shook her head again. "Only from torturing Keller. I think he was trying to steal some sort of power from his brother. That's all I could gather. I just know that, right now, the most important thing is for us to get ourselves and Keller out of his reach. It's all right, Keller. Everything will be good now. No one will ever hurt you again."

"Oh, thank you!" said Keller. He let go of Tara-lin's hand and decided to hug her. Fortunately, Cuthlin stepped to her side and took the elf-sword out of her hand before he cut himself on it.

"Well," said Eldor, "we can find our way out. I and Lìrulin snuck around here quite a lot over two decades ago, and I still remember the lay of the place pretty well."

"Can you get that big baby off of you so you can take this sword again?" asked Cuthlin. "I like its steady light."

"Steady," laughed Tara-lin. "Let go of me, Keller," she said, and struggled free of his arms. She took the sword from Cuthlin, and it burst again into purple flames. She realized belatedly that she, wearing the Starweave, was not affected by the dark, but her human companions could probably barely see at all.

They set off, Keller on one side of Tara-lin, Eldor on the other side, and Cuthlin and Namdon in the rear.

"Are you okay, Dad?" asked Tara-lin after a few minutes. "Did they hurt you?"

"I'm just tired. I haven't slept since –"

"It's probably the night after the night you were taken," interjected Tara-lin.

"Well, since the night before that. I've not eaten, either. We did manage to get a drink."

"Have the rest of my water," said Tara-lin. "I'm so ashamed. I've slept and eaten a little – I barely could – since then. But have they hurt you?"

"No more than orcs normally do carrying one off like that. They aren't gentle or kind creatures, but no, not really. And don't be ashamed, Tara-lin. What else were you supposed to do? Having your mind foggy wouldn't help you find us. I doubt it helps you work magic. Each must make do with the best he can," said Eldor wearily.

"All right. I'm glad they didn't beat you or something," said Tara-lin. She stopped and took her bag off her shoulder. "Drink!" she said.

They passed it between themselves, taking a few mouthfuls each, then returned it to her. She did not think she could argue with them. Keller was urging her to get moving.

"We shouldn't talk more than necessary," said Eldor. "It makes sound by which we can be found or followed. See if you can get Keller to quiet."

"If you want to carry him?" suggested Tara-lin.

"We'll carry him if that's what it takes," said Eldor. The other two echoed the sentiment.

"Really?" asked Tara-lin. She stopped again and looked at her father. "You look ready to drop."

He smiled wanly. "You look pretty exhausted, too, but yes, we'll carry him. It's better than being found by all that noise he makes."

"Very well," said Tara-lin. She stopped and began to sing softly.

As soon as she began to sing the sleep song, the half-elf threw himself at her. "No!" he screamed. "Don't hurt me! Don't! MOM! Please! Why are you doing this to me?!"

Tara-lin stumbled and fell under his weight, her song broken. The three Valor Knights threw themselves on top of Keller then. They wrestled him to the ground and one covered his mouth to muffle his terrified cries. Tara-lin's heart wrenched; she pitied him and did not wish him this anguish. She took up the song again and concentrated, effectively blocking out his muffled screams and the sound of the struggle on the floor at her feet. It was one of the hardest things she had done yet to concentrate the sleep song on one man and leave the other three untouched. She was not sure she could completely do it, but as exhausted as they all were, she knew she must do what she could to keep her friends from being affected by it. It would take longer to take effect on Keller, too, since he was so awake and so scared and fighting so hard.

Slowly, his screams become softer, quieter, more indistinct – though they were already quite muffled and indistinct because of the hand on his mouth. His struggling grew weaker, then ceased altogether. Tara-lin barely noticed that the men had stood and moved to position themselves as guards around the two half-elves.

She sang for fifteen more minutes, then let the last note fade away. "There!" she said. "That should hold for a few hours, but I should refresh it before it's done if we still need it. Much easier that –"

Tara-lin stopped mid-sentence. Two guards appeared out of the light of the nearest torch.

Eldor turned to her. "Can you hide us?"

"Not fast enough."

He motioned to his comrades and they quickly formed together and charged the guards. Tara-lin glanced quickly around, wondering what she should do. Should she help them fight? Should she stay with Keller – in case a guard pair came from the other direction?

Knowing that the light would benefit her father and his comrades, but not the orcs, she closed her eyes and sang, expanding and steadying the light of the torch. The song absorbed her attention, and she did not at first notice when the men came back towards her.

After a moment, Tara-lin did notice. "There you are!" she said. "How long was that?"

The men looked confused by her question. They arranged themselves to pick up Keller between two of them. Then Eldor motioned to her, and Tara-lin understood that they wanted her to lead since she carried the sword. He moved to the back and took up the rear-guard position.

How do they do it? wondered Tara-lin. *I'm almost falling asleep even while I'm singing! They're moving with military efficiency and formation. I wouldn't have thought of a rear-guard... I wish I could talk. But maybe that's part of why it's Dad back there. He doesn't want me to be tempted to talk to him. Or maybe it's because he's too tired to help carry Keller.*

Tara-lin's thoughts were running away with her. She kept thinking back to the combat in Anakrim's magical torture chamber – for that was how she thought of it, and, clearly, Keller dreaded it greatly. She was sure the Starweave did more than allow her a new power of vision, protect her from the Corruption, and allow her sword to kill wraiths. She was certain it added power and direction to her song. She had no doubt that, with the Starweave, she could open the gates of Nightshade.

She wanted to ask them how they had escaped their captors *inside* Nightshade Castle.

They came to a corner and Tara-lin stopped. "Which way?" she whispered. "Dad?"

"The left. And, if you can do so while walking, since you said you have a song to help you know which way to go, why don't you sing that?" Eldor whispered back.

Tara-lin nodded, then thought he would not be able to see her nod, especially from his position in the back. "Yes," she whispered back, turning her head for a moment. Then, after a moment's thought, she stopped again and turned around. "How necessary is it, do you think?" she asked. "Songs take energy, and I'm tired, even though I shouldn't be as tired as you are."

"I'm not completely confident of my ability to navigate this maze," Eldor whispered back. "Also, there might be short cuts you can take, I wouldn't know of."

"They won't help if they run us straight into a cloud of nightmares," responded Tara-lin.

"Then − if you can − add something to the song to help it not direct you into the enemy," said Eldor. "Ultimately, this has to be your decision, though. You know your abilities and limitations far better than any of us do."

"I'm not sure about that," muttered Tara-lin. She scarcely had any idea what she could and could not do or why.

"What was that?" asked Eldor.

"Nothing important," said Tara-lin. She tried to clear the fog from her mind and started to sing softly as she continued down the hall.

At one corner, they found orc guards. In a moment, Cuthlin and Namdon laid Keller down, and all four of them fought the orcs. It was over quickly. Tara-lin shook her head as they rearranged themselves. *I am so tired*, she thought. *I shouldn't feel like falling asleep right after fighting...*

This time Cuthlin took up the rear-guard position. They had only moved a few steps when her father's whisper came to Tara-lin's ears. "Are you all right?" he asked. "Did you get hurt in that last skirmish?"

She stopped at once and Eldor almost slammed into her. "What do you mean?" she asked.

"You're limping."

"Oh, I hurt all over. It was that blast earlier."

"Okay. Let's keep moving."

"I think I really need to sleep," said Tara-lin. "I don't know how you all can make do with less sleep than I have got, but I think I need to."

"Can you wait a moment?" said Eldor. "I'm almost certain we're almost to the gates."

"If I have to fight, I think we're going to all die," said Tara-lin, "but, yes, I can't wait to be out of here. It just feels evil. It's almost frightening to think of falling asleep in here. It feels like we're in the belly of some *horror.* Let's go, then."

Not long later – though it felt like a long time to Tara-lin – they faced what was almost certainly the gates. On either side stood a pair of orc guards.

Tara-lin let the men lead the charge. The orcs focused on them, and then she stepped softly and slowly forward while they fought against the orcs. Sneaking up behind where two of them battled Eldor, she drove her sword into the back of one's neck. A moment later, the other fell.

Tara-lin straightened and looked around. Namdon had slain his orc and was just coming up to help Cuthlin finish his. She winced. Her father's question about her well-being might have been warranted. Every step, almost every movement, was pain. Perhaps that contributed to her exhaustion. But, she could not believe that they had not been manhandled and hurt by their orc captors. She never got a good view as to how uncomfortable they were, since they were almost always either behind her or fighting for their lives.

She thought how much kinder they were to her weaknesses than she had been to Alis' difficulties, at least to begin with.

"Why don't you try to open the gate, Tara-lin?" said her father.

"Right," she said, and nodded. The elf-sword still naked in her hand, she approached the huge black gates while her comrades again picked up the Prince Keller. Standing before the gates, she sheathed the elf-sword and placed both her hands on the black stone. She shuddered for a moment at the contact, then sang.

Slowly she began, but gathering strength. It might have been harder, in the sense of requiring far more difficult concentration and discipline, to sing the sleep upon Keller without sending her father and his friends to sleep also, but this required more power, for the gates were warded with black magic. She did not think it would be possible, at any rate with her current knowledge, experience, and level of energy, to do this, if it were not for the Starweave. As it was, she was almost certain of success.

Tara-lin felt the power build in her song and built upon it. Her voice thrummed with the summoned power, and soon her body responded to the power as well. She could feel the gates vibrate under her hands. She knew a presence far mightier than herself, and also far better and cleaner than herself, stood beside her, the source of all power. She wondered how her heart could ever have quailed at the sight of the Nightshade Castle, for she felt as if around her rose a fortress of indomitable goodness, radiating unlimited power.

She concentrated on the song. Almost without realizing it, she shifted from the common language of Ellenesia into the ancient tongue of Elethri. Her voice soared with the powerful magic and it became uncomfortable. She concentrated harder. She had to ignore the discomfort in her voice and build the power and the song to carry it.

Tara-lin's body grew taut as she sang. The contest between herself – her song – and the gates with their dark magic grew more pronounced, more dynamic. A kind of exultation poured through her body, but it was not the exultation of victory, or not yet.

Then she stepped back. "Push it open! NOW!" she screamed.

The men dropped Keller and ran at the dark doors, throwing their bodies into them. The gate swayed at the impact and, for one horrid instant, Tara-lin thought it would not open. She swayed, too. Darkness encroached on her vision, and she sank to the ground.

A moment later, Tara-lin sat up. Through the gates, she saw stars in a sky that seemed unusually light for the time of night. She stood, and almost passed out again. Cuthlin and Namdon took up Keller again, and she walked, almost leaning against Eldor, out of Nightshade Castle.

It took her a long moment of confusion and bewilderment to understand what she saw. The night was almost over. Dawn spread its rays above the mountains in the east.

Above her, flying south, what was that shimmering, glittering monstrous thing? It could not be a dragon, could it?

Then Tara-lin's eyes resolved what she was seeing. It was not one huge glittering thing. It was multitudes of wings, each flashing or reflecting a shifting, shimmering light. Were some of them gryphons? She could not see them clearly, but she was almost certain some of them were of horrible aspect and nature, though this was hidden by the shimmering colors.

"What are we going to do now?" she gasped, breathless.

When Tara-lin again came to herself, she was laying in a cave. Beams of sunlight coming through the mouth and landing on her face had awakened her. She turned her eyes away from the brightness, but not before she saw one of the men standing guard at the mouth.

How could I have been so unkind to Alis? she wondered to herself. *It couldn't possibly have been nearly as hard for me then as it is now for Dad and Namdon and Cuthlin. Yet they haven't scolded me for being a burden or for slowing them down or for needing more sleep or for anything, not a single time! They must be so tired. How in the world was I so rough with Alis?*

Tara-lin sat up. She winced. She had grown so much stiffer overnight! After a moment, she stood, carefully and painfully, and walked over to where Cuthlin stood guard. Without turning his face from the Icecrown Vale, he acknowledged her. "Hi, Tara-lin. You finally woke up."

"What – what time is it? How long has it been?"

"It's morning of the day after we came out of Nightshade Castle. We're out of food and water. Namdon went out to hunt some animals. Hopefully he can get a few rabbits. He'll come back with water soon, even if he doesn't succeed at hunting."

"Then we'll need to be able to start a fire in order to cook them," said Tara-lin, "but I want to get out of here."

"We all share that sentiment," said Cuthlin.

"I could watch, while you could go gather wood," said Tara-lin.

"Certainly," said Sir Cuthlin. "I will leave you here with your father."

He clambered down out of the cave mouth. Looking at the slope – nearly a cliff – Tara-lin thought, *How did they ever manage to get themselves – and me – and Keller – up here?*

She looked behind her and saw her father laying wrapped in his cloak in one place and Keller in another. *How did they get Keller to go to sleep?* she wondered. She sat down on the edge of the cave and settled herself to observe the area. Looking around, Tara-lin judged that it was a very good choice. The slope leading up to it was completely bare, and mostly of a whitish rock. It would gleam even in starlight. Only on the darkest nights would it be difficult to observe a shape crawling up it – unless that shape were clothed in an Elethrian cloak and moving carefully. Boulders around her made a natural barrier to anything trying to climb in, and the slope was such that any man or orc, or even elf, would have difficulty keeping his footing. One man could stand in the gap between the boulders, and only one foe could fight him at a time.

Tara-lin took out her sword and laid it naked across her knees. Somehow, she felt more comfortable that way. She tried to ignore her thirst. She hoped Namdon would come back soon with water.

The vale below her was beautiful. The surrounding mountains were covered in snow and ice. Cloud hung to some of them. The others were a bluish color in the shade cast by the rising sun; elsewhere, the hills and valleys were illuminated by the reddish-tinge of dawn. Woods and grassy meadows clothed the hilly vale, which looked like it ran up between the mountains in several directions. Blue streams ran hither and thither and poured into lakes. Many of the trees were evergreens, but many were also deciduous and their leaves were beginning to be tinged with fantastic colors, ranging from red, to gold, to purple. Up on the sides of the mountains there were a fair number of these. But the whole scene was marred by the bulbous labyrinthine monster, like the heart and mother of all evil, or the egg out of which all evil hatched, laying against the mountain. The vale was also marred by an unusual number of dead or nearly-dead trees.

Suddenly, Tara-lin realized something she had not seen before. The ridges that connected the outer ring of Icecrown to the mountain out of which or against which lay Nightshade Castle, like some horrible sore, were lower than either that mountain or the outer ring. This vale was one of at least two vales arranged around the central Icecrown Mountain and separated from each other by high ridges, spurs that came out from the central Icecrown Mountain and connected with spurs that came out from the outer ring. *How interesting,* she thought.

Then Tara-lin noticed that the tone of the dryads' song had changed. She was not certain if it was any stronger, but after listening to it for a long time she decided it was no longer a deathsong. They were once again both sinking and drawing life, through their roots, out of the soil. They were once again gathering strength from the sunlight and the air. Listening to it still longer, she felt certain that the general song a grove emanated would usually be slightly different in spring than in autumn, different yet in the winter.

Footsteps behind her caused Tara-lin to turn. Her father had risen. He still looked so tired, and she was certain now that he had been hurt. She could see a green bruise along one side of his face. "Why are you up, Dad?" she asked. "Sleep more."

"I don't feel like sleeping right now," he said, settling himself next to her. "I want to sit with my Tara-lin."

She smiled up at him. "I'm glad you love me so much."

"And I'm glad you love me, too. You wanted to talk to me in private?"

"Keller's in there," said Tara-lin.

"You don't need to be concerned about that," said Eldor. "He woke up and was completely unmanageable yesterday. I used some of the herb lore Lìrulin taught me, and found an herb to put him to sleep with. He was hungry enough to eat the food we mixed it with, and he won't wake for another three hours at least."

"I'm so sorry, Dad," said Tara-lin. "How did he not wake me up?"

"You were really out," said Eldor. "You're young. Your mind and body are still growing. And you've been using magic, magic you aren't really used to yet. That tends to make people *very* tired."

Tara-lin leaned her head on his shoulder.

"So, what did you want to ask me about?" he asked.

"I mostly did. I just kind of found myself asking, on the ridge – it feels like yesterday, but it wasn't. When I first laid eyes on Nightshade Castle." She paused for a moment, then said slowly and softly, "What do you know of Shallim-Araldor."

He jerked away from her and looked her in the eyes. "Shallim-Araldor?"

"Yes, Shallim-Araldor. Do you know the name then?" she asked.

"I heard my wife speak it once. I don't know if she was dreaming or speaking to a dryad or what. I asked her once what it meant. She told me only that it was the name of the King of the Dryads. I felt certain there was more, and I asked her 'I thought you told me dryads don't have kings or queens.' 'Not that kind of king,' was her reply. I never pushed for more. She seemed unwilling to tell me more, and I was certain until she was willing to tell me, it would do no good for me to ask. So far, she never has told me more," said Eldor. "What do you know of Shallim-Araldor?"

"I was first introduced to the name by being told he was King of the Dryads, too. I don't know. I've seen a lot of things. I know he has something to do with the Starweave – this thing, that isn't a thing in the normal sense of the word, that I have bound around my head. I'm sure it had something to do with the power and effectiveness of my song, among other things. I think he might have something to do with that thing you told me about finding something you could hold to and that held onto you even in the morass of evil. I don't know how he's related to all that. The dryads say he values compassion, mercy, pity," said Tara-lin.

Eldor nodded. They settled against each other again.

"How did you escape the orcs *inside* Nightshade of all places?" asked Tara-lin.

"I had a dagger on me in a place they didn't search," said Eldor. "My cloak might have had something to do with it. Cuthlin knows how to pick locks, and we managed to unlock the dungeon door. I remembered where weapons were put from my previous exploration of the castle, and so we were able to recover our swords and bows. We were just coming back from that, and discussing what to do in order to meet back up with you, when we met."

"And your face?" asked Tara-lin.

"Orcs are not gentle. That's all. You, however, are a mess. All those bruises on your body might have contributed to your need to sleep, too, you know."

"Even I don't know what it looks like under my clothes," said Tara-lin. "I'm just really stiff."

"I carried you, girl," said Eldor. "Of course I wouldn't let anyone else do *that*. And I tried to do it gently."

"I bet you're being stupid," said Tara-lin. "I bet the orcs beat you up as much as I'm bruised from that blast. They might have simply been displaying typical orc rudeness and lack of gentleness, and not trying to hurt you or anything, but I really bet you're at least as uncomfortable as I am."

He shrugged stiffly. "Who knows?"

"I really want to get out of here," said Tara-lin. "Anakrim might have left with a horde, but this is still a haunt and fountain of evil."

"I agree," said her father. "And your description of Nightshade Castle as a monster is apt. I see now, though, why you didn't want to call the Icecrown gryphons. It looks like there were a lot of them in that horde of Anakrim's, if my eyes served me right. Cuthlin and Namdon agree."

"So do I," said Tara-lin. "There *were* gryphons. But I wonder what he's doing...? It can't be any good."

"No, it can't be," said Eldor, "but I don't think talking about it will help. There's not much we can do right now except survive and get out of this vale."

"Unless we need to survive and go back *into* Nightshade in order to do something?"

"Like what?"

"I don't know," said Tara-lin. "I know the dryads don't seem to be dying anymore. Their life is still slowing, for the most part. They know winter is coming. But I don't feel – it's hard to describe. Their deathsong was beautiful. It didn't suggest the kind of feelings we human-kin tend to feel about death. It's like dryad-death and tree-death is a completely different thing from death as human-kin know it. Their song helped to protect me from the nightmare until I was within Nightshade Castle itself. But it just – it no longer feels like their life in this world is failing, it just..."

"It's okay," said her father. "You don't need to be able to describe to me. I can't see why that would make you think you need to go back into Nightshade, though? It would seem almost as if you'd been successful."

"I don't know," said Tara-lin. "Anakrim left. Maybe he's going to go steal the life from dryads in a different place? I don't know what all those instruments did that I shattered, though... Maybe, he couldn't do whatever it was he was doing without them? I don't know."

"If you want to go back in, we'll go with you," said Eldor. "And I see now why you didn't want to call the gryphons. Given that Anakrim has such a liaison with them, it was almost certainly the right choice. If you had spoken to the gryphons in these mountains, they would have told him."

Tara-lin nodded. "I'd just rather not have to hike out now," she said.

"We might have to," said Eldor, "but it wouldn't be so bad. We'd be going *out*, instead of in."

"There is that," said Tara-lin. "I'm so tired."

A few moments later, she sat straight up. "You know what the *real* reason is? – Keller!"

"And how exactly are gryphons going to help with that?" asked Eldor.

"We can tie him onto the gryphon!" said Tara-lin.

"With *what?*" asked her father.

"I don't know! Something!" said Tara-lin.

"I don't know how well that would work," said Eldor.

"Oh," said Tara-lin with a sigh.

Several moments passed, then Eldor said, "I have something I want to ask you, Tara-lin."

"Yes?"

"You told me many times 'that's a long story' when I asked you questions about what happened between when I departed the Valor Hall and when we met up almost a week ago now. Care to tell me now?"

"Oh, yes! Those're some of the things I didn't want to talk about around the others, at least until some other things were settled, and we'd been in and out of Nightshade. I convinced a girl named Alis Luela who didn't want her family to marry her off, and didn't want to join a monastery either, to run away with me – only, she was running away, and I was running *to.*"

"Ah, I remember that practice," said Eldor. "I never thought much of it, and I've forgotten it these past decades, living in Elethri. It wasn't much of a thing where I grew up."

"It wasn't?" asked Tara-lin.

"No. There were men and women dedicated to the service of the gods and goddesses, but they chose to do so because they wanted it. I don't think there was much of a concept of women neither serving the gods nor being married, but arranged marriages there are... mostly just a formality. The fathers don't really choose their daughters' spouses. I hear in some countries of the Valor Alliance arranged marriages aren't even a formality."

Tara-lin wondered if Alis knew this.

Speaking lower and slowly, Eldor said, "But, after my experience with the nightmare, when I thought I was lost forever, I lost all interest in the gods."

"Did you ever have any?" asked Tara-lin.

"The usual," said Eldor. "More or less."

Chapter Twenty-Three - Of Bandits and Knights, Dryads and Wights

Tara-lin was still telling her father about Alis and about their wild adventures, running from the Valor Hall and being welcomed by dryads, when Sir Namdon appeared. They waved to him, seeing him coming out of the woods, and he managed a wave back.

He climbed up most of the way to their cave, and there Eldor and Tara-lin took his burdens from him. When they had done so, they stepped aside and let him scramble all the way up. Standing there, he said, "It's good to see both of you awake. Where is Cuthlin?"

"He went out to get firewood," said Tara-lin. She had already picked up the water-skin. "I've drank from the stream down there already," she said.

"I'd still prefer to wait for Cuthlin and boil it," said Eldor.

"All right," said Tara-lin, dropping down into a sitting position. She leaned back against a boulder and closed her eyes, trying to ignore her thirst. Her head throbbed already. She wondered how her father managed it, since he was telling Namdon about her and Alis' escapades. That made it harder for her to ignore her thirst, and every time she got excited it did not help her headache. Namdon's responses were hard for her to read; they seemed non-committal. That worried her.

Then, when Eldor finished telling about the encounter in the tavern, Namdon laughed.

Tara-lin opened her eyes. "What?!"

"That's just funny. Her father bellowing at them about how you were a witch, and the common folk being like, 'umm, what business does he have here?' It was something I began to notice as the years wore on. I was supposed to be a Valor Knight – champion of the weak, defender of all, not least the common folk, but in many places there was a certain guardedness towards me. It wasn't towards me in particular. In places where I got to be known I was usually accepted. It was towards Valor Knights in general – the Valor Hall. Of course, there were some places where we were all lauded as heroes. It was all very strange. I think the real giveaway was when I went to one town, and the people were pretty reserved, except for a few little boys – children, really – who wanted me to teach them how to be knights. They had a problem with bandits and thieves waylaying their wagons on the way to market, and a girl had been stolen. I was there to deal with it, find the girl, arrest the bandits, and all that. I'd a few younger knights with me. It didn't warm them up to me at all that I was there to help them."

Tara-lin had closed her eyes again. She was trying to listen without listening in order to avoid her headache.

"As we were wrapping up the bandit problem, I made casual conversation with them. I made them understand that I didn't need special quarters – whatever they had for themselves was good enough for me. In fact, I was happy sleeping on their hay – that way, if the bandits came to steal their animals or anything they stored in or around their barn, they'd meet *me!* I tried to make them feel comfortable around and about me. I wasn't there to impose on them or their wives or make them my servants. I'd eat whatever they ate whenever they ate. I'd even help them carry their goods in or whatever I could do to help them with their farming. I'd chat with them when we were working together to catch or find the problem-makers. I didn't see myself as part of a separate class than themselves. I wasn't there to lord it over them because I was a Valor Knight who'd dedicated my life to protecting them, while they were only simple farmers and work-people."

He paused, taking a deep breath, but Tara-lin felt like he was going to continue. She did not want him to. She wanted to try to sleep until the water was deemed fit for drinking by her father and his comrades – her comrades, now.

"Eventually, they told me some things. Surreptitiously at first, but I began to piece the puzzle together. I think at first they were afraid I'd side with the Valor Hall against them. Valor Knights traveling through the region demanded to be treated like royalty – or at least as much like royalty as these simple farmers and tradesmen could imagine. They probably didn't know how the royalty *really* lived. Apparently, some Valor Knights were no better than bandits. One young woman confided in me that she was almost afraid when she learned the Valor Hall had been notified of the problem and was sending a team. Her best friend had married a man in a village two days' walk away. One Valor Knight had come through and demanded one of the girls in the village. When her brother told him off, he challenged him to a duel and killed him – which was a matter of course, since the man was a farmer and could fight with a pitchfork about as well as with a sword. 'But,' she added, 'people often feel abandoned out here, like the Valor Hall doesn't care about us, we're small and insignificant. When we do report problems, they usually go for years, without the Valor Hall ever taking notice. All that stuff about orcs and problems in the mountains – isn't it just stuff you make up to feel important, while you abandon the real work? How many Valor Knights really die or are wounded fighting in Icecrown or fighting things that come out of Icecrown? Isn't it all trumped up stories so that your fellows can feel good about themselves and be honored by us, while they live in luxury and, sometimes, cowardice? They ride around so much, can they really be fighting in Icecrown all the time? Is Wizard Falkur really our problem? Is the real reason we don't see nightmare creatures around here because of the valor of yourself and your comrades, or because Falkur is a recluse in some mountains who really isn't here to cause anyone trouble?'

"I told her I didn't know. I *had* fought a band of orcs in the foothills of Icecrown once. It wasn't completely trumped up, but I didn't know how big of a problem it was. I didn't know if she had a point. When I left, I started investigating how farmers and villagers felt about us, how city-folk felt about us, how people on the edges of the wilderness felt about us." There was a pause. "It looks like she's gone to sleep again, and you already told me the story, Eldor. How about you continue telling me about the adventures of your daughter and Alis?"

Tara-lin sighed softly.

She was disturbed from her doze by Cuthlin clambering in.

"When will the water be ready?" she asked.

"Not too long now," said Eldor.

A minute later, she heard Namdon saying, "Shouldn't we try to hide it somehow?"

"Not really necessary," said her father. "Orcs build fires, too. Orcs'll even cook over fires. Let's just *try* to keep it from smoking too badly."

It felt like a long time later to Tara-lin when she was finally gulping down very warm water. It was almost hot. She was so thirsty, however, that she hardly minded.

"Stop it! Stop it! Where am I?"

The yelling voice woke Tara-lin. For a moment she wondered whose it was. *Keller!* she thought, almost instantaneously. That same moment she noticed the smell of cooking meat.

She opened her eyes and sat upright. Keller was definitely yelling and screaming. She could not understand what about. "Keller!" she said.

His yelling changed to cries of "I'm hungry! Please feed me!"

"The food isn't ready for you to eat yet," said Tara-lin, rising. "Is it?"

He did not appear to hear her, but continued to yell. "You're starving me! Stop it! Stop starving me! I need to eat too! I –!" He sputtered.

Namdon climbed up and looked at Tara-lin. "Can you do something about this? His screams will surely attract the interest of any nightmare creatures around here."

Tara-lin nodded. Her brain was still fuzzy. "I'll... see what I... can do," she said. She rested her hand on the boulder and thought, trying to focus.

She began to sing, once again in the ancient language of Elethri, weaving a spell to capture and muffle the sound in a ring around their cave and the open area before it. As she sang, another thought came to her, and she added a thought, to obscure the fire – using an element not entirely unrelated to those used in the Elethrian cloak – and to send the smoke in a circuitous route, diffusing it. Once she was done, no orc would find them except by chance. Almost with surprise – surprise muted by her involvement in the spell – she realized that this new addition fit on perfectly to the previous form of the song. It cost hardly any effort to meld the two.

Absorbed in the song, Tara-lin did not notice when food was brought before her and laid on a rock next to her. It was cool when she opened her eyes.

"Oh!" she said. "I am so hungry!" She tore a chunk off the portion of rabbit before her and began to devour it.

"What did you do? It took a long time," said Cuthlin.

"A lot of things," said Tara-lin, with her mouth full. "Whatever noise Keller makes shouldn't go far now. Our fire shouldn't be seen either, and the smoke won't leave a trail."

"What did she just say?" asked Cuthlin, turning to Eldor.

Her father shrugged. "I think she said that she did what we asked and some more things, as well. Something about no one seeing the smoke."

Tara-lin nodded. She swallowed, then shoved more meat directly into her mouth. "Pretty much, and some more," she said, again with her mouth full. "The fire shouldn't be seen, either."

After a couple minutes, she said, "Keller's not screaming

anymore. Why is that?"

"He ate a ton. Someone is going to have to go out and get more. It was difficult keeping him from eating the food we set aside for you. He's gone to sleep now," said Eldor.

"He was quite thin," said Tara-lin.

"None of us are fat," said Namdon.

"True," said Tara-lin, again around a mouthful. "And we're working, whereas he is only a nuisance. I feel sorry for him. I feel sorry for his brother, too. How do you *not* go crazy if you're raised – if you're born and live your whole entire life – inside that monster?"

"You do have a point," said Eldor. "We never thought of that, but you're right. How did we never think about the obvious – that these half-elves were raised inside Nightshade Castle?"

"I thought of that while talking to some dryads," said Tara-lin. "They tend to have a most interesting and unique perspective."

"Tend to?" asked Eldor.

"Well, there seems to be a... commonality, sort of, a continuity, a similarity, certainly, between their perspectives, but so many of them have such unique perspectives! It's not like there's one dryad perspective on things. They're always so interesting and unique," said Tara-lin.

"And humans and elves aren't?" asked Namdon, smiling.

"No. Human-kin can differ a lot, too. But, mostly I've only known very young humans and elves and the thing about dryads is, even though they tend to live at somewhat of a slower pace, they live a really long time. So their perspectives, personalities, are quite developed. And, for some reason, they tend to be less bad, less corruptible than we are. I've met a few bad dryads, but those aren't the rule. Most dryads seem to be almost completely immune to the influence of the nightmare. They don't understand it at all. They don't know fear, and they don't know... *death.*"

"Well," said Eldor, "we don't really know death either. We know what dead bodies are like. None of us here has experienced death or knows what really happens to *you* – one, when one dies."

"I think it's mostly an unknown to the dryads, too, but they don't fear unknowns. For the most part, they seem to have a strong confidence, a certainty even, in the basic goodness of reality."

"That would be grand," said Cuthlin.

"We'll talk more later," said Namdon. "It's your turn to catch some food."

While Cuthlin turned to do so, Tara-lin said, "We're not leaving today?"

"No. We talked this over. Things are pretty dangerous until you get down out of Icecrown into the Northridge Plain. This cave we have is pretty secure. We were going to stock up on food a little, and try to make the journey out in as little time as we can manage. Since you added the spell around this cave, that idea seems still better to us," explained Eldor.

"The spell won't stop orcs – or anything else – from happening upon this place. I'm not willing to try that yet. I might lose *us*," said Tara-lin.

"No, but it's a better camp-site than almost any we might choose and, given the time it took for you to sing the spell over this place, we can't ask you to do it around any camp-site we choose. We definitely need the sound-barrier or whatever it is, with all of Keller's screaming," said Cuthlin.

"I agree about *that*," said Tara-lin.

Cuthlin waved, then stepped out.

"I hate sitting and doing nothing," said Tara-lin.

"Gather your strength," said her father, seating himself next to it. "We will all need it for the trek out of here."

Tara-lin sighed. "I don't look forward to that either. This is part of why I wanted to ride gryphons!"

"All in all, this has not been that bad," said Namdon. "Nightshade Castle was an... experience, and no one enjoys being carried off by orcs, but... I expect complications. I expect something to go wrong yet."

"Like some orcs that heard Keller's screaming before I contained it, and are on their way right now?" asked Tara-lin. "Or what about an army of those ice-wraiths?"

"Wraiths? Ice-wraiths? What is this?" asked Eldor.

Tara-lin told them about her battle with the wraith in the tunnel and then again at the door to the chamber in which she had found both Anakrim and Keller.

"Oh yes!" said Eldor. "The wailing wights, the Elven Bane."

"The Elven Bane?" asked Tara-lin.

"You've not heard all stories yet, have you?" he said, chuckling a little. "In the legends, they're said to be the lesser kin of the Abysstreaders. I doubt Abysstreaders even exist. If any such thing did exist, they would be terrifying and I don't know what power could stop them. Anything they touch becomes... nothing. But the Elven Bane is real. However, I doubt there's an army of them around. They don't seem to be that common. I fought one once, in Nightshade. I should say I tried to fight it. I didn't seem to be getting anywhere, and it was a horrible experience. Ice-wraith is accurate. It felt like it was freezing me to death, and my sword hardly seemed to deter it at all. I did have frost-blisters left over from the encounter, which lasted at least several minutes. Eventually, it left. I have no idea why, but it wasn't destroyed.

"Legend calls them the Elven Bane because it is said no other of the nightmare creatures have such power against the elves as the wailing wights. Some say no elf has ever survived an encounter with them. They are barely more affected by the fire of the elf-sword than by the steel of any other blade. One legend tells of an elven singer in the dawn of Ellenesia who is reported to have banished one, but I'm surprised you met two. It's also very interesting you could kill them. I'm inclined to think you're right, and it has to do with the Starweave but, given that legend, it could also have something to do with the fact you're a singer. Other legends say that wailing wights are the ghosts of elves taken by wailing wights, which leaves open the question of what was the first wight? I could tell you more sometime, but I doubt any of this speculation is much use to us right now. Lìrulin could probably tell you the story of the elven singer who, as the legend states, alone among elves lived through an encounter with a wailing wight."

"Is it an elf story?" asked Tara-lin.

"Yes. I told her about what I'd fought in the corridor, and she said, 'Oh, a wailing or frozen wight!' I'd never heard of such things before," said Eldor.

"How did I not hear about all these things that happened to you before?" asked Tara-lin.

"We didn't want to tell you everything. Remember, we thought you were very young. You still are very young in a lot of ways, and we didn't want to tell you about the wights. There's some horrible stories about them."

"Like what?" asked Tara-lin. "Aren't *all* the nightmare creatures horrible?"

Eldor sighed. "I guess I have to tell you.... One legend says that the wights turn the souls of elves into themselves by inducing the elves to kill themselves on their own swords. Another legend says the only way for an elf to escape the fate of becoming undead is to kill himself on his sword instead of letting the wight kill him in its cold embrace. One variation of this legend says this suicide only works if the sword is one of the elf-swords." He sighed again.

"You don't think it's true, do you?" asked Tara-lin.

"Which one?"

"The one about having to kill yourself – I mean, if you're an elf – to escape undeath."

"No, I don't." He looked up at her and forced a smile. "After all, you've already fought two of these things – my, that's hard to believe, but the first at least had to be a true wailing wight – and you're alive."

"I have the Starweave," said Tara-lin. A horrible thought occurred to her. "What if wailing wights are those dryads who... fear death and become corrupted?"

Her father shrugged. "I wouldn't know. What good do these suppositions do?"

"None, really," said Tara-lin. "It just... explains their... I can't call it *song.*"

"Well, it might be. It might not. We might as well not think about it. But I seriously doubt there's another wailing wight out there waiting for us, let alone a whole army of them, Tara-lin, if that's any comfort to you."

She shrugged. "I guess. But if two, why not more than two? Anyway, you're right. This conversation isn't doing us any good. Still, the story about committing suicide to avoid wighthood just doesn't sound right. Kill yourself to avoid undeath? Huh? The other one, about the wights convincing the elves to slay themselves, sounds more like it."

"I agree with you," said Eldor. "That one rings more true, whereas the other rings wrong... especially after some things I've experienced. But reality is often so strange, much stranger than we imagined it could be."

"I don't believe it," said Tara-lin, "and, the more I think about my own encounter with the first wight, the more it feels like... inducing elves to kill themselves would be in its... function."

"You would know that better than I," said Eldor. "You're elf – or half-elf."

"Elf, but I don't know if being more human and less dryad would affect this or how," said Tara-lin.

"All right, elf," said Eldor. He smiled at her.

Watching him lapse into silence, Tara-lin said, "You're *still* upset I'm here."

"I suppose I am, Tara-lin," said her father. "I love you."

"I know that," she said. Then, "We're going to leave tomorrow morning, right?"

"That's the plan," said Eldor.

"We're leaving tomorrow morning," pronounced Tara-lin.

Namdon cast a questioning look at Sir Eldor.

Tara-lin turned away and buried her head in her cloak.

"You still haven't told us how you got the elf-sword," said Namdon.

"I stole it from the Valor Hall. You guys have a whole bunch of them laying on a table doing nothing," snapped Tara-lin.

Chapter Twenty-Four - Song of the Dryads

Darkness. Cold.

Despair. Terror. Rage.

Senselessness.

Cold.

Tara-lin woke. She recognized in a moment the presence, the incorporeal song, of a wraith, a wailing wight.

She rose, unsteady on her feet. Darkness pressed around her on all sides. Why could she not see the stars?

Despair and darkness pressed in on her mind. For a moment she wondered why. Since she had bound the Starweave about her head the presence of wraiths and other nightmare creatures had affected her almost not at all. Had it slipped loose?

No. Tara-lin knew at once it was still there. Why could she not see?

Fear swept over her. She groped her way along the cavern towards the entrance.

She must keep the wailing wight from Keller. There was no way he could fight it.

Tara-lin sank to her knees and clutched her temple. Misery. Sheer misery. Her head throbbed as if pierced with a thousand icy knives. She tried to scream in agony, but her cry was muffled and floated away on a frozen breeze.

Again she felt the embrace of darkness, of evil so pure it no longer knew any good, anything at all, to hate or fear. With a last, failing thought, Tara-lin wondered why the Starweave no longer protected her. Why had Shallim-Araldor, why had all that of which Alai-ie-a sang and the dryads spoke, forsaken her?

The void reached out for her soul. The pain in her head grew and enveloped her entire body and maybe more.

There was no way she could stop the wraith from reaching Keller. Even her body in the way would not stop it. It could simply float around her or over her, maybe even through her.

Tara-lin could not even scream in the extremity of her torture. Her mind withered before the pain, as her entire being cried out against the touch and embrace of the cold wight. At the same time, she fled from the torment.

There was no bliss behind it. Despair. Blackest despair. Nothing at all. There was nothing, good *or* evil to hate. There was no threat or change to fear. There was no hope of which to despair.

Coldness. Numb. Painless. Pain without any comfort or pleasure or rest against which to be torture. Darkness without any light without which to be dark. Hate without any love against which to be hate. Despair without any hope against which to be despair. Evil without any good against which to be evil. Void, nothingness, without any*thing* against which not to be.

The torture did not pass from her mind and body. Tara-lin tried to cry out, but she could not do so. Slowly, as if her body were made of ice, she fell to the ground, but she could not move. The agony gripped her like a vice.

Darkness passed over her.

No!

The word rang in her mind like one triumphal trumpet.

This is death. This is the death worthy of fear. Nothing else.

But I should not fear?

This is not death.

Tara-lin rose to her knees. She almost fell again from the increased intensity of torment. A thought floated before her in the darkness, the emptiness, the nothingness, a single glimmer of light.

In the darkness, a shining green plant, not two inches tall, sporting one radiant, vibrant leaf. The darkness around it pulsed with song and became an aura of light.

Light. Life. Hope. Joy. Rest.

Tara-lin formed one single word and let it out on a soft, high note, the first beginning of a song.

The void swam around her. Waves of darkness, shadow, fear. Abandonment. Where was anything?

The light was still before her, the radiant seedling. It stabilized the void in her mind, provided something steady amidst the dizzying torture of cold and of evil that made such a whirl-storm of her mind. Almost her mind withered from the evil, but she grasped the song again. She focused on the image. *Life.*

As Tara-lin sang, the pain receded. Back and forth it surged, like the waves on the sea, sometimes dragging her under yet again, almost drowning her. Somehow, she held on. *Life. I want to live. Love. Happiness. Alai-ie-a.*

It must not get to Keller!

Tara-lin recognized now an opposing song. The wraith struggled. It was a struggle, so much a struggle it did not know it, so much was it in torment. She did not pity now, not exactly. Pity and hate were one. It must go. It must not come closer. It must be bound. Its being – its non-being – fought her song with what little remained of its existence. This wraith of song was powerful, and almost Tara-lin felt it overpower her and her song.

She was standing now, fighting the shadow in the very mouth of the cave.

You will not kill.
Death is not what you are.
Life will endure.
We will live.
The seedling sprouts after the ice of winter thaws.
The tree leafs up as the snow melts once again.
The seed is cut off from the tree.
It passes through a bird or falls into the earth.
It withers, is scoured and frozen.
It sprouts, sends out roots and a tiny leaf.
It was not quite alive when it hung from the tree.
It seemed dead later.
Now it is alive.
It will live and live and live.
It will pass through the dry heat of summer.
It will pass through the bare cold nights and the frozen storms of winter.
It will grow and live and rejoice in the life of the sun.
We are with it.
Why are you not with it?
Go!
Let go and live!
Let go!
Pass into life and abundance of life.

We are seeds.
Life beckons us.
Spring beyond the cold of winter.
The air and the sun after the darkness and confines of the beast's belly.

Life, sap running through us, growth, after the shriveling and drying and falling from the branch of life.

"You *must fight and overcome, yourself.*"

Tara-lin breathed a deep sigh. She did not know if the shade was gone for good or for a time.

She swayed for a moment, not knowing what she had done. Then, realizing that an ice-wraith had found them, that she had barely lived through the battle – her whole body was only now beginning to shake and burning pain of coldness, of limbs awakening out of its icy vice, shot through her body. She wanted to wail from the pain. Instead she called, "Awake! Get up! We must go!"

"It's still dark, Tara-lin," said Cuthlin. "What are you doing awake?"

"Are you really telling me you didn't notice what just happened over your head?" asked Tara-lin. She stomped, then winced and cried out softly from the pain in her cold foot and legs.

"I was awake. To be sure, it is very icy, and I cannot describe the feel. It is as if a storm is coming, and it was hard not to sleep. But I am alert. Fearing that my uneasiness might have something to do with the approach of a nightmare creature, I unsheathed my sword and stood ready."

"Yeah, there you are!" said Tara-lin, noticing him now, standing before the opening. "I fought an ice-wraith right over your head."

"It seems," said her father's voice behind her, "that wailing wights may not be as rare as we thought. For the most part, their presence seems to be only fully felt by those with elven blood. But, Tara-lin, are you sure we should go now and not wait for the dawn? Darkness is the time when the nightmare creatures fight best and we fight worst."

"A wailing wight found us. It may have called to the nightmares and summoned more horrors. They will come and trap us. We must be gone!" said Tara-lin. She only barely remembered not to stamp for emphasis again. Her eyes watered from the pain.

She wanted to cry. She felt no triumph, only an anguish and horror of some unfathomable not-quite-remembered wrong and an unknown depth of something she could only identify as loneliness.

Keller woke when the men went to pick him up.

"Sshh!" said Tara-lin as he began yelling. "We're taking you to a good place. Be nice and come along quietly."

She was sobbing as they made their way down the incline. "What is wrong?" Eldor asked her quietly, putting his arm around her.

"I – I don't know. It's awful. I felt like I was going to be taken again. It's..." Her voice trailed away.

"Well, you're safe now," said Eldor, squeezing her gently.

"Not until we're out of these accursed mountains," said Tara-lin, her words punctuated by sobs.

"No cry, Mommy not cry!" said Keller. "Or is he going to do bad thing to you? Is he going to do bad thing to me?"

"No, no, Keller," said Tara-lin. "No one is going to do bad thing to me or to you. These men here are all nice. And I'm not your mom."

"Who are you then?" asked Keller.

"Nice woman. Not Mom," said Tara-lin. "Call me Tara-lin."

"Nice woman!" said Keller.

Soft laugher passed through the group.

Half an hour later, Tara-lin was thinking that Keller was an inferior woodsman to even Alis, even though he had the dryad blood in him. Then she thought, *But what do you expect of someone who never saw the sunlight and grew up in Nightshade?*

In one clearing, he stopped. "Those are... stars?" he asked, pointing to the eastern portion of the sky. The rest of it was dark, covered with clouds.

"Yes, Keller, those are stars," said Tara-lin. "Now, be quiet and stop talking. Bad things can find us more easily if we talk too much. We're running away from the bad things and they want to find us."

"We're running away from the bad things? Finally!"

"Yes, we're finally running away from the bad things," said Eldor and Tara-lin together. "Now sshh."

The dryads sang around her, Tara-lin realized. They sang of life, of light, of rest, of calm – of sanity. She hoped they would be able to help Keller. She just wanted to run away... At least, the song of the dryads comforted her, as well.

Dawn found them climbing up out of the valley. As the sun rose over the mountains, Keller stopped and looked around. Wild delight was evident on his features. He raised his arms to the orb of light, its rays splashing over and around the mountains with abundant glory, and cried out in a voice of sheer and unbelieved pleasure, "The sun! The *day!*" He sounded as if he were near tears.

The day, thought Tara-lin. *I never knew what that meant until I'd been into and out of Nightshade. The day. The dawn. What must it mean to him? How long has it been since he's seen the light – except for that little bit in the cave when he woke up frightened and hungry?*

"We must keep going," said Namdon, after Keller had admired the rising sun for a minute.

Just then, Keller ducked his head and keened. "It hurts my eyes!"

"The sun will do that if you look straight at it," said Tara-lin. "Let's go."

"I don't want to! It's so bright. I like the light! But it's too bright to look at. It hurts my eyes. Why?" asked Keller.

"Even I can't look straight at the sun," said Tara-lin. "Come. We can talk about the sun when we get further away from here. The bad things are still just down there." She pointed.

Apparently he understood. He took off running in the opposite direction of Nightshade Castle.

He seems a lot saner than he did a day or two ago, thought Tara-lin.

They followed after him, wishing he went slower. Nonetheless, they knew they would find him very quickly. He made a great deal of noise tearing across the ground. He was no woodsman and they could hear, almost see, his motion. He was only barely out of sight. He would also tire very quickly. On the trek here, he had moaned regularly about how tired he was. Apparently, he understood what the Nightshade Castle was, for it inspired fresh terror and energy in him. He was most motivated to get as far away from it as possible.

They caught up with him, but he still led, despite his lack of skill. Several times, Tara-lin had to direct him to go in a different direction than he was inclined. "No," she said. "*That's* the way away from Nightshade."

On the top of one ridge, he stopped and looked around. "I still see it, the horrible thing!" said Keller. "The prison, the dungeon!"

Tara-lin nodded. "We will have to go farther," said Eldor. "We can make it. We know the way."

Keller stood for a moment, as if lost in deep thought. Then he said, "No, we've been doing this all wrong. We have to go towards the sun."

The first snowflake fluttered down and settled on Tara-lin's arm. "That won't work," she said. "The sun moves across the sky, and we can't get into the sky. We have to go that way." She pointed again.

Keller looked confused. "But the sun..." he began.

"We didn't always live in this valley," said Eldor. "Where we used to live, you can never see Nightshade Castle. Come with us. We know the way."

"We really do," said Tara-lin, but her words were cut short by alarm. Out of the clouds between them and Nightshade Castle dropped a battalion of winged creatures.

"We have to go, Keller. *Now,*" said Namdon. He grabbed the man's arm and began pulling him along. "Is there anything you can do, Tara-lin?" he asked, as Keller screamed and yelled things Tara-lin didn't understand.

"I suppose," she muttered, following her comrades down the ridge and across to the next, her eyes trained behind her on the pursuit. She saw now that it had distinct portions. One wing of the flying army was composed of gryphons, and the other of the dreadful vampires.

At least we have the day, she thought. *Vampires are said to hate day, possibly like none of the other nightmares.*

Then she saw the storm. It was still rolling towards the east and descending. The sun was moving towards the west. They would meet shortly. Even with the day, she had no idea how to fight so many vampires... and gryphons! There had to be a way to convince the gryphons to turn against the vampires...

A few more snowflakes settled on her cloak. *The storm,* Tara-lin thought. Could she do something with the storm? It was certainly ripe to turn into a monstrous wind from the look of it. Such a wind would batter the wing-borne creatures to bits, possibly killing most of them, but Tara-lin did not really want to kill gryphons. Furthermore, it might result in a blizzard down here. She did not know if they could survive a blizzard, and they certainly could not travel through one.

Tara-lin looked ahead and realized she had fallen behind. She ran to catch up. Just as she did so, she heard Eldor moan, "No! We're surrounded. Tara-lin, is there anything you can do?"

"Where?" Tara-lin asked.

Cuthlin was pointing. A flight of gryphons was coming in over a gap in the southern mountains towards which they were making.

With her elven sight, Tara-lin descried a rider on one of the gryphon's backs. She stood, watching intently for a moment. *It can't be,* she thought. *It must be illusion.* Then, *It's our only hope. It's the direction we need to go, and it's a smaller force than the one coming at us from the other way.*

Should I call the storm down on us? Is that the best option? Hopefully, maybe, most of the gryphons will be able to get back to their eyres.

"Oh no!" cried Keller. "The sun is going to disappear. I told you, we need to go towards the sun!"

"No," said Tara-lin. "We go that way. I don't think those gryphons are against us. I know it's hard to believe."

She pushed her way forward, past the standing men, and began to lead. For a few minutes the gryphons ahead vanished from view, while the winged hordes behind continued to gain on them, though those were sometimes obscured by the fog coming down from the storm-clouds.

The snow fell harder and faster. "What's this white stuff? Is it good?" asked Keller.

"It's not bad, but it's cold. We don't like it," said Namdon.

Above the trees, Tara-lin saw the gryphons from the south growing rapidly nearer. She was certain now, as she strained to see. Her friend Alis sat astride that brown one with the golden mane! *How in the world?!* she wondered.

As Eldor came up beside her, she said, "It's Alis I see riding that gryphon. How likely is it to be an illusion?"

"Illusions do happen," said Eldor. "I really don't know. It would be unheard of..."

"I'm trying to ask the dryads, but they aren't responding to me. I don't know if they hear me," said Tara-lin. "We keep going, though."

"No!" said Keller the very same moment that the light of the sun vanished from the valley, obscured by the storm. "We need the sun!"

"We need to get *out*," said Tara-lin. "Let's hope the storm-winds slow our pursuers down but don't make it harder for us to get out." Panting as she climbed, she called down to him, "You can't see the sun right now, but it's still day. Look how light everything around us still is." She noticed even as she spoke that it was darkening by the minute. This storm could get very dark.

It wouldn't turn into a blizzard even without her intervention, would it?

Tara-lin sang as she climbed, hoping her song would be enough to tilt the weight of the storm.

Calm around us, away from us
Fly with your winds and fierceness
Down in the valley a whirl of storm
Cloud and wind and power of storm
Whirl around in the valley low

Tara-lin stopped, realizing she did not know what to sing or what she was doing. How would she keep a storm quiet on the hillside she was climbing up but feed the fierceness into it over *there,* behind and above her?

She thought maybe she could do it if she could stand still and give all her attention to the song, maybe close her eyes and hum to the storm. She could not do it while hiking and plotting the best course to the next ridge.

They weren't at the ridgeline, but the trees opened out ahead of her. She could see the gryphons drawing rapidly nearer again. She stepped forward and waved, trying to catch Alis' attention. The others filed up and stood behind her. "What are you doing?" asked Eldor.

"We wait here for the gryphons," said Tara-lin. "Don't speak to me until they land." She closed her eyes and hummed. She felt the air vibrate in tune to her hum. Slowly, she adjusted it, reaching out to feel the storm. With a tingling sensation that ran through her whole body, she realized she experienced something not unlike what Beriririkirkirkitira spoke of, about knowing what other dryads on other continents knew. She reached out and gathered some idea of the storm through the knowledge of all the reviving dryads throughout the massive Icecrown Vale. She returned her attention to the song.

"It's getting darker! We need to find the sun and go to him!" said Keller. His voice barely disrupted her concentration.

Tara-lin did not need her father to tell her when the gryphons landed. She felt their large bodies and the wind generated by their massive wings. She turned and opened her eyes as they landed. "Alis!" she cried, seeing her human friend dismount. So many emotions clashed on Alis' face, pride, pleasure, concern, excitement, the desire to share, curiosity, worry, fear. "Tara-lin!" she cried in response. "I've come!"

"I can see that," said Tara-lin. "No time to explain now." She pointed towards the approaching horde.

"I can tell," said Alis.

"Explain to Keller that he needs to get on one of these beasts and cling to his mane, and that's how we're going to find the sun," said Tara-lin.

"You're as good at explaining things to him as any of us," said Cuthlin.

"It's okay," said Keller. "I heard. The beasts will fly us to the sun where he's hidden behind the clouds."

Not exactly, thought Tara-lin.

"What's going on with him?" asked Alis. "He's a grown man but talks like a baby."

"As I said, explanations later," said Tara-lin. "Which gryphon should he ride? By the way, he's a half-elf."

Alis stood for a moment with a thoughtful expression on her face. "That one," she said, pointing to a dark brown gryphon with a mane just as dark.

A few moments later, Tara-lin looked up at Keller, seated on the gryphon's back. "As I said, remember to hold tight. Grip with your legs. Hold tight!"

Keller nodded, but she was not sure if he understood.

A moment later, Tara-lin was seated on the back of another gryphon. She leaned forward and crooned into the beast's ears. Then a thought struck her. "Alis!"

"Yes?"

"Can you tell the gryphons behind us not to pursue us? That we're not enemies? That they should go home to their eyres and care for their young? That they have no friendship with vampires?"

"You don't need to go on," said Alis. "I'll try."

A moment later, they were airborne. Six gryphons bore riders, and around them flew four more who were riderless. Not, thought Tara-lin, that they were riders exactly, except perhaps for Alis. The rest of them were passengers.

The gryphons carried them rapidly. Tara-lin was almost certain Alis had asked them to fly as hard as they could. The cold wind rushed past her. Snowflakes melted against her face. She shivered and tried to dig deeper into the gryphon's mane. Her feet hurt, and she tried to dig them into the beast's fur. Her hood came loose, and she was afraid to put up her hand to pull it back over her head.

Tara-lin risked a glance behind her, and saw the vampires rushing down out of the storm. She did not see any gryphons...

She re-connected with that sense she had through all the dryads, and sang, hoping to thicken the storm around the vampires, but to provide the gryphons with a favorable wind. She did not know if she could do it, but she must try.

Lightning flashed through the clouds. Tara-lin did not think it had anything to do with her song, but she adjusted slightly, hoping to guide the lightning.

The gryphons crested the ridge. Looking ahead, Tara-lin could see the Northridge Plain spread out before her and the beginning of the Malaitha Mountains. Far out upon the plains she could see the light of the sun gleaming on grass, on fields ripening for harvest, on orchards and farm-steads. Looking behind, she got a glimpse of the huge storm rolling in from the northeast.

An idea came to her. She took up her song again, singing to the air and the storm. If only she could do with the storm something like what she had done with the sound around their cave only, instead of muffling sound, she now meant to increase the turbulence of the wind!

Tara-lin only hoped this would not harm the dryads left in Icecrown. If she succeeded, it would be one massive storm back there...

She would try to focus the turbulence high in the air, to keep the winds on the ground relatively quiet and smooth.

For a moment, Tara-lin saw the sun behind and above the storm. She saw Keller wave one hand in the sky and heard him exclaim something. She *thought* she caught the word 'sun'.

She yelled back to him without taking *her* hands out of the great beast's mane. "Hold on with both hands!" Then she closed her eyes and focused on the enchanting song.

Chapter Twenty-Five – Gryphon-Rider and Dryad-Brood

A few of the vampires got through. Half an hour later, the gryphons were engaged in an aerial combat, their passengers clinging to and gripping them as hard as they could, as the gryphons wheeled and dropped, banked and dove, and jerked a great deal. Even though the four who bore neither human nor half-elf tried to fight the vampires before they could get to the burdened gryphons, and to keep them away from the same, all the gryphons had to fight a little.

Several times in the battle, Tara-lin thought about drawing her elf-sword. Each time she thought better of it. She was not even sure how to draw it from its sheath without at least risking falling off in the chaos. If she *did* manage to get it out without falling to her death, she probably could not avoid hurting or killing the very gryphon on which she rode with it. Better to let the gryphons fight as well as they could, unassisted.

Then the last of the vampires were gone, and they continued their flight.

By evening, Tara-lin could tell that the gryphons were tired. Their wings beat slower and sometimes a little unsteadily. She crooned encouragement and gratitude to the beautiful beast who bore her.

The gryphons circled down and landed on the very edge of the foothills of the Malaitha Mountains. It was night, some hours after sunset.

Tara-lin dismounted and stumbled as she hit the ground. Her legs ached. She could hear Keller crying and sobbing. "The sun is gone!" he moaned.

"The sun will be back," Alis assured him.

When everyone was dismounted, Tara-lin saw Alis go round to each of the gryphons and perform some sort of ritual with them, which ended in her giving the gryphon a hug, and the weary gryphon flying away.

"Do they still have enough strength left to reach their eyres tonight?" asked Tara-lin.

"They could if they had to," said Alis. "Some of them are flying back to the eyre, which was left in the charge of a pair of old gryphons. Others of them will roost for the night on rocks and cliffs on top of hills, which are closer than the eyre, then hunt and fly home tomorrow."

"How did you do it?" asked Tara-lin.

"To be honest, I don't really know," said Alis. "I climbed up the mountains. In some places, it was rather precarious. I climbed into one of their caves. It was unattended at the moment, but I could guess it was a gryphon cave from its contents. There was an egg in there, which I sat down next to and put my arm over. I must have fallen asleep, since, next thing I knew, there was a gryphon chick, or a gryphonet, or a gryphling, or whatever you call the thing. Soon, I discovered that the gryphon flight had left the egg just the day prior, since it was way past its hatching date, but apparently it was just a late hatcher. After that, I discovered that I can speak to and hear the gryphons. That's pretty much how it happened."

"That's wonderful, just wonderful!" said Tara-lin. "You're a gryphon rider now, Alis!"

Alis smiled. "Yes, I am. The first human girl gryphon rider ever? Maybe? Anyway," she said, yawning, "I'm hungry, and far from the dryads who were housing me."

"I think we still have some left-overs," said Tara-lin.

"That we do," said Cuthlin.

A few moments later, they passed the water-skin between them. When Alis saw the food, she almost jumped in the air. "More meat?" she asked. "I always feel starved for meat!"

"Can you not convince the gryphons to hunt for you, when you could convince them to fly into Icecrown?" asked Tara-lin.

"I couldn't *cook* it, if they *did* hunt for me," said Alis.

"Oh, I'd forgotten," said Tara-lin. "I am tired."

Keller's sobs about the vanished sun and day ceased as soon as he had his hands and mouth full of boiled connie.

"Couldn't you ask one of the dryads to take us in for the night?" asked Alis.

"I don't know," said Tara-lin. "I'm sure they'll offer us some protection, some shielding against discovery, but I doubt they'll reveal themselves or want to bring us food. They tend not to like being seen by too many people."

"Oh," said Alis.

"Don't you need to see your gryphling?" asked Tara-lin.

"I'll go see him tomorrow. I can talk to him from here without any difficulty at all. He misses having me next to him, but the other gryphons will keep him warm for me." She yawned again. "You know, I think I really should finish this and go to sleep."

A few minutes later, Tara-lin rose on shaky legs. She sought out a nearby clump of trees and, entering deep into their darkness, requested an audience with their dryads, assuring them the humans could not see or hear them in here. When they appeared, she could barely see them. "I don't ask you to show yourselves to my friends," said Tara-lin, "but can you provide us protection against discovery?"

"As much as it lays in our power to do this," said a tall female dryad, the one most visible to Tara-lin, since her skin was pale and her hair and covering was a very pale, almost glowing, green. "You know we cannot always guarantee this?"

"I know it is not a certain guarantee, but that there is very little which will simply wander through the magic of so many dryads," said Tara-lin, curtsying. "Thank you."

The dryads all expressed their agreement.

Tara-lin went to the edges of the thicket and called her comrades to come in.

Alis came last. She looked around, then said, "I don't want to sleep so near to so many men."

"Is it the number of men that bothers you?" asked Tara-lin.

"No... What kind of a stupid attempt at humor is that?... Well, is there anything you can do?"

"Yes," said Tara-lin. "Follow me."

Yawning again, Alis followed. "You know," she said, "I'm going to get hurt stumbling around on these branches. It's so dark. Can't you hear what's going on where the men went?"

"Yes, I can. Sorry, Alis." Tara-lin stopped to pull out her sword. "Is this better?"

"Barely. Go slowly."

"It's really not that bad," said Tara-lin. "The dryads are trying to welcome us. But I wouldn't want you to trip anyways."

"Where are we going? What are we doing?" asked Alis.

"Just over here, this way, a little," said Tara-lin. "We're so close to civilized regions, I don't want to leave the thicket. I know we used to sleep under individual trees – usually it was more like a copse, during the day – but circumstances are such I'd rather not do even that right now. Not with all of us here, certainly."

"Why? What happened? All those Valor Knights with you – none of them are going to try to take me back, right? There's more than just your father," said Alis.

"No, none of them will kidnap you or take you back. However, the Valor Hall might execute *them.*"

"Why? For harboring me?" Alis' voice was full of the fear and concern Tara-lin had previously known her to exhibit.

"I don't know if harboring you would be crime enough under the code of the Valor Hall, but, no. Quite apart from you," answered Tara-lin. "Here."

She placed her hands on the trunk of the tree. "Nyi-availa!" said Tara-lin softly. "It's just me and my friend Alis here right now. Can you provide us some privacy and a good place to sleep? The men are our friends, but Alis and I are women, and they are men."

"What does that have to do with anything?" asked Nyi-availa. Her pale skin and leaves shone a strange color in the light of Tara-lin's sword.

"Human things," said Tara-lin.

"Very well," said the pale dryad. "I can't claim to understand such things, but very well. You may not have fully succeeded, but you have done well, and you have helped us. Our kin in Icecrown even now strengthen themselves."

"Is it not too late in the year, with the winter coming on?" asked Tara-lin. The thicket around her rustled.

"No. Any deciduous dryads who were on the brink of death will simply retreat with their trees into the roots and come back next year. It's perfect for them. I don't know about the evergreens so much, but I don't think it will hurt them. Anyway, there you go."

"Thank you," said Tara-lin. She sheathed her sword and lay down. For a moment Nyi-availa remained, a splash of light in the utter darkness, then she vanished.

"What did you do while you were in Icecrown with those men?" asked Alis.

"I don't really know," said Tara-lin. "One of them always stood watch. Speaking of which, let me go and tell them they don't have to put up a watch tonight. The dryads will do as well as they could, and will certainly be able to wake me if there is need!"

When Tara-lin returned a moment later, Alis, yawning, repeated her question.

"I told you, there was always a watch. Does that count for nothing? And Sir Eldor is my father. I think that counts for something.

Also, I'm half-elf," said Tara-lin.

"What does that have to do with anything?" Alis' words were slurred by sleepiness.

Tara-lin shrugged. "I'm a singer, too."

"And what does *that* have to do with it, either?" asked Alis.

"Don't worry, Alis. I haven't done anything. It may not have been the best situation, but it's over now, and it was necessary."

"Oh, I wouldn't care if you *had* done anything," said Alis. "Just wait until I tell you..."

All right. She's gone to sleep now, so I can, too, thought Tara-lin. She lay down. *What has got into Alis? Even I am disgusted by that idea. How has she suddenly ceased to be?* So wondering, she fell asleep.

The world swam around in her slow, rhythmic undulations, waves of something Tara-lin could only think of as light, predominantly of deep green color, but there were too many colors – they were not all green, though they seemed all to be out of or within green. No, not really green. She just associated it most closely with green light. It throbbed gently but with a strong pulse that seemed as if it must come out of the heart of some giant – some giant whose heart was as large as the earth, whose heart *was* the earth.

A voice, a signature, something like a voice. She thought it came to her through Nyi-availa, but it bore the signature of many more, perhaps the consensus of the dryadic race.

We have named you Dryad-Friend, Tara-lin. As Dryad-Friend, you know many of our secrets, but we require that you not share them with others in whom flows the blood of men. You are as one of us, though not as one of us, Singer and Dryad-Brood.

Tara-lin acknowledged the pronouncement. She sensed her own ripple, or wave, or undulation of its own unique color, go out, merging with the rest of that world. Her consciousness departed that mode of perception.

In the early hours of the dawn, Tara-lin found herself in a state between waking and sleeping. She was not fully awake, but she thought coherently. Why herself? Why should she be invited into the world of the dryads? Why herself and not another? She was rather confident that among the secrets she was bound to keep was that which she had fully realized only yesterday – that she could feel the world through other dryads. For whatever reason, they did not want men and elves to know that they were not separated by space and continents as were men and elves. The extremity of the difference between dryads and men began to dawn on her. Their very methods of communication and relationship were different, and, as yet, Tara-lin had scarcely even begun to perceive the subtleties of this mode. She did not think she was required to keep secret any word of Shallim-Araldor, despite the dryads' reluctance to share it with even her. After all, all Alai-ie-a wanted to do was share her own dream or song with the children of men. Shallim-Araldor was not so much a *secret* of the dryads, as some knowledge they had, albeit in various ways and to various degrees, and which, by general consensus, they *tended* to think was better not told.

Tara-lin's mind returned to the question of, *Why me?* Why should she, among all the children of men, be welcomed into the world of dryads? Then again, there were humans, and there were dryads. So why not her? She had a strange feeling... that as the children of dryads could walk the earth as men, perhaps the children of men could also enter into the dryad world? Was there a dryad equivalent to the elves? But, why should she get to live in both worlds, to walk the earth as a human, and also to sing with it as a dryad?

Unless... what if she lived between worlds? What if there was as much in the world of men that lay beyond her comprehension and touch as there was in the world of dryads still beyond her comprehension and touch?

Tara-lin knew that the wailing wights had no power over the dryads such as they had over the elves. It seemed that the wailing wights were the peculiar bane of her race, though she had the impression that elves tended to be less affected than full humans by many of the nightmare races.

Alis' voice rang above her. "The dryads *did* bring us their food!"

Tara-lin opened her eyes to see her stouter friend examining the contents of a large, slightly curved, piece of bark. It was almost a platter.

"Did I wake you up?" asked Alis, seeing Tara-lin stir.

"I don't know," said Tara-lin. She sat up and helped herself to the food the dryad had brought. "You know I really should check and make sure my father and his friends – and Keller – have food, too, but let me ask you this: what has changed, Alis? You, and your views, seem to have changed a great deal in the last week."

"It really has been about a week, hasn't it?" asked Alis. "Well, I – I've met Shallim-Araldor, kind of. I can't really talk about it, very much, but I *know* now that our religion is false, our gods are no gods. Men and women are alike before Shallim-Araldor." She laughed lightly. "None of us are much. But he sustains the world and all that lives within it. At any rate, now I shall *never* worry again about being cast into the netherhells because I wanted to think and choose for my own self. But that seems the least important part of it now..."

"What did you mean when you said you didn't care what I'd done with men?" asked Tara-lin.

"Oh, that!" said Alis. "Did I offend you?"

"I'm – I mean, no, it's just strange. *I* am disgusted by the idea," said Tara-lin.

"Well, it's not like... not like it's my business to pry into other people's affairs," said Alis. "It's not like I'm... Shallim-Araldor. It's just... You've got to take up what you think, what you want, whatever you think is right or wrong, yourself. I'm not... You're not me. Your body isn't my body. You were friends with me back when I was almost crying about how afraid I was that I'd go to hell for running away." She shrugged. "And I still don't want to have anything to do with men – in any way that has anything to do with marriage or stuff like that – at all, either way. But, really, I didn't say that because I've changed... because I've met Shallim-Araldor. I said that because... I would've said that when we were first getting to know each other, Tara-lin. Many of my people think that if people do certain things, they should be slain or otherwise punished – that it is the duty of the temples, the brothers and the sisters, to see to it that they are made to suffer. *Justly*, they say. I don't. I never have. I'm a rebel, myself, after all, right?" Here she laughed again. "So, *of course*, I said that. It just means I'm not siding with..."

"You don't need to go on," said Tara-lin. "It just means you wouldn't think anyone should *do* anything to me if I had."

"Pretty much," said Alis. "It only means what I *don't* think. It doesn't mean anything about what I *do* think. Now, go and check on the men if you're going to!"

Tara-lin rose.

Once she left the bower Nyi-availa had made for herself and Alis, she heard clearly the voices of the men, talking while they ate.

Namdon was saying, "Look, we went into Icecrown because Tara-lin wanted to. If she doesn't anymore, what more have we to do with this crazy mission given out in order to *kill* us?"

"More to the point," said Cuthlin, "where are we going to go now? There's always Elethri, but technically Elethri is part of the

Alliance. I don't think they would offer safe haven to Valor Knights-turned-traitors, and it's hard to just disappear and blend into... Eldor, how many humans are there in Elethri? Would it be possible to blend in?"

"No." Eldor's tone of voice was dry and weary. "I was a real oddity. I'm not the only human to take up living in Elethri for a time. Some want to learn the wood lore of the elves or come for some other reason, and some of these fall in love with the woods and nature or the animals and stay there. I'd say, at any given time, there are less than a hundred humans living throughout the length and breadth of Elethri, more if you count tourists and others just passing through."

He noticed Tara-lin. "Hey!" He waved. "Come on over. How are you and Alis?"

"Alis is eating," said Tara-lin. "I just came to be sure you had plenty of food, because otherwise we would share."

Keller, who had been staring at his food and slowly eating, looked up at her. He looked pitiful, dejected, morose. "This is strange," he said. "You're all strange."

"That's true," said Tara-lin. "We're strangers. We don't know you, and you don't know us. But look around. The sun is risen. I told you it would come back."

"I wish the sun stayed always," said Keller.

"I gather you've heard our discussion?" Tara-lin's father asked her.

"The last minute of it," said Tara-lin. "Basically, we're fugitives now, all of us, since Alis ran away from her parents, and I helped her, and, what else? Oh yes, and you've all decided that the Valor Hall is corrupt and you can't be part of it anymore, so you have to leave."

"Do we?" asked Cuthlin. "Couldn't we say our companions were lost, and we tried to look for them, but it was paramount we get into Nightshade Castle and find out what we were sent to find, and do what we could?"

"And what?" asked Sir Namdon. "They'll only try to kill us again. Remember: they were already looking for a way to kill us. That's why this whole mission happened in the first place. They'll find out Alis' 'kidnapper' is Tara-lin, Sir Eldor's daughter, and it was she who got us into Icecrown, and they'll have our heads. Sooner or later, one way or another, we'll all be dead."

"Speaking of that," said Tara-lin, "we're not too far away from where we departed from – where I sang the traitors to sleep. Shouldn't we do something about it?"

"Isn't it confusing? Who's the traitor? Did we betray the Valor Hall, or did the Valor Hall betray us? It makes it hard to know what one is talking about!" Namdon asked. On a more serious note, he answered, "These mountains are pretty big. We're not actually that close to the spot. There're no trails to this place, and they probably won't be looking for us anyways. In fact, moving around might endanger us more than staying for the moment? Shouldn't they have woken up by now?"

Tara-lin shrugged. "I lose track of the days. I couldn't imagine my song lasting more than a week. Alis thinks it's been about that long."

"It's been exactly a week, if my memory serves me right," said Namdon.

"Anyway," said Tara-lin, "aren't there some southern nations that aren't part of the Alliance?"

"Yes," asked Cuthlin, looking at her intently. "What are you thinking?"

"Couldn't we go south and hide there?" asked Tara-lin.

"We've discussed that, and we're not too thrilled with that idea," said Namdon. "Any of the southern nations which would welcome fugitive Valor Knights would probably want to involve us with their own politics and spy networks and that whole mess. As for *hiding,* how do you hide an elf and a half-elf? You might pass for human on a cursory inspection, but you won't pass for human long."

"Her mother certainly wouldn't," interjected Eldor.

"Furthermore, we'd be different enough to attract attention down there. Most of the southern people are darker than any of us," finished Namdon.

"Well, we don't have to decide right now," said Tara-lin, "and we have to find Mom and let her know what's going on, too. But, why don't we see if Alis can convince the gryphons to take us in?"

"You'd think you'd be suggesting that *you* ask the dryads to take us in," said Namdon.

"I told you already, dryads don't like lots of people. I think in part it's too much noise for them and, in part, they don't fully trust humans. At any rate, remember when that one didn't want to be seen while he made the cloaks for all of you?" asked Tara-lin.

"They ought to be able to understand our need," said Eldor.

"I think it's not in their way to interfere in human society very often or much," said Tara-lin. "But I suppose I can ask. I can ask if there's a secluded valley or portion of mountains or something somewhere where we can go, that they can put their magic around to deter others from finding or entering. It's not like we need them to interact with or feed us." She rose. "As I said, this doesn't have to be decided today, does it? And I should go see Alis again and eat."

"Enjoy!" said Eldor, waving her away.

Meanwhile, Keller just sat staring off into nothing.

When Tara-lin stepped through the branches, Alis looked up. "I thought you were never going to come back."

"Is there still food left?"

"Yes," said Alis. "I'm pretty hungry myself, but I figured you were hungry, too."

"I am," said Tara-lin, sitting down.

After Tara-lin helped herself to some food, Alis asked, "So, what is it with that man, Keller?"

"He's a half-elf, actually. I don't know what his past is. He's the brother of Prince Anakrim and, as you could tell, he's kind of crazy. He's actually acting less crazy than he was when we first found him."

"Really?" asked Alis.

"Oh yeah." Tara-lin told her about it.

"That's... that's horrid," said Alis.

"Not as horrid as ice-wraiths or wailing wights," said Tara-lin.

Alis raised her eyebrows.

"I don't want to talk about it."

"All right," said Alis. "Makya and Vonë are still with some dryads who promised to take care of them for me, and I'd really like to see Kushon today."

"Kushon?" asked Tara-lin.

"That's the name I gave my gryphling. He's so cute!" said Alis.

"I'd love to see him," said Tara-lin.

"Maybe I can convince the gryphons it's okay for me to take you with me. After all, he's the only young one at the moment."

"It's pretty amazing that one hatched this time of year at all," said Tara-lin. "I'm surprised."

"Maybe Shallim-Araldor arranged that just for me?" asked Alis.

"You think so?" asked Tara-lin.

Alis shrugged.

"Or it could have been his Ellenari, I suppose," said Tara-lin.

"Same difference to me," said Alis. "*Someone* told me to persuade the gryphons to go with me into Icecrown to rescue you. If someone did that, why not arrange the circumstance that allowed me to even speak to gryphons?"

"I guess. Anyway, remember when you told me it seemed I was good at everything and you were good at nothing?"

"Yes?" asked Alis.

"You found a gryphling and you can talk to gryphons!"

Alis smiled. "Yes, I can. It's wonderful. I really love Kushon, and he misses me so much. I've got to get up there today, but it is *such* a climb."

"I can imagine," said Tara-lin.

Chapter Twenty-Six - Getting Alis' Gryphon

Half an hour later, they gathered together in the thicket. "Couldn't you ask some gryphons to carry us up?" asked Cuthlin. "Then, we'd be farther into the mountains, farther away from people, farther away from our ex-comrades. Wouldn't one of the gryphons gladly come and take you up to your gryphling, anyway?"

"It's bad enough I have to ask them to feed him, when you see it from a gryphon's perspective," said Alis. "Not that they mind feeding him. But they're exhausted. Can you imagine what I asked them to do yesterday? What that looks like from a gryphon's point of view? And *I* do not want to ride a gryphon again today. Are you not sore?"

"She – you – rode twice as far as we did," said Eldor.

Alis nodded. "But, no, that is not an option, and I don't want to ask," she said. "If I ask for too much... they'll get tired of listening to me."

"I wonder how Anakrim does it," muttered Cuthlin.

"Sorcery. Witchcraft," said Tara-lin. "You'll notice the gryphons didn't have much commitment. As soon as Alis told them they should all go home, they were happy to do so. Maybe he threatened them?" she asked, turning towards Alis.

Alis shrugged. "Maybe. I don't know why you're all asking me?"

"Because you're the only one here who has bonded to a gryphon and, as far as we know, no one else has achieved what you can do – speaking to other gryphons you're not bonded to," said Tara-lin.

"You've done it," said Alis. "Apparently, Anakrim has, too."

"Not really," said Tara-lin. "I can sing to them and ask them to do things for me. I can't talk with them like you can. As for Anakrim, I'll figure he didn't speak to them at all. I'll figure he used that stolen power of his to... manipulate them, make them think it was their idea. Then, when you talked to them, that kind of woke them up, reminded them what sorts of things really are *their* idea."

"Anyway," said Alis, "I'm going up to see Kushon. I should start sooner rather than later. I invited Tara-lin to come with me."

"Then go ahead!" said Eldor. "The sooner you start the better. But will we be safe here?"

"I think so," said Tara-lin. "Keller's pretty sleepy. I'll figure the dryads are helping you with that. We'll go on when we come back down. If that's okay?" She looked around.

"I just don't know how we're going to take care of a gryphon," said Namdon.

"As long as we don't have to carry Keller, too, we can carry a gryphling," quipped Cuthlin.

"All right," said Eldor. "Go then! And come back as quickly as possible."

"Early afternoon, tomorrow," said Alis. "Maybe more like evening, since we'll have to take Kushon down with us." She turned to Tara-lin and flashed a shy but confident smile. "Come!"

The two young women had scarcely left the thicket before it began to drizzle. There was a slight breeze, and Alis asked Tara-lin, "Do you think it's going to storm?"

"I don't know what you mean," said Tara-lin. "I definitely think this is going to turn into heavy rain. It's going to be a rather uncomfortable, slippery climb. As for lightning and thunder, which would make this truly dangerous... I don't know."

Tara-lin was right. Within half an hour it was pouring. An hour after that, the ground was slick and rivulets were running here and there. Both girls were soon soaked. "Are you sure this is a good idea?" asked Tara-lin.

"I'm going, for sure," said Alis. "I need to see Kushon."

"Then I'll go with you," said Tara-lin.

"I'm glad of that," said Alis. "If this storm gets dangerous, I'm sure I'm safer with you, anyway."

"It's not as simple as that," said Tara-lin. "For one thing, up in those rocky heights, the dryads won't be with me to join their song with mine. For another, you have to sing *with* the world. You can't... no, it's too hard to explain. But, yes, I suppose your characterization *is* correct enough."

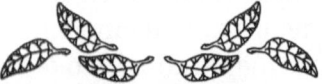

Late in the afternoon, they were making their way up a narrow ravine, when Tara-lin stopped.

"What is it?" asked Alis.

A moment later there was a flash of untold bright blue radiance through the blue mist and pouring rain. Thunder rumbled so loudly they put their hands over their ears, and the earth under their feet shook.

When the thunder faded away, Tara-lin said, "You sure this is a good idea, Alis?"

"I have to see Kushon," said Alis. "I'm not sure it's safer to go back, now that we've gone this far. This ravine takes us most of the way to the eyre."

"Okay," said Tara-lin. She was still very uncomfortable with this. "Are you sure?" she asked again.

Alis shrugged. "I'm going. I have to see Kushon."

"Can't you wait till tomorrow?"

"We can't get down before it's dark, anyways," said Alis.

"I can find a dryad and ask her – or him – to shelter us," said Tara-lin.

"You can go back and do that, if you want," said Alis. "I'm going."

"I shouldn't have asked to come with you," said Tara-lin. They continued forward.

The lightning did not strike close to them again, though they heard thunder several more times and saw lights flash in the sky. It grew very dark before they reached the gryphon eyre, and Tara-lin drew her sword to light the way for them.

They were scrambling up a steep incline on the side of the ravine. Suddenly, a rank of gryphons blocked their way. Low growls emanated from their throats and their eyes flashed back the light of the elf-sword. Their beaks and bared claws flashed with the same light. Tara-lin stood still, while Alis stepped forward. Tara-lin saw the gryphons acknowledge her, but they maintained their threatening stance. More gryphons threatened them from above.

Alis stepped forward again and stroked under the mane of one of the gryphons. She spoke softly, and, even in the pouring rain and the whistling, howling wind, Tara-lin caught most of her words. "I've just brought my friend to see Kushon. You shouldn't be afraid for him; you've been helping me, but he is, after all, my gryphling, and this is my eyre-mate."

After a little more coaxing, and after sniffing Tara-lin and licking her forehead once or twice, the gryphons allowed both girls to pass. Gratefully, Tara-lin sat down against the rough stone wall of their cave. Alis went in a little deeper and soon returned, a gryphling in her arms. The light was such that Tara-lin could not see him well, but she pet him and talked to him for a few minutes. Then she found a place comfortable enough to lay down and went to sleep. *This is strange,* she thought, as she closed her eyes. *Delightfully strange. Alis has found her... well, whatever it is she was looking for, I think. Her expertise. What she's good at and comfortable with. For the longest time, it seemed like I was the one who knew what I was doing and she was incompetent. Now... well, that situation isn't reversed, but she has discovered her competence... and more. She's discovered Shallim-Araldor. At any rate, she's much more herself, much more like what she was supposed to be, than when I met her.*

Alis stayed up longer, playing with her gryphling.

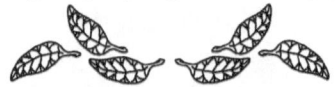

Tara-lin woke early in the morning. The light of day revealed Kushon's colors with clarity. He was a dark liver brown color, with wings of a slightly lighter, more chestnut, brown. He lay next to a sleeping Alis, one eye open.

Tara-lin woke Alis. While the girl rubbed her eyes, she said, "We have to start early if we're going to make it back tonight. I don't know how late it was when we finally got in here last night, but it was at least an hour past sunset."

Alis nodded. "It's farther from where we landed than I thought." She yawned. "I'm so tired."

"When did you go to sleep?" asked Tara-lin.

"I don't know."

They ate and drank what they had brought with them, then began their way down the mountain. Alis was stumbling over her own feet, and so Tara-lin had to carry Kushon most of the way. The gryphons attended them for the first several hours; they seemed, Tara-lin thought, to have some attachment to Kushon, despite the fact that they had abandoned his egg for lost and he had bonded to Alis on hatching.

The ground was slick and slippery, and sometimes Tara-lin wondered if she should have let Alis sleep longer, since it was so hard for her to keep her footing. It was still drizzling, so there was no hope of the ground even getting drier as the day wore on. As a result, they went slowly, so that Alis could manage, and not slide or fall down and hurt herself. Tara-lin's arms were soon tired from carrying Kushon, especially since he squirmed a fair amount. She was relatively confident that he both did not appreciate being carried so much, instead of waddling around on his own four feet, and that he would have been happier in Alis' arms, but Alis was far too tired to carry him and also navigate wet rock and clay. Even with Kushon's weight and wiggling greatly complicating matters, Tara-lin was able to manage somewhat better than Alis.

Tara-lin thought that Alis had probably hardly slept at all. Maybe she had gotten about two hours of sleep, but probably she had stayed up almost all night playing with her gryphling. Sometimes, when the going was especially rough, or when she saw how much Alis was stumbling, or when Kushon wiggled in her arms, she found herself growling under her breath. *How stupid*, she thought. *She should have gone to sleep, happy she could go to sleep with her gryphling cuddled against her, and happy she was taking him down so they wouldn't have to be parted anymore, instead of staying up all night and making this harder and more dangerous than it was already going to be!* She noticed that Kushon was disturbed when she growled, so she tried not to express her frustration, but she still felt it.

Added to this was another uneasiness. Her frustration reminded her of the horrors that had begged entrance to her mind and soul, and sometimes gained it, when she had been in or around Nightshade Castle. Tara-lin wondered whether the two were only superficially related to each other in her own mind and experience, or whether the frustration and unhappiness she now experienced was, in fact, related to the nightmare. Would it make her more vulnerable to the assault of the nightmare, or did it only feel like it would make her more vulnerable? Was it, in itself, a mild assault of the nightmare, or did it only feel like one? She definitely *seemed* to have a good reason for it, but, then again, half the time, when one was under the influence of the Nightmare, one *seemed* to have a very good reason for the feelings it aroused, the hatred, the fear, the despair, the whole gamut of horrors it tried to thrust upon one's soul and bury one in.

In the evening the clouds in the west cleared up and the sun came out. For a few minutes, whenever they chanced to look behind them, they saw a brilliant full rainbow arcing across the mountains and the sky. It grew almost impossibly bright, and a very bright double rainbow appeared above it, the purple at the top and the red at the bottom. Alis gasped when she saw it.

"It is *very* beautiful," Tara-lin agreed. "Even I don't know if I've ever seen such a beautiful rainbow, but we're late already. I don't want Dad and the others to worry about us. We've got to go on."

"Yeah," agreed Alis sadly.

After a few minutes, the rainbow began to lose brightness, for the sun was setting. Soon, it was gone altogether. Stars began to come out in the west, but the rest of the sky was overcast. It was quite dark.

Tara-lin put Kushon down. The gryphon squeaked and waddled around a little. "Do you think you can manage to carry him?" the elfling asked as she drew her sword.

"Yes, it's a lot less steep here," said Alis, her words muffled by a large yawn.

Tara-lin led, the sword casting a purple light at their feet. It was well past dark when they finally arrived at the thicket, Alis stumbling and dragging her feet through the leaves and branches.

"Thank Overion, you're here!" Namdon's voice could be heard saying.

"Are you hurt? Did anything happen?" asked Tara-lin's father.

"Nothing happened except the storm and Alis staying up with her gryphon all night," answered Tara-lin.

"Is there food?" asked Alis, after putting Kushon down.

"Yes, and there's even food for the gryphon," said Eldor. "Cuthlin shot a rabbit."

"Good," said Alis with a sigh of relief.

"How's Keller?" asked Tara-lin.

"Sleeping right now, I think. Sometimes, he sits against a tree and just cries his heart out. Sometimes, he rants and raves. Some of it we understand, some of it we don't. Several times he threw himself on us and attempted violence, but we're fine. He's not that strong," said Eldor.

"Oh," said Tara-lin.

"Why?" asked her father.

"Just wondering how things are with you."

"Well enough for the moment. Let's all talk tomorrow. Both of you sound very tired," said Eldor.

"We are," said Tara-lin, laughing a little.

Alis fed her gryphon. While Kushon tore apart the rabbit, making himself a bloody mess, Alis and Tara-lin moved where they would not have to watch to drink and eat their own meal. Then they slept.

It was light, but still almost cold, when Tara-lin woke. Alis was snoring softly a few feet away, and Kushon was ambling around and over her. Tara-lin wondered how he did not wake her up. He was sticking his beak into everything and she saw him step on Alis' face.

I really bet she didn't sleep more than an hour or two that night, thought Tara-lin. She found that food had been again provided and ate half of it. The sounds of men talking reached her ears and she rose, leaving Alis, and went towards the men's voices.

Their voices led her to the edge of the thicket. They were looking south and conversing. When they caught sight of her making her ways towards them, they stopped talking. "Good morning, Tara-lin!"

Keller stood up, too. "Who is it? Oh, you!"

"Good morning, Dad," said Tara-lin, continuing to walk. Keller made his way towards her. When they were a few feet apart, she said, "You recognize me? You remember me?"

He cocked his head in a strange gesture. "I'm... not sure. You... don't look like Mom."

"That's because I'm not," said Tara-lin.

He continued to maintain that strange attitude of consideration. "But... you do look like... Mom. Like... not like these others." He waved his hand to indicate the men.

"Is that because I'm an elf or a woman?" asked Tara-lin.

Keller's face crumpled in total confusion. After a few moments, he stammered, "E-e-lf? W-wo-woman?"

Tara-lin wondered if he didn't know the words or if he couldn't remember or comprehend the concepts at the moment. She didn't know how to ask or explain. "It's okay," she reassured him. "You don't have to know right now. I was just curious." She smiled at him, then turned to her father. "What's the plan today? What do you want to do?"

"Go east, around the mountains, and then travel the mountains into Elethri, and find Lìrulin." he said. "Maybe she will have an idea what we should do. It is really something of a... dilemma isn't quite the word, that we have here. But, I'm not in a hurry. We'll leave when Alis wakes up."

"*If* she wakes up today," said Tara-lin. "Anyway, what is this problem that's not really a dilemma?"

"Namdon, why don't you tell her?" suggested Eldor.

Namdon held out his hands and examined his fingernails for a moment. Then, he spoke. "We swore oath to the Valor Hall – we dedicated our entire lives, as we thought it was, to the purpose of keeping peace for the free peoples of the Coalition of the North. We gave our fealty, allegiance, to the Valor Hall as – well, as that, as representative of that, as the way we would serve that. It's hard to know anything, now." He paused for a long moment, during which he again appeared to be examining his fingernails. "It's hard when you gave your life to something to just... throw it away. Up till now, we had not really broken with our oath or our mission. We went up into Icecrown and investigated what was going on in Nightshade Castle, then escaped with our lives after discovering... not that much, but we have something to tell, and we definitely have to tell that the Prince is gone. Under normal circumstances, we would ride back as fast as we could to the nearest courier post to deliver our message, which would then be carried, assuming general integrity, back to the Valor Hall with as much speed as possible.

"Now, it appears the Valor Hall wants us dead. We've talked through a lot of things, and we wonder if the *first* attempt to send Sir Eldor, your father, into Icecrown was an attempt to kill him and Se'lorn, one which only partially succeeded because the interference of your mother was not anticipated. We don't have anything conclusive, but we have to consider that as a distinct possibility, though perhaps not a probability.

"But we swore oath. What is our obligation? What is our word? How do we fulfill the oath we swore? Is it possible? Cuthlin has expressed a potential desire to go back to the Valor Hall, to try to tell people what is wrong, and to gather together those who might have some integrity, some actual faithfulness to their oath, which brings us to another issue that now shakes our world: how can so many men swear such an oath with no intention of abiding by it? That one or two infiltrators might do so we can understand, and that another one or two might be turned we might also be able to accept, but that almost everyone is an infiltrator or turned? That is... it goes against our whole sense of reality. What does one do in such a world? Especially when, hitherto, one's whole identity has been centered around being a Valor Knight. Where do I go? Do I and Cuthlin go into the south, and try to work our way through the mess of politics in those nations, see if we can find some refuge somewhere, and try to gather together people to help us return the Valor Hall to men of integrity? Is that even possible? Are there enough men of integrity?

"In short, we feel like traitors. If we were – Heavens forbid – to return to the Valor Hall and serve it, knowing it to be entirely corrupted, we would be breaking our oath. If we do as we are now, fleeing from the Valor Hall and trying to find a place to hide and survive, or even to work against it, we would be breaking our oath in another sense. It is clear, to me, which path is better, but it does not entirely make me comfortable. I can see why Cuthlin considers the thought of returning and trying to work for a return of integrity from within the Valor Hall, though I am almost certain such a path leads very quickly to death on the edge of a sword, not that that is a reason against it. As Valor Knights, we always knew our lives could easily end on the edge of a sword. Such a path *seems* to satisfy both senses of our oath. But does it? Can it be followed, knowing the extent of the corruption in the Valor Hall? Wouldn't it be better to publish freely, if we can find somewhere from which to do so, our experiences of the corruption in the Valor Hall and, hopefully, gather to us those who will, instead of gathering them right under the nose of those who would kill us? Though that path raises its own problems, for the rulers and powers of the southern nations are certainly corrupt, even if not *quite* as corrupt, and will be trying to use us for the advancement of their own nefarious goals. So, what do we do?"

"I have nothing to add," said Cuthlin. "Except that, while I am thoroughly convinced of some high level corruption or infiltration, and probably collusion with Wizard Falkur and, at least, with Prince Anakrim, I simply cannot believe that *all* or almost all of the Valor Knights, except for the three of us here and a handful who may have been murdered as we almost were, are corrupted."

"Not a handful," said Namdon. "I've reasons to suspect at least a hundred deaths I've noted were murders of Knights with some integrity."

"That's beside my point," said Cuthlin. "That's still less than one out of twenty."

In the pause that followed, Tara-lin turned to her father. "Do you feel this way?" she asked.

"Less so. *Much* less so," he answered. "You should be able to understand why."

"You dwelt for over twenty years in Elethri with Mom. That's a long time, away from the Valor Hall, and with something else and other ideas," said Tara-lin.

"Something very much like that," answered Eldor.

"Well, I'm sorry," said Tara-lin.

"Don't be," said Namdon. "You saved our lives. It's better for us to be alive, to face this problem and do whatever good we can, than dead, even if we don't have to deal with these questions. Besides, it might feel rather bad to know you've died, not in a noble cause, but because the whole organization to which you gave your life was corrupt from the inside out."

"Still," said Tara-lin, "I can't really empathize, but I'm sorry about the whole situation."

Alis woke sometime in the afternoon. They traveled for several hours, then made camp again, if one could call it a 'camp'.

The next day, they continued south for a few hours to pick up Makya and Vonë. Then they turned north and east, to get around the tip of the mountain range, and then south the following day, and continued to travel in that direction. Every evening, one or another of the men went hunting to get something for Kushon and, hopefully, for everyone else as well. They tried to make as good time as they reasonably could, since Eldor was worried about his wife. He did not know if the Valor Hall would hunt them yet. They might operate on the assumption that they had died in Icecrown. However, he was uncomfortable, feeling that going south along the Malaitha Mountains into Elethri was entirely too predictable. Tara-lin tried to assure him that, as long as no elves were sent after them, she and the dryads would have no difficulty hiding their presence.

One day, Tara-lin took some of the standard Northern currency from the Valor Knights and went east, to find a village from which she could purchase horses. That day, she bought one horse and rode him back. Several days later, she went down again, to buy another horse. A day later she journeyed farther east and purchased another horse. A few days later, she bought a fourth horse for Keller to ride. She spent all the Northern currency they had on the horses, but that did not matter, since they did not need the money for traveling through the wilderness of the Malaitha Mountains, and, even keeping to the hills, they were able to travel faster riding. The problem with this was that Keller had to be taught to ride but, all in all, he really fell in love with the horse and enjoyed riding. In a few days, he wanted to sleep with his horse. The other problem was that Kushon absolutely detested the experience. Alis told them that he expressed to her his hatred for everything about the horse's gaits. Someone offered for Alis to ride a different horse, but Kushon hated the gaits of all the horses at least as much, and sometimes more, than he hated Makya's.

As the days went on, it seemed to Tara-lin that he was slowly getting used to it. At least, he did not squack as much, and he did not look so unhappy at night when they stopped or in the morning when they mounted again as he had at first.

At night, Tara-lin continued to dream dryadic dreams, impossible for her to fully remember or articulate when awake. Bits and pieces of knowledge came to her and then vanished, incomprehensible as they were to her part-human mind. Mostly, the senses she received were almost incomprehensible to her but, to the extent to which she did understand them, bursting with life and peace and goodness.

Chapter Twenty–Seven – Refuge

They had hardly been riding for a month when, one day, Tara-lin motioned for them to stop. "What is it?" asked Eldor.

"Listen!" She said.

They heard it, then. It was the sound of a company moving through the forests.

"What should we do? How do we hide?" asked Eldor.

Tara-lin did not speak for a few moments. Instead, she extended her consciousness through that bond she had with the dryads. When she withdrew her mind from the matrix of the dryads' life, she wondered how she would tell her friends it was okay and also keep her other friends' secrets safe. She looked around, then said, "I'm almost sure it's all right."

"How?" asked Eldor.

"It's a feeling, like that sense I got that we shouldn't call the gryphons to carry us into Icecrown."

Even as they were speaking, the approaching company grew nearer. Tara-lin could tell that some were mounted, and that some were on foot, and that they spoke amongst themselves. She turned to the others. "Hide if you will. I will ride out to them. If they do turn out to be foes, I will lead them away from you and then escape."

"You can do that?" asked her father.

"Yes," said Tara-lin. "I got into Icecrown. I am a singer. The dryads will help me. With only myself to be concerned over, I might be able to foil capture by any elf, and I can certainly escape any human."

"Not if there is a wizard," said Eldor.

"Not if there is a wizard," agreed Tara-lin. "If there is a wizard with those approaching us, we are doomed already." She nudged Vonë slightly with her heels and trotted forward. After a few strides, she nudged him again, and he picked up a gentle canter.

In a couple minutes, she saw the company. It was as she had surmised, a host of elves, many, but not all, of them mounted. Her mother rode in the first row of riders and beside her rode Earnrìl. Both of them called out, "Tara-lin!"

Lìrulin said, "Are you alone?"

"No. Dad is with me, and some others. I just..." said Tara-lin.

"It's okay," said Lìrulin. "You felt like running ahead a little."

"Yes," said Tara-lin. "But what is wrong? Why are you here?"

She had drawn Vonë up and was riding him side by side with Lìrulin and Earnrìl's steeds.

"Elethri has been overthrown. Queen Alaria and King Orenduil took sick and died within weeks of each other. Many of their closer cousins, nieces, and nephews have also died. Prince Anakrim appeared, saying that he had responded to a request to appear before the Elethrian court, in view of the fact that the King and Queen were aging and he was the only living heir, despite his disreputable parentage, and expressed his regrets that he had arrived too late to meet his grandparents before they died. He is already beginning to take over the governance of Elethri," answered Lìrulin.

"Oh my!" said Tara-lin. "I didn't think the elves would accept him?"

"Many of them will. He promises to help them regain their lost arts and magic, something many of the elven youth very much appreciate. Some of them, however, are wary of him. You can see what is here with me, and I am sure there are more. We fled in a hurry. But let's wait until we find your father. I don't want to repeat everything twice."

"That's fine, Mom," said Tara-lin.

"Tara-lin, I'm so glad you're here!" said Earnrìl. "When Lìrulin told me it was almost certain you had followed your father towards Icecrown, I was really scared. Then she told me the dryads said you were alive and well, but that didn't totally ease my discomfort until I saw you riding up that hill towards us!"

"Cool!" said Tara-lin. "I didn't know you missed me that much. After all, you've known me for only a little while, since I've grown up very quickly."

"Why do you think I liked going down to the sea with you so much?" asked Earnrìl.

Tara-lin shrugged. "I thought you had other friends."

"Not that many," began Earnrìl, but Tara-lin interrupted her. "My Dad and his friends should have seen us by now." She took a deep breath and readied herself to call, when she saw Alis step out from under the shadow of a tree, leading Makya. The gryphling, not yet ready to fly, followed at her feet.

Earnrìl squealed. "A gryphling! How did she get to be a gryphon rider?"

"More than a gryphon rider," said Tara-lin. "She can speak to any gryphon in the vicinity."

"What?!" asked Earnrìl.

"Yes," said Tara-lin, "but her name is Alis, and the gryphon's name is Kushon."

From slightly different directions, the rest of Tara-lin's companions appeared, all of them with their horses.

Lìrulin slid, somewhat awkwardly since she was encumbered by the child growing in her belly, from her steed's back. She and Eldor embraced for a long time. Then they stepped apart from each other, and he said, "What has brought you here?"

Lìrulin began to narrate her story, while Namdon and Cuthlin gathered close to her and Eldor to listen. Keller stood, looking almost lost, with a strange expression on his face, one of mixed confusion, recognition, and, Tara-lin thought, a sense of delight and safety, but also a fear that the safety might be false. He certainly seemed to know his mother had loved him, and she wondered if he recognized his mother's people.

She was soon distracted from watching and thinking about him, for right next to her Earnrìl and Alis were excitedly talking. Alis was answering Earnrìl's questions about how she had managed to be a gryphon rider, and Earnrìl expressed her surprise. "It's something of an achievement for an elf to be a gryphon rider! In fact, it's considered somewhat impressive for an elf to even try! I've never heard of a human..."

"Well," said Alis, shyly, "there's got to have been a first human gryphon rider or so. Why not a second, like the first?"

"Not necessarily!" said Earnrìl. "What if the first human got his gryphon from the elves much as humans bond to gryphons hatched from the eggs of another bonded gryphon? But it's absolutely astounding that you can speak to other gryphons than Kushon! I've never heard of that happening before... not even in the legends."

Tara-lin interjected. "Elves are definitely superior to humans when it comes to wood lore and woodcraft and understanding growing things, but I think the elven superiority with animals is a result, largely, of the fact that most elves live rather close to nature and the wild and the animals, much closer than all but a very few humans, and, also, that elves have a lot longer to learn things."

"That definitely could be," acknowledged Earnrìl. "Humans might not be very good at getting gryphons because they just... don't try very much." Her voice took on a sad tone. "It looks to me like elves, in general, are getting more like humans in these bad ways. Most of the elves don't... try things, anymore. They go about whatever is usual, and they don't... try things, do things, explore outside the norm of their lives."

"But isn't that what Prince Anakrim is baiting them with? The opportunity to explore what the elves used to have but has passed outside of the norm? The opportunity to try things?" asked Tara-lin.

"Not the opportunity to try things," said Earnrìl. "They could try things all on their own, if they wanted. They don't need him to provide the opportunity. They need him to sanction the opportunity, to make it not an exploration, an adventure, but a teaching, a norm, something that might feel a little like an adventure, but isn't really one. Nothing prevents them from trying to re-develop elven magic on their own, aided, perhaps, by what knowledge remains of what was done and, less, of how. They could study our remaining magic artifacts and try to create artifacts of their own... artifacts not of the past, of another's imagination, but of their own imagination and their own interest. No. That's not what he's baiting them with. He's baiting them with something that *looks* a little like that, but really isn't."

"That makes sense," said Tara-lin. "But what are we going to do?"

"I don't know," said Earnrìl. She shrugged. "Find a place to hide? Hope more elves realize what's wrong and that some of them find us? Some of us could go and try to invite others to see what's wrong and come. I'm so happy to find you, Tara-lin, again, and meet you, Alis, and Kushon. By the way, do you know, Tara-lin, that your mom found a princess of the royal house? She realized that the deaths around her were unexplained very early on and, somehow, managed to escape. I think she's like an eighth cousin to King Orenduil, one or two times removed. She's not that much older than we are."

"You mean than you are," said Tara-lin.

"Yes, I just forgot that," said Earnrìl. "We might as well be about the same age."

That night, they camped in the place where they met. The following morning, they set off towards a valley deep within the Malaitha Mountains to which the dryads had directed Lìrulin. According to her, she had been directed by a dryad to lead those elves she found who had rejected Prince Anakrim north, in search of her daughter and husband and, when she found them, to take them all to a high valley where their magic was strong and ancient. It happened that the valley was a couple weeks south of where they had met, just on the border of Elethri.

It turned out to be a very large, forested valley, and high indeed. The first snows had fallen when they reached it and, where the trees did not cover the ground, it was dusted in a couple inches of snow. Nonetheless, it was rather temperate for the altitude and time of year, being almost a canyon, and so shielded from much of the wind that blew across the peaks and bare shoulders of the mountains, but open on its southern end to receive the light of the winter sun. As they rode up towards it, alongside a river, Alis suddenly exclaimed.

Tara-lin looked and saw what she meant. A herd of gryphons circled in the sky above the valley. Tara-lin turned her head and smiled at Alis.

Alis leaned across the space between their horses and whispered to Tara-lin, "I wonder if there's a better way for people to become gryphon riders... a way to convince the gryphons it's good for their hatchlings to bond to humans, instead of stealing their eggs." Tara-lin knew what she was thinking. *What if the gryphons were, naturally, protective of their young, and someone stole a gryphon hatchling, and then the gryphons decided, again quite naturally, that human-kin were not to be trusted around their young ever again? What if there was a better way – one in which one convinced the gryphons that one did not come to steal and enslave their hatchlings, but to form a relationship with them and take care of them?*

They lived peacefully in the valley. Under the advice of the dryads, and with their help and guidance, Tara-lin sang wards around the entrances to the valley and along the ways that led to it. At first she barely under-stood the songs. Though she discerned that they hindered and deterred those recognized as enemies or unwelcome, in much the same way as the Elethrian cloaks repelled the recognition of the eye, yet they would guide those recognized as welcome and friends, she did not understand how the ward recognized into which class a person might fall. Eventually, she wondered if the ward did not recognize it at all, but was a matrix of power anchored by and under the influence of the dryads.

The first winter was somewhat hard. The dryads revealed that they had limited ability to supply food, and the elven and human refugees had no food stores of their own. They did have some ability to hunt, and Alis convinced the gryphons to help them. Tara-lin thought the dryads might have helped her with this.

Now and then, an elf or two would seek them out and find them, but the low numbers of these disappointed Tara-lin and Earnrìl. The two of them, with Alis – Tara-lin and Alis were the real leaders in these conversations – sometimes discussed Tara-lin's desire, shared strongly by Alis, to find a way to reach other girls in positions much like Alis and offer them a life where they could discover who they really were, marrying if they desired, but not being forced into a life of another's choosing.

A couple weeks after they settled in the valley, Lìrulin went into labor one morning. In the evening, Tara-lin's younger brother was born. After he nursed, and after his father got to hold him, Tara-lin held him for a few minutes. *I wonder what he will look like,* she thought. At the moment, his eyes were a dark slate gray and his hair was a surprisingly similar color, but she knew those things changed. She held him for a moment, gazing on him with sisterly love, when Keller came by.

He stood for a moment looking at her and her brother, then an expression of fright crossed his face. Tara-lin scrambled away, just in time, for he threw himself at her, crying, "No! No! No!"

Eldor and several elven men subdued him and asked him what the problem was. After minutes of struggle, Keller lay still. "You won't... love him more than me, will you?" he asked.

Tara-lin, who was still near, did not know whom he addressed. "He's my little brother," she said. "What sort of a question is that? What are you afraid of?"

He broke down into tears again, then said, "*He* used to love me. Until my brother came."

So far, it was the most Keller had ever expressed about his fears and past. Tara-lin, looking into his eyes, shuddered at what she knew lay there. She was certain he had been tortured, possibly to some extent – as certainly by his brother – as a magical experiment, probably at times because Falkur had been frustrated at his lack of buy-in into Falkur's ways, possibly at times simply as a way to take out demented anger and rage. What kind of life for a child was that? How could he even have survived it? No wonder his mother, Princess Ithrìl, had thought him dead when he was taken from her. For what could he possibly have been taken from her?

The next day, looking on her baby brother while he lay asleep in the arms of his sleeping mother, Tara-lin said to Eldor, "He'll be young when you are old. Do you understand, now, why I and Lìrulin did not want you to go – wanted you to find any other way?"

"Tara-lin," said Eldor, "I understood even then, to some degree, but I did not know what was right, what I should do, how I could not follow through on my oath." He stopped speaking. Tara-lin knew he had more to say, more that he was thinking, but she did not ask. He was probably unwilling, or unable, to share.

Instead, she asked, after a few minutes, "What will his name be?"

"I will have to talk it over with your mom. I am thinking of calling him Lyan."

"I like that name," said Tara-lin. It turned out that Lìrulin agreed, and so Lyan became the name of Tara-lin's brother.

In the spring, Tara-lin followed one of the rivers out of the valley, and went to visit with the dryad Aumoura.

When she approached, the dryad materialized out of her tree. "Greetings, Tara-lin!" she said in her musical, resonant voice, a voice rich with the feel of the sun and rain and growth of years spoken in a few seconds.

"Hi, Aumoura," returned Tara-lin. "You're the first dryad to speak to me, so I... thought I'd come back."

"I am pleased," said Aumoura. "But, though you have done all that we could expect, I fear that, through the ages to come, the dryads and the elves will grow estranged. Anakrim is no friend of ours, and, as a whole, the elves have gone after him. Many of us think the best way to avoid such potential threats and horrors in the future is to have no further contact with the elves. There are some who think that we, dryads, would still be close to humans if none of us had ever grown so close, in such a manner, as to have off-spring descended of both our races. But, do not fear, Tara-lin. Only a very few corrupted dryads will ever shun you and, while you live, many of us will continue to speak with and interact with the elves."

Tara-lin thought of Alai-ie-a, and thought that nothing would ever change the willingness of her, and dryads like her, to sing to other races and try to draw them into the happiness and life she knew. Even if she did not know of Shallim-Araldor by name, she had something it seemed the rest of the world had mostly missed. "I know the dryads will not abandon me," said Tara-lin. "They speak to Lìrulin also, and they have offered the refugees of Elethri haven."

"I know," said Aumoura, "but tell me why you have come to me."

"Mostly," said Tara-lin, "to thank you. It was you who first began the process of teaching me to sing as dryads sing."

"You are most welcome," said Aumoura, with a strong, clear laugh. "You have learned very well. A dryad of your years would do no better."

"But I shall never live as long as a dryad," said Tara-lin, "or learn as much as most of you learn before you, so to speak, die."

"What else have you come for?" asked Aumoura.

"To ask you a question, since you know more of what may be done with the dryad power than I. Anakrim was doing something to Keller when I found them, something Keller hated. What could it possibly have been? It wasn't any... ordinary torture. I can only think of it as some form of... magical experiment, I think. At least, I thought something like that once."

"I cannot answer you," said Aumoura. "I know little of what the power of our life can be when it has passed through such twisted hands and into such a twisted form. But I will try to receive it if you share with me what you saw."

Tara-lin reached for Aumoura, as she now knew how to touch the matrix of the lives of the dryads and trees, and called up what she remembered of what she had seen and felt when she stepped into the room where she had found Anakrim.

"I do not know," said Aumoura, "except that there is dark magic there. The place is full of the nightmare magic, if magic it can be called, and I cannot see through it well. There may be other dryads who might know better than I, however."

"Well, thank you," said Tara-lin.

"Rather, it is we who thank you," said Aumoura.

"I'm not sure if I even did anything," said Tara-lin. "I think he might have already gotten what he wanted."

"I seriously doubt that," said Aumoura. "I doubt that he has, even now, gotten what he wants. Whatever else you did or did not do, you destroyed some at least of what he was using for his magic. That much I know from what you have shared with me."

To Be Continued ...

In Legend of the Singer Book Two
Sorceress of the Dryads

Tara-lin reached the cliff-like walls and began to climb them, throwing all her nervous energy into the effort. She was hanging on when a voice above her suddenly asked, "Tara-lin, what are you doing?"

Tara-lin almost lost her footing. "Coming up here," she panted. She continued to climb, scrambling up the incline. Finally, she dropped herself down on a ledge. Alis stood next to her, and beside Alis stood her mighty brown beast, the gryphon Kushon.

"Something is wrong, Tara-lin," said Alis. "This is not usual behavior."

Get *Sorceress of the Dryads* here: https://books2read.com/legend2

Sign up to be notified about new releases:
https://books2read.com/r/B-A-OUYQ-HMXXB

Follow me on Goodreads:
https://www.goodreads.com/author/show/20243136.Raina_Nightingale

Follow me on BookBub:
https://www.bookbub.com/authors/raina-nightingale

Or, if you like weekly reviews, ramblings of all sorts, and occasional art posts, you can follow my blog:
https://enthralledbylove.com

And if you liked *Children of the Dryads*, please leave an honest review on your favorite book platforms. It really helps readers and independent authors to find each other.

www.ingramcontent.com/pod-product-compliance
Lightning Source LLC
Chambersburg PA
CBHW030141180626
46812CB00002B/789